A MARKHAM SISTERS COLLECTION - ABCD

DIANA XARISSA

ISBN: 1530965691
ISBN-13: 978-1530965694

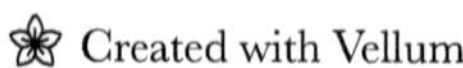

Contents

The Appleton Case

A MARKHAM SISTERS COZY MYSTERY NOVELLA

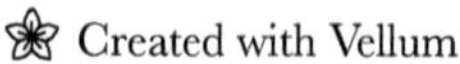
Created with Vellum

For my sister. Sisters are a wonderful blessing!

Acknowledgments

This novella, like my other works, is the result of the hard work of many people. Thanks to Denise, my editor, who managed to fix most of my mistakes. I know a few will have snuck in, most likely because I keep making changes after she's done!

Thanks to my beta readers, Charlene and Janice, who agreed to try out this first book in my new series without really knowing what they were letting themselves in for.

And thanks to my readers, those who found this book through Bessie (or something else I've already published) and those who are trying me for the very first time. I truly appreciate each and every one of you and would love to hear from you. My contact details are at the end of the book.

Author's Note

Starting a new book is always both exhilarating and terrifying in pretty much equal measure. Starting a new series takes both of those emotions to a new level. Let me start by thanking you for giving this book a try.

The Markham sisters made their first appearance in *Aunt Bessie Decides,* book four in my Isle of Man Cozy Mysteries series. There the sisters were having a lovely holiday on the Isle of Man and met Bessie Cubbon on Laxey beach. That book took place in June 1998, so that has rather determined the start date of this series.

Janet, the younger sister, has stayed in touch with Bessie, and each book will open and close with parts of her letters to their new friend on the Isle of Man. You don't need to read the Isle of Man Cozy Mystery Series to enjoy this series. The letters to Bessie provide a short introduction and wrap-up to the story here without giving any details from the Bessie series.

The Markham sisters' mysteries take place in a fictional Derbyshire village and they are novella length, so somewhat shorter than the Bessie novels.

As with the Bessie books, I've used English spellings and terms and have provided a glossary and notes in the back of the book for readers outside of the United Kingdom. The longer I live in the US, the greater the chances that Americanisms may slip into the text, and I do apologise for any that have snuck past me.

This is a work of fiction and all characters are a creation of the author's imagination. Any resemblance that they may share with any real person, living or dead, is entirely coincidental. As I said, the village in Derbyshire where they live is also fictional. Some of the shops and restaurants may bear a coincidental resemblance to some real-life counterpart, but that is wholly unintentional.

I'd love to hear from you. My contact details are in the back of the book. I hope you enjoy reading the story at least as much as I enjoyed writing it!

3 August 1998

Dearest Bessie,

It was such a great pleasure getting to know you and your lovely island in June. Joan and I often talk about what a wonderful holiday we had. We are planning another visit, perhaps next spring, and hope to get to spend even more time with you then.

I especially enjoyed hearing about your involvement in figuring out what happened in the unfortunate death of that young man off the telly, and about your other recent investigations.

Joan and I actually had a similar experience lately, looking into a mysterious death here in Derbyshire. It all started just after we returned home from our holiday, when Joan, usually the sensible one of the two of us, had a rather startling idea.

Chapter 1

"Where are we exactly?" Joan asked in a calm voice.

"We're right here," Janet answered, waving the map in the air. "At least I think we are." Janet held her breath, knowing what was coming.

"We're lost, aren't we?" Joan asked, her tone somewhat less calm.

"Maybe just the tiniest bit," Janet admitted, glancing at her sister in the driving seat.

Joan sighed deeply. "I'll just find a place to pull over," she muttered.

A few moments later a large pub appeared on their left and Joan pulled into the car park. She turned towards her sister in the passenger seat and smiled.

Janet wasn't fooled. She knew the smile was fake and that Joan was cross with her. "I did suggest that I drive and you read the map," she said quietly, handing the map to Joan.

"Yes, well, it's rather too late for that, isn't it?" Joan looked at the map for a moment. "Where are the directions from the estate agent?" she asked eventually.

Janet handed her the step-by-step directions that she'd taken over the phone from the man. Joan read through them while looking over the map and then shook her head.

"These directions don't make sense," she said angrily. "There isn't any third turning after you leave the motorway."

"That's what I said," Janet agreed, happy to have her sister angry at the estate agent rather than her.

"Didn't you look at the map when you were talking to the man?" Joan asked sharply.

Not out of the woods yet, Janet thought. "I just assumed, since he's getting paid to show us the house, that he'd want to give us proper directions," Janet replied.

"Yes, well, one of us shall have to go into the pub and ask for directions from here," Joan announced. "I suggest you go."

Janet opened her mouth to argue and then shrugged. She didn't mind doing it and she'd probably do a better job than her older sister anyway.

"I'll just turn the car around, ready to leave," Joan told her as Janet opened her door.

Yes, I suppose we must be ready for a quick getaway, Janet thought to herself, rolling her eyes at her sister when she was sure Joan couldn't possibly see her.

The middle-aged man behind the bar in the empty pub was kind enough to trace the correct route on Janet's map for her and she was thrilled to find that they weren't all that far away from their destination.

"Come back for some lunch later," he suggested. "We've cottage pie and chips on special today."

Janet nodded. She'd love to come back, but Joan didn't really enjoy pub food. She preferred to eat what she'd prepared herself. As Joan was an excellent cook and an even better baker, Janet never complained.

With the new directions, the pair found their destination only a few minutes later.

"It looks really large," Janet said doubtfully, looking up at the guesthouse that they'd come to see.

"Well, we can't very well run a bed and breakfast from a tiny flat, can we?" Joan asked. She climbed out of the car, leaving Janet shaking her head.

"I never wanted to run a bed and breakfast," Janet muttered towards her sister, who was walking rapidly towards the front of the home. "This was your crazy idea, remember?"

Joan was knocking on the front door when Janet caught up to her. By the time she'd climbed the two steps to join her sister on the small porch, the door was swinging open.

"Ah, Ms. Markham? I'm Henry Fitzsimmons. We spoke on the phone."

The man who opened the door looked exactly the way Janet expected him to from their short phone conversation. He had to be somewhere in his mid-twenties and he looked uncomfortable in his suit and tie. His dark brown hair needed cutting and his thick glasses magnified his brown eyes. He was at least a few inches shorter than six feet tall, but that still made him half a foot taller than the two women.

"I'm Joan Markham," Joan answered as she shook the man's offered hand. "But you spoke to Janet on the phone."

Janet smiled brightly as she took her turn shaking hands with the man. "It's nice to meet you," she said, politely ignoring the fact that he'd given them the wrong directions.

"It's nice to meet you as well," the man muttered as he took a step back into the house. "Come on in and have a look then," he suggested.

Joan followed him inside quickly while Janet took a moment to turn back to see what the view from the porch was like. There was just enough room for a few chairs, and Janet smiled to herself as she looked out across the Derbyshire dales. Maybe this bed and breakfast wasn't such a bad idea.

She turned back and stepped into the house, pushing the door shut behind her.

"I think I'd quite like to simply go around by myself," Joan announced in the spacious foyer.

"Yes, well, that is, um, I don't know, I mean, I suppose you can," Henry sputtered ineffectually.

Janet chuckled silently. If Joan wanted to look around by herself, the young man would be smart to simply stay out of her way. Of course, Janet had sixty-plus years of experience with her older sister; she was much better equipped at dealing with her than the young man was.

"There's really no point in you following me around and saying things like 'this is the en-suite.' If I can't work that out for myself, I've no business buying a bed and breakfast, surely?" Joan asked.

"Well, yes, I mean, I suppose so," the man's eyes darted between the two women a bit desperately.

"Why don't you tell us the basic specifications and then we'll have a look," Janet said in her very kindest primary schoolteacher voice.

"Of course," Henry said. "Doveby House was built in the late seventeenth century as a sort of manor house for the wealthiest farmer in the area. It sits on the outskirts of Doveby Dale, which is a small village just up the road. Doveby House remained in the original owner's family for many generations before the family died out and the property was sold. In the last hundred years or so it has had many owners. The last owner, a Mrs. Margaret Appleton, was the one who converted it into a bed and breakfast. She turned the six-bedroom, one-bath home into a four-bedroom, four-bathroom property."

"So every bedroom has its own en-suite?" Joan asked.

"Yes, that's really necessary these days," the man replied. "Guests, especially guests from the US, expect it."

"Indeed," Joan nodded. "Is there anything else we should know before we have a look around?"

"The property has been somewhat neglected in the last year or so and could probably do with a fresh coat of paint and some modernising," Henry said. "But it was originally done up to a very high standard and you certainly won't need to replace any bathrooms or the kitchen."

"Good to know," Joan said. "Anything else?"

"The property is being sold fully furnished, from the beds, tables and chairs to the dishes and glasses in the kitchen cupboards. It also includes a small coach house at the back," Henry said, speaking quickly. "It's just being used for storage at the moment, but it could be converted and used as additional guest space."

"I don't imagine we'll need additional space for guests," Joan said. "Two bedrooms for letting should be more than enough."

"There are three guest bedrooms," Henry said. "And a large owner's suite with a bedroom and a private sitting room."

"Yes, but Janet will need a room," Joan pointed out.

"Oh, you'll be buying the house together, then?" he asked.

Janet and Joan both laughed.

"We've lived together pretty much our entire lives," Joan told him. "I can't imagine that changing any time soon."

Henry smiled. "I couldn't live with my sister," he said. "But we never got along, not even as children. Anyway, how about having that look around?"

Joan headed out of the foyer with Janet on her heels. She glanced back at Henry and saw that he'd sat down on the small bench by the front door and already had his mobile in his hand.

The foyer opened into a large and comfortably furnished sitting room. Henry was correct that the space could use a coat of paint and some of the furniture was getting a bit shabby, but it still looked comfortable. Perhaps it could simply be reupholstered rather than replaced, Janet thought.

"I don't recall telling him that we're sisters," Joan remarked.

"Everyone always says we look so much alike that it's obvious we're sisters," Janet replied.

Janet could feel Joan looking at her hard. "I don't see the resemblance," she said eventually, before heading off through the door at the back of the room.

Janet shrugged and then wandered over to inspect the two doors in the one wall. A small closet was behind the first door, and Janet wondered what they might keep in it. It was empty, so she had no idea what the previous owner had used it for.

The second door opened into a small cloakroom and Janet took advantage of the mirror over the sink to finger comb her hair. Then she studied her face, wondering just how much she really did resemble her sister.

They were both grey-haired, with the same bright blue eyes that they'd inherited from their father. Where Janet was plump and always smiling, Joan was slender and more serious, but they were almost the exact same height. Neither had ever married, although Janet had considered it on more than one occasion. They'd both been schoolteachers in their local village school for their entire working lives, and now they'd both retired.

Janet pulled her jumper down, smoothing it over her hips. It didn't seem fair that Joan was the one who cooked and baked while she was the one who gained weight, she thought. At least now she could dress for comfort, rather than in the more formal outfits she'd worn for teaching. Of course, Joan didn't feel the same way, still dressing in skirts or smart trousers every day as if she were just about to have a classroom visit from the head teacher and the school governors.

"Janet, where have you wandered off to?" Joan's voice carried through the rooms.

"I'm just looking at the cloakroom," Janet called back, emerging back into the sitting room.

"Well, come and see what I've found," Joan said.

The excitement in her sister's voice surprised Janet and she quickly followed Joan into the next room.

This room was also spacious and was set up as a television lounge, with a small television sitting on a stand against the back wall. Again, the furniture wasn't new, but it looked comfortable.

"What's so exciting?" Janet asked, looking around, trying to spot what had excited Joan.

"Not this room, that's for sure," Joan told her. "Come see what's back here."

Janet followed her sister through a small door and sighed with delight. "It's a tiny library," she said softly.

It seemed as if every inch of wall space was covered with shelves and every shelf was full of books. Janet stepped forward and pulled a random title from the closest shelf. "Agatha Christie," she told her sister.

"There doesn't seem to be any order to the collection, but there are some very good books here," Joan told her. "I've found several old favourites."

Janet knew that that meant the classics. They were just about all that Joan read.

"But surely they won't be including the books in the sale of the property," Janet said with a sigh.

"Actually, the current owner is willing to include them in the sale price," Henry told them from the doorway.

"They're including all of these books?" Joan asked. "But some of them may be valuable."

Henry shrugged. "The current owner is a trust that isn't interested in taking the time to go through the whole house in case there might be something with a bit of extra value hidden away," he said. "I think the books came with the house when Mrs. Appleton bought it anyway, and she left it just the way she found it."

"Well, we'd love to have them," Joan said. "Didn't Mrs. Appleton have any family to leave things to?"

The man frowned. "She has a son called Gavin," he said after an awkward pause. "I gather they didn't get along well and she decided to leave everything to Doveby Trust instead of him."

"Does he live nearby?" Janet asked.

"Not far away," Henry admitted. "But he won't be any bother."

That Henry didn't meet her eyes when he said that had Janet wondering if he was lying to them. She couldn't help but worry that Gavin Appleton might want all of the lovely books and that he might find some way to claim them.

"I suppose we should look at the rest of the property," Joan said after several more minutes spent inspecting the library.

The sisters left the room reluctantly.

"There's a conservatory off the television lounge," Henry pointed out as Joan opened the door into the glass-walled room.

It was small, but it had lovely views of the beautifully kept gardens behind the house.

"Those gardens will take a lot of work," Janet remarked.

"Actually, they're currently being kept by one of the neighbours for a nominal sum," Henry told her. "I don't know if you noticed the small semi-detached homes across the street, but they don't have very much garden space. I've been told that one of the residents used to be a professional gardener and he enjoys taking care of the gardens here in his spare time."

"That's handy," Joan said.

The other door off of the television lounge opened into a small dining room. Beyond that was a reasonably large kitchen.

"It's nicely up-to-date," Henry pointed out.

"It is," Joan agreed mildly.

Janet hid a smile. The kitchen was probably twice the size of their current kitchen and much more modern. Joan would love cooking and baking in this beautiful space.

The owner's suite was next door with a small bedroom and equally tiny sitting room. A compact bathroom completed the suite.

"I suppose I should have the owner's suite," Joan said. "As I'll be one making the breakfast every morning, it just makes sense for me to be nearest to the kitchen."

Janet nodded. She'd expected her sister to claim the owner's suite; at least she hadn't used her usual "I'm the oldest" excuse for demanding the best.

Upstairs there were two adequately sized guest rooms, each with its own small bathroom. The third guest room was larger, with its own fireplace and a spacious bathroom with a large and deep bathtub. It had wonderful views out across the dales from its many windows and Janet sighed with delight as she imagined herself living in the room.

"This will do nicely," she told her sister as they looked around the beautiful room. It was painted a lovely soft lilac colour that exactly suited Janet's taste.

"Oh, we should use this as a guest room, surely," Joan protested. "You can have one of the other rooms."

Janet shook her head. "As this whole bed and breakfast thing is your idea, and you've already claimed the owner's suite for yourself, it's only fair that I get this bedroom," she said firmly. "Half the money is mine, after all."

Joan opened her mouth and Janet glared at her. After a moment Joan shrugged and walked out of the room. After another look around the space that Janet was already beginning to think of as "hers," she followed Joan back down the stairs into the sitting room.

Chapter 2

Henry had stayed on the ground floor while they'd explored the first floor. Now the women found him sitting in the conservatory, talking on his mobile phone.

"So, what's the asking price again?" Joan asked him once he'd hastily ended his call.

"Um, you haven't seen the coach house yet," Henry reminded them.

"Oh, yes, we must do that, mustn't we?" Joan said. There was a door to the garden from the conservatory and the sisters followed Henry out onto the beautifully manicured lawn.

"This is beautiful," Janet said after she'd inhaled the scent of the gorgeous assortment of flowers that surrounded them.

"It is quite nice," Joan agreed.

The coach house was off to the side of the property and Henry opened its side door.

"There used to be large doors on the front, apparently," he told them. "But when they no longer needed to store coaches inside, they walled up those doors and just left this side one."

Joan and Janet followed him into the building. Janet found

herself blinking in the dimly lit space after the bright sunshine outside. After a moment, her eyes adjusted.

"It is rather a mess," she said. The building was essentially a large single room that was poorly lit by a single dangling bulb hanging from the ceiling. There were piles of old boxes lining every wall and a few pieces of broken furniture dumped into the middle of the room.

Janet took a few steps forward and then sneezed.

"Bless you, dear," Joan said. She was offering Janet a tissue before Janet was even sure she was finished sneezing.

"Thank you," Janet muttered, taking the tissue. "It is quite dusty, isn't it?"

"Yes, rather," Joan replied.

"But it's a very large space that you could use for many things," Henry said brightly.

He took a few steps forward and began to gesture towards the back wall. "You could easily fit an en-suite against this back wall and turn the main space into a large...."

He was interrupted when the door suddenly slammed shut. Everyone jumped and spun towards it. Henry walked over and rattled the knob. The door remained firmly closed.

"I left the keys in the lock on the outside," he told the sisters. "We appear to be locked in."

"I suggest you ring someone, then," Joan said. "In the meantime, we can spend rather more time than necessary inspecting the coach house."

Janet joined her and they made a slow circuit of the room while Henry made a few phone calls.

"I have a colleague on his way with the second set of keys," he said eventually. "But it will take him about twenty minutes to get here."

Joan and Janet exchanged glances. Janet could see that her sister was not pleased.

"What did you say the asking price was?" she asked Henry, hoping to distract her sister.

He named a price that made Janet wince. "But of course you'll have the income from the bed and breakfast to help with the expense," Henry added.

"It seems quite dear, considering the amount of work the house needs. Not to mention the deplorable state of this coach house," Joan said.

"That is just the asking price," Henry said. "There may be some negotiating room in there. I believe the property has been on the market for some months, since the previous owner's unfortunate and unexpected passing."

"What happened to her?" Joan demanded.

"Oh, I'm not quite sure," Henry stammered. "I just know…."

"Hullo? Is there anyone there?" a loud voice suddenly interrupted.

"Hello, we're locked in the coach house. Can you get us out?" Henry shouted back.

"Oh, aye," came a cheery reply. "Hang on a minute."

A moment later the door swung open. Henry was quick to exit and the sisters didn't delay in following him.

Janet took several deep breaths of fresh air. She felt as if she were covered in dust herself after being trapped in the grimy coach house, even though they'd only been in there a few minutes.

"Thank you so very much," Henry was saying to the tall man who had opened the door.

Janet inspected him as she waited for Henry to stop babbling so she could add her own thanks.

He had to be nearly six feet tall, with dark brown hair that was clearly dyed. There was no way he'd managed to get to his age without going grey, she decided. He appeared to be somewhere in his sixties and his dark eyes sparkled with amusement as Henry continued to thank him.

"It's fine," he said when Henry paused for a breath. "I was just going to do a bit of weeding and I heard voices. I thought I'd better check things out."

"I'm just a tiny bit claustrophobic," Henry explained. "I was feeling quite, um, unhappy in there. I don't understand how the door came to blow shut, though, it isn't windy."

"No doubt it was the ghost," the man told him. "I shouldn't worry about it."

"But where are my keys?" Henry demanded, looking around on the ground outside the coach house door.

"I didn't see any keys when I got here," the man said. "Luckily I have my own set. I store some of the gardening things in the coach house, you see."

"I'm Joan Markham," Joan inserted herself into the conversation. "My sister Janet and I are considering purchasing this property. I take it you're the neighbour who is currently looking after the garden?"

"Yes, that's right," he said, smiling as he shook Joan's hand and then Janet's. "I'm Stuart Long and I live across the road with my wife, Mary. I'm very fond of the gardens here and I hope to continue looking after them once the new owner has purchased the place."

"As far as I'm concerned, if we end up buying the property, you'd be more than welcome," Janet said firmly.

Joan frowned at her. "Of course, nothing has been decided yet," she said sharply.

"Yes, well, if you have any questions about the neighbourhood or anything, I'm happy to answer them," Stuart said.

"That's kind of you, but I don't think we have any questions at this point," Joan answered before Janet could say anything. "We have a lot of talking to do between ourselves."

"In that case, I shall walk you back to your car," Henry said. "I have a sheet with all of the particulars of the property for you, if you'd like it. I also have some information about other bed and breakfast properties in the area, if you'd be interested in seeing what else is out there."

Joan nodded and the sisters fell into step with Henry, walking through the gardens back to the property's small car park. Henry handed Joan an envelope and she handed it to Janet before the sisters climbed into the car. As Janet began to open it, Joan pulled carefully away from Doveby House.

"Well, that was an interesting way to spend a morning," Janet said after a moment. She'd given up on the envelope, not willing to risk the inevitable car sickness she'd experience if she tried reading while the car was moving.

"It was indeed," Joan agreed. "What did you think of the house?"

"It was very nice and I loved the library."

"Can you see us running a bed and breakfast?" Joan asked.

"What's put this idea into your head?" Janet had to ask. Joan had announced the previous day that she'd made the appointment to see a bed and breakfast property that she thought they ought to consider buying, but hadn't been willing to answer any questions from Janet. Now that they'd seen the place, Janet thought it was time for some answers.

Joan sighed. "I don't know really," she said after a moment. "We've had that bit of money from Great Aunt Mildred and we've no idea what to do with it."

"I thought we were going to travel and just enjoy being retired," Janet replied.

"I know we were both looking forward to retiring," Joan said, "but I think, well, I suppose I'm just the tiniest bit bored. Travelling is all well and good, but we can't simply travel all the time. I just started thinking about trying something completely different. I've always loved cooking and baking, so I thought about opening a restaurant, but they're very hard work with very long hours. I thought a bed and breakfast would be easier."

"Except that you're essentially on call twenty-four hours a day when you have guests," Janet pointed out.

"Well, yes, but we could be very careful about who we would accept as guests," Joan replied. "We wouldn't absolutely need paying guests all the time, or even most of the time. Most of the time we could use the guest rooms for our friends, but once in a while we could extend that to friends of friends or others who've been recommended to us. We could still plan various holidays for ourselves and just shut whenever we want to get away."

"I think it will be much harder work than you realise," Janet said.

Joan laughed. "This is quite odd," she said. "Usually I'm the one trying to talk you out of doing silly things, but this time it's the other way around."

"Give me some time to think," Janet said after a moment. "Let's listen to some music and relax for the drive home."

Neither sister was worried about maps and directions for the journey back to their cottage. Joan had an excellent sense of direction, so simply reversing their earlier journey was easy for her. Janet was okay with finding her way to and from most places, but she sometimes found that her mind wandered and she missed turning at the right junction or drove right past her destination. Either sister was happy to drive their shared car, but Joan usually drove when they went anywhere outside of what was familiar territory to Janet.

Now Joan turned on the radio, tuned to a station they both liked. Classic hits from the sixties filled the car for the next twenty minutes. They were nearly home when the news began.

"Here are the headlines. A man's body has been discovered in a flat in Derby. Police are on the scene. Reports of stolen cars are up twenty-five per cent throughout the county. Police are reminding everyone to keep their cars locked whenever they are parked. A three-year-old has gone missing from her child minder's home in Clowne. Police are investigating. The weather will…."

Joan parked in front of their cottage and turned the car off. She shook her head. "Why is the news always bad news?" she asked Janet.

Janet decided it was a rhetorical question. She climbed out of the car and headed towards the front door. It was nearly time for lunch and she was starving.

Half an hour later Joan had lunch ready. Janet sat down at their kitchen table and frowned. It looked as if Joan had prepared all of her favourites.

"What's for pudding?" she asked suspiciously.

"Apple crumble with custard," Joan answered.

"You really want to buy that house, don't you?" Janet asked.

"I certainly want to discuss it," Joan replied.

"You don't make my favourite pudding for discussions. You only make apple crumble when you want something."

"That's not true. I make apple crumble a lot. It's quick and easy and delicious and almost good for you, with all those oats and apples."

"Do you think we should look at a few other bed and breakfast properties that are for sale?" Janet asked.

"I really liked Doveby House," Joan replied.

"But there could be other places that are just as nice," Janet said.

"But Doveby House has a library."

Janet opened her mouth to reply and then shut it again. Joan was right; the library was a powerful attraction.

"I've been going over the numbers," Joan said after she'd served the crumble. "If we get a decent selling price for this house, we can afford Doveby House and have enough left over to paint and redecorate, on a small scale anyway."

The sisters had both been very frugal during their working years. Aside from a short holiday each summer break, they'd spent little on anything other than necessities. Their current cottage, while small, was in an area that was increasingly in demand. With their recent inheritance and what they had saved over their long working lives, they wouldn't need to worry about keeping the bed and breakfast full of guests.

"Buying a bed and breakfast just seems like a rather surprising thing to do, that's all," Janet said after a moment.

"So? Let's be impulsive for once," Joan replied.

Janet stared at her sister for a long time. "I can't believe you just said that."

"No, I can't quite believe it myself."

The sisters talked for some considerable time about the proposed move. Janet had always liked their little cottage, but Doveby House was much larger and would be far more comfortable. The chance to have her own en-suite was enough to tempt her away from their current home. She was tired of sharing their single bathroom with her sister.

"How did you even come to find out about Doveby House?" she asked Joan.

"I was in town the other day and I walked past the estate agency on the high street," Joan replied. "I always glance in their windows to see if there's anything interesting on the market. Doveby House was in the centre of the commercial property section, looking exactly like something out of a BBC drama about village life."

"Or an Agatha Christie mystery," Janet interjected.

"Exactly, it's the perfect seventeenth-century manor house and it's within our budget. I couldn't resist having a look at it."

"I'm still not sure about actually running it as a bed and breakfast," Janet said with a frown.

"I suppose we wouldn't have to," Joan replied. "Although I think it would be fun and interesting. I would much rather run it as a bed and tea, though, if such things existed. I hate getting up early in the morning, even though I love to cook and bake. I'd be much happier making a fancy tea for our guests every afternoon than making them breakfast."

Janet laughed. "We could advertise it as the world's first bed and tea establishment and see how many guests we get," she suggested.

"Let's start by putting in an offer," Joan replied. "We'll worry about the finer details later. I'm more than a little worried about the previous owner's son."

"I'm more concerned about the ghost," Janet said. "I can't believe you didn't ask Stuart about the ghost."

Chapter 3

After some additional discussions, the pair agreed to put in a rather low offer on Doveby House. While they waited to hear back about that, they asked Henry to give them another tour of the property. Janet was determined to find time to chat with Stuart Long this time around.

"But what's going on?" Joan asked as she pulled into the car park at Doveby House the next morning.

Henry was standing on the small front garden. He was waving his arms and seemed to be shouting at a large man whose back was to the car park. Joan and Janet were quickly out of the car.

"You had your day in court," Henry was saying. "If you want access to the property, you'll have to contact the Doveby Trust. They own it now, at least until these ladies buy it." He gestured towards the Markham sisters, who were approaching cautiously.

The man who turned to face them was scowling. He looked to be in his forties and was of medium height and nearly as wide as he was tall. He seemed to be made of solid muscle and Janet found her steps faltering as he glared at her. His jet-black hair seemed to match his eyes. She noticed that his fists were clenched as she stopped and grabbed her sister's arm.

"You aren't buying me mum's house," the man told them. "You've no right."

"They've every right, I think you'll find," Henry said, his voice only quavering slightly as the man glanced back at him. "The courts have already decided the case. Doveby Trust owns the property and they've just accepted an offer from these two ladies."

Janet and Joan exchanged glances. While she was glad to hear that their offer had been accepted, Janet couldn't help but wish she'd been told under different circumstances.

The man drew a deep breath and then smiled tightly. "Look, ladies, I don't mean to argue with anyone," he said. "I'm Gavin Appleton, Margaret's son. Here's the thing. My mother left some very personal things in that house. Things she meant for me to have. All I want is a chance to go in and get them. I only need five minutes, maybe ten, and then I'll be out of your way forever. What do you say?"

"The property isn't ours yet," Joan answered in a firm voice. "I'm sure if you contact Doveby Trust they'll be able to make those arrangements for you."

"Except they won't," the man said. He shook his head. "I'll admit I may have shouted at the woman in charge a little bit. It was such a shock, mum leaving the property to them and not me. But that doesn't excuse my behaviour, I'll admit that now. Anyway, they've made it clear that I'm not welcome at their offices and they certainly won't let me in the house."

"Yes, well, I'm sorry to hear that, but it really doesn't concern us," Joan told him. Janet hid a smile as she saw her sister give the man her very best serious teacher look. Stronger men than this one had backed down from that.

"Once you've purchased the property, you'll let me have a minute, won't you?" he said plaintively. "It's just that mum died so suddenly, you see. She meant to give me some things and she never had the time."

The catch in his voice might have impressed Janet if she hadn't noticed how keenly he was watching to gauge their reaction to it.

The sound of a car door shutting had them all turning towards the car park. The man walking away from the police car had an amused look on his face. He didn't look much older than eighteen, with short brown hair and hazel eyes. He was tall and looked physically fit, but Janet couldn't help but think that Gavin could knock him out with a single punch.

"Now Gavin, I thought we'd agreed that you'd stay away from Doveby House," he said when he reached the small group.

"Aye, we did at that," the man replied, looking down at the ground. "I just want my things."

"Yes, but the courts have decided that they aren't yours. Everything in your mother's house was given to the trust and it's their right to do what they like with it," the policeman replied.

"That don't make it right," the other man snapped.

"He has my keys," Henry said in an angry voice. "He must have locked us in the coach house yesterday and stolen them."

"Gavin, do you have Mr. Fitzsimmon's keys?" the policeman asked.

"I found them," Gavin told him, reaching into his pocket. "I was just walking through the garden, looking at the house, and I tripped over them."

"You stole them yesterday," Henry accused him.

"If I stole them yesterday, I'd have let myself in last night and found what I'm looking for," Gavin shot back.

"Perhaps you could give us a list of the things you're after. If we come across them, we could get them to you," Janet found herself offering.

"Nah, never mind," the man said, turning away.

"Now Gavin," the policeman said in a stern voice. "The lady made you a good offer. Why don't you tell her what you're so desperate to get your hands on and see if she can find it for you?"

"Ah, it was just letters and stuff," the man said with a shrug. "It doesn't much matter, I suppose."

"Give the lady your contact details," the policeman suggested. "If they find any letters with your name on them, they can send them to you."

The man hesitated for a moment and then shrugged again. He

reached into a pocket and pulled out a business card, turning it over in his hand and then handing it to Janet.

She read it slowly. "Gavin Appleton, Doveby Dale Garage."

"If your car needs work, come over," he told her. Then he turned on his heel and stomped off towards the car park before anyone else spoke.

The policeman sighed as they watched him drive away.

"Sorry about that," he said to Henry and the sisters as Gavin's new sedan disappeared in the distance. "He's not supposed to be coming here, but he doesn't seem to want to listen."

"I found him trying to get the front door open," Henry told him. "He had my keys. The ones that went missing yesterday."

"I have to believe that he'd already have been through the house if he'd found them yesterday," the policeman said. "He may well have really just tripped over them this morning."

"What's he after?" Janet asked.

Both men shrugged. "It certainly isn't letters," the policeman told her. "I'm Robert Parsons, by the way. I'm the village constable, but I'm only here part of the time, as I also cover the next village. Usually one constable is more than enough between the two places, but Gavin is making me work hard at the moment."

The sisters introduced themselves.

"Well, ladies, it's nice to meet you, and welcome to Doveby Dale. I hope this is the last I ever see of you," Robert said, smiling.

"Indeed," Joan said crisply. "I can't imagine us needing a police constable in the future."

"I'll just give you my card, in case you are bothered by Mr. Appleton any further."

The sisters each took one of his cards before he headed back towards his car.

"Sorry about that," Henry said as they turned to look at him. "I believe I mentioned yesterday that there were some difficulties with the previous owner's son."

"You did," Joan said. "I do hope it's all sorted now. Did you say our offer has been accepted?"

"It has," the man confirmed.

Janet and Joan exchanged glances. They hadn't really been expecting the trust to agree to their low offer. They'd thought that reaching an agreement would take rather more time. Now it seemed as if they were about to own a bed and breakfast, ready or not.

They took their time going back through the property. Janet found herself seeing it with different eyes, as they had now agreed to purchase it. By the time she'd made two complete circuits of the home, she was very happy with the decision she and Joan had made.

"It's just about perfect," she told Joan as they joined Henry in the conservatory. "I think I love everything about it."

"Yes, well, we'll need to do a great deal of painting and decorating," Joan said. "And we'll have to recover some of the furniture."

"I love my bedroom just the way it is," Janet said. "I don't want to paint it or change any of the furniture."

"We'll have to get rid of your current bedroom furniture, then," Joan pointed out.

"Or we could use it in one of the other bedrooms, where the furniture isn't as nice," Janet said. "Let's not worry about that for today. I want another look in the coach house and then I want to meet the neighbours."

Henry let them into the coach house and then remained outside while the two women had a quick look around.

"What did you want to see in here?" Joan asked after a moment.

"I don't know," Janet admitted. "I just felt as if I wanted another look." They both headed towards the open door just as the light went out.

Joan grabbed Janet's arm. "I didn't think that single bulb was providing that much light," she said as they both stood still in the suddenly very dark room.

"No, it seemed quite ineffectual until it went off," Janet agreed.

The pair moved cautiously towards the open door that seemed brightly lit compared to the darkness within the space. Janet tripped once on a broken piece of furniture and Joan slipped on a piece of paper that managed to get under her foot, but eventually the two made it more or less unscathed to the door.

Henry was sitting on a bench in the garden, talking on his phone, apparently unaware of the situation.

"Did you turn off the light?" Joan demanded of him when he jumped up.

"Turn off the light? In the coach house? Why would I do that? You were still in there."

"Well, someone turned it off," Joan told him.

Henry walked over to the door and found the light switch. He pushed it and the bulb inside the coach house flickered on again.

"I was sitting right here the whole time," he told the sisters. "No one has been anywhere near that door."

Joan looked at Janet and rolled her eyes. Perhaps young Henry was feeling bored and had turned off the light to hurry them along, Janet thought.

"You can lock everything up now," Joan told the man. "We're just going to have a chat with the neighbours."

"Did you want me to come along?" Henry asked as he locked the door to the coach house.

"Of course not," Joan told him.

Doveby House sat at the end of a very short road. It branched off from a rather busier road that came off of the main road through Doveby Dale. There were a few houses scattered along that busier road and quite a few along the main street. Doveby House, itself, was almost alone on its short street. Only a single semi-detached property sat opposite it.

Joan and Janet made their way to the semi and knocked on the door to house number one. After a few moments, the door opened and Janet found herself smiling at a rather handsome gentleman. He appeared to be in his mid-sixties and was only a few inches taller than the sisters. His completely bald head was covered in a smattering of freckles and his brown eyes were warm.

"Ah, good morning," he said brightly. "I take it you're the ladies who might be buying Doveby House? Very kind of you to drop by."

"Yes," Joan answered for them. "We've just had our offer accepted."

"How nice," he replied. "I'd invite you in for a cuppa, but I'm just on my way out to the shops. Promise you'll come back and visit another time?"

"Of course we will," Janet said quickly. "And you must come and visit us once we're settled in. Joan is wonderful at baking. You must come for tea."

"I'd like that," he replied. "Oh, I'm Michael Donaldson. I nearly forgot to mention that."

The sisters introduced themselves and then Michael excused himself to finish getting ready to go out.

"Well, he seemed very nice," Janet said as the pair walked down the short path from his door to number two.

"He did indeed," Joan murmured. She knocked on the door at number two and after a moment it swung open.

"Ah, the ladies from yesterday," Stuart Long said. "Do come in and meet the wife, won't you?"

The sisters followed him down a short corridor and into a large sitting room.

"Mary, we have guests," Stuart said.

The woman who was sitting on one of the couches looked up and frowned. "The house is a mess," she protested.

"It's fine," Stuart said. "These are the women who are buying Doveby House."

"Oh, really? In spite of all that trouble with the Appleton lad? I wouldn't want to get on his bad side, I can tell you," Mary said.

She stood up and Janet studied her as she took a step towards them. Mary Long looked to be a few years younger than her husband. She was about the same height as the sisters, and slender with grey hair and brown eyes. When she'd taken a few steps, she held out her hand.

"I'm Mary Long. It's lovely to meet you," she said to Janet.

Janet shook her hand and supplied her own name. Joan did the same in turn.

"Welcome to the neighbourhood, I suppose," Mary said after insisting that the sisters sit down.

"Stuart, why don't you make the ladies some tea?" she suggested.

"Oh, we're fine," Joan assured her. "We just wanted to ask a few questions about the area and that sort of thing."

Mary nodded. "Very sensible," she said. "Always better to know what you're getting yourself into."

"So, how much of a worry is Gavin Appleton?" Joan asked.

The couple exchanged looks.

"Robert is on top of it, I think," Stuart said after an awkward pause. "Gavin never visited his mum, so I can't imagine what she had over there that he's after."

"He told us he was looking for some letters," Janet said.

"I find that hard to believe," Mary said. "He doesn't seem like the type to write letters to his mother."

"I'm not sure why he'd bother. He lived in the same town, after all," Joan interjected.

"He hardly ever visited her, though. Maybe he sent her some threatening letters and he's eager to get them back before the police see them," Stuart offered.

"He'd have visited more if he'd known she was going to die so suddenly," Mary said. "He'd have wanted to make sure of his inheritance, if he'd known."

"What happened to Mrs. Appleton?" Janet asked.

Again the couple exchanged looks and Janet was desperate to know what they were thinking while they did so.

"No one seems to0 sure about that," Stuart said eventually. "You could ask young Robert, I suppose."

"Only she wasn't technically Mrs. Appleton anymore," Mary added. "She may never have actually been Mrs. Appleton, for that matter."

"What do you mean?" Janet asked.

"She was married a couple of times during the years she was here. Her husbands were both much older men who left her a good deal of money when they passed on. I gather she had a different husband before she moved here. It was him that left her the money for Doveby House," Mary told them.

"So what was her proper name?" Joan asked.

Mary shrugged. "She had everyone call her Mrs. Appleton, or

Maggie. She said it was easier to have the same name as her son, and she never managed to be married long enough to bother getting everything changed."

Now the sisters exchanged looks. Janet shook her head. Sometimes other people's behaviour still surprised her.

"Anyway, Gavin was her only child. No doubt he expected to inherit everything," Stuart said.

"But she left everything to the Doveby Trust instead, as I understand it," Joan replied.

"Yes, well, I gather she and Gavin had a disagreement about something a while back and she was just angry enough to change her will. She may well have changed it back again once they'd made up, but she didn't get the chance."

"How unfortunate for young Gavin," Janet murmured.

"But fortunate for you," Mary pointed out.

They chatted about the neighbourhood and the location of the closest grocery shops and other shops for a few minutes before Joan glanced at her watch.

"My goodness, we really have taken up far too much of your time," she said to the couple. "And we have an appointment with our solicitor to get to. Thank you so much for talking with us."

"It was our pleasure," Stuart said. "We're both retired, so guests are always welcome."

"You must come and visit us once we're settled in," Janet said as she rose to follow her sister from the room.

"We'd like that," Mary said.

The pair walked to the door behind the sisters.

"Oh, yesterday you said something about a ghost," Janet said to Stuart. "What ghost?"

Mary laughed. "You mustn't listen to that nonsense," she told Janet firmly. "Stuart has some crazy ideas sometimes, that's all."

Stuart opened his mouth and then snapped it shut.

"We really must go," Joan reminded her sister.

Janet followed Joan out reluctantly. She really wanted to hear about that ghost.

Chapter 4

"I wanted to hear about the ghost," Janet complained as they drove back towards home.

"You know I don't believe in such things, really," Joan told her. "And clearly Mary didn't want Stuart to tell us anything. We'll have to get Stuart alone and ask him."

Janet shook her head. It seemed strange to hear Joan planning such things. It was usually Janet who went chasing after ghost stories and other oddities. Clearly retirement was bringing out a different side in her elder sister.

"What if Mrs. Appleton is haunting the house? Maybe Gavin murdered her and that's why no one knows what happened to her," Janet suggested.

"Maybe you have an overactive imagination," Joan replied. It wasn't the first time she'd said such a thing to her sister.

The next fortnight flew past as the sisters put their cottage on the market and began to pack their belongings for their move. While they had lived in the cottage for more than twenty years, neither was particularly sentimental about things, so besides books, they found they had little to sort through. Most of their furniture they arranged to donate to a local charity that helped families in crisis situations.

As Doveby House was fully furnished with good quality items, they were happy to share their good fortune with others.

Their cottage sold almost immediately and the new owners, who had just been transferred to the area for work, were eager to move in quickly. Doveby Trust was happy to agree to a quick sale as well, and by the middle of July the two women found themselves the proud owners of their very own bed and breakfast.

Some old friends threw a small party for them, with everyone promising to stay in touch. Doveby Dale was less than an hour from their previous home, and both sisters hoped that some of their friends would come and stay with them once they were settled.

The sisters hired professionals to paint every room in the house except for Janet's lilac bedroom, and once that was done, they moved in. They had little to do besides arrive with their suitcases, as all of the furniture was already in place. They hired a man with a van to follow them to Doveby House with the boxes and boxes of books that the sisters had decided to keep. Once he'd stacked the boxes in the library for them to sort out later and left, Joan found the kettle in the cupboard and made tea. They'd brought a small box of grocery items with them, little more than what they needed for a first cup of tea in their new home.

"Welcome home," Joan said to Janet as the pair sipped tea in the conservatory a short time later.

"I feel as if I should pinch myself," Janet said. "It doesn't quite feel real."

"No, it really doesn't," Joan laughed. "It all happened rather very quickly, didn't it?"

"Yes, perhaps too quickly. I'm sure I shall get lost on my way to the loo in the middle of the night tonight."

Joan laughed again. "Just don't tumble down the stairs," she cautioned.

"That's another good thing about my bedroom," Janet told her. "It's quite far from the stairs, really."

"So what shall we do first?" Joan asked after she'd refilled their cups.

"You should start baking," Janet told her. "You haven't baked any biscuits or treats in weeks. I know we've been busy, but I can't go much longer without some shortbread or at least a flapjack."

"I suppose we need to find the nearest grocery shop, then," Joan replied.

They finished their tea and headed out. When they'd talked with Stuart and Mary several weeks ago, the couple gave the sisters directions to the centre of Doveby Dale where there was a small grocery shop. The sisters decided that that would do for today. They'd need to find the larger shop eventually, to do their larger weekly shop, but for today they didn't need much.

Janet drove as they both tried to remember exactly what Stuart had said. The road was straight and he'd told them to simply follow it. A small single-story building that was completely lacking in any architectural style appeared alongside the road as they drove.

"Doveby Dale Garage," Janet read off the sign that was hanging at an awkward angle from a bent post.

"So that's where Gavin Appleton works," Joan said in a thoughtful tone. "Interesting."

"I always thought garages sold petrol," Janet said.

"All I saw were three garage doors in a row," Joan told her. "They were all shut, so I suppose the garage isn't open."

"It's the middle of the day, why would it be closed?"

"Maybe he doesn't have any business," Joan suggested.

"Well, he's not likely to get any if he's shut up when customers come calling, is he?"

Just around the next bend was the small main street of Doveby Dale, with shops and cafés dotted along it. At the far end of the street was the grocery shop they were looking for. The prices in the shop were higher than they would have been at a larger chain shop, but the sisters knew they were paying for convenience. The closest big name grocery shop was several miles further down the road in a somewhat busier area. They practically had this shop to themselves as they filled a shopping trolley with far more than they'd intended to purchase.

"We shouldn't shop when we're hungry," Joan said as they watched all their shopping adding up at the tills.

"But we have nothing to eat at the house," Janet countered. "I suppose we could have stopped and had lunch at a pub somewhere and then come shopping."

Joan wrinkled her nose. "I suppose we'll get through all this food eventually," she said as they loaded the bags into the car.

"Of course we will," Janet agreed. "I intend to get through a good deal of it today, even."

As they drove back past Gavin's garage, the rolling overhead door in the centre of the building began to rise. A very new-looking dark-coloured sedan pulled out of the garage and turned in the opposite direction. The sisters could see a man pulling the door back down behind the car.

"Gavin was driving that very fancy car," Joan told her sister.

"He must be repairing it," Janet said. "That isn't what he was driving the last time we saw him."

"I certainly can't see him owning something that luxurious," Joan agreed.

Back at home the sisters had a light snack before Joan began to bake. Janet left her sister doing what she loved best, deciding that this was the perfect time to do some exploring around their new home. She needed to do something while she waited for some delicious treat to be ready.

After pretending to consider looking around the guest rooms, Janet headed straight for the library. The boxes of books that they'd brought with them caught her eye, but she ignored them for the moment. Unpacking was boring, even if it needed to be done.

She started at the door and worked her way slowly around the room, pulling odd books from the shelf, curious as to what exactly they'd purchased with their new home. All of the books were hardcovers and most were in excellent condition. The more Janet looked around, the less she could understand how the books were arranged, however.

They were clearly not alphabetical, either by title or author, and they didn't seem to be arranged by subject matter, either. After an hour of trying to work out a pattern, she decided that, for some strange reason, the books had been shelved entirely at random.

"Well, that will never do," she said out loud. One of her favourite jobs as a teacher at their small village school had been running the tiny school library. Now she sat down at the small desk in one corner to think about how she'd like to arrange her new favourite place in the world.

After a while, she decided she needed to start taking notes. Joan would probably have her own ideas as well, so Janet wanted to be sure she knew exactly what she wanted to do before she talked to her sister. She pulled open the top desk drawer and found a pen amid the pencils, paper clips and other office supplies that were scattered inside.

The first side drawer held sheets of plain white paper and Janet pulled one out and began to make notes. After several minutes, she frowned. She'd been so distracted by all the glorious books that she hadn't given any thought to being nosy. But what else was in this desk?

She pulled open the middle side drawer and laughed. So much for being nosy, she thought as she stared at boxes of envelopes. That left only one more drawer. This is more like it, she thought as she pulled a pile of file folders out of the drawer.

Margaret Appleton's solicitor had given them a few boxes of paperwork that related to the running of the bed and breakfast. Those still needed to be gone though, but maybe that meant that this paperwork was more personal. Janet opened the first folder eagerly.

Inside were several letters from someone called "Jack," who wrote of his undying love for "his dear Maggie." Janet blushed and stopped reading the first letter after a particularly racy section. She shut the folder, surprised that no one had removed such personal correspondence from the house before it was sold. Perhaps this was the sort of thing that Gavin was looking for?

Three more folders were full of similar letters from "Simon," "Edward," and finally, "Kenneth." Janet did no more than skim the first letter in each pile, finding that they were all very intimate. Reading any more would have felt too invasive of the dead woman's privacy.

She opened the last folder, expecting more of the same, but instead she found letters that were all signed "Gavin." She began to read the first one, dated some ten years earlier, with some interest.

"Mother, I'm fine and I think I'm going to like living in Devon. I don't suppose you'll miss me all that much, as you're rather busy with all of the men in your life. Let me know when the next wedding is going to take place and I'll send a card. Gavin."

Janet sat back in the desk chair and closed her eyes. These letters were far less personal than the others, but Janet still felt that she really shouldn't read them. They must be the papers that Gavin wanted to collect, she thought. Perhaps she and Janet ought to take them to him.

"Dinner's ready," Joan called from the kitchen.

Janet dumped all of the files back in the bottom drawer and slid it shut. She was surprised to find that the entire afternoon had flown past. But she'd worry about the letters another time. The smells coming from the kitchen were more important.

Joan had made cottage pie with a rhubarb crumble for pudding.

"That was delicious," Janet said after she'd swallowed her last bite of crumble. "Not as good as apple, but nearly."

Joan laughed. "I'm glad you enjoyed it," she said. "Tomorrow I plan to start making biscuits and cakes and all the lovely things I usually make all the time and have quite neglected in the last few weeks."

"Oh, thank heavens," Janet told her. "All of my trousers are getting rather loose on me. I'd hate to have to go clothes shopping."

Janet could tell that her sister wasn't sure if she was kidding or not, but she just smiled at her.

"I found some letters from Gavin to his mother in a drawer in the desk in the library," she said after they'd done the washing up. The kitchen had a dishwasher, but neither sister was ready to try it out just yet. No doubt it would come in handy if they ever had a house full of guests, though.

"You didn't read them, did you?" Joan asked.

"I just skimmed through the first one," Janet said defensively. "Anyway, it was really short and didn't really say anything."

"I suppose our first job tomorrow should be to take the letters to Mr. Appleton, then," Joan said.

"I suppose," Janet agreed, hating to have to spend the time doing that when they could be doing so many more interesting things.

With the kitchen tidied, they both found books in the library to curl up with for a few hours and then headed to bed.

"I hope I can sleep," Joan said as Janet headed up the stairs. "It's always difficult in a strange place."

"I'm sure you'll be fine," Janet replied. "Just pretend you're on holiday."

Janet washed her face and brushed her teeth and then changed into her favourite nightgown. She crawled into bed and was asleep in minutes.

Some time after midnight, she came awake suddenly. She sat up in bed and listened. The loud scream that had woken her was repeated as her heart pounded in her chest.

Chapter 5

With her senses on full alert, Janet slowly slid out of bed and found her slippers and her bathrobe. She tiptoed across the bedroom and then stopped at her door. After the second scream, she'd heard nothing but silence. She turned the doorknob, wincing as it squeaked under her hand. Holding her breath, she slowly pulled the door open.

The moon, shining through a small window at the top of the landing, was providing the only illumination in the short hallway. Janet looked up and down the hall, but it was empty. After a moment of indecision, she headed for the stairs. Better to get Joan to join her before checking the other bedrooms. As she descended the stairs, she started to worry about her sister. Where was she? Surely the screams had woken her as well.

Janet expected to run into to Joan at any second, but she reached the ground floor without hearing another sound or seeing her sister. She walked down the corridor to the owner's suite and tapped gently on the door. After a moment, she knocked again, with more force. Getting no reply, she gave up on knocking and opened the door.

"Joan?" she called out quietly. "Are you awake?"

The sound of snoring coming from the bedroom answered that question for her. Janet shook her head and then stomped across the floor.

"Joan? Didn't you hear the screaming?" she asked loudly, right next to her sister's ear.

Joan sat up in bed, nearly bashing heads with Janet. "Janet? What are you doing here? What time is it?"

Janet glanced at the clock. "It's two-fifteen," she told her sister. "And I was woken up by screaming, so I came down to get you so we could check the house over together."

"Screaming?" Joan echoed. "I didn't hear anything."

"You were snoring too loudly," Janet replied.

"I don't snore," Joan told her stoutly. "I suppose you won't be able to sleep until we check the house, though, will you?"

Janet thought about it. "Not really," she said. "I definitely heard someone screaming. Maybe we should ring the police, now that I think about it."

"Let's look out the front window, first of all," Joan suggested. "Maybe something has happened across the street or something."

Joan put on her own slippers and robe and the two sisters headed towards the front of the house. The more awake she became, the more Janet began to doubt what she'd heard. Outside, the street was dark and nothing seemed to be moving.

"Are you sure you weren't dreaming?" Joan asked as they began to walk through the downstairs, switching lights on and off in each room.

"I'm sure," Janet replied, even though she was feeling less certain every second. She peeked into the small cloakroom, but it was as empty as every other room on the ground floor had been.

"Just the first floor to check," Joan said.

The two guest bedrooms and bathrooms were quickly inspected and found to be empty. Janet switched on her own lights and walked through her bedroom and bathroom.

"Nothing," she said quietly as she sat down on her bed.

"Perhaps you had a bad dream," Joan suggested. "You sometimes do in strange places."

"Yes, but I've never dreamed that I've heard screaming before," Janet argued. "It's very strange."

"I think we should both get back to sleep," Joan told her. "Would you like a cup of tea before you go back to bed?"

Janet shook her head. She'd caused enough fuss and bother for one night. "I'm sure some more sleep will do me a lot of good," she told her sister. "Sorry about waking you."

"That's no problem," Joan assured her.

Joan gave her a warm hug. Janet sat on the bed, listening to her sister's footsteps getting further away. After several minutes, she switched off the lights and curled back under the covers. Sleep was elusive and erratic and morning seemed to arrive far too quickly.

When she got downstairs for breakfast after a shower that did little to wake her up, Janet was pleased to find that Joan had made coffee. Both sisters preferred tea, but this morning coffee was definitely called for, at least as far as Janet was concerned. Joan didn't look the slightest bit tired.

"Did you manage to get back to sleep?" Joan asked as Janet filled the largest mug she could find to the very brim with hot coffee.

"Not really," Janet told her. She took a small sip and sighed. Although logic told her that the caffeine couldn't possibly have done anything yet, even that single sip seemed to make her feel more alert. By the time she'd emptied the mug, she felt almost like her usual self.

"I made oatmeal," Joan told her, filling a bowl for Janet.

Janet felt her emerging good mood vanish. She hated oatmeal and Joan knew it. Joan, on the other hand, not only loved it, but also seemed to feel that it had its own restorative qualities. Every time Janet was tired or poorly, Joan made her oatmeal for breakfast.

The sisters sat at the table together and ate their breakfast. Joan ate with enthusiasm, while Janet worked her way through her bowl resignedly.

"So, I suppose we should go and see Gavin Appleton this morning and give him the letters," Joan said as Janet did the washing up.

"Should we read them first?" Janet asked, hoping her sister would say yes, but fairly sure she wouldn't.

"That would be wrong," Joan said primly. "They aren't ours to read."

"They came with the house," Janet reminded her.

Joan shook her head. "We know that Gavin wants the letters back," she said. "Perhaps he's embarrassed by things he said in them. It isn't our place to read them."

"I'll go get them," Janet said, swallowing a sigh. It wasn't that she was especially nosy, she just had a healthy sense of curiosity, she told herself as she headed into the library. The folders were exactly where she'd left them and she flipped through them, pulling the bottom one out and returning to the kitchen with it.

"I'll just glance through the pile and make sure that they're all from Gavin," she told her sister, sitting down at the table. "We definitely shouldn't give him anything that isn't his."

Joan didn't object, so Janet quickly went through the small stack. It only took a moment to check that all of the letters were indeed signed "Gavin." There were only about a dozen letters in the pile and, as Janet closed the folder, she began to regret that she hadn't taken the time to read her way through them the previous evening, before she'd told Joan about them.

They agreed to stop at the man's garage on their way to the grocery shop. Now that Joan was feeling more settled in the house, she wanted to start doing a great deal more baking. Janet grinned as she climbed into the car. Joan's mood had all the hallmarks of a baking frenzy, something that happened once or twice a year to her sister, usually after some small upset.

The frenzy always started with Joan pulling out a number of cookbooks, looking for new and interesting recipes to try. Janet had spotted several of Joan's old favourites on the kitchen counter, along with a new American one that she'd purchased only a few weeks earlier.

If Janet was correct, the trip to the grocery shop would be an expensive one, but once they were home again Joan would start baking everything from bread to pies to biscuits and cakes.

We'd better invite the neighbours around for tea soon, Janet thought, otherwise we'll never eat it all. Joan usually baked for three or four days before she ran out of ingredients or recipes she wanted to try or both. Then she'd go back to her normal pattern of baking just a little something every day.

Joan drove today and Janet enjoyed the scenery that she hadn't really noticed on their last trip when she'd been driving. When they arrived at the garage, one of the large overhead doors was open.

"Oh, good, someone is here," Joan said as she turned into the car park.

"I hope it's Gavin," Janet said. "I don't want to leave these papers with a stranger."

Joan parked and turned off the engine. "I suppose we should both go in," she said in a reluctant voice.

"Unless you'd rather go alone," Janet said, suddenly wishing they'd just turned the papers over to the police to return to Gavin.

"Let's go," Joan said.

"Okay," Janet replied with forced enthusiasm.

"Hello?" Joan called as they approached the door. There was no reply. The sisters reached the door and peeked into the garage. A large black car was parked in the space, but no one was around.

"I think the office is over there," Janet whispered, pointing towards the back corner of the garage.

"Why are we whispering?" Joan hissed at her.

"I don't know," Janet replied in a hushed tone.

Janet took a deep breath and then strode purposefully towards the door. As she got closer she noticed that a small, hand-lettered sign that read "office" was stuck to the door. Stopping when she reached it, she knocked hard. The sound seemed to echo through the large space.

"It's open," a voice shouted from behind the door.

Janet glanced at Joan and then turned the knob, frowning as her hand encountered something sticky on its surface. She pushed the door open and forced herself to smile at the four men who were looking at her in surprise.

"I'm so sorry to interrupt," Janet said. "Only we found some letters in the house and we wanted to give them to you."

She addressed her remarks to Gavin, who was sitting facing the door at the large round table that took up most of the office space. The other three men, who looked considerably younger, had glanced at the two women and then turned away.

"Oh, great," Gavin muttered, jumping up from the table. "We can talk about that outside," he said, crossing to the sisters and ushering them out of the room.

"There isn't really anything to discuss," Joan said. She stopped in the middle of the garage and reached into her large handbag and pulled out the folder. "These are the letters we found. They're all from you to your mother."

Gavin frowned. "You didn't read them?" he demanded.

"No, of course not," Janet said indignantly. "I just flipped through them to make sure they were all from you. We didn't want to give you the wrong letters, now did we?"

"No, right, well, thanks then," Gavin said, opening the folder and flipping through it. "Is this all the letters you found?" he asked after a moment.

"So far, at least," Janet replied. "Why? Were you expecting there to be more?"

"Well, yeah," Gavin said. "I mean, I wrote to mum a lot. I thought there'd be a lot more."

"If we find anything else, we'll be sure to drop it off to you," Joan said.

"Yeah, or just ring me and I'll come get whatever it is," Gavin told them. "I don't want you to have to keep coming by here."

"It's no problem," Janet said. "You're on our way to the grocery shop, anyway."

"Yeah, well, thanks, then," Gavin said. He took them each by an arm and led them out of the garage.

"Those young men looked very young," Joan remarked as she dug in her handbag for her keys.

"I run a sort of apprentice-like scheme," Gavin muttered.

"There aren't a lot of good jobs around here, but people always need someone to repair their cars, you know?"

"Indeed," Joan said. "And how nice of you to help out future generations."

The sisters climbed into their car. Before Janet shut her door, Gavin grabbed it.

"I really want the rest of my letters," he told her intently. "Why don't I stop over tonight and see if I can find them myself?"

"That's not necessary," Janet answered. "If they're there, we'll find them eventually."

Gavin frowned and for a moment Janet felt a flash of fear. Before anyone spoke, Joan started the car's engine. Gavin opened his mouth and then snapped it shut. He pushed Janet's door shut and stepped away from the car.

Joan pulled away, back onto the road, headed for home. For several minutes neither woman spoke.

"I thought we were going grocery shopping," Janet said eventually.

"I was afraid that if Gavin thought the house was empty, he might try to find whatever it is he's after himself," Joan told her.

"Good thinking," Janet said. "He scares me a little bit."

"He scares me a lot," Joan told her.

"You don't think he killed his mother, do you?" Janet asked.

"We don't have any reason to believe that she was murdered," Joan pointed out. "But if she was, he'd be my first suspect."

"I suppose there's nothing wrong with them taking a break from working on that black car," Janet said after a moment.

"I'm not sure it's strictly legal to be playing poker with your apprentices in the middle of the afternoon," Joan suggested.

Janet laughed in spite of her unease at the man's behaviour. "There seemed to be an awful lot of money on the table. I didn't know apprentices were that well paid."

"So what do you think Gavin's really after?" Joan asked. "More letters or something else?"

"He seemed excited when we said we'd found some letters," Janet replied thoughtfully. "But then disappointed when he saw what we'd brought. Maybe there's something in one of the letters that gives Gavin a motive for murder. I wish I'd read them now."

"Whatever your suspicions of the man, reading the letters would have been wrong," Joan said firmly.

"But maybe it would have helped us work out what Gavin is looking for," Janet replied.

"Maybe Stuart will have some idea of what Gavin's after," Joan suggested as she pulled into their car park.

"Why don't you run to the grocery shop while I talk to him?" Janet replied as she too spotted the man, who was busily watering the flowering shrubs along the side of Doveby House.

"Okay," Joan agreed. "There are a few little things I really wanted to get today."

Janet smiled to herself as she got out of the car. Her sister would be baking up a storm before lunch.

Chapter 6

"Another lovely day," Stuart said as Janet joined him in the garden.

"It's so nice to have all this sunshine," Janet agreed. "I hope it isn't too much extra work for you."

Stuart laughed. "I love watering the flowers," he told her. "I don't get to do it very often. We usually have plenty of rain."

"Everything looks gorgeous," Janet told him, taking a moment to truly enjoy the beautiful flowers that seemed to be blooming everywhere in their garden.

"It's come a long way in the last few years," Stuart told her. "When I took over there was nothing here but grass and mud."

"Do let us know what we need to pay you for looking after all of this," Janet said. "I just hope we can afford you."

"I'm sure we can come to some sort of agreement," Stuart said with a wave of his hand. "I love the job."

Janet smiled and then tried to think of a way to gradually bring the conversation around to the various things she wanted to ask the man. After a moment, she shrugged. It would be easier to simply be blunt.

"We found a few letters in the house from Gavin to his mother," she said.

Stuart stopped watering the roses and looked at Janet, clearly interested in what she was saying. "Did you now?"

"Yes, we've just dropped them off to him at his garage," Janet replied. "But he seemed quite disappointed with them. I gather he was looking for something other than those particular letters. Do you have any idea what he might be after?"

"I never believed it was letters he was after," Stuart said in a quiet voice. "I think his mother left something really valuable in the house, but only Gavin knows what it is."

"Like what?" Janet asked.

"I don't know," Stuart shrugged. "She married a succession of very rich men. Maybe there's some jewellery or a vase from ancient Egypt or something."

"I haven't seen anything that looks valuable," Janet said. "Although we haven't been through every drawer in every room yet."

"You may not even recognise the thing as valuable," Stuart suggested. "But I bet Gavin knows exactly what it is. I think his problem is that he isn't sure where it is."

"Has he been in the house since his mother died?"

"Not as far as I know," Stuart said. "I'm not exactly sure what happened to Margaret, but the first we knew about her passing was when a man from the trust showed up with a solicitor. The trust had the locks changed and the man asked us to keep an eye out for Gavin in case he came around."

"Which he did."

"Yes, later that same day he was over there, trying to get in," Stuart told her. "I rang young Robert and he came and had a word with him."

"So he didn't know about his mother's death until that day, either?" Janet asked.

"I suppose not," Stuart said. "He and Margaret had had a big fight about six months before she died and Gavin hadn't been around to see her after that. Like I said, I'm not really clear on what happened to Margaret."

"Surely the trust had someone go through the house and remove anything of great value?" Janet asked.

"They did, that's why I reckon whatever Gavin's after is either hidden or doesn't look valuable, but is," Stuart told her. "I don't know how careful the trust was, anyway. They were so excited at getting the house, I don't think they gave much thought to the contents."

"What does the Doveby Trust do, anyway?" Janet asked.

"As I understand it, they run a scholarship programme for kids from the Doveby Dale area," Stuart told her. "They encourage young people to go to university and then come back to the area to work. Doveby Dale is too small to give jobs to all of them when they finish, but they try to get the kids to come back to somewhere in Derbyshire anyway, rather than seeing them all move to London or some other big city in the south."

"And Margaret supported what they're doing?"

"I didn't know Margaret even knew they existed," Stuart replied. "I've no idea why she left them anything, let alone her entire estate."

Janet frowned. The more questions she asked, the more complicated everything became. "Did you hear someone screaming last night?" she asked, changing the subject completely.

"It was the full moon, wasn't it?"

"The full moon was screaming?"

"No," Stuart smiled at her. "Which bedroom are you using? I bet I can guess. I bet you're in the purple bedroom, aren't you?"

"I am, yes," Janet admitted.

"Every time there's a full moon, the ghost in that bedroom screams twice right around two in the morning. At least that's what Margaret told us. After a while she stopped renting that room when the moon was due to be full. She said it wasn't worth the bother."

"There's a ghost in my bedroom?" Janet felt a strange mix of fear and excitement.

"Oh, there are ghosts all over Doveby House," Stuart replied cheerfully. "It's been there for a long time and lots of things have happened within its walls. You have to expect a ghost or two in a house that old, don't you?"

"I suppose I'd never thought about it," Janet said slowly.

"And the estate agent wouldn't have mentioned it," Stuart said. "He wouldn't have wanted to risk putting you off the place."

"So is the ghost in my bedroom going to scream every time there's a full moon?" Janet asked.

"Apparently so. As long as you don't paint."

"What do you mean by that?"

"Margaret tried painting that room blue once, and apparently the ghost cried every night until she covered the blue with purple again."

Janet shook her head. There was a part of her that didn't believe a word Stuart was saying and a part of her that was keeping an open mind. She did hear the screaming, after all.

"We aren't planning on painting the room, at least not for now."

"Good, so you only have to worry about full moons," Stuart said with a grin.

"What about other ghosts?" Janet asked.

"Oh, well, there's one in the coach house, of course," Stuart replied. "And one in the library."

"Stuart? Aren't you done yet?"

Janet spun around and forced herself to smile at Mary, who was quickly crossing the grass towards them.

"I thought we were going into Sheffield for lunch," she said crossly to her husband. "You said you just needed five minutes."

Stuart flushed. "Sorry, love, but I got busy chatting with Janet and lost track of time. Give me two more minutes and I'll be ready to go."

He gave Janet an apologetic smile and turned back to the flowers. Janet walked back towards the car park with Mary.

"Sorry about that," she told the other woman. "Joan and I had just been to see Gavin and I was curious if Stuart had any idea what Gavin might want in our new home."

"I expect he's got some drugs hidden in there somewhere,"

Mary told her. "You need to look out for things that look like medicine or strange powders."

"Really? Gavin does drugs?"

"I expect so," Mary replied. "He seems like the type and he and his mum had a huge fight about something. I reckon she found his secret stash in her house and got mad."

"Surely if she found it, she would have made him get rid of it," Janet suggested.

"Maybe she only found part of it," Mary said with a shrug. "Or maybe she was using it to keep Gavin in line or something."

"Okay, I'm ready to go," Stuart came up behind them. "I've left the hosepipe out," he told Janet. "I'm going to have to water more later."

"No problem," Janet replied. "Thank you both for taking the time to talk with me. I'm sure I'll see you soon. Have fun in Sheffield."

She watched the pair walk back to their house, wondering what her sister would make of the different ideas about Gavin that they'd shared with her. She didn't have long to wait to find out. Joan pulled into the car park only a few minutes after Janet had gone inside. Now she rushed back out to help Joan unload the car.

"Any sign of Gavin?" Joan asked as they worked together in the kitchen, unpacking the groceries.

"No, although Mary and Stuart both had different theories about what Gavin might be after," Janet replied.

"Such as?"

Janet told her sister everything that the Longs had said, except for what Stuart had said about the ghosts. Joan always said she didn't believe in such things and Janet was reluctant to bring the matter up, at least for now when they had other things to worry about.

"So they both think there's something hidden in the house that Gavin wants, even if they don't agree on what it might be," Joan concluded. "I think after lunch we need to search the place. Maybe we can find what Gavin wants."

Joan made a light lunch and the pair ate quickly. Janet wasn't convinced that they would find anything, but they really should have taken the time to go through the whole house as soon as they took possession. With the lunch dishes washed and put away, Joan headed to the owner's suite, while Janet climbed up to the first floor.

She did a quick tour of her room, fairly certain that she'd inspected it thoroughly when she'd moved in. There was nothing under the bed. The wardrobe was full of her clothes, and she was positive it had been empty when she'd unpacked. There were no obvious hiding places in the bathroom, but she poked around anyway, checking the empty medicine chest and even lifting off the back of the toilet. There was nothing hiding there.

Across the hall, she checked the smaller of the two guest rooms. There were a few hatboxes in the back of the wardrobe, and Janet felt her heart racing as she peeked inside the first one. The large black hat that occupied the box wasn't worth the excitement she'd felt. The other two boxes were also, disappointingly, full of ugly old hats. A quick look around the en-suite bathroom revealed nothing and left only the final guest room to check.

This time Janet started with the bathroom, fairly certain that she would find nothing, which proved to be the case. In the bedroom, the small chest of drawers and the bedside table were both empty. The wardrobe, however, had a few small boxes piled up in the back of it. Janet pulled the boxes out one at a time. She was about to open the top one when she heard her sister calling.

"Janet? Have you found anything interesting?"

"I'm in the larger guest room," Janet called back. "We really do have to give these rooms names or something."

"Yes, well, I'll leave that to you," Joan told her as she walked into the room. "You'll come up with something far more interesting than I would. I'd probably call them the blue room and the green room or something."

Janet frowned. "I'm sure we can do better than that," she told her sister. "I just need to do some research. Maybe someone famous once stayed in one of the rooms or something."

"I rather doubt that," Joan replied. "I'm sure the estate agent would have mentioned it when he showed us around, if that were the case."

"Maybe he didn't know," Janet answered, unwilling to be discouraged.

"Anyway, I found a few boxes in the back of one of the cupboards downstairs," Joan told her. "What have you found?"

"A couple of boxes as well," Janet replied. Joan crossed to her and Janet opened the first box.

"Are they car parts?" Joan asked as they stared into the box.

"I've no idea," Janet answered. The box was full of metal plates in various sizes as well as assorted screws, washers, and other metal parts that the sisters couldn't identify. Janet poked around inside the box, but recognised nothing.

They set the box to one side and opened the next one. It seemed to be full of old papers. Janet flipped through the pile. "Gas bills, electricity bills, car registrations, receipts for big-ticket items, notes from former guests, and the like," she told her sister. "I don't see anything especially interesting here, do you?"

Joan glanced at the top couple of sheets and shook her head. "It all looks to be at least a couple of years old, as well as uninteresting. We should go through the lot though, at some point, just in case there's something important in the pile."

"Maybe not today," Janet suggested. She shut the box quickly, hoping her sister might forget about the boring task of sorting someone else's old paperwork into some sort of order.

Janet was disappointed to find that the third box was more of the same. "Surely she could have at least sorted this into categories," Janet grumbled as she riffled through old bank statements and grocery shop receipts.

"Like we do?" Joan asked with a laugh.

Janet shook her head. She knew that somewhere in the handful of boxes the sisters had brought with them was one box that was full of nothing but unsorted paperwork. Both she and Joan always intended to go through it and file everything neatly into separate folders, but neither sister ever seemed to find the time to get the job done. Instead, box after box got filled with papers. When they'd moved, they'd sent several boxes of older papers away to be burned.

"Maybe we should just turn them all over to Gavin," Joan suggested. "He can have the fun of looking through them all."

"He'd just burn the lot," Janet said.

"And that would be bad because?"

"You never know," Janet said. "There could be information about past guests or even about our ghosts."

As soon as the words left her mouth, Janet wished she could take them back. Joan's reaction was pretty much what she expected.

"Our ghosts?" Joan asked. "Surely you don't believe such nonsense?" Joan gave her a piercing look. "Who's been telling you about ghosts?"

"Stuart just said a few things," Janet answered. "I gather, from what he said, that Margaret Appleton believed in the ghosts. I just thought there might be something in here that gives us more information."

"To entertain the tourists with, you mean," Joan suggested.

"Exactly," Janet agreed eagerly. One look at her sister's face told her that she hadn't fooled Joan. Janet didn't really believe in ghosts, but she was more willing to consider the possibility of them than Joan. She'd heard the screams, after all. If there was anything in the paperwork they'd found that could tell her more about that, then going through them would be well worth it.

Janet carried the box of metal bits down the stairs and put it on the kitchen table. Joan followed with the two boxes of papers. Then the pair inspected the boxes that Joan had found. All three contained papers, and Janet swallowed a sigh as they opened the last box.

"More papers," she said. "Going through all of this is going to be a job."

"I suppose something in one of the boxes could be what Gavin is after," Joan said. "Maybe there are valuable stock certificates hiding in between the credit card statements and the telephone bills."

"Maybe," Janet said doubtfully. "What about the box of metal parts? Do you think that's what Gavin wants?"

Joan shrugged. "I don't know, I suppose it could be."

"Maybe we should take that box to the police," Janet suggested. "I can't imagine we have any use for it. Perhaps Constable Parsons will know what all the bits are."

"Let's take it now," Joan replied. "Then, when we get back, I'll make dinner."

Chapter 7

The Doveby Dale branch of the Derbyshire Constabulary was housed in a tiny building that had once been a miner's cottage. A sign on the front gave the hours that the building was staffed.

"That seems foolish," Janet remarked as they walked from their car to cottage door. "Surely they're as good as telling the criminals when there won't be any police about."

The cottage had originally been one large room, but now it was partitioned off into a tiny reception area with two offices behind it. Janet felt claustrophobic as soon as she stepped inside the front door. She imagined that she would confess to just about anything if she'd been forced to spend any time in one of the tiny and enclosed offices.

"Can I help you ladies?" A middle-aged woman was sitting at the reception desk. She'd been knitting when the sisters arrived, but she put her needles down and looked at them expectantly. Her hair was platinum blonde and her eyes were a lovely shade of green.

"We'd like to see Constable Parsons, please," Joan told her, setting the box on the desk.

"Oh, I'm terribly sorry, but he isn't here right now. Did you have an appointment?" the woman asked.

"No, I didn't realise we needed one," Joan replied.

The woman chuckled. "Oh, you really don't, at least not normally. But we've had a call about a missing child, you see, so Robert, er, Constable Parsons is out investigating."

"A child missing from Doveby Dale?" Janet asked.

"Indeed," the woman replied solemnly. "I don't know if you heard about the little girl who went missing in Clowne a short time ago, but there are similarities between the cases."

"And that little girl hasn't been found yet, has she?" Janet held her breath as she waited for the reply, hoping she was incorrect.

"No, she hasn't," the woman answered. "Her mother is quite frantic."

"I can't even imagine," Janet told her, shaking her head.

"If you absolutely have to see Constable Parsons, I can ring him and see when he thinks he might be back," she suggested.

"Oh, no. If he's looking for a missing child, that's far more important than what we wanted," Joan said firmly. "We'll just leave this with you and you can tell him all about it."

"What is it?" the woman asked, a worried look on her face.

"We've just purchased Doveby House," Joan told her, adding their names to the introduction.

"Oh, it's very nice to meet you," the woman replied. "I'm Susan Garner. I do hope you're going to get the bed and breakfast up and running again quickly. Margaret Appleton used to sell my crafts for me to her guests." She gestured towards the knitting that she'd put down on the counter. "I wasn't getting rich, but it was a nice little bit of extra income for me."

Janet and Joan exchanged glances. "I didn't realise that the previous owner did that," Janet said. "It may be a while before we get the place open for business again."

Susan nodded. "Well, when you do, I'd love it if you'd display and sell some of my blankets and jumpers again."

"Of course we will," Janet assured her.

"Margaret kept ten per cent of the sales, which seemed more than fair to me," Susan continued.

"I'm sure we can work something out once we get back in business," Joan said, clearly putting an end to the topic. "When we were going through the house we found this box of car parts," she told Susan. "We wondered if this is what Gavin Appleton is after. He seems quite determined to get inside the house."

Susan opened the box and looked inside. "Are you sure they're car parts?" she asked, poking a finger randomly into the box.

"No, not at all," Janet replied. "But we thought they might be and that Constable Parsons might know why Gavin wants them."

Susan shrugged. "I'll have him take a look when he gets back," she said. "I know there was a case in Derby a few years ago where a garage owner was making cheap car parts himself and fitting them, while charging his customers for proper parts from the manufacturers. It was only when the parts started falling to bits and causing accidents that someone worked it out and rang the police. Maybe Gavin is doing something similar in his garage. Robert can certainly check it out."

The sisters went back to their car and headed for home.

"She was very nice," Janet commented once they were underway, with Joan at the wheel again.

"Yes, and her knitting was lovely," Joan replied.

"I didn't get a close look."

"I did. She's very talented. I can see why Margaret was willing to sell her things at Doveby House."

"But we aren't necessarily going to be taking on paying guests," Janet said.

"Once we've worked out exactly what we are going to do, we'll have to talk to Susan again and then go from there."

"Do you think that Gavin's making his own car parts?" Janet asked.

Joan shrugged. "I don't know. There were a lot of nuts and bolts and screws and things in the box. Maybe he's making those sorts of little things."

"I can't imagine there's much money in nuts and bolts," Janet mused.

"But neither of us knows anything about cars," Joan pointed out. "I don't even go over the bill when we take the car to the garage for oil changes and the like. Maybe we're paying a lot for little bits and just don't realise it."

"So maybe we should visit Gavin again," Janet suggested. "We could have a look around the garage and see if there are any suspicious looking parts."

Joan laughed. "That is one of the worst ideas I've ever heard from you, little sister," she said. "We wouldn't know a badly made part from a brand-new one from the manufacturer. What would we even look for?"

"I don't know," Janet admitted. "But we could have a look around."

"How exactly?" Joan asked. "If Gavin is there, he isn't exactly going to take us on a tour, and if he isn't there one of his intimidating apprentices will be, or the place will be shut."

Janet didn't answer, but her mind was racing. There had to be a way to snoop around the garage. She just had to work out what it was.

Back at Doveby House, Janet paced around in small circles in the library, thinking about Gavin, while Joan made dinner. After they'd eaten and Janet had washed up, the sisters settled in to watch a bit of telly and relax. Before the programme they planned to watch had even started, though, they heard someone knocking at their door.

"Who could that be?" Joan asked as she got up from the couch.

"Maybe Constable Parsons came over to talk about the box we left for him," Janet suggested.

Both sisters were surprised to find Michael Donaldson on their porch.

"Mr. Donaldson, do come in," Joan said.

"I hope I've not come at an inconvenient time," the man said as he stepped inside. "I've been meaning to come over for a chat for days but I've been rather busy."

"You're always welcome," Janet assured him.

"Oh, thank you kindly," the man beamed at her.

"Would you like some tea and biscuits?" Joan asked. "I baked shortbread and oatmeal raisin biscuits today."

"I don't want to cause you any bother," Michael replied.

"Oh, please," Janet said with a laugh. "We bought a bed and breakfast so my sister can bake for more people than just me. Come and have tea and biscuits. We'll never eat everything she made today and she'll be baking more tomorrow."

In the kitchen, Janet filled the kettle while Joan piled biscuits onto a plate. Within minutes the trio was seated around the table enjoying their snack.

"These are very good," Michael said after he'd had one of each biscuit.

"Please, take more," Janet suggested. "And then you can tell us all about yourself."

"That seems a fair trade," Michael replied, his eyes twinkling. He ate his way through a couple more biscuits, washing them down with tea, before speaking again.

"I haven't had a very exciting life," he told them in an apologetic voice. "I was born and raised in Doveby Dale and aside from university, I've never really left."

"It's a lovely place," Janet said.

"It is," Michael agreed. "My wife was from the village as well. We met in primary school and started seeing each other when I was sixteen. I never really went out with anyone else. We got married as soon as I graduated from university. Unfortunately, we were never blessed with children, and my wife passed away a few years back."

"What did you study at university?" Janet asked.

"I trained as a chemist," he replied. "I had my own little shop in the village for nearly forty years, but I retired last year and shut the shop."

"We're both retired as well," Janet told him. "We were both primary schoolteachers."

"And now you're going to start a bed and breakfast," Michael said. "Are you fulfilling a lifelong dream?"

"Yes, rather," Joan answered, earning a surprised look from Janet.

"Well, if there's anything I can do to help, just ask," he said. "I'm usually home and often bored. Being retired is rather dull. This last week I was filling in at one of the chemists in Derby. I do that from time to time."

"That's very good of you," Joan said.

"I was thinking that I should find a part-time job," he told them. "Just a few hours here and there, but something to get me out of the house. I don't suppose you'll need someone to help with serving breakfast and the like?"

Janet and Joan exchanged glances. "I don't think so," Janet said after an awkward pause. "I mean, we haven't actually given the business side of things any real thought."

"I've given it quite a bit of thought," Joan said sharply. "But we have some way to go before we're ready to start taking on guests. We will certainly keep you in mind if we find that we're needing additional staff, as we go on."

Michael smiled. "Good, well, I suppose I should be getting home. It's getting rather late."

The sisters walked him to the door, where he paused.

"I don't suppose, that is, well, I was wondering, that is, Joan, would you like to have dinner with me tomorrow night?" he asked.

Joan flushed. "I don't know, that is, um, we're just getting settled in and…."

Janet held up a hand. "She'd love to," she told Michael. "You can pick her up at seven."

"Smashing," Michael replied. He thanked them for the tea and biscuits and disappeared down the steps towards his home.

Janet shut the door behind him and turned to her sister. "Well, he's very nice, isn't he?"

"He asked me to have dinner with him," Joan said in a weak voice.

"I'm sure you'll have a lovely time," Janet said brightly.

"I'm not," Joan answered. She grabbed Janet's hands. "I've never been on a date," she reminded her. "I don't know how it works."

"It's just like having dinner with a friend," Janet told her. "You eat, you talk, you laugh, that's all."

"But he isn't a friend," Joan snapped back.

"Not yet, but I think he will be," Janet told her. She looked at her sister's face and sighed. Joan looked halfway between terrified and furious. "Let's have some more tea," she muttered.

Back in the kitchen, Janet pushed Joan into a chair and then refilled the kettle. She busied herself with meaningless tasks until the kettle boiled and she could make the tea. She put a great deal of extra sugar in her sister's drink before she handed it to her. Anything that might help sweeten her sister's mood was worth trying.

"I'm sorry," Janet began with after she sat down across from Joan. "I shouldn't have just agreed on your behalf like that, but you were babbling and I thought the poor man needed an answer."

"You should have said no," Joan told her quietly.

"Why? He seems very nice and he must be smart if he was a chemist. What's wrong with him?"

"I don't know, but there must be something or he would have asked you out and not me," Joan said sulkily.

Janet shook her head. "Don't start with that," she told her sister sternly. "You could have had lots of boyfriends when you were younger, but you never gave anyone a chance."

"It was more fun watching you go out with every man you met," Joan shot back.

Janet laughed. "I had lots of fun, but never got serious about anyone," she replied. "I didn't want to get married and be expected to give up teaching to raise a family."

"I didn't either, so it was easier to not even date."

"But going on dates was really good fun," Janet told her. "And now we're both retired, so we can date as much as we like. We could even get married if we wanted to."

Joan shook her head. "I'll have dinner with Michael tomorrow since you've told him I would, but then I'm done. One date in my lifetime is more than enough."

"We'll see about that," Janet answered.

Chapter 8

Joan was less certain about even having that one date the next day. Janet felt as if she spent all of the time from lunch until seven o'clock talking her sister into going.

"This is a bad idea," Joan said as the sisters waited for Michael to arrive.

"This is one dinner, two hours, out of your life," Janet said for the five-hundredth time. "Just go and have fun and stop making such a big deal out of it."

"That's easy for you to say," Joan muttered, plucking at her skirt.

"Stop fussing. You look lovely," Janet said soothingly. She took both of her sister's hands and looked into her eyes. "Really, you look wonderful, and you'll have fun, I promise."

"Make sure your mobile is on," Joan told her. "I might want you to come and get me."

"Do you want me to ring you every half hour to make sure things are going okay?" Janet asked.

"Would you?" Joan replied.

"No," Janet said firmly.

Before Joan could argue further, someone knocked on the door.

Janet watched all of the colour drain from her sister's face. She shook her head and headed towards the door.

"You're way too stressed about a simple dinner," she told Joan just before she opened the door.

Michael stood on the other side, a bouquet of flowers in his hand.

"Ah, good evening, Janet," he said with a small bow. "These are for you."

He handed Janet the flowers. She took them, feeling confused.

"I remember you said that Joan does most of the cooking," he told her. "I thought you deserved a little something for my making you get your own dinner tonight."

"That's very kind of you," Janet told him, giving him bonus points for being so thoughtful. She looked over at her sister. Joan looked more pleased than Janet had ever seen her look before.

"I did make sure she'd have something to eat," Joan told Michael. "I made soup. She just has to heat it up."

Michael laughed. "But she'll miss out on your company," he pointed out. "Surely that warrants a few flowers."

"Whatever the reason, they're beautiful and I very much appreciate them," Janet said. "Now off you two go. Have a wonderful time."

Janet nearly shoved her sister out the door. Michael took Joan's arm and escorted her down the steps to the pavement. Janet watched as they crossed the road and Michael helped Joan into his car. Only then did she shut the door.

For a giddy moment she felt like shouting. From what she'd seen, Michael was a lovely man and he and Joan seemed well suited. She just hoped her sister would get over her nerves and actually enjoy herself.

In the kitchen, she arranged the flowers in a vase and then heated her soup. She sliced some fresh bread to have with it and washed the meal down with a cup of tea. After washing up, she sat back in her chair, uncertain of exactly what she wanted to do with an evening to herself. Before she'd made up her mind, she heard a knock on the door.

"Constable Parsons, this is a surprise," she said when she'd opened the door.

"I just have a few questions about the box you brought in to me," the young man replied. "Can I have a few minutes of your time?"

"Certainly, do come in," Janet offered.

"I'm sorry I've come by so late," he said after he'd taken a seat in the small sitting room. "I was rather busy yesterday, and today was one of my days to be in Little Burton. It was only an hour ago that I stopped back at the station and found the box."

"What about the missing child?" Janet had to ask.

"She was at her grandmother's house," the policeman replied. "It was all just a big misunderstanding."

"And what about the little girl from Clowne?"

"That child is still missing," he said with a frown. "It's quite sad and a very difficult case, but that isn't why I'm here."

"No, of course not, sorry," Janet said. "What did you want to ask me?"

"Is your sister at home?"

"No, does that matter?"

"I suppose not. Do you mind if I ask where she is?"

Janet frowned. "I suppose not," she answered slowly, wondering why the man was asking. "She's having dinner with a friend."

Robert nodded. "As you both were parties to finding the box, I'd like to hear the whole story from each of you. I suppose it's better that she isn't home. I can interview her separately another time."

"So what we found is important?" Janet asked.

The man shrugged. "I just want to be clear on how you came to find it," he said. "I haven't gone through the whole box yet, but at first glance it seems as if some of the contents might be interesting."

"Interesting in a criminal context?"

"Let's just leave it at interesting, shall we?"

Janet felt a hundred questions flood to her lips, but she rejected most of them before speaking. "What do you need to know?" was the question that she finally let out.

"Where did you find the box?"

"It was in the back of the wardrobe in one of the guest rooms," Janet answered.

"Were there other boxes there, or just that one?"

"There were two others, but they just contained paperwork."

"Can I have a quick look at the other two boxes?"

Janet thought for a moment, but couldn't think of any reason not to let the man go through the boxes. "Let me go and get them," she told him.

They'd left the boxes in Joan's small sitting room. Janet carried them both into the main sitting room. Constable Parsons was sitting exactly where she'd left him when she returned.

He quickly took the boxes from her and then set them on the coffee table. He sat down and opened the top box. After only barely glancing inside each box, he was back on his feet.

"Thank you," he said. "I think I've seen enough for tonight. I'll probably be back tomorrow to have a better look at what you have there."

Janet opened her mouth to reply, but the man was already leaving. She hurried behind him, getting to the door after he'd already pulled it open.

"Thank you for bringing me that box," he said as he headed across the porch. "We'll get everything sorted tomorrow, I imagine."

Janet shut the door behind him and sighed. Get what sorted? And why tomorrow and not tonight? What had the man seen in the papers that Margaret had left behind?

Back in the sitting room, Janet flipped through the first box, looking for a clue as to what the policeman had seen. Nothing in the pile of utility bills and correspondence caught her eye. She opened the second box and looked at the first few sheets. The third item in the box caught her eye.

The paper was thick and felt expensive. It was from "Powell, Brown, Abbot and Grey, Solicitors."

Without her sister there to stop her, Janet read the letter, which simply confirmed that Margaret had made an appointment to make changes to her will. The handwritten note in the margin was more interesting.

"Maggie, I know you and Gavin are not getting along at the moment, but to suggest that he might do anything to harm you seems extreme. We'll talk on Monday about the changes you want to make. George"

The letter was signed by "George Abbot" and his signature seemed to match the handwritten note. Janet sat back and tried to think. The appointment mentioned in the letter would have taken place after Margaret's death, so presumably the woman never made whatever changes to her will she was planning.

Janet paced around the room, wondering what Margaret had been intending. Had Gavin known about the appointment and killed his mother to prevent her keeping it? Perhaps Gavin didn't realise that his mother had already cut him out of her will. Perhaps he thought she was going to do that with this appointment. Would that have led Gavin to murder her?

When she couldn't answer any of those questions, Janet switched to thinking about the box of car parts. Was Gavin doing something illegal or unethical at his garage? Was it possible that his mother was threatening to go to the police with the box of parts?

Janet sighed and sat back down on the couch. Joan was on her mind at least as much as Gavin and his mother. Was her sister having a good time? Janet could only hope that Joan and Michael would find things to talk about and have a good meal. She looked at the clock.

It was only half eight and way too early to think about heading to bed. She wandered into the library and pulled down a book at random. It was an old detective story and Janet flipped through the pages, unable to actually concentrate on the story. A passage caught her eye.

The police don't seem interested in anything I tell them. I think it's time to do some of my own investigating.

Janet read the lines again and then frowned. Such behaviour was always a bad idea in these sorts of books. She shut the book and slid it back onto the shelf. There was no way she was contemplating such an action herself. She didn't even know what she ought to investigate. She couldn't very well tell the police that she thought

Gavin might have murdered his mother when she had no idea how the woman had died.

In the kitchen, she made herself a cup of tea. She pulled out a box of biscuits and frowned. Digestives just didn't sound good. She wanted custard creams. She dug through the cupboard, but there weren't any custard creams hiding at the back. As she sipped her tea, she nibbled her way through a digestive, but it wasn't the same.

Five minutes later she found herself in the car, heading to the nearby grocery shop. It wasn't like her to be out and about at nearly nine o'clock, but she wouldn't sleep until her sister was home anyway, and she'd feel much better once she'd had a few custard creams.

She slowed down as she passed Gavin's garage, wondering to herself if driving past the garage was the real reason she'd come out. She pushed the thought from her mind and drove on to the grocery shop. As she had no idea where the man lived, she couldn't snoop any further than she had, pointlessly driving past the garage that had been dark and shut up tight.

She pulled out a trolley and made her way through the shop, randomly selecting everything that sounded good. Ten minutes later, at the tills, she giggled to herself. Joan would have a fit when she saw all of the unhealthy food Janet had picked out. Janet knew that Joan would eat her fair share of the crisps, cakes, chocolate and biscuits, however much she complained.

"Having a little party?" the cashier asked as she packed everything into bags.

"Just a small one," Janet answered, hoping she wasn't blushing as much as she felt she was.

"I love these, " the girl said, holding up a box of cakes. "I could eat this whole box in one sitting."

"At my age, if I did that, I'd gain ten pounds," Janet told her with a rueful smile.

"Oh, I know. My mum keeps telling me that I won't be able to keep eating like I do in a few years," the young girl said cheerfully. "I'm studying to be a dietician at university, anyway, so I do try to eat healthy most of the time. It would easier if fattening food didn't taste so good."

Janet laughed. There was no way she could argue with the girl.

"Let me get Jack to walk you out," the girl insisted. "He can load up your car."

Janet protested, but the girl had already buzzed the office for assistance. Jack turned out to be a tall and gangly young man who looked no more than sixteen. He blushed bright red when the cashier spoke to him.

"Jack, can you please help this lady to her car and load everything into her boot?" she asked

"Sure," he muttered. He walked ahead of Janet out of the shop, pushing her trolley for her.

She unlocked the car and then opened the boot for him. It only took Jack a few moments to load the bags into it.

"Thank you kindly," she told the boy.

"You're welcome," he mumbled.

"My sister and I have just bought Doveby House," Janet said. "I suspect you'll be seeing a lot of us here in the future."

"Doveby House? From Gavin Appleton?"

"Well, from his mother's estate," Janet replied. "Do you know Gavin?"

"Not really, but I know a few of the guys who work for him," Jack said. "I'd advise you to stay away from them, really. They aren't nice guys."

"They aren't?"

"I thought about applying there. Gavin seems to pay really well, but he hired some old schoolmates of mine that I'm not eager to spend time with," Jack explained. "This place doesn't pay nearly as well, but I like everyone I work with."

Janet wanted to ask the boy a dozen more questions, but he glanced back at the shop and then grabbed the now empty trolley.

"I'd better get back to work," he said. "I expect I'll see you around."

Janet nodded. "I'm sure you will."

She climbed into her car and sat behind the wheel for several minutes, thinking about what Jack had said. She was surprised to hear that Gavin paid well. The garage didn't look as if it were that successful. Shaking her head, she started the engine. She'd met some of Gavin's staff, and she had to agree with what Jack had said. They didn't seem like nice young men.

She headed for home, eagerly anticipating not only custard creams, but a few other little treats while she waited for her sister. Almost unconsciously, she found herself slowing down slightly as she approached Gavin's garage. She was startled to see one of the overhead doors open and lights on inside the building. Slowing down even further, Janet tried to see who was at the garage and what they were doing.

Without giving herself time to think, Janet indicated and then turned into the car park for the garage. She drove to the far end of the lot, pulling into a space as far from the building as she could get. None of the light from inside the garage reached this far and there were no streetlights along this stretch of road. Janet turned off her car's engine and sat in the darkness, trying to work out what she was going to do next.

Chapter 9

After watching the garage for several minutes, she didn't see anyone moving around inside it. Rather quickly, she began to get bored. The sensible voice inside her head told her to go home and eat biscuits. Janet chose to listen to the other voice that suggested she should check things out.

She opened her car door and stepped outside, shutting the door behind her as quietly as she could. The noise felt loud to her, and she waited for someone to come rushing out of the garage to investigate, but no one appeared. She walked quickly from her car towards the edge of the building, trying to keep to the shadows. Feeling somewhat ridiculous, she crept along the building's side wall, stopping to listen every few seconds.

The third garage door, furthest from the office, was the open one. When she reached the open door she stopped and listened carefully. She couldn't hear anything except the pounding of her own heart. The sensible voice told her to go home.

"Hello?" she called softly, stepping into the garage. A couple of cautious steps later, she called again. "Hello? Is there anyone here?"

The bay with the open door was empty, but there were cars parked in the other two spaces. Janet knew very little about cars, but they both looked relatively new. Janet wondered what was wrong with them. They seemed too new to be in the garage for repair.

After a moment's indecision, she headed towards the small office where they'd found Gavin the last time they'd visited. The door was open, but the room was dark. Janet didn't dare turn on any lights, but she had a quick look around. There was no sign of the poker game they'd interrupted. In fact, the table in the centre of the room was completely bare, as was the top of the desk along the back wall. Janet thought about seeing what was in the desk drawers, but she wasn't brave enough.

She sighed and headed back towards the open garage door. If she wasn't brave enough to snoop properly, she might as well go home. She'd only taken a few steps when she heard the sound of a car engine. Without thinking, she dashed back into the office, hoping she would be out of sight there.

A car swung into the last empty bay. Janet watched as someone switched off the engine and climbed out. In the rather dim lighting, Janet thought she recognised the man as one of young men who had been playing cards with Gavin on her last visit to the garage.

He stood quietly, looking out the door for a few moments, as if waiting for something. Then Janet could hear another car approaching. She watched as the man walked to the door of the garage and then disappeared through it. After a moment, she saw someone pull down on the overhead door.

Janet suddenly realised that she was in danger of being shut up inside the garage. Now she hurried towards the closing door, but she was torn between shouting and not wanting to be found. She felt helpless as the door banged into place, leaving her standing between two cars. She heard a car engine race and listened to the sound as it got further and further away.

There has to be a way to open the garage doors from the inside, she told herself, ignoring the part of her that was panicking completely. She walked towards the door, looking all around for some handle or something that could be used to open it. A sudden noise behind her had her jumping. Her heart beat faster as she stood still, uncertain of which was to go next.

Another sudden noise startled her. It was the loud click that indicated that the overhead light had just switched off. Janet froze in place as the entire garage was plunged into darkness.

For several minutes, Janet didn't move. Her heart was racing and she felt terrified. As her eyes struggled to adjust to the darkness, her fear was replaced by anger at her own stupidity and embarrassment at the predicament she now found herself in.

With a deep sigh, she dug into her handbag and found her mobile phone. It lit up as she tapped in her pin code, the bright light making her blink in the otherwise dark space.

"Joan, it's me. I'm awfully sorry to interrupt your date, but I'm afraid I need a bit of help."

Janet explained the situation and then leaned against the closest car as her sister launched into a lengthy lecture about her foolishness. When Joan paused for a breath, Janet jumped in.

"Why don't you wait and yell at me when you see me?" Janet suggested. "For now, I'd much rather you find a way to get me out of here."

Janet heard Joan sigh deeply. "Hold on," she instructed her sister.

"Like I've any choice," Janet mumbled. She could hear her sister talking with Michael. After what felt like at least an hour to Janet, Joan's voice came back down the line.

"I'm afraid we can't come up with anything besides ringing Robert Parsons," Joan said. "We'll ring him and I'll let you know what he says."

Joan disconnected before Janet could speak. She pressed the off button on her phone and watched as the handset went dark. She very nearly began to cry in the silent blackness.

Later Janet would discover that Joan, Michael and Constable Parsons arrived less than twenty minutes after that call ended. If you'd asked Janet, she would have said it was more like five or six hours. All Janet could think about what how stupidly she'd behaved and the custard creams that were sitting in her car just outside.

The next time I go snooping, I'm going to bring snacks, she decided as she waited. Of course, I'm never snooping again, she added. After a short time she tried walking carefully around the parked cars. But it was too dark and there were too many obstacles along the floor to make it safe for her to move around. After tripping over something unseen for the second time, Janet decided to stand absolutely still and wait to be rescued. She heard the car before she heard voices.

"Janet? Can you hear me?" Joan's voice sounded muffled, but even so Janet could tell that her sister was angry.

"Yes," she called back. "But if you're angry, you can go away again."

"Of course I'm angry," Joan shouted. "I leave you alone for a few hours and you find yourself locked inside a garage you shouldn't have been anywhere near."

"I stopped to ask Gavin about the box we found," Janet lied. "But I couldn't find him anywhere. It's hardly my fault that I got locked in while I was looking for him."

"Ms. Markham? It's Constable Parsons. I've rung Gavin and asked him to come down and open up the garage for us. He should be here soon."

"Thank goodness for that," Janet called back. "I'm ever so sorry to have caused all this bother."

"Yes, well, we'll discuss that later," the constable told her.

Janet suspected he was angry as well, but she didn't know him well enough to be certain from his tone of voice. She sighed. She was at least as angry with herself as everyone else was with her.

The sound of another car arriving made Janet feel hopeful. Surely Gavin had to be the new arrival.

"Ah, Constable Parsons, I'm not sure why Ms. Markham felt the need to involve you in this. I'm happy to let her sister out once she explains what she was doing here tonight."

Janet heard Gavin's voice, but the initial relief she felt was replaced by fear when she heard his words.

"I don't think we have to worry about that, at least not right now," the constable replied. "Let's get the door open, shall we?"

"As I said, you're not really needed here," Gavin repeated himself. "You certainly don't need any reinforcements. Once you've all gone, I'll open the door and the Markham sisters and I can have a cuppa in my office."

"I'm not going anywhere," the policeman said. "Open the door, please."

Janet could hear Gavin's deep sigh from her side of the garage door.

"Look, this is silly," Gavin said. "I don't think this is a police matter, that's all."

"You're entitled to your opinion," the other man replied.

"What was your sister doing here, anyway?" Gavin asked.

"I've no idea," Joan answered.

Janet could tell her sister was losing patience.

"Now quit arguing and open the door," Joan added.

Janet smiled to herself. Now everyone could tell that Joan was losing patience.

"Yeah, sure," Gavin muttered. "I'll just open it a few feet and your sister can duck out. No point in opening the door all the way or anything."

"Don't be ridiculous," Joan snapped. "Just open the door."

From inside the garage, Janet couldn't make out anything that was being said for several minutes. Finally, she heard Robert Parsons speaking quite loudly.

"Gavin Appleton, I don't need a search warrant to search these premises if I have reason to believe that someone's life is in danger. Janet Markham is an elderly lady who is believed to be trapped inside the building. For all I know, she's had a heart attack from the stress of the situation and is in desperate need of medical attention. If you don't open one of these doors in the next thirty seconds, I'll open one myself."

Janet thought about calling out to reassure the policeman that she was just fine, and mostly bored, but she decided against it. Gavin was clearly reluctant to open the doors, presumably because he was hiding something and he didn't want the police to find it.

After a few more minutes of muffled conversation, Janet heard one of the garage doors begin to move. As it lifted, an interior light came on and Janet felt a rush of relief at being able to see once more. The garage that was opening was the furthest from where she was standing, but she didn't rush towards the door. If Robert Parsons wanted a good look around, she'd give him every excuse to come inside the garage.

As it happened, she needn't have bothered. When the garage door was finally open, she could hear the policeman shouting. "Stop him!"

Janet walked slowly towards the open door, listening intently to the commotion outside. When she reached the door, she found her sister and Michael standing to one side, both staring with shocked faces at Gavin Appleton who was on the ground with a large policeman lying on top of him.

Robert Parsons walked over and pulled the policeman to his feet. Gavin looked up and sighed deeply.

"You're under arrest," Robert told the man.

Gavin climbed to his feet slowly, moaning and groaning the whole time.

"I think he broke my ribs," he complained once he was upright.

"You shouldn't have run," the policeman replied.

"No, I suppose not," Gavin said. "I mean, I haven't done anything wrong, have I? I was just startled, that's all."

"Save the story for your solicitor and the jury," Robert suggested. "I'll be taking you down to the Derby station for processing."

"Surely that isn't necessary," Gavin said. "I'm sure we can work something out."

Robert didn't answer. Instead, he walked past Janet and into the garage. After a few moments he walked back out, shaking his head.

"All three of the cars in your garage were reported stolen in the last twenty-four hours," he told Gavin. "I'm sure you'll have some sort of explanation all ready for the inspector when you get to Derby. There's no point in wasting it on me."

Gavin opened and then closed his mouth. He glanced over at Janet and frowned.

"This is all your fault," he shouted. He moved towards her, but was held in place by another policeman. “What were you doing at my garage, anyway, you nosy old biddy?”

“I wanted to ask you if you killed your mother,” Janet snapped at him, feeling brave because they were surrounded by police officers.

Gavin began to laugh. After several minutes the laughter trailed off and he shook his head. “It isn’t funny, really,” he told her. “But on the other hand, the accusation is quite amusing.”

Janet looked at her sister and shrugged. After everything that had taken place, they still didn’t know what had happened to Margaret Appleton.

Chapter 10

Robert Parsons escorted Gavin to a waiting police car and then walked over to Janet, who was standing next to her sister trying to look inconspicuous.

"I'll be at Doveby House at nine tomorrow morning to get statements from both of you," he said to the sisters in a no-nonsense voice. Before they could speak, he'd turned on his heel and strode away.

"Why don't we head for home?" Michael suggested.

Janet smiled at him. "I'll drive myself home. You two can finish your date. I'm awfully sorry I interrupted it."

"It's fine," Michael assured her. "At least I got a front row seat for the most exciting thing that's happened in Doveby Dale for years."

Janet walked over to her car and climbed in. She sat behind the wheel for a minute, gathering her thoughts. It was all she could do to start the engine and drive sedately away. What she really wanted to do was open the boot and dig out her custard creams.

Back at Doveby House, Janet carried her groceries into the kitchen and unpacked the bags, suddenly grateful that she'd resisted the urge to add that tub of ice cream to her selections. Joan wouldn't have been understanding if they'd needed to clean up melted ice cream from the boot of their car.

Now that she was so close to her treat, Janet dragged out the anticipation just a little bit longer. She made herself a cup of tea and then sat down at the table with it and three biscuits on a plate. Her first bite was interrupted by Joan's arrival.

"The kettle's just boiled," she told Joan before her sister could speak.

"Lovely," Joan replied. "And we appear to have quite a few snacks to enjoy with the tea now."

"That's why I went out," Janet explained, hoping that her sister wasn't as angry as she seemed. She hated when Joan was too calm. "I wanted some custard creams, you see."

"And you didn't think it was rather late to be out shopping for biscuits?"

"It was, but I just couldn't get them out of my mind," Janet said.

Joan nodded. "Well, I hope Constable Parsons likes that excuse when you talk to him tomorrow."

Janet frowned. Maybe she'd better come up with something better, she thought, even though it was the truth.

The sisters sipped their tea and Janet ate her biscuits in silence. Janet knew her sister was mad and she didn't really blame her.

"How was dinner?" she asked as she ran the water for washing up.

"It was very nice," Joan replied. "Michael is a very nice man who was very understanding when our evening was so rudely interrupted."

"I'm glad," Janet said, blushing. "And I'm very sorry as well," she added.

"We'll talk tomorrow," Joan told her. "I'm tired and no doubt you are as well after your ordeal."

Janet was sure she could hear sarcasm in her sister's tone, but before she could answer, Joan left the room. Janet finished the washing up and headed to bed.

It was a much later night than normal for both sisters and Janet found herself scrambling the next morning in order to be ready when Robert Parsons arrived. She barely had time to say much more than "good morning" to her sister before she heard the knock on the door.

"Ah, good morning," the young policeman said tiredly when Janet opened the door.

"Do come in," Janet said. "Would you like some tea or coffee?"

"I'd love some coffee if you have it," the man replied. "I didn't get much sleep last night."

Joan already had coffee brewing when Janet showed Robert into the kitchen. She'd also put out a plate full of biscuits and cakes, and the young man looked delighted when he saw it. Joan handed him a small plate and he quickly filled it with a little of everything.

"Sorry, I didn't get any breakfast, either. Things are quite busy at the station this morning," he explained.

Joan handed him a cup full of coffee and he added a splash of milk before taking a sip.

"Ah, that's wonderful," he said with a sigh.

Janet poured herself a cup of tea and then sat down at the table with him. Joan handed Janet a plate for biscuits before making her own tea and sitting down as well.

"The first thing I have to make perfectly clear is that you were in great danger last night," Robert said to Janet. "If Gavin Appleton had found you snooping around his garage, there's no telling what he might have done."

"I wasn't really snooping," Janet said defensively. "I stopped because I saw the lights were on and I wanted a quick word with Gavin. I was hoping to get a better idea of what papers he was looking for, as we'd found so many boxes full of paperwork."

"Yes, well, I know exactly what he was looking for," Robert told her. "And he wouldn't have told you."

"I wasn't to know that," Janet said. She sipped her tea, hoping the man believed her.

"Gavin could press charges against you for trespass if he wanted to," he said.

"I wasn't trespassing," Janet insisted. "The lights were on and the door was open. I just walked in, looking for someone, and while I was doing that someone locked the door behind me."

"Well, you must never do anything like that again," Robert said sternly. "If you have concerns about someone, you must come to the police and let us handle things. I'd be even more angry if there hadn't been such a successful outcome, of course."

"The cars in the garage were all stolen?" Joan asked.

"Yes, and one of the young men who was working for Gavin has filled us in on the whole scheme. Gavin hired a number of young men and used them to modify the stolen vehicles. He usually did the actual stealing himself, apparently, but in the box of parts that you found were vehicle identification plates. Gavin was making his own and replacing the genuine ones with his."

"Wow, it's like something from telly, not real life," Janet remarked.

"It is rather," Robert agreed. "He started out small and at some point his mother found out what he was doing. Apparently that's when she cut him out of her will. Anyway, lately he'd increased his little operation, bringing in more staff and stealing more cars."

"So he was after that box of parts," Janet said. "That's why he wanted to get into the house here."

"Not just that box of parts," Robert told her. "Where are those boxes of papers you found?"

Joan carried the boxes in from her sitting room. He quickly flipped through the first box, pulling out several sheets of paper as he did so.

"Blank registration papers," he explained, showing the sheets he'd taken to the women. "All Gavin had to do was fill in the blanks and he could claim to be the owner of each stolen car. Somehow Margaret got her hands on a large number of these and that box of parts. Gavin won't tell us how she got them, but apparently she used to visit him at the garage from time to time before their falling out."

"But he didn't kill her to get them back?" Janet asked.

"No, Margaret wasn't murdered," Robert told her.

"So how did Margaret die?" Janet demanded.

Robert frowned. "I'm afraid I can't answer that question," he told her. "You'd have to ask Gavin."

"But he's locked up," Janet said with a sigh. "I know it isn't really any of our business, but I can't help but be curious about it."

"Well, rest assured that Gavin had nothing to do with it," Robert told her. "He wasn't anywhere near her when she died."

The policeman took a few photos of the wardrobe where they'd found the box of car parts and went through all of the boxes of papers, removing several more of the car registration pages.

"These are issued by the DVLA. The Derby CID is working with them to find out how Gavin managed to get his hands on blank ones," he commented as he slid all of the sheets into a large envelope.

"So it was good that I was stuck in the garage last night," Janet suggested as the man was preparing to leave. "Otherwise you wouldn't have found the stolen cars."

"Actually, we'd requested a search warrant, based largely on the box you'd given me and the papers I saw when I looked through the boxes here. We were going to execute it this morning anyway," Robert replied. He left before Janet could point out what a big help she and Joan had been in turning the box over to him.

"I am really sorry I spoiled your date," Janet said to Joan after Robert was gone. "I didn't intend to."

"It's okay," Joan replied after a moment. "It was getting a little bit awkward, anyway."

"But you had fun? Are you going to go out with him again?"

"I did have fun and if he asks, I will go out with him again," Joan told her. "But he might not ask."

"Of course he will," Janet insisted. "You're wonderful and he's just about smart enough to have noticed."

"After lunch we need to talk about getting the bed and breakfast up and running," Joan told her sister as Janet headed up to her room to curl up with a book.

Janet made a face at no one. She wasn't in any hurry to start their business. If they had guests now, she certainly wouldn't be able to just curl up with a book all morning.

Lunch was over far too quickly for Janet's liking.

"Let's sit in the sitting room and talk," Joan suggested.

Janet followed her and sank down on a couch. A moment later the doorbell rang.

"Ah, Michael, what a lovely surprise," Janet exclaimed, ushering the man into the house, feeling as if just about anyone would have been welcome just then.

"I just stopped over to thank your sister for a lovely evening," he told Janet. "That is, thank you," he said to Joan with a small bow in her direction.

Joan flushed. "I should be thanking you," she replied. "Dinner was wonderful."

"I understand the police have arrested Gavin," Michael said. "Apparently he was behind a rather large car theft ring. I can't quite believe it. Nothing that exciting ever happens in Doveby Dale."

"Margaret Appleton died suddenly," Janet said. "Surely that was a little bit exciting."

"But she didn't die in Doveby Dale," Michael told her.

"She didn't?" Janet asked. "Do you know what happened to her, then?"

Michael looked at each sister in turn. "You didn't hear the story?" he asked.

"No, no one seems to know the story," Janet said in frustration.

Michael chuckled. "Well, I know the story, but I suppose that's because I know the gentleman she was with when it happened. I didn't realise it wasn't more widely known."

"What gentleman? What happened to Margaret Appleton?" Janet took a deep breath to stop herself from shouting. "Sorry, but we've been wondering what happened to her since we bought the house, but no one seems to know."

"It was a tragic accident," Michael told her. "She was in Ibiza with a gentleman friend. I won't give his name, as it isn't relevant to the story, but he is somewhat younger than Margaret was."

"We don't need to know his name," Joan said. Janet just resisted the urge to stick her tongue out at her sister. She wanted to know who the man was, even if Joan didn't.

"So what happened?" she prompted the man.

"They were at a nightclub just after they arrived in Ibiza. Margaret was dancing on a raised platform in six-inch heels. When the foam party started, the platform got very slippery and she fell off and landed on her head. I understand she died instantly."

"I'm sorry, but how old was Margaret Appleton?" Joan demanded.

"Sixty-four," Michael told her.

"Foam party?" Janet said faintly.

"Six-inch heels?" Joan murmured.

So you see, dear Bessie, Margaret Appleton wasn't murdered at all, but Gavin was mixed up in something rather criminal anyway. I've taken to calling our little adventure "The Appleton Case," which seems to annoy Joan for some reason.

As for the foam party and the high heels, Joan and I have agreed that, even though we are around the same age as Margaret was, we're quite happy to stick to sensible shoes and to stay out of nightclubs.

Joan continues to see Michael about once a week. We've begun some minor redecorating in the two guest bedrooms and we would like nothing better than for you to be one of our first guests (of course we wouldn't allow you to pay for your stay).

We've yet to see or hear any more from our resident ghosts, but we haven't had another full moon yet either, so you never know.

Anyway, with The Appleton Case behind us, no doubt we will now be quietly settled in Doveby Dale for many uneventful years to come.

Yours truly,

Janet Markham

Glossary of Terms

- **biscuits** — cookies
- **boot** — trunk (of a car)
- **car park** — parking lot
- **chemist** — pharmacist
- **chips** — french fries
- **crisps** — potato chips
- **cuppa** — cup of tea (informal)
- **estate agent** — realtor
- **estate agency** — real estate agency
- **flat** — apartment
- **fortnight** — two weeks
- **head teacher** — principal
- **high street** — the main shopping street in a town or village
- **holiday** — vacation
- **jumper** — sweater
- **loo** — restroom
- **midday** — noon
- **motorway** — highway
- **pavement** — sidewalk

- **petrol** — gasoline
- **primary school** — elementary school
- **pudding** — dessert
- **queue** — line
- **shopping trolley** — shopping cart
- **telly** — television
- **till** — check-out (in a grocery store, for example)

Other Notes

In the UK dates are written day, month, year rather than month, day, year as in the US. (April 2, 2015 would be written 2 April 2015 for example.)

The "cloakroom" on the ground floor of Doveby House is what in the US would be described as a half-bath.

In the UK when describing property with more than one level, the lowest level (assuming there is no basement, very few UK houses have basements) is the "ground floor," and the next floor up is the "first floor" and so on. In the US, the lowest floor is usually the "first floor" and up from there.

An "en-suite" is a bathroom attached to a bedroom.

A semi-detached property is one that shares one common wall with a neighbour. (Generally called a duplex in the US.)

The DVLA is the "Driver and Vehicle Licensing Agency."

When referring to time, in the UK they say "half something" rather than "something thirty". (For example, half seven is seven thirty.)

Foam parties were popular in Ibiza in the nineties, where foam canons or foam generators pumped out huge quantities of foam all over the dance floor.

It has been pointed out to me that I talk about different biscuits, but don't explain them. Digestive biscuits (usually just called digestives) are round, hard, slightly sweet and probably the most common biscuit in the UK. The closest US equivalent that I can come up with is a graham cracker, but digestives are less sweet and have a harder texture. You can find them covered with a layer of chocolate or even caramel and chocolate. Custard Creams are sandwich biscuits with a creamy custard flavoured centre.

The Bennett Case

A MARKHAM SISTERS COZY MYSTERY NOVELLA

Created with Vellum

For everyone who loves to read, everywhere.

Acknowledgments

I am always so grateful to the many people who devote their time and energy to help make my books the best they can be.

Thank you to my editor, Denise, who patiently corrects my grammar and punctuation mistakes, time and time again.

Thank you to my beta readers, Janice and Charlene, who offer insightful feedback on my early drafts.

And mostly, thank you to my readers. You are why I do this! I'd love to hear from you. My contact details are in the back of the book.

Author's Note

Welcome to the second novella in the Markham Sisters Cozy Mystery series. You don't have to read the books in the series in order, but the characters will develop as the series goes along, so I recommend that you do. Like the Bessie series, the novellas will be alphabetical.

The Markham sisters first appeared in *Aunt Bessie Decides,* book four in my Isle of Man Cozy Mysteries series. Since Janet has stayed in touch with Bessie now that the sisters have returned to Derbyshire, each book opens and closes with Janet's letters to Bessie. You don't need to read the Bessie books to enjoy this series, however. The letters to Bessie provide an introduction and conclusion to each "case" but really have nothing to do with the Bessie books.

As with the Isle of Man Cozy series, I've used English spellings and terms and have provided a glossary and notes in the back of the book for readers outside of the United Kingdom. The longer I live in the US, the greater the chances are that Americanisms may slip into the text, and I do apologise for any that have snuck past me.

This is a work of fiction and all of the characters are a creation of the author's imagination. Any resemblance that they may share with any real person, living or dead, is entirely coincidental. The village in Derbyshire where the sisters live (Doveby Dale) is also fictional. Some of the shops and restaurants may bear a coincidental resemblance to some real-life counterpart, but that is wholly unintentional.

2 September 1998

Dearest Bessie,

It sounds as if you've been having quite a difficult time of things lately and I urge you once again to come and stay with us for a while. We are still busy working towards getting the bed and breakfast up and running, but we could certainly accommodate you at any time. Just let me know when to expect you.

After the excitement we had when we first arrived, Joan and I have been enjoying the quiet pace of life in a small village. We've been redecorating and fixing up the two guest rooms in the house, ready for paying guests at some point in the future.

Things were moving along quite nicely last month until we had a very unexpected visitor. Little did we know that his arrival was just the first in what would begin to feel like a rush in newcomers to the neighbourhood.

Chapter 1

"I think the guest rooms are as ready as they'll ever be," Janet said over breakfast on a sunny morning in the middle of August.

"I'd like to hang some paintings on the walls," Joan replied.

"It would be nice to use local artists. I wonder if there's a local gallery nearby."

Joan shrugged. "I suppose I could ask Michael over lunch," she said casually.

Janet grinned. "Why don't you do that?" she replied.

Janet resisted the temptation to tease Joan about her lunch date. Her older sister had only just begun dating for the first time a few weeks earlier. As the two women were in their sixties, Janet tried hard to resist doing too much of the sort of teasing she might have done when they'd been in their teens.

After the breakfast dishes had been washed and put away, the two women climbed the stairs. They'd only owned Doveby House for a little more than a month. Joan was the more eager of the two to begin running the small manor house as a bed and breakfast. The former owner had apparently been quite successful at doing so, and Joan was keen to emulate her success.

"I think we need a nice painting on this wall," Joan told Janet, gesturing towards the only wall in the smaller guest room that didn't have a window or a large furniture piece along it.

"You could be right," Janet said, looking around the room. "I'm surprised Margaret Appleton didn't have any art in the guest rooms."

"Maybe she did and the trust that inherited the property removed the pictures before they sold us the house," Joan suggested.

The sisters moved across the hall to the larger guest room.

"This room needs a large painting on that wall and a smaller one over here," Joan announced, showing her sister where she wanted them.

"See what Michael says," Janet replied. "If there's a local gallery that showcases local artists, that should be our first stop."

"Perhaps we could find a local artist who would like to loan us his or her work in the hopes that someone might buy something," Joan said thoughtfully.

"That's a great idea," Janet said. "And it would save us some money as well."

The sisters had been able to purchase Doveby House thanks to a small inheritance and the sale of the cottage they used to own. While they were both generally frugal with money, they'd spent a great deal of it in getting the house fixed up and ready for guests. A few paying customers, at least now and then, were starting to sound better and better to both sisters.

"Otherwise, the rooms look good," Janet said as they walked back down the stairs. "As does the rest of the house."

They'd had every room painted and had much of the furniture, which had been included in the sale of the home, reupholstered or refinished.

"We should do something with the library," Joan said, opening the door to the small room that was tucked into a corner at the back of the property.

Janet stepped into the library and sighed deeply. She'd refused to consider doing anything in this room. The shelves were crammed full of books that had apparently been positioned in a completely haphazard fashion. Organising the library was on Janet's mental list of jobs and she wanted to do it all herself.

"I'll get around to it," she told her sister now. "I'm saving it for a rainy day."

"More like a rainy month," Joan replied. "It's going to take some considerable time for you to take all of the books down and clean properly. That needs to be done before you even think about reorganising the shelves."

Janet frowned. Joan was right, but she wouldn't be rushed. The library was her favourite place in the whole world, even as it was. She would make it perfect, eventually, but there was no rush. Their guests wouldn't be coming to look at books anyway; they'd be coming to explore Derbyshire.

"Don't you need to ring the doctor about your knee?" Janet asked her sister, hoping to change the subject.

"Oh, yes, I suppose I do," Joan replied with a sigh. Both sisters were in excellent health, but Joan had tripped on a loose bit of carpet a few days earlier and twisted her knee. The pain didn't seem to be getting better, so she'd finally agreed she ought to let a doctor have a look at it.

With Joan out of the room, Janet ran her fingers lovingly along one of the shelves. She counted slowly to ten and then pulled out the book closest to her hand.

"*Jack Spry, Extraordinary Spy,*" she read off the cover. She flipped it open and checked the copyright date. The book had been published in 1957. She read a few paragraphs of the first chapter and then shook her head. Clearly the author had read some of Ian Fleming's books and decided to try to write something similar.

The book opened with Jack romancing a beautiful blonde woman. As Janet read on, Jack drank and flirted, while at the same time he was eavesdropping on a conversation across the room, thanks to a sophisticated listening device he conveniently had with him. Janet shut the book as Jack led the blonde up to his room, stopping on the way to inform the bartender, who was also apparently a spy, all about the top secret plans that the men on the other side of the room had just made.

She slid the book back into its place and sighed. Not every book in the room was going to be wonderful, she knew that, but it seemed that most of her random selections lately had been disappointing. She'd never realised how many truly awful books had been published.

"Janet? Are you still in the library?"

Janet gave up on finding another book and headed out to find her sister.

"I'm coming," she called back, heading towards the kitchen. She ran into her sister in the corridor.

"Ah, there you are," Joan said. "The doctor has an opening in his schedule now, so I'm going to pop over and get this knee looked at. I'm sure I'll be there for ages, so I've told Michael that I'll meet him at the restaurant rather than having him collect me here. I'll see you sometime this afternoon, after my lunch with Michael."

"Good luck with the doctor, and have fun at lunch," Janet told her. "Ring me if you need anything."

"You don't mind me taking the car, do you?"

"I wasn't planning on going anywhere," Janet assured her. "There's plenty in the kitchen for my lunch. I think I might start working on the library while you're out."

As the sisters had always worked at the same primary school together, they'd only ever owned one car that they shared. It hadn't been a problem before they'd both retired, but now Janet was starting to think that she'd quite like a little car of her own. Today she really didn't mind her sister taking the car, though. She really did want to spend some time in the library, even if all she accomplished was finding a good book to read.

"Good. I'll see you later this afternoon, then," Joan said. "Perhaps, instead of the library, you'd like to spend some time sorting through all the paperwork from the bed and breakfast," she called back over her shoulder as she headed towards her room.

"Perhaps not," Janet muttered as Joan disappeared into the large owner's suite. Along with furniture and books, the house had also contained several boxes of paperwork when they'd purchased it. Both sisters knew that they should take the time to sort through it all. No doubt it would provide useful information for them as they prepared to reopen to paying guests. Already they'd had a handful of letters and phone calls from former guests, requesting bookings. Both sisters were reluctant to accept any until they'd been through the papers, though.

"There might be a list of former guests who were difficult or unpleasant," Janet had pointed out to her sister the last time the subject had come up. "We don't want to open our home to just anyone."

Joan had agreed, but now she'd taken to reminding Janet of the need to sort the papers nearly every day. When Janet suggested that Joan could start the task, Joan always found something more pressing that needed doing, generally in the kitchen.

As Joan was an excellent cook and baker, she'd always done all of the food preparation for them both. Now that she was dating, however, Janet found herself on her own for meals more often than usual. She hadn't mentioned it to Joan yet, but Janet was finding that she quite liked doing a bit of cooking now and then. Of course, some of that was probably due to her tendency to cook only her very favourite things, often conveniently forgetting to add the vegetables that her big sister always insisted on including in every meal.

Today Joan had left a bowl of soup in the refrigerator for Janet, so Janet simply had to reheat it when she got hungry.

Janet sat down in the comfortable sitting room and picked up the book she'd left on the coffee table. She read a few paragraphs, but it really wasn't holding her interest. Putting her finger in the book to hold her place, she sat back and stared out the nearest window at a beautiful summer day.

"Janet, I'm going now," Joan said from the doorway. "I've left a box of papers on the kitchen table with the blank file folders. I'm sure the sorting won't take that long once you get started."

She was gone before Janet could reply. Janet stuck her tongue out at her anyway. Then she put a bookmark in her book and put it back on the table, reluctantly heading to the kitchen. Joan had put the box at the place where Janet habitually sat, spreading file folders across the rest of the table. Janet would have to move things around in order to eat her lunch.

And while I'm at it, I may as well do a bit of sorting, Janet thought, knowing that was exactly what Joan had envisioned.

An hour later, Janet had a half-empty box and a pile of neatly labelled file folders. Most of what she'd found had been old utility bills, receipts for purchases of everything from groceries to furniture, and bank and credit card statements. A few notes from former guests had proven more interesting, although ultimately fairly useless. Janet had put them all in a separate folder and now she read through it a second time.

Maggie, Thanks for a lovely time, as ever. Yours, Dave.

Maggie, Doveby House is gorgeous, thanks for sharing it with us. See you next year, Bob and Sue.

Maggie, We had a wonderful time at Doveby House. You'll be seeing us again. Matt and Dawn.

There were a handful more, but they were all similarly short and had all been signed with only Christian names. Janet set the file folders to one side and put the box on the counter. She knew that there were several more boxes like it in the small storage closet in the sitting room, but now it was time for more pressing concerns, like lunch.

She heated her soup and ate it with a slice of crusty bread smothered in butter. Joan tutted when she put too much butter on her bread, but Joan wasn't home to notice. Janet glanced down at her curvy hips and thought for a moment that she was lucky her sister didn't go out more often. She'd probably gain a great deal of weight if Joan wasn't around to nag her to eat healthily.

After eating, she washed up her lunch dishes, drying them and putting them away. Sorting more paperwork held no appeal for her, but she wasn't really in the mood for poking around in the library either. The sun was shining brightly and Janet thought it would be the perfect afternoon to sit in their garden and enjoy the weather. She was heading towards the conservatory, to go out through the French doors there, when she heard someone knocking.

"Ah, but you aren't Maggie," the man who was standing on the small porch said when Janet pulled the door open. "But never mind, I guess the important thing is that I'm here. I can wait a little while longer to see my Maggie."

Janet opened her mouth and then snapped it shut again as she studied the new arrival. He appeared to be somewhere in his sixties, with short grey hair and light grey eyes. He was taller than Janet, but most people were. This man was maybe five feet seven or eight. His dark grey suit looked to have been tailor-made to fit his still athletic build.

Janet took all of this in as quickly as she could, all the while ignoring the one thing that her brain was most concerned about. Next to the man on the small porch were a number of large suitcases.

Chapter 2

While Janet stood there, trying to figure out what to say to the man on the doorstep, he grabbed one of his cases and smiled at her.

"This is the heavy one. Grab whatever you can manage and then I'll come back for the rest."

With that, he stepped around Janet and strode into the house as if he owned the place. Janet grabbed the smallest of his bags and followed him into the sitting room, suddenly finding her voice.

"Oh, but you can't, that is, we aren't open for business yet," she told him.

He ignored her and returned to the porch where he picked up the last of his bags. He stopped and carefully shut and locked the door before returning to the sitting room.

"Am I to stay in the purple room again?" he asked brightly.

"No, that is, you aren't to stay at all," Janet said in her firmest voice. "We aren't open for business, you see."

"Oh, but Maggie will sort it all out," the man said with a wave of his hand. "She always has room for me. I'm sure she has something in mind."

"I'm rather certain she doesn't," Janet said coolly. "Mrs. Appleton passed away some months ago."

The man stared at her for a moment, the colour draining from his face. "Maggie's, but, Maggie's dead?" he muttered.

Janet found herself pushing him into a chair. "I'm sorry if this comes as something of a shock," she said, not really feeling sorry for him in the slightest.

"It's a huge shock," the man told her. "I think maybe a cup of tea…." he trailed off and gave Janet what she assumed was a hopeful look.

"I think you need to figure out where you're going to stay before you worry about tea," Janet said, unwilling to leave the man alone while she fixed the tea. She was worried he might start unpacking if she turned her back.

"Well, I'll stay here," he replied. "Maggie was expecting me. All of the arrangements were made. If you've taken over the bed and breakfast, surely you have to honour existing reservations?"

"We don't, actually," Janet replied, hoping she was right. "We aren't open for business. In fact, we don't even know if we are going to reopen. My sister and I have purchased the house and we might just choose to live here by ourselves."

"But if it's just you and your sister here, you must have spare bedrooms," the man said softly. "I'll pay well for a few nights in one of them. You don't even have to provide breakfast. I just need a place to stay for a few days."

Janet shook her head. "We simply can't," she said firmly.

The man reached into his pocket and pulled out a wallet. "Two hundred pounds a night for three nights," he said, taking note after note out of the wallet. "I'll pay the lot in advance and if I decide to stay longer, I'll pay three hundred pounds a night after that."

Janet looked at the pile of twenty-pound notes the man had put on the coffee table. Six hundred pounds was a lot of money, but she wasn't comfortable with the idea of a total stranger staying in the house.

"Do Stuart and Mary Long still live across the road?" the man asked. "I'm sure they'll vouch for me. I used to stay with Maggie quite regularly."

Janet took a deep breath, wishing Joan were there to help with the decision. "We really aren't equipped for guests," she told the man.

"Look, there's Stuart now," the man said, jumping up from the sofa. He'd been sitting facing towards a side window. Now Janet looked and saw their tall and dark-haired neighbour walking along the side of the house.

Stuart had been a professional gardener, and since he had retired he looked after the extensive gardens at Doveby House in exchange for a small fee and a great deal of tea and biscuits.

The strange man was walking through the house towards the conservatory and the glass French doors that opened into the garden. Janet rushed after him, angry at his overconfident behaviour. He had the doors open before Janet reached him.

"Stuart, how are you?" he called to the man who was just opening up the coach house.

Stuart spun around. "Edward? This is a surprise. I thought you and Maggie parted ways ages ago."

The stranger shrugged. "You know how it is," he said with a chuckle. "We had a disagreement, but we'd been writing again and I told her I'd come see her this month. It was all arranged."

"You heard she, well, she passed?" Stuart asked.

"I did," the man said sadly. "I've been out of the country for most of the year and I came straight here when I got back. It was a huge shock."

"Well, I'm sure the Markham sisters will make you feel welcome," Stuart said heartily. "Joan, the older sister, is brilliant in the kitchen. Maggie was a great person, but she wasn't a very good cook. Joan is much better."

"Excellent," the man beamed. He turned to Janet. "I assume you're not Joan, then?"

"Haven't you introduced yourself?" Stuart asked. "All the travelling around the world hasn't improved your manners." Stuart turned to Janet. "Janet Markham, this is Edward Bennett. He was a dear friend of Maggie's for many years. Edward, this is Janet Markham, the younger of the two lovely sisters who have just recently purchased Doveby House."

Edward bowed deeply. "It is a great pleasure to meet you, Ms. Markham. I do hope you'll be able to find a room for me."

Janet opened her mouth, not entirely certain how she was going to say "no," but she was interrupted.

"Janet? What's going on?"

Joan was coming down the steps from the conservatory, the pile of banknotes that Edward had left in the sitting room clutched in her hand.

"Ah, this must be the lovely Joan," Edward said. He turned and bowed to Joan, offering his hand when he straightened. "I'm Edward Bennett. I was a friend of Maggie's and I had a booking for this week for the purple guest room. I was just asking Stuart if he'd vouch for me, as your charming sister seems reluctant to accommodate me."

Joan looked from Janet to the collection of notes in her hand. "I'm sure we can work out something," Joan told the man. "Although I'm afraid the purple room is out of the question, as that's Janet's room now."

"Ah, of course, but that's no problem. I'm happy anywhere. Maggie used to have me sleep on the couch in the sitting room if the guest rooms were all full," Edward replied.

"Well, that certainly won't be necessary this time," Joan said. "We have two perfectly lovely empty guest rooms. You can have your choice between them."

"I think he should go in the west room," Janet said loudly. Not only was it the smaller of the two rooms, it was further from her room.

Joan looked as if she might argue, but Janet didn't let her.

"Come along, then, I'll show you to your room," Janet said to Edward. She headed off towards the house, not caring if the man was following or not. Behind her she heard him saying a few words to Stuart. When she reached the French doors, he jumped ahead of her.

"Allow me," he said, holding the door while she walked through it.

Janet muttered "thanks" under her breath and then walked back to the sitting room. She grabbed the lightest of the man's bags and headed for the stairs.

"I take it you don't have any staff around to help with bags?" Edward asked as he looked at the other three bags that remained.

"We aren't open for business," Janet reminded him tartly.

"In that case, just leave the bags and I'll take them up one at a time," he suggested.

"This one isn't heavy. I'll take it up," Janet replied. "You can do what you like with the rest."

In the short upstairs corridor, she made sure her bedroom door was shut before opening the door to the smaller guest room. She dropped the man's case on the bed and turned to leave. Edward was right behind her, carrying the two largest cases.

"I do hope this is okay," Janet said, not caring if it was or not.

"It's fine," Edward assured her. "I assume the door locks and you have a key for me?"

Janet frowned. "Of course we do," she said uncertainly. She knew she'd seen keys somewhere, but she simply couldn't remember where as the man stared at her.

"Here we are," Joan said from the doorway. "I'm fairly certain this is the right key, but let me check."

Janet watched as Joan tried the key, which turned easily.

"Mrs. Appleton had it labelled as "blue room," but, of course, we've had it painted," Joan told Edward.

"I like the new colour," he replied. "And you've had the furniture fixed up as well. Maggie was allowing things to get a bit shabby around here."

Joan beamed. "We've tried to make everything as nice as possible," she said. "I've always wanted to have a little bed and breakfast, you see."

"What did you do before this?" Edward asked.

"Janet and I were both primary schoolteachers," Joan told him. "We retired last year and did some travelling, but I felt like it was time for a new adventure."

"How very fortunate for me," the man said. He smiled brightly at both women, but only Joan returned the look.

"We'll let you get settled in," Janet said, walking quickly to the door. The room was definitely too small for three people, she thought as she hurried out of it. She walked down the hall to her own room with Joan right behind her. When she hesitated outside her door, Joan opened the door and pushed her inside.

"Here," Joan hissed, handing Janet a key ring.

"What is this?"

"The key to your door," Joan told her. "I thought you'd want to keep your door locked now that we have a guest."

"I most certainly do," Janet agreed. Aware that she was nearly shouting, she made an effort to lower her voice. "Why on earth did you tell him he could stay?" she demanded of her sister.

"Did you see all the lovely money?" Joan asked. "And besides, what's the point in having a bed and breakfast if we aren't having guests? Stuart knows him; it isn't like he's a total stranger or anything. Besides, he seems charming."

"He was one of Maggie's old boyfriends," Janet said.

"You don't know that for sure. He just said they were friends," Joan countered. "Anyway, so what if he was?"

Janet shook her head. She hadn't told her sister about the letters she'd found in the desk downstairs. They were very racy letters that various men had written to Maggie Appleton over the years. Janet was sure that one of the authors had been a man called Edward. She hadn't read more than a few lines of any one letter, but that had been enough to make her feel uncomfortable about their unexpected guest.

"I'm going to lock up the empty guest room as well as the library," Joan told her sister. "If Mr. Bennett wants to look at the books, he can ask one of us to open the door. I've also locked up my suite, of course."

Janet nodded. She felt better knowing the library was going to be locked. She didn't want the man to find the letters he'd written, if he was indeed the Edward in question.

"How's your knee?" Janet asked as she suddenly remembered that her sister had been to the doctor.

"It's fine," Joan told her. "The doctor did a bunch of poking and prodding and said he thinks it's healing fine. I just need to be patient and careful with it."

"Well, that's something good today anyway," Janet muttered as Joan let herself out of the room.

While Joan headed back downstairs to start preparing dinner, Janet had a sudden thought. What if Edward actually knew that Maggie had died and he'd come looking for the letters he'd written to her? Maybe she needed to talk to Joan about the letters after all.

An hour later, when Joan knocked on the door to tell her dinner was ready, Janet still hadn't figured out what she wanted to do about the letters. She followed Joan down the stairs and then frowned when she saw Edward already sitting at the small kitchen table.

"I'm sure you don't mind that I invited Edward to join us for dinner," Joan said. "It's just cottage pie with veggies and I always make too much for just the two of us."

Janet forced herself to smile. It's fine," she muttered, taking the seat opposite the man who was, at least as far as she was concerned, an unwelcome guest.

Joan frowned. "That isn't your usual place," she said as she began to serve.

"Nothing wrong with a bit of variety," Janet told her sister.

"I'm sorry," Edward said. "I didn't mean to cause trouble between you two. Clearly I'm intruding where I'm not wanted. I can leave, if that's what Janet wants."

The man looked at Janet and then reached across the table and took her hand. He stared intently into her eyes. "I'm not such a bad person, once you get to know me," he said softly. "Please, give me a chance."

Janet breathed in slowly, trying to think as she felt herself getting lost in the man's gorgeous eyes. He tightened his grip on her hand and Janet felt her heart skip a beat.

"You can throw me out after dinner if you still want to," he said. "But for now, please let me eat. Everything smells so good."

Janet pulled her hand away and then took a large drink of water. The man was too charming and too sophisticated for her. She looked over at Joan, who was glowing as Edward kept up a steady stream of compliments on her cooking.

After a moment, Janet began to feel ignored as Edward and Joan chatted lightly about nothing much. For the first time in a long time, Janet didn't really feel hungry. She ate a few bites of the cottage pie, which was, as always, expertly prepared, but she felt slightly unwell.

"Are you okay?" Joan asked her, pulling Janet back from her wandering thoughts.

"I'm fine," Janet said a bit too loudly. "I think I'm just a little bit overtired. We've been so busy lately, getting the house ready and everything."

"Yes, well, maybe you should have an early night," Joan suggested.

"Do you have a date?" Janet asked. She felt as if Joan had almost been flirting with their guest, which annoyed her.

"Michael said he might stop over to watch a bit of telly with us later," Joan said, her eyes moving from Janet to Edward and back again.

"Don't tell me you're dating Michael Donaldson from across the road?" Edward asked with a bark of laughter. "You're much too good for him."

Joan flushed. "We've gone out a few times," she muttered. "He's a nice man."

"Oh, he is at that," Edward agreed. "And I'm sure he'll treat you well. He has to know you could do much better if you wanted to."

"Michael's smart and funny and he treats Joan like a princess," Janet said tartly. "I don't think she'd be able to find a kinder or more understanding man."

Edward smiled at Joan. "I guess if you get tired of Michael, your sister wouldn't mind dating him herself."

Janet turned bright red. "Not at all," she said hotly. "He isn't my type, but he's perfect for Joan and you shouldn't be rude about him, that's all."

"I didn't think I was being rude about him as much as complimenting your sister, but let's not argue. I'm still hoping you won't want to throw me out after pudding," Edward said in a teasing tone.

"Are you staying for pudding?" Janet shot back.

"Janet!" Joan said sharply. "That's enough. Edward is our guest. Our paying guest at that. If this is how you're going to treat paying guests, perhaps we need to rethink our plans to reopen the guest house."

"As they're your plans, not mine, I don't suppose it much matters what I think. I'll be in my room. I'm not feeling well." Janet got up from the table and headed for the stairs.

"I made apple crumble," Joan called after her.

Janet's steps faltered. Apple crumble was her absolute favourite pudding, and Joan didn't make it nearly often enough.

"Apple crumble is my favourite," Edward said.

That was all Janet needed to hear. She stomped up the stairs and carefully and quietly opened and closed her bedroom door. She wasn't going to give the man the satisfaction of hearing her slam it like she wanted to. Falling onto her bed, she waited for the tears to come.

After a moment, when they failed to materialise, she sat back up. She knew she was behaving badly and out of character, but she wasn't quite sure why. The handsome and worldly Edward Bennett was the cause of her disquiet, she knew that, but she couldn't begin to understand why he bothered her so much. Maybe it was time to read through all of the letters that Edward had written to Maggie, she decided.

Chapter 3

Doveby House was quiet just after midnight. Janet lay in bed, trying not to think about apple crumble. Joan had come up to check on her around nine.

"Are you okay?" Joan had asked, looking concerned.

"I'm fine. I think I might be brewing something, that's all," Janet replied.

"Well, you were very rude to Edward," Joan scolded. "I hope you'll make an effort to be nicer to him tomorrow."

"Did Michael come over?" Janet changed the subject.

"He did. He and Edward and I watched some telly and had biscuits. It was a very pleasant evening. Tomorrow night you should join us."

"I might," was as far as Janet was willing to concede. "I'll either be feeling better or definitely ill by then."

Now, three hours later, the only thing she was feeling was hungry. She could almost hear the apple crumble calling to her softly from the kitchen. No doubt it was feeling rejected after she'd turned her back on it earlier.

She rolled over and punched her pillow into shape. After a moment she pushed back the top layer of covers and rolled to her other side. Several minutes later she gave up. There was no way she was going to get any sleep until she'd had her share of the apple crumble. Muttering darkly about unwelcome guests causing unnecessary inconveniences, she pulled on her bathrobe and tucked her feet into her slippers before exiting her room. She locked her door behind her and then slipped the key ring into her pocket.

Living for the past month in Doveby House had taught her how to get down the stairs without making noise. As the house had been built in the seventeenth century, there were many creaky steps and floorboards throughout it. Experience had taught Janet that her sister could sleep through just about anything, but she'd still taken the time to learn where to step as she went up and down the stairs, so that when they had paying guests she wouldn't have to worry about disturbing them if she wanted a midnight snack. Tonight she was glad she'd done so.

In the kitchen, she quickly pulled the remains of the apple crumble out of the refrigerator. She frowned when she saw how little was left. Clearly Edward had enjoyed more than his fair share, she thought. Not wanting to make any noise, she didn't bother to heat it, simply spooning a large portion onto a plate. She added a dollop of custard and then sat down at the table and dug in.

A few minutes later she was feeling much better. She put her plate and utensils in the sink, sticking her tongue out at her sister in advance. There was no doubt that Joan would complain about it in the morning. Janet headed for the stairs, but paused before she got there. Since she was up anyway, maybe she ought to have a look at those letters now, she thought.

She pulled the keys from her pocket. In addition to the key to her room, Joan had included a master key that opened all of the doors in the house. Janet turned and headed for the library. As she pushed open the door to the television room, she gasped.

"I hope the telly didn't disturb you," Edward said, looking up at her from his seat on one of the comfortable sofas. "Joan said I could stay up and watch as long as I liked."

"I didn't know you were here," Janet replied.

"Came down for your apple crumble?"

"I was hungry." Janet was angry with herself for feeling defensive. This was her house and she could do what she pleased.

Edward stood up and switched off the television. He crossed over to the doorway and stood facing Janet. "We seem to have started off on the wrong foot," he said quietly. "I'm sorry if I did or said anything to upset you. I know I can be rather demanding and difficult, but I'm grateful to you and Joan for letting me stay."

Janet focussed her eyes on the far wall of the room to avoid meeting Edward's eyes. "It's fine," she said after a moment. "I hope you enjoy your visit to Derbyshire."

"I'm sure I will," Edward replied. "Perhaps you'd like to do some sightseeing with me?"

"Oh, I'm afraid I'm rather busy at the moment," Janet answered quickly. Something about the man made her feel uncomfortable and she wasn't about to spend any more time with him than absolutely necessary.

"Well, the offer's good if you change your mind," Edward told her. "I suppose I'll say good night, then."

"Good night," Janet muttered. She began to turn back towards the stairs, but Edward put his hand on her arm. When she stopped and looked at him, he smiled.

Before Janet had time to think, Edward leaned towards her and kissed her very gently on the lips. By the time she'd registered what had happened, he'd walked past her, heading for the stairs. Janet stood and listened to his soft footsteps as they faded behind her. It wasn't until later that she realised that he'd climbed the stairs without a single creak.

Janet went back to bed, all thoughts of reading Maggie's letters gone from her head. She was certain that she'd never manage to sleep with her mind racing and her emotions raging, but she slept as soon as her head touched the pillow, and she woke later than usual the next morning, only when someone knocked on her door.

"Janet, it's breakfast time, what are you doing still in bed?" Joan demanded when Janet pulled open her bedroom door. "We have a guest, remember? You're meant to help with breakfast when we have guests."

"Sorry," Janet muttered. "I'll just grab a quick shower and I'll be down."

Joan tutted her disapproval, but Janet shut the door in her face and rushed to her adjoining bathroom. It had been a while since she'd woken up late and had to hurry through her morning routine, but many years of practice meant she had it down to an easy system. She was showered, dressed and ready to go in just fifteen minutes. In the bathroom, she studied her reflection for a moment.

She'd always considered her blue eyes her best feature and her grey hair seemed to complement them nicely. She and Joan shared their hair and eye colour and everyone who met them seemed to think that they looked alike, but neither sister ever really agreed. Although they were both around five feet, three inches, Joan was slender with pronounced cheekbones where Janet was more generously padded. Today she frowned at her curves, wondering for the first time what Margaret Appleton had looked like. They'd never seen a photograph of the woman, she realised. Perhaps one of the neighbours had one they could show her.

In the kitchen, Janet squeezed oranges into juice and put it in a pitcher, then she went out into the garden to cut some fresh flowers for the kitchen table. She arranged them in a vase while Joan dashed about anxiously.

"He said he'd be down for breakfast at eight," she told Janet. "I thought I'd fix him a full English breakfast. But what if he would prefer something else? Maybe you should run to the store and get some more jam. We only have strawberry and raspberry. What if he asks for orange marmalade? Do you remember where I put that cookbook all about omelets? What if he requests an omelet? I can't remember how to make them."

Janet tried to ignore her, but after twenty minutes of endless babble from her sister, she was actually relieved to see Edward coming into the room.

"Full English?" Joan greeted him with. "Or would you prefer something else?"

"Full English sounds wonderful," the man said with a huge grin.

"I've been out of the country for so long, I think I've quite forgotten what a full English breakfast is like."

Joan smiled and quickly got busy.

"Freshly squeezed orange juice?" Janet asked as the man sat down at the table.

"Oh, yes, please," Edward smiled at her.

She filled a glass and handed it to him. He took it and then quickly captured her hand.

"I hope you slept well," he said quietly.

"I did, thanks," Janet muttered. "Did you?"

"I always sleep well," he replied with a chuckle. "It's supposed to be a sign of a clear conscience."

Janet opened her mouth and then snapped it closed. She wasn't sure what she'd been about to say, but something told her not to say it.

"Janet, can you fix the toast?" Joan asked without turning around.

Janet pulled her hand away from Edward's. She busied herself with the toast until Joan was finished with the rest of the man's breakfast. As Joan delivered a plate full of food to Edward, Janet dropped the toast rack next to it.

"You don't need us both watching you eat," she said. "I'm going to go and run a few errands."

Joan frowned. "Don't forget that we're having Michael over for lunch," she told her sister. "He'll expect you to be here."

Janet nodded. "I'll be back. I just need a few things from town."

As Janet left the room, she heard her sister talking to Edward.

"Of course, you're more than welcome to join us for lunch as well," Joan was saying.

Janet made a face and only just barely managed to not slam the front door as she left the house.

In the centre of Doveby Dale, Janet parked the car and wandered around the shops. She didn't actually need anything but to get away from Edward Bennett, but now she felt she needed to buy something to justify leaving her sister to deal with their guest. By dawdling in every shop she entered, Janet managed to fill the morning, finally heading back towards home just a short time before lunch would be ready.

She parked her car in the small car park outside the house and headed inside, certain that Joan would be cross that she'd been gone so long. As she opened the door, she made sure she had all of the bags that contained the various bits and pieces she'd purchased. There was no one in the small sitting room, so Janet headed up to her room to freshen up before she hurried down to the kitchen to help her sister with lunch, carrying the new vase that she'd decided they needed with her.

"Ah, there you are," Joan said testily. "I didn't know you were planning to be gone all morning. Another pair of hands would have been useful around here."

"Sorry," Janet replied quickly. "I only went to town for a few things, but I had trouble finding what I wanted. You know what the shops are like in Doveby Dale."

"I don't suppose you considered just leaving it for today?" Joan asked. "Our guest is only here for a few days. There will be plenty of time for shopping once he's gone."

"Sorry," Janet repeated herself. "I'll plan on staying close to home from now on until Edward leaves."

The knock on the front door interrupted their discussion.

"You go and let Michael in," Janet told her sister. "Just tell me what to do while you're gone."

"Everything's done," Joan replied grumpily. "You can set the table, I suppose." She swept out of the room.

Janet pulled down three plates and three sets of cutlery. Joan hadn't told her whether Edward was joining them or not, so she chose to assume he wasn't. If her assumption made him feel somewhat unwelcome if he did join them, well, that was too bad.

She set the table and then headed out into the garden to cut some flowers to put in the new vase. Back in the kitchen, she arranged them carefully and added water to the container. But what on earth was keeping Joan, she wondered. She was halfway to the door, going to find out, when the door swung open. Edward walked in and gave her a big smile.

"I do hope you had a nice shopping trip this morning," he told Janet.

She forced herself to smile back at him. "It was fine," she muttered. A moment later the door swung open again. This time it was Joan, and she looked even less happy than she had when she'd walked out. Behind her, Michael entered the room, and behind him was another man of a similar age who smiled faintly as he crossed the threshold.

Michael was only a few inches taller than Janet. She considered him quite handsome, with his bald head and his intelligent brown eyes. The man with him was no taller than Janet herself, and considerably heavier. He had a bulbous nose and a handful of stray hairs that had been carefully arranged around his head to try to fool people into thinking he wasn't bald. Janet took an instant and irrational dislike to him before she even knew who he was.

"Ah, Janet, this is my old school friend, Leonard Simmons. He's just up from London for a few days," Michael said. "I thought maybe the four of us could have dinner together somewhere tonight."

Chapter 4

Janet stared at Michael, unable to come up with a suitable reply. While Leonard was probably a lovely man, she really didn't want to have dinner with him, not even if Joan and Michael came along.

"Ah, what a shame." It was Edward who broke the awkward silence. "Janet just this minute agreed to have dinner with me tonight," he told them.

Janet turned her stare towards him and he winked at her.

"Oh, that is a shame," Michael said. "I hope Joan won't be too bored, listening to us talk about our school days all night."

"Maybe I should just stay home and let you two go out on your own," Joan said stiffly.

"If you're sure you wouldn't mind, that would be great," Michael replied, clearly not understanding Joan's tone.

"I haven't set nearly enough places for lunch," Janet said, eager to stop the argument that was brewing. "But the table in here only seats four. Let's move lunch into the dining room."

Joan frowned, but Janet didn't give her a chance to speak. "If everyone gives me a hand, we can have the table set up in there in no time," she told the men. Janet left her sister standing in the middle of the kitchen with an angry look on her face. With the men's help, it only took a few minutes to set the table in the dining room.

"Sit down and introduce yourselves all around," Janet suggested. "I'll go and help Joan with the food."

"I'm happy to help as well, if you'd like," Edward replied.

"No, no, I'm sure you'll find plenty to talk about," Janet replied. She was pretty sure Joan was about to explode in the kitchen, and she didn't want their paying guest to witness the fireworks.

Janet rushed back to the kitchen as the men began to settle in around the table.

"What can I do to help?" she asked Joan, who didn't appear to have moved in her sister's absence.

"Tell them all to get out of my house," Joan suggested.

"It's my house, too," Janet replied. She could tell that Joan was feeling hurt by Michael's behaviour. Clearly he hadn't bothered to mention that he had a friend coming to visit. If that wasn't bad enough, he'd made no effort to hide the fact that he'd rather have dinner with his friend than with Joan.

"We can't throw anyone out," Janet said, giving her sister a hug. "You promised them all lunch."

"I invited Michael," Joan retorted.

"And Edward," Janet reminded her.

"Yes, but I certainly didn't invite Leonard," Joan grumbled.

"You would have invited him if Michael told you about him, though," Janet said. "Anyway, it's no good complaining. He's here now and we have to give him and the others lunch."

Joan sighed deeply and then opened the oven. A gorgeous lasagne was bubbling away inside it.

"That looks wonderful," Janet said happily.

"I suppose you can take the salad through," Joan replied. "I'll bring the lasagne and the garlic bread in a few minutes."

"You are going to come and have some salad, though, right?" Janet demanded. "You aren't going to leave me with the three of them on my own."

Joan sighed again, even more dramatically. Janet just looked at her.

"If I must," Joan said after a moment.

"You really must," Janet said emphatically.

Grabbing the salad bowl, which was full of an assortment of mixed greens, tomatoes and cucumber tossed in a light dressing, Janet headed back into the dining room. She could hear Joan sliding the lasagne out of the oven behind her.

"Here we are," she said brightly, setting the salad in the middle of the table. "Everyone help yourselves. I'll get some drinks. What can I get you all?"

She headed back towards the kitchen with the drinks requests, nearly knocking Joan over as she went.

"We need to get everyone drinks," Joan hissed.

"I'm working on that," Janet answered her. "You go and sit down and have some salad. I'll bring the drinks."

Joan clearly wanted to argue, but as they were standing in the dining room doorway in full view of the others, she refrained. Janet continued on to the kitchen and quickly collected the cold drinks that had been requested. She added a cup of tea for her sister and a cold drink for herself to a small tray and then carried it all back through. Joan was sitting at the head of the table, between Michael and Leonard, but she jumped up to help Janet serve.

"Now you sit down and have some salad," Joan said. "I'll finish up in the kitchen."

Janet sank into a chair next to Edward and used the salad tongs to put some salad on her plate. Michael and Leonard were talking loudly about their university days, so Janet nibbled at her food quietly. Every so often Michael would say something about being sorry for excluding others from their conversation, but neither he nor Leonard seemed willing to actually change the subject.

"Aren't you glad you're having dinner with me?" Edward whispered to Janet during one particularly long anecdote about some party that had taken place forty years earlier.

Janet quickly took a drink to avoid having to answer the question. The truth was, she wasn't sure how she felt about having dinner with the man.

Joan carried in the lasagne and then a plate full of garlic bread.

The men all murmured appreciatively, which at least earned a tiny smile from Joan. Leonard reached for the spatula to start serving himself, but Michael interrupted.

"Ladies first," he said, smiling at Joan.

Janet relaxed slightly when Joan gave him a slightly larger grin before she helped herself to lunch.

Michael appeared, throughout lunch, to try to include everyone in the conversation, but Leonard seemed to have a one-track mind. Janet was quite happy to just sit back and let the boorish man monopolise the conversation, even though nothing he said was even remotely interesting. The food was wonderful and she didn't really have anything to say to any of their guests, anyway.

Joan served tea and biscuits for pudding. Janet was sure she'd seen a Victoria sponge on the kitchen counter and could only assume that Joan had decided to save that for another day. Perhaps one when Leonard would be absent.

"We ought to stay and help with the washing up," Michael said, his tone apologetic. "But I promised Leonard a trip into Derby."

"Have fun," Joan said flatly.

Michael looked as if he wanted to say more, but Leonard grabbed his arm.

"Let's get going, shall we?" he asked. "Lots to do."

Michael shrugged and followed the man from the room. Joan busied herself with clearing the table, so Janet followed the two men to the door.

"Tell her I'm really sorry," Michael whispered to Janet at the door. "He just showed up out of the blue and I couldn't think of a polite way to get rid of him."

A few ideas sprang to Janet's mind, but the two men were disappearing down the pavement before she could reply. She watched them cross the road back to Michael's home before she shut the door.

In the kitchen, Joan was loading all of the dishes into the dishwasher.

"Are you sure that's wise?" Janet asked. The machine had come with the house, but they hadn't actually tried it yet.

"I'm not doing all that washing up by hand," Joan said crossly.

"Let me help," Edward said from the dining room doorway. He was carrying a stack of dishes and he quickly crossed to Joan. "It's best to put them in this way," he explained, loading plates and then glasses and mugs onto the various racks. Within minutes he had everything tucked up inside the machine. Joan handed him the box labelled "dishwasher tablets" that had come with the house. He showed her where to put the tablet and then shut the machine's door and switched it on.

"It should take about an hour," he said. "And everything will be quite hot when it's finished."

"Thank you," Joan said. "And thank you for helping to clear everything up as well."

"I'm always happy to help," the man replied. "And now, if you ladies will excuse me, I have a few errands to run." He bowed to them both and then headed towards the kitchen door.

"I'll make a dinner booking for seven," he told Janet on his way past her. "If you can be ready for half six?"

"Fine," Janet muttered, thinking this was the perfect opportunity to cancel their date, but failing to do so.

"Good."

The sisters were quiet as they heard him moving around the house for a few minutes before they heard the front door open and close. Janet blew out a breath she hadn't realised she was holding.

"You didn't tell me that you and Edward were dating," Joan said as she tidied up the kitchen.

"We aren't," Janet replied. "I don't even like the man."

"And yet you're having dinner with him tonight," Joan replied.

"Apparently," Janet muttered.

A knock on the front door disrupted their chat. Janet rushed to open it, happy with the interruption.

"Constable Parsons, this is a surprise," Janet said to the young man on the doorstep.

They'd met the town's only policeman before they'd even purchased the house, after an altercation with the previous owner's son. Although he was only in his mid-twenties, Robert Parsons was responsible for policing both Doveby Dale and neighbouring Little Burton. As nothing much happened in either small town, he usually managed the job easily. Today his brown hair looked in need of a cut and his brown eyes looked tired. He was, as always when Janet had seen him, neatly dressed in ordinary clothes rather than a police uniform.

"Can I come in for just a minute?" he asked politely.

"Of course you can," Janet said. "Would you like some tea and a biscuit?" she added as she showed him into the sitting room.

"I'm afraid I haven't much time," the man replied, looking disappointed.

"What can we do for you, then?" Joan asked from the doorway.

"I just wanted to warn you that we've had a report of a possible fugitive in the area," he told them.

"What sort of fugitive?" Janet asked. "Are we in great danger?"

"I don't think so," was the vague reply. "The man in question is called Peter Smith, but that won't be the name he's using. He's a con artist who was in prison in London, but, through a series of unusual circumstances, managed to escape or get let out. I'm not clear on the details and that's all still being investigated at that end. Anyway, he's known to have ties in the Derbyshire area, so we've all been put on alert. It seems unlikely that he'll come here, but anything is possible. As you run a small guesthouse, even if you aren't taking guests at the moment, I wanted to let you know. It's just possible he might turn up here looking for a place to stay."

"Do you have a photograph?" Joan asked.

"I have several, but I don't know that they'll do you much good," Robert told them. He reached into his coat, pulled out a small envelope, and handed it to Joan.

She flipped through the contents. "But these are all different men," she protested. "Which one is the man you're looking for?"

"That's the problem," Robert told her. "They're all the same man. He's excellent at disguising his appearance."

Janet looked through the photos herself. Joan was right; they looked like several different men. At the same time, there was nothing particularly noticeable about any of them. They all looked like average men of around sixty.

"We have a guest right now," Joan told Robert. "He arrived yesterday."

"I'm sure Edward isn't an escaped fugitive," Janet said hastily. "He's an old friend of Maggie's after all."

The policeman frowned. "I don't know enough about the missing man to be certain. Tell me about your guest, please."

Janet wasn't happy to sit there and listen as Joan told Robert everything they knew about Edward Bennett. It wasn't as if she even liked the man, she reminded herself, it just seemed unfair to be suggesting to the police that he might be a criminal. As Joan talked, Janet had a sudden thought. Once Joan was finished, Janet jumped in.

"Michael, across the road, had a guest turn up unexpectedly today," she told Robert. While Joan frowned at her, Janet told the policeman the little that she knew about Leonard Simmons.

"If any other men around that age suddenly turn up, please let me know," Robert told them as he rose to his feet. "I'm going to stop over at Mr. Donaldson's house and see if I can have a quick word with Mr. Simmons."

"They were going into Derby," Janet told him. "I doubt anyone is home."

"Well, thank you for your help," he said. "I'll keep you informed if we find the man."

Joan walked Robert to the door, letting him out and then carefully locking the door behind him.

"I can't believe you told the police that Michael might be harbouring a fugitive," Joan said angrily when she returned to the sitting room.

"You told him we might be harbouring a fugitive," Janet shot back. "I'm sure Edward isn't anything of the kind."

"Considering you spent most of yesterday insisting you didn't like the man, you suddenly seem very cosy with Mr. Bennett," Joan said.

"He's growing on me," Janet admitted. "Anyway, he's an old friend of Maggie Appleton's. He can't be a criminal."

"We don't know what sort of friends Mrs. Appleton had," Joan countered.

Janet thought about the lascivious letters that were still in the bottom desk drawer in the library. The sisters knew that Mrs. Appleton had had several husbands over the years. Was it possible that she was also involved with criminals?

"I'd like to see a picture of her," Janet said, as the thought crossed her mind again.

"Of Maggie Appleton?" Joan asked.

"Yeah, I wonder what she looked like?"

"What difference does it make?"

"I'm just curious," Janet replied.

"And you want to know what Edward saw in her," Joan said, as if the idea just hit her.

"Not at all," Janet replied, looking out the window towards the garden.

"Perhaps Stuart has some old photos," Joan suggested, presumably seeing the same thing Janet had through the sitting room window.

Stuart was on his way into their garden again.

"I think I'll go and ask him," she told Joan, heading towards the conservatory.

Chapter 5

"How are you?" Janet greeted their neighbour when she found him in the very back corner of the large garden.

Stuart smiled at her. "I'm well," he replied. "I saw some weeds coming through back here and I figured I'd better tackle them before they got out of hand."

Janet looked at the rolling expanse of grass. "It looks just about perfect to me," she told the man.

He dropped to his knees and pointed to something. "See? This shouldn't be here. If it's left to grow on its own, it will soon take over."

Janet leaned down and studied the area he was pointing to. All she could see was grass. "I see," she said after a moment. "Well, it's a good thing you're here to keep track of such things, then."

"Did you need something else doing?" Stuart asked, sitting back on his heels.

"I just had a quick question," Janet replied. "We were talking about Maggie Appleton and I realised that I've no idea what she looked like. Do you have any photos of her?"

"Maggie didn't like having her picture taken," Stuart said. "We don't take a lot of photos ourselves, Mary and I, but we had the camera out one day when the grandchildren were due for a visit and I tried to get Maggie to pose with Mary. She very politely refused."

"So in all the years she lived here, you never got a single photo of her?" Janet asked, disappointed.

"As I said, we don't take a lot of photos, and once I knew Maggie didn't like having her picture taken, I never tried again. You should ask your guest. If anyone has pictures of Maggie, it would be him."

"Edward? Why?"

"He and Maggie were a couple, weren't they? He used to visit pretty regularly, that's for sure. They used to go sightseeing together and all sorts. You should ask him."

Janet nodded slowly, her mind racing. Edward was the last person she wanted to ask about Maggie Appleton.

"Was there anything else?" Stuart asked, glancing at his watch. "I really need to get some weed killer mixed up and applied, and I promised Mary I'd only be a few minutes."

"No, sorry, that was all," Janet told him. "Sorry to interrupt your work."

She headed back inside feeling dissatisfied. Perhaps she needed to go through the rest of Maggie's old paperwork. She hadn't noticed any photos in the boxes, but there could be some somewhere. Joan was eager to get away to do some grocery shopping at the large store outside Doveby Dale, which left Janet alone in the house.

Unable to think of anything better to do, and not wanting to think about her dinner plans, Janet settled into a comfortable chair in the sitting room with one of Maggie's boxes of papers and a pile of file folders. She sorted out piles of old bills, receipts and the odd note from a happy (or not so happy) former guest at Doveby House.

By six o'clock she was feeling fed up and bored, but she'd managed to empty the box. She was just tidying everything neatly away when Edward let himself in the front door.

"That seems like a lot of paperwork," Edward said cheerfully.

"We found several boxes of papers in various places when we

bought the house," Janet explained. "We're taking our time, sorting through them all."

"Maggie's papers?" the man asked.

Janet frowned, wishing she'd done the sorting in her room instead. "Yes," she replied. "But they're nothing exciting." She suddenly recalled the letters that were locked up in the library. Those were considerably more exciting, but she was even more reluctant to go through them than she was to sort out the bills and things.

"If you'd like a hand, I'd be happy to sort through a box or two for you," Edward said.

His tone was casual, but Janet couldn't help but feel like he was really interested in getting his hands on the boxes.

"That's very kind of you," she replied, getting up from her seat and dropping the file folders into the now empty box. "But Joan and I are getting through them. We're hoping they might help us with getting the business going again, so we're being very careful as we sort."

"Very sensible, I'm sure. Have you found anything interesting so far?"

Janet shook her head. "Not unless you consider old utility bills interesting," she replied. "Although Joan certainly does. She's trying to work out what our bills will be like, especially in the winter months when we'll have this big house to heat."

"I suppose I can see Joan's point, but no, I don't find old utility bills the least bit interesting. And that's all you've found?"

"That's all, aside from a few notes from former guests," she told him, watching him closely. His face didn't give anything away, but Janet still thought he seemed disappointed.

"Well, I'd better go and get ready for dinner," he said after a moment. "I have a hot date."

"Lucky you," Janet retorted.

Edward winked at her. "You'll be ready by half six, won't you?" he checked.

"Of course." Janet glanced at the clock and frowned. It was later than she'd realised.

"Can I carry that box somewhere for you?" Edward asked now, as Janet lifted the box filled with the sorted paperwork.

"You go and get ready," she replied. "It's fine." She waited until she heard his footsteps on the stairs before she headed to Joan's suite. With a guest in the house, they had moved the boxes into Joan's small sitting room, but Janet didn't want Edward to know that. She put the box back with the others and then rushed upstairs to get ready for dinner, pausing just long enough to make absolutely certain that the door to Joan's suite was locked behind her.

"I'm sure you'll have a lovely time," she told her reflection. The face in the mirror didn't look convinced. Janet added a bit of makeup and then shrugged. She didn't even like the man; there was no point in fussing with her appearance. Still, it was a date, the first she'd had in many years. She added a quick coat of lipstick and decided that was enough.

"Janet's always late for dates," Joan's voice carried down the corridor as Janet approached the sitting room. "When we were younger and she was going out every night, I swear I spent more time entertaining her dates than she did."

Janet heard Edward chuckle. "I hope she isn't too late," he replied. "I've made a booking at my favourite local restaurant."

"I'm not late," Janet said from the doorway, ignoring the clock on the wall that suggested she was, in fact, about five minutes behind schedule.

"And you look lovely," Edward said, getting to his feet. "Shall we?"

Janet took the arm he offered and then made a face at her sister behind his back. Joan shook her head and Janet knew she was wondering when her younger sister might actually grow up. As far as Janet was concerned, she was as grown up as she needed to be.

Edward escorted her to his car, a nearly new saloon car that Janet recognised as a luxury model. She settled in her seat and then Edward shut her door.

"This is very nice," Janet said once Edward was behind the driver's seat.

"I like cars," he replied. He glanced over at her and then

grinned. "I won't bore you with any details, but I've always tried to buy the best car I could afford. When I was younger, I drove fast sporty cars, but now I find I prefer comfort and performance instead."

"I just like to get from place to place," Janet replied. "We've been buying pretty much the same car every four or five years since we bought our first car."

Edward laughed. "That's one way to do it."

"It works for us," Janet told him.

The drive to the restaurant wasn't a long one, but by the time they arrived, Janet was rethinking their commitment to the manufacturer of their current car. Edward's car purred along quietly, absorbing the bumps in the road and leaving her feeling almost as if she'd floated all the way there.

"What does a car like this cost?" she asked as Edward helped her from the incredibly comfortable leather seat.

The number Edward gave her made her laugh and then shake her head. So much for that little fantasy. She and Joan would never be able to afford a car like his.

The restaurant was a small French one that Janet had passed more than once but had never been inside. It was dimly lit and looked expensive, where Janet and Joan tended to look for bright and cheerfully economical on the odd occasion when they ate away from home.

The host greeted them warmly. "Ah, Mr. Bennett, it's such a pleasure to see you again. And with such a lovely companion this evening."

He showed them to a quiet table in the back corner of the restaurant and left them with the gorgeously handwritten menus.

Janet scanned the menu quickly. The entire menu was written in French. Besides that, there were no prices on it, and that worried her. She felt completely overwhelmed by the entire place and the man sitting opposite her. She found she was suddenly wishing that Joan would call and interrupt things before they went any further.

"Do you need any help with translating the selections?" Edward asked.

Janet felt a flash of temper and reminded herself that she didn't like the man. She took a deep breath and smiled sweetly at him. "I think I'm okay," she said softly.

When the waiter arrived he and Edward had a lengthy conversation about wine without including Janet. She bit her tongue, as she didn't particularly care what wine they had with dinner. She wasn't planning on drinking much.

The man returned with the bottle Edward had selected and went through the ritual of having Edward taste his choice. Janet ignored the whole thing. When the waiter then asked if they were ready to order, Janet put her menu down.

"Are there any specials today?" she asked in perfectly accented French.

The man smiled and read off the list of specials from a card. Janet asked several questions about how certain dishes were prepared and about the various accompaniments, carrying on the entire conversation in French, before she ordered. Edward added his choices to the order, his own French accent almost as good as Janet's, and then handed their menus to the waiter who bowed before he walked away.

"I'm an idiot," Edward said in a conversational tone as Janet took a sip of wine. "I don't blame you for thinking that I am."

"Not at all," Janet replied with a shrug.

Edward chuckled. "I didn't expect you to speak French, let alone speak it so very well. I suspect you're going to continue to surprise me."

"I'm a very ordinary retired primary schoolteacher," Janet told him. "There's nothing surprising or even interesting about me."

"So where did you learn to speak French so beautifully?"

"When we were much younger, Joan and I spent a few years teaching English in a small French village," Janet explained. "And I taught French at our village primary school for many years as well."

"I underestimated you and I'm sorry," Edward said. "I like to think of myself as rather old-fashioned, but that doesn't excuse me acting like we're still living in the nineteen-fifties when it comes to how I treat people."

"So what is it you do that lets you buy fancy cars?" Janet asked, changing the subject.

"I work in imports and exports," Edward answered vaguely. "Although I'm mostly retired now."

"How does 'mostly retired' work?" Janet had to ask.

"I guess I should say that I'm supposed to be retired," Edward replied with a smile, "but I get called every now and then to deal with various little things."

"And you were good friends with Maggie Appleton?" Janet asked.

"We knew each other for a long time," Edward said, not really answering the question. "But I travel a lot. I spent the last year in America," he added in an exaggerated American accent. "I guess that's how I missed hearing that she'd passed away."

"I don't suppose you have any photos of her," Janet said, trying to sound uninterested.

"I doubt it," Edward replied. "Maggie didn't like having her picture taken. In fact…."

He was interrupted by the arrival of their starters and for the next hour and a half Janet found herself forgetting all about Maggie Appleton as she enjoyed the delicious meal. She drank well over half of the bottle of wine, as well.

"I'm driving," Edward reminded her when she pointed out that he wasn't drinking his fair share.

The food was fabulous and Edward spent the meal telling her many stories about his travels over the years. He switched accents along with locations and Janet found herself laughing frequently as he talked of strange wildlife encounters in Australia, odd people encounters in the US, and freak weather happenings in Canada.

By the time she'd eaten the last bite of her chocolate mousse, Janet couldn't quite remember why she hadn't like the man. He was charming and erudite as well as quite handsome. She held his arm a little more tightly as he escorted her back to his car.

"It's a lovely night for a drive," Edward said after he'd climbed into the driver's seat.

Janet burst out laughing. The wind had picked up and it was raining heavily. The sentiment was romantic, but it was a crazy idea.

"Yeah, okay, maybe not," Edward said with a chuckle. "I'm just having such a wonderful time, I don't want the evening to end."

"It's getting late," Janet said, glancing at her watch. "I have to get up early to help Joan get breakfast for our guest."

Edward frowned. "Don't worry about breakfast for me," he told her. "Not if it means you have to get up early."

"I always get up early," Janet told him. "Joan and I have always been morning people."

"I'm a night owl," Edward replied. "And right now I'd like nothing more than to sit up all night getting to know you better."

Janet blushed. "I'm flattered, but I'm also very tired," she said. "I think I need to call it a night."

"I guess I shall have to simply extend my stay," he said as he put the car into gear. "I was only going to stay one more night, but that isn't nearly enough time to get to know you properly."

Janet sat back in her seat and thought about his words. She'd enjoyed the evening far more than she thought she would, but thinking about getting to know Edward better was worrying. Not only was he rather more sophisticated than the men she had dated when she was younger, there was also still the remote possibility that he was the escaped fugitive Robert Parsons was chasing.

She thought about their conversation and the ease with which the man used various accents. Was it possible that he hadn't heard about Maggie's death because he'd been in prison for the last year?

Chapter 6

Once Edward parked the car, Janet climbed out quickly.

"Thank you for a lovely evening," she called, heading towards the house before he'd even finished getting out of the car.

"You're very welcome," he answered smoothly, catching up to her with a few long strides. He took her arm and helped her up the steps to the front door.

Before Janet could find her keys, the door swung open.

"There you are," Joan said. "I was just heading to bed and saw the car lights."

Janet grinned and then stepped into the house. "We had such a wonderful meal," she told her sister. "Come up to my room with me and I'll tell you all about it while I get ready for bed."

Joan locked the front door and the two sisters headed for the stairs, leaving Edward standing in the middle of the sitting room.

"Thank you again," Janet said with a small wave as she exited the room.

Upstairs, Janet told her sister about the evening, focussing on the food but also repeating a few of Edward's stories about his travels.

"So do you think he's Peter Smith?" Joan asked when Janet had finished.

"I don't know," Janet answered anxiously. "I suppose he could be, but he's so very charming as well."

"But con men have to be charming, don't they?" Joan countered.

"I guess that rules Leonard Simmons out, then, doesn't it?" Janet asked, giggling.

"You could be right," Joan said with a smile.

After Joan left, Janet locked her door and got ready for bed. She climbed into bed and grabbed the book that was on her nightstand. Feeling far too restless to sleep, she decided to read a few chapters before she turned out the light. Ten minutes later she was fed up with the book and feeling even more unsettled than she had before she'd crawled into bed.

"There's a whole library full of books just downstairs," a little voice in her head whispered. Janet told the voice to be quiet and read another paragraph, but it was no good. The book was one she had read before and it couldn't hold her interest. All she could think about was the shelves and shelves of books on the floor below her.

"It's my house," she said loudly to no one. "If I want to go and get a book, I can."

She opened her door as quietly as she could and then looked up and down the short corridor. Nothing was moving, so she slipped out of her room and shut her door behind her. She locked it carefully and then crept to the stairs. Stepping carefully to avoid making any noise, she made her way down to the ground floor. It was dark, but there was enough light from the moon streaming in various windows that Janet felt fairly confident that she could move through the house without turning on any lights. She reached the television room without incident and was relieved to find it empty.

Just as she was about to cross to the library door, she heard a faint creaking noise. Stepping back into the sitting room, she slipped behind the door between the two rooms. The library door opened slowly, creaking again as it did so. A moment later Edward emerged from the room. He turned and did something to the door that he'd closed behind him. After glancing left and right, he made his way through the television room and then through the sitting room.

Janet held her breath as he walked past her and then headed up the stairs. She listened to his footsteps on the stairs as they faded away. Making her way to the library, she checked the door. It was locked. Did Edward have his own key or had he somehow broken in and then managed to lock up behind himself, she wondered. She stood at the door, debating what to do, for several minutes. The sound of a car driving slowly past the house spooked her just enough to send her back up the stairs to her bedroom.

She climbed the stairs as quietly as she could, slipping into her room. As she pushed her door shut, she was certain she heard the door to the west room across the hall opening. Turning her key in the lock as quietly as she could, Janet stood for several minutes listening. When she heard nothing at all, she sighed to herself and headed for bed. It seemed only a few moments later that the alarm she'd actually remembered to set for a change woke her.

Joan was already working on preparing breakfast when Janet joined her at half seven.

"I thought you might lie in after your late date," Joan said as a greeting.

"I didn't think you'd approve," Janet replied.

While Joan did the cooking, Janet went out in the light rain to cut some flowers for the table. She was just arranging them into vases when Edward came into the kitchen.

"Good morning, ladies," he said with a bright smile. "I hope everyone slept well."

"Very well, thanks," Joan answered.

"Yes, very well," Janet muttered as she slid bread into the toaster.

"Excellent," he replied.

Joan and Edward chatted about nothing at all over breakfast. Janet ate her share of everything, but she felt tired and out of sorts as she did so. Joan had made both tea and coffee and Janet found herself drinking cup after cup of coffee, hoping the caffeine would make a difference.

"Are you okay?" Edward asked, his voice full of concern, as Janet began to clear the dishes from the table.

"I'm fine," Janet replied. "Just a little tired."

"Does that mean you don't want to have dinner with me again tonight?" he asked quietly.

Janet glanced at her sister, but Joan was busy at the sink, running water for washing up.

"I think I need an early night," Janet replied, hoping he would accept the excuse.

"Perhaps we should have lunch together instead," he suggested.

"I have to help Joan with things most of today," Janet said, desperately trying to think of a more believable pretext to offer.

Before Edward could reply, a chime sounded.

"What's that?" Joan asked.

"It's the bell on the conservatory door," Edward told her. "You have a visitor."

"I didn't know there was a bell on those doors," Joan said.

Janet headed for the French doors, eager to get away from the conversation she'd been having. Stuart was standing outside the French doors with another man Janet had never seen before.

"Hello, Stuart, how are you?" she asked after she'd opened the door.

"I'm very well," Stuart replied. "I just wanted to introduce you to someone. This is James Abbott. He's Mary's brother-in-law and he's just here visiting for a few days."

Janet smiled and shook hands with the man. He looked to be somewhere in his sixties, with short grey hair in an almost military-style cut. His eyes were brown. He was around Stuart's height, and looked similarly fit and healthy.

"You're Mary's brother?" Janet asked, not sure she'd understood Stuart.

"No, I'm her brother-in-law from her first marriage," he explained in a soft voice. "Actually, I'm more like her step-brother-in-law or something like that, but we've never worried about the finer details."

Janet laughed. "Today's modern families," she said.

"Exactly," the man replied with a grin.

"James will probably be helping me while he's here, just so he has something to do," Stuart told her. "He worked in the gardens of a few stately homes over the years, so he's very well qualified. Anyway, I didn't want you to see him poking around behind your house and worry about who he was."

"That's very kind of you," Joan said from behind Janet.

After everyone had been properly introduced, the two men turned towards the garden. "We're just going to check on those weeds," Stuart told the sisters. "They might need a second treatment."

The light rain had stopped and the sun was at least trying to dry things out. Janet and Joan headed back inside.

"Another man around the right age to be the missing criminal," Joan remarked.

"Surely he can't be if he's Mary's brother-in-law," Janet replied.

"It seemed a tenuous relationship, from what he said," Joan said. "If they aren't close, maybe she doesn't know about his criminal history."

"Or maybe Edward is the man the police are looking for," Janet suggested.

"Or Leonard," Joan added. "Don't forget to add Leonard to the suspect list."

Janet laughed. "You don't like him much, do you?"

"Michael called this morning and said he was going to take Leonard into Sheffield for some sightseeing and lunch. They're going to some sporting event later and having dinner at some pub. He did invite me to join them for the latter two things, but I politely declined."

"He's only here for a few days, right?" Janet asked. "I'm sure Michael will make things up to you once Leonard has gone."

"If I give him the chance to do so," Joan said grudgingly.

"But where is Edward?" Janet asked, suddenly noticing his absence.

"He was right behind me when I followed you to the door," Joan replied. "I don't know what happened to him."

Janet walked into the sitting room just in time to watch Edward's car driving away from Doveby House.

"I guess he changed him mind about lunch," Janet said, feeling hurt.

"Maybe someone rang him or something," Joan suggested.

"Maybe." Janet shrugged. "I told him I was busy, anyway."

"Why?"

"He makes me nervous," Janet replied. "And he could be a conman. And he was in the library last night."

"What do you mean, he was in the library last night?" Joan demanded.

Janet told her what she'd seen when she'd come downstairs in the middle of the night.

"Do you think he took anything?" Joan asked.

"I think we should check," Janet replied.

In the library, Janet headed straight to the desk, while Joan scanned the shelves.

"There don't seem to be any gaps anywhere," Joan said after several minutes. "But I suppose he could have switched something on our shelves with a different book and we'd never notice."

"I will organise the books one day," Janet said. "I wasn't expecting guests, remember."

Joan nodded. "Let's not argue about that," she said. "I assumed we didn't need to worry as we can lock the library. I don't know how Edward managed to get in, but clearly the lock wasn't able to stop him."

Janet had been going through the desk drawers, but nothing seemed to have been touched. She opened the bottom drawer and pulled out the file folders inside it.

"What do you have there?" Joan inquired.

"Some very personal letters that Maggie Appleton received from various suitors," Janet told her. "I haven't read them, but I did glance through them all. One set came from a man named Edward. Maybe that's what he was after."

Janet flipped through the folders, but nothing seemed to be missing. The letters from Edward were still there.

"Is anything missing?" Joan asked.

Janet shrugged. "I didn't count the letters or anything. He could have taken a few, I guess, but from what I remember everything is here."

"So why was he in the library?" Joan wondered.

Janet sat in the desk chair and looked slowly around the room. Nothing looked any different to the last time she'd been in there.

"Once he's gone, we need to make sure we take a proper inventory of the whole house before we have any more guests," Janet said.

"That painting is crooked," Joan pointed out. She walked over to the small painting that Janet had barely noticed. It was hanging on the wall, sandwiched between shelves, not just on either side of it but also above and below it.

Joan pushed up on the bottom right corner of the picture, causing it to swing off-centre in the other direction. She tried again, gently attempting to straighten the artwork, but again she failed.

Janet had joined her by now and she reached over and pulled the picture off the wall. Both women gasped. Behind the painting, built into the wall, was a small safe.

"I suspect we might have just found what Edward was doing in the library," Janet said in a whisper.

"How would he even know this was here?" Joan asked. "And why didn't anyone tell us?"

"He and Maggie were very close, apparently," Janet replied, aware that she sounded quite cross as she spoke. "And perhaps no one else knew about the safe," she added.

Joan reached out and pulled on the safe's door, but it didn't open. She spun the dial a few times and then sighed. "Want to guess the combination?"

Janet sighed as well. "We could guess a million times and never get it right," she said grumpily. "We don't even know how many numbers are in the combination."

"You could ask Edward," Joan suggested.

"No way," Janet replied. "We'll have to hire someone to open it for us."

"That will probably be costly and ruin the safe," Joan argued. "I'll ask him if you won't. I'll just mention that we found the safe and wondered if he knew the combination, that's all. He doesn't have to know that you saw him coming out of here last night."

Janet sighed again. She couldn't explain to her sister exactly how she felt. She wasn't even sure herself. The thought that Edward might know the combination to Maggie Appleton's safe just made her feel uncomfortable. It suggested an even greater intimacy than she'd already assumed they'd shared. The letters spoke of physical closeness, but sharing the combination to a hidden safe suggested a more serious commitment.

Before the sisters could discuss things further, they heard someone knocking on the front door.

"I'll tidy up in here," Janet told her sister. "You go and see who's at the door."

Joan headed out while Janet quickly rehung the painting. She collected the folders full of letters and dropped them into the bottom drawer, sliding it shut. After a quick glance around the room to make sure she hadn't missed anything, she switched off the light and shut the door.

"Hardly worth locking it," she muttered to herself as she turned the key in the lock.

She could hear her sister's voice coming from the sitting room, along with a deeper voice that she didn't recognise.

"I'm sorry, but I don't think so," Joan was saying as Janet entered the room.

Joan was standing in the centre of the room with her hands on her hips. She didn't even glance at Janet, instead keeping her eyes pinned on the man standing across from her.

Janet studied the stranger. He was another grey-haired man who looked to be somewhere in his sixties. He was dressed in a dark grey suit that fit him perfectly and he was clearly trying to smile in the face of Joan's upset.

Chapter 7

"What's going on?" Janet asked.

"Good morning," the man said, giving Janet a smarmy smile. "You must be the other Markham sister. I've heard so much about you both."

"Really?" Janet replied. "I hope you didn't believe any of it."

The man laughed, an annoyingly grating sound. "I only believed the good things," he said.

"Who are you?" Janet asked, tired of being polite.

"How remiss of me," the man said. "I introduced myself to your sister, of course. I'm William Chalmers." He said it as if she ought to know the name. Then he offered his hand and Janet took a few steps towards him to take it.

"I'm Janet Markham," she replied. He held her hand for a moment or two longer than she felt was necessary. As soon as he let go, she took a step backwards.

"I'm sorry, but your name means nothing to me," she told him, watching him closely. Something like annoyance flashed over his features before his artificial smile slid back into place.

"I had hoped that the small business owners of Doveby Dale

would stick together and support one another," he replied. "Perhaps that was overly optimistic of me."

"I'm not sure what your aspirations have to do with us," Janet said.

"As the owners of the village's premier bed and breakfast establishment, surely you are both deeply interested in the sorts of shops and restaurants that Doveby Dale has to offer," he intoned.

"As we aren't actually open for business yet, I suppose the thought had yet to cross our mind," Janet replied. Although the man was hugely annoying, she still had no idea what he'd said to upset Joan.

"Yes, well, I suggest you start paying attention to what's happening in the village," William told her. "The wrong sort of shops could be seriously detrimental to your guesthouse. You don't want to start attracting the wrong sort of people, now do you?"

Janet forced herself to smile. "Thank you for the advice," she said. "If that was all you needed, I'll see you out. Joan and I are quite busy. I'm sure you understand."

"Oh, but that isn't why I'm here at all," William replied. "I came to buy some books. I was told that you have a small library full of old books, and I need some. I'm opening a very exclusive antique shop, you see, and I want to scatter a few old books among the bookshelves and desks that I'll have for sale."

Well, that explained Joan's upset, Janet thought. The library was a large part of the reason why they'd purchased Doveby House in the first place. Both women were hugely fond of the space, even if they had yet to go through the books that had been included in the sale of the house.

"Were you looking for any particular books or authors?" Janet asked, curious what the man was planning.

"Oh, goodness, no," William exclaimed. "I just need about eighteen inches worth of old hardcover books, that's all."

"You want to buy books by the inch?" Janet asked, incredulously.

"Sure, why not?"

Janet exchanged looks with her sister. "I'm sorry, but we aren't planning on selling any of the books in our library," she said after a moment. "We haven't been here long enough to even begin to catalogue what we have. There's certainly no way we could just choose a random selection and sell it to you."

"I won't be opening for business for several weeks yet," the man said. "If you find some books you don't want, do let me know."

He reached into a pocket and pulled out a silver card case. "My card," he announced as he handed a card to Janet. She glanced at it and then put it down on the closest table.

"If I were you, I'd start looking elsewhere for books," she advised as she walked with him to the door. "I can't imagine we'll want to get rid of any of ours."

"What an unpleasant man," Janet said to Joan after she'd locked the door behind their unexpected visitor.

"He was worse before you came in," Joan told her. "He started out by giving me a lecture about all of the things we're doing wrong here and then he demanded that I show him the library."

"My goodness, I'm glad I came in when I did," Janet said. She crossed the room and gave Joan a hug. "Let's look on the bright side, maybe he's Peter Smith."

Joan chuckled. "Now I'm feeling quite torn," she replied. "I was hoping Leonard would turn out to be the conman so that he'd go away, but now I do rather hope it is William Chalmers. I hate the thought of him having a business in Doveby Dale."

Another knock on the door interrupted their conversation.

"If it's him again, don't let him in," Joan told Janet as Janet headed towards the door.

"I definitely won't," Janet said emphatically.

She was quite happy to see Constable Parsons on their doorstep. "I do hope you've come to tell us that Peter Smith is once again safely behind bars," she said after they'd all taken seats in the sitting room.

"Unfortunately not," he replied. "I just wanted to check in on your two. It rather worries me, the two of you living here on your own."

"Did you worry about Maggie Appleton?" Joan asked sharply. "She was completely on her own."

"Maggie nearly always had a husband here with her," he replied. "They never seemed to last long, but she always had a replacement ready when one left. Anyway, there was no doubt in my mind that Maggie could take care of herself."

"And you don't think we can do the same?" Janet asked before Joan could start shouting.

"I'm not saying that," the young man said, flushing. "But with Peter Smith possibly in the area, I just thought it would be wise to check on you, that's all."

"That's kind of you," Janet told him, shooting Joan a "keep quiet" look. "We've been meaning to ring you anyway. We've met a few more men that could fit Mr. Smith's description."

The constable pulled out his notebook. "We are still checking, very discreetly, into the two men you told me about last time," he told them. "As it's very likely both men are exactly who they claim to be, we don't want to upset them."

"Yes, well, perhaps you should do the same with James Abbott, who is staying with the Longs. He's meant to be a step-brother-in-law or some such thing to Mary Long," Janet said.

Robert made a note. "Someone mentioned that the Longs had a guest, but they didn't have any details."

"The other man who bears some investigating is a Mr. William Chalmers," Joan said. "He claims to be opening an antique shop in the village, and he's thoroughly unpleasant." She handed Robert the card that William had given to Janet.

"Perhaps he's the man who's leased the old greeting card and gift shop on the high street," Robert replied. "It's been empty for a few years, and I noticed the other day that someone had cleared some of the mess out of it. I'll have to stop by and introduce myself to him."

"I doubt he's doing the work himself," Janet said. "He doesn't seem the type to clean anything."

Robert nodded and made another note on his pad. "Thank you

for the information," he said. "I do hope you're both locking your bedroom doors at night while you have a guest."

"We are," Janet assured him. "And we both double-check all of the outside doors before we head to bed as well."

"Modern security systems are quite useful," he suggested. "You could track movement around the inside of the house as well as monitoring the exterior doors and windows."

"I'm not sure our guests would feel especially welcome if we told them that they couldn't move about the house after a certain time at night," Joan replied. "Part of the whole bed and breakfast experience is feeling like you're staying in a home rather than a hotel. If someone fancies a midnight snack or wants to watch a bit of telly after Janet and I are in bed, they should be able to move around without ringing alarms or bringing the police."

"I suppose that makes sense," the man conceded.

"You really mustn't worry about us," Joan told him. "We're a lot tougher than we look."

"I'm sure you are," Robert replied, but he didn't look convinced.

"Maybe I should take some karate classes or something," Janet said after she'd locked up behind the policeman.

"I wonder if we could," Joan replied, surprising her sister.

"Seriously?"

"It's something to think about."

Joan disappeared into the kitchen, leaving Janet blinking in astonishment. Retirement was changing her older sister in all sorts of ways. After a moment, she followed Joan into the kitchen.

"The coach house is open, which means Stuart and James are still working in the garden," Joan said. "I thought I would take them some tea."

"I'll help," Janet offered.

Joan arranged a pot of tea on a tray, with milk and sugar in tiny containers. She added two cups while Janet piled biscuits onto a small plate. Joan carried the tray, while Janet opened the French doors for her. They crossed the garden to the coach house where Stuart stored some of his gardening equipment.

"Hello? Stuart? Are you here?" Joan called as they approached the coach house door.

Stuart's head popped out of the coach house. "We're in here, trying to reorganise some hose pipes," he replied.

"We've brought you some tea and biscuits," Joan said. "You've been out here all morning."

Joan and Janet walked into the coach house, which was dimly lit by a single bulb. Joan set the tray down on a rickety table near the door.

"One of these days we have to start clearing this place out," Janet said, looking around the large, dirty, and cluttered single room.

"We certainly do," Joan replied. "We've been too busy with the house thus far."

"I hope you aren't planning to fix it up as a guest room," Stuart said. "It's handy having storage space for my tools and things."

"We just need to clear out the junk and then clean the whole room," Joan told him. "I can't imagine we'll ever use it for anything more than storage."

"I saw you had a visitor," James emerged from a dark corner in the room. "Who was that, then?"

"The local police constable," Janet told him. "He was just checking in on us."

"That was kind," the man said. "He's gone now, though?"

"Yes. I think he was off to Little Burton, actually," Janet said. "He covers both villages, you see."

"Hmmm," the man mumbled around a biscuit.

Stuart and James quickly finished the plate of biscuits and the pot of tea while Janet and Joan looked around the coach house. Janet opened a few boxes that were stacked in one corner and found books.

"We should take these in and go through them," she said to Joan.

"We still have to sort out the ones in the library, not to mention the boxes of books we brought with us from our old cottage," Joan pointed out. "These have been in here for some time. We can go through them after we've figured out a system for cataloguing what we already have."

Janet nodded reluctantly. Joan was right, but somehow these books, hidden away in the coach house, seemed more interesting than the ones neatly shelved in the library.

"We'd better get back to work," Stuart said. "Thank you for the tea break."

"Any time," Joan told him. She picked up the tray and she and Janet headed back towards the house. Janet could hear the men talking in low voices as they walked away, but she couldn't make out what they were saying.

In the kitchen, Joan pulled out some cold cuts and bread for sandwiches. "I'll cook something nice for dinner," she said. "I hope a light lunch is okay."

"It's fine," Janet agreed. She wasn't really hungry. Her mind was on too many other things.

"I'll make a steak and kidney pie for later," Joan said. "Is Edward going to be joining us?"

"I don't know," Janet snapped. "He certainly didn't tell me his plans."

Joan patted her arm. "Never mind. I'll make two pies so we're sure to have plenty. If it's just the two of us, I can freeze the second one for a rainy day."

After their lunch, Joan got to work on the pies while Janet made her way back to the library. She spent several minutes twisting and turning the dial on the wall safe that they'd discovered, occasionally attempting to open the door. It was a pointless exercise and she knew that, but she couldn't stop herself from trying.

The letters in the desk seemed to be calling to her, teasing her and tempting her to read them. She felt a curious mix of curiosity and dread whenever she thought about the letters from Edward.

They may not even be from Edward Bennett, she told herself, as she headed towards the desk. Edward is a common name, after all. She sat down in the desk chair and pulled open the bottom desk drawer. The folders were right where she'd left them, and she quickly found the one that she was looking for.

"Here goes nothing," she muttered to herself as she opened the folder.

Half an hour later she shut the folder and pushed it away from her. While the letters were less explicit than she'd feared, it was clear from reading them that Edward and Maggie had been lovers. What she couldn't be certain of was whether this Edward was Edward Bennett. All of the letters were simply signed "Edward" or even just "E," which was no help.

They were fairly short and said little more than how much Edward missed Maggie and what he was planning to do with her when he saw her again. If the author had deliberately tried to avoid providing any information about himself, he couldn't have done a better job of it.

Already feeling uncomfortable about reading someone else's private correspondence, Janet opened the next folder and read through some far more graphic notes from someone called Simon. There were only a few of them, but the content left her blushing. They also gave her a surprising amount of information about Simon. While the letters weren't long, Simon managed to mention his job (dentist), where he lived (Bristol), and with whom he lived (his wife, who didn't understand him).

Janet felt struck by the contrast between Simon's correspondence and Edward's. She sighed and shook her head. Maybe she was creating something from nothing. The Edward in the letters might not be the Edward who was staying with them anyway. She put all of the folders back in the bottom desk drawer and stood up. She'd be better off helping Joan fix dinner than sitting here snooping through Maggie's past.

Chapter 8

Joan already had the pies in the oven, so Janet decided to curl up with a book for a short while. She felt unsettled and a bit cross with the world. By the time Joan called her down from her room for dinner, she was feeling a bit more like herself. She'd lost herself in one of her favourite classic detective stories and now felt as if Sherlock Holmes would be most welcome at the moment. No doubt he'd be able to open the library safe and spot Peter Smith with no difficulty whatsoever.

When Janet joined Joan in the kitchen, the two pies had just come out of the oven.

"They look wonderful," Janet said. "And they smell even better."

"I am rather pleased with them," Joan admitted. "The crust has browned quite nicely. I wasn't sure about this oven, but it does a very nice job."

"Something certainly smells good," a voice boomed from the front of the house.

The sisters exchanged glances. Edward had a key to the front door, but the voice sounded like Michael's, and he did not. A moment later, all was revealed as Edward, Michael and Leonard all appeared in the kitchen.

"I was coming up the walk just as Michael was about to knock," Edward explained. "I figured I might as well let them in."

Janet glanced at Joan. From the look on Joan's face, Edward's decision hadn't been a good one.

"Of course," Janet said loudly before her sister could speak. "We're always happy to see Michael."

"And his friends," Joan added icily. "I thought you two had plans for today."

"We changed our minds," Michael said. "We decided we'd rather stay closer to home. I came over to see if you both wanted to join us for dinner."

"As I've just finished cooking, it's a bit late for that," Joan replied.

"I see that," Michael said. "And I smell it as well. Those pies smell beautiful."

"Thank you," Joan said shortly.

Janet could tell that the compliment had done little to soften her sister's annoyance with the man. Of course, the polite thing to do would be to invite them all to stay for dinner, but Janet was hesitant to upset her sister further. She glanced at Joan and raised her eyebrows. For a moment it seemed as if Joan was going to pretend not to understand the unspoken question, but then Joan sighed deeply.

"We've plenty if everyone would like to stay for dinner," she said in a grudging tone.

"Thank you kindly," Michael said. "We'd love to, wouldn't we, Leonard?" Leonard grunted something that didn't exactly convey enthusiasm.

"Am I invited as well?" Edward asked, taking Janet's hand to get her attention.

"As Joan said, we have plenty," Janet replied, pulling her hand away and ignoring the tiniest bit of regret as she did so.

"You'd better get yourselves settled in the dining room," Joan said. "Janet and I will serve."

"I'll help," Michael said. "It's the least I can do."

Joan opened her mouth and then snapped it shut. "In that case,

Janet, you go and get everyone settled in the dining room. Michael and I will serve."

Janet led Edward and Leonard into the dining room. Janet quickly laid the table with cutlery from the sideboard and then they all took seats. Leonard sat across from Edward, who'd taken the chair next to Janet's once she'd sat down.

"Maybe we could go down to the pub for a drink after dinner?" Edward asked Janet.

"I think, after this lovely meal, I'll be too tired to go out," Janet replied. Determined to change the subject, she smiled at Leonard. "I do hope you're enjoying your visit with Michael," she said brightly.

"It's fine," he muttered.

"What have you two been doing?" Janet asked.

"Not much," the man said with a shrug. "I'm here to get away from things at home. I'm not much for sightseeing or whatever."

"But there are some lovely old castles and stately homes in the area," Janet told him. "You should at least visit Chatsworth and Hardwick."

Leonard shrugged. "I'm happier just keeping to myself," he said.

Janet was trying to think of something else to discuss when the door to the kitchen swung open and Michael entered with several plates full of food. He put one down in the front of Janet and then served Edward and Leonard before returning the kitchen. Only a moment later he was back with plates for himself and Joan. Joan followed with tea for everyone.

"I hope you don't mind. It was easier to plate everything in the kitchen," Joan explained as she took her seat. No one objected.

For several minutes the room was mostly silent as everyone enjoyed the delicious pies. Joan had added salad to each plate as well, and Janet noticed that Edward was the only man who ate his.

As everyone finished eating, Michael insisted that Joan remain seated while he cleared away the dirty dishes. He was back with a plate of biscuits a moment later. Janet tried to make conversation again as everyone sipped tea and nibbled biscuits.

"That was very good," she told her sister. "And your lemon biscuits are the perfect final course."

"Thank you," Joan replied.

"Everything was wonderful," Michael said, beaming. He patted Joan's hand. "I'll take you somewhere for a meal to thank you properly one day soon."

"We'll see," Joan said, pulling her hand away.

Michael frowned. "Just as soon as Leonard has gone, we'll go to your favourite place," he said firmly.

"Thanks," Leonard muttered.

Michael shook his head. "You know what I meant."

"I did, and I'm sorry if I'm in the way," Leonard replied. "You know things are, well, difficult, right now. I'm sure I won't have to hide up here forever, though. Just a few more days, I hope."

Michael nodded. "You're welcome for as long as you need to stay," he told his friend.

"Ta," Leonard said before he piled another six biscuits on his plate.

"Joan, I hope I'm welcome a little bit longer, as well," Edward said now, with a smile. "My plans changed rather suddenly and I'd like to stay a few more nights."

"Of course you can," Joan said. "You're more than welcome."

An awkward silence followed Joan's pronouncement until Janet couldn't take it any more.

"I'll just get started on the washing up," she announced, getting to her feet. "No, you visit with our guests," she told her sister. "You've done all the hard work so far today."

"And I've done nothing but eat," Edward said with a chuckle. "I'll give you a hand," he told Janet.

Janet frowned to herself as she carried her biscuit plate into the kitchen. She was trying to avoid Edward.

In the kitchen, the pair soon had the dishwasher loaded up and ready to go once the final pudding plates had been added.

"I wonder what or who Leonard is hiding from," Edward remarked as Janet began hand-washing the pie tins.

"What do you mean?"

"He said something about not hiding up here forever. I just wondered what happened that he needs to hide at all."

Janet shrugged. "Maybe he forgot his wife's birthday," she suggested. She'd been thinking the exact same thing, but she didn't want Edward to know it. The last thing she wanted to discuss with Edward was the missing conman, since it was still quite possible Edward himself was the man in question.

The pie tins didn't take long to wash, but by the time she'd finished them Joan had brought in the rest of the dishes.

"Leonard and Michael have gone," she told Janet. "Michael did mention that he might stop over later tonight, though. Apparently there's something on the telly that Leonard never misses, so Michael might just leave him to it and come over for a cuppa while it's on."

Janet smiled at her sister, who was clearly in a better mood. "Hopefully Leonard will be heading home soon," she said to Joan.

"Indeed," Joan murmured.

Joan set the dishwasher running and the trio walked out of the kitchen and into the sitting room.

"It's too a nice an evening to stay inside," Edward said. "Let's take ourselves down to the pub or something."

"I have a few things I need to do around here, and then Michael might be stopping by," Joan said. "You two go, though."

A knock on the door interrupted Janet's flustered attempts to get out of the trip. She rushed over and threw the door open.

"Mr. Chalmers? What can we do for you?" she asked, surprised to see the man back on their doorstep.

"I was just visited by a police constable," the man said angrily. "What do you mean sending the police to my store? He asked all sorts of incredibly prying questions."

"We didn't send the police to your shop," Janet said firmly.

"As you're the only people I've spoken to about my new business, it must have been you," the man retorted. "This constable person knew far too much about me. You must have told him everything I said when I was here."

"Do you have something to hide?" Edward asked, coming up behind Janet.

"Who are you?"

"I can't see why that's any of your business," Edward said smoothly. "But the name is Edward Bennett. And you are?"

"William Chalmers," the other man replied. "In answer to your question, I've nothing to hide, but I also don't want everyone in town talking about my new business. Not yet, anyway. It's going to take some time to get everything arranged exactly right before I can open. If another, similar shop were to open between now and then, it would be catastrophic."

"Perhaps you shouldn't be going around telling people about it, then," Edward suggested mildly.

"I'm not," William replied hotly. "I told two people. I certainly didn't expect them to call the police about it."

"We didn't call the police," Janet protested. "Constable Parsons was here to see us about something else and we happened to mention your visit, that's all. We certainly didn't send him to question you and we haven't mentioned you at all to anyone else."

"Yes, well, see that you don't talk about me," the man said haughtily. He turned on his heel and stomped back down the steps. Edward and Janet watched him walk to the small car park and climb into a fairly new estate car.

Janet winced as the man accelerated out of the car park at high speed. He turned onto the main road, nearly striking a car that was coming towards him. Janet shook her head and then shut the door.

"What an unpleasant man," she said.

"Another man who's hiding something," Edward commented. "Or hiding from someone. He was very upset that the police came to speak to him."

"I almost wish we had sent Robert Parsons to see him," Janet remarked. "I do hope he doesn't come back again."

"Don't let him in," Edward said sternly. "I don't trust him."

And I don't trust you, Janet thought sadly.

A ringing noise startled them all.

"My mobile," Edward explained as he reached into a pocket. He disappeared down the corridor with his phone in hand. A few moments later he was back.

"Sorry, we'll have to do the pub another day," he told Janet as he headed for the door. "Something's come up rather suddenly."

He was out the door and down the steps before Janet could reply.

"Well, that was rude," Joan said as Janet shut the door behind Edward.

"It was, wasn't it?" Janet said thoughtfully. "He keeps pointing out how other people are hiding things and then he behaves mysteriously himself."

"I like him," Joan told her. "But I'm not sure I trust him."

"I like him as well," Janet admitted. "And I'm very sure that I don't trust him."

The sound of the bell on the French doors startled them both.

"It's just going to be one of those days, isn't it?" Joan muttered as the sisters headed towards the conservatory.

Stuart smiled at them through the glass as he waited for them to open the door.

"Have you seen James?" he asked as Janet opened the door.

"No, have you lost him?" Janet asked.

"We went in for dinner and then we were going to do some weeding in the flower beds on the south side of the garden. I gave Mary a hand with the washing up and James said he was going to get started. I can't seem to find him anywhere, though," Stuart replied.

"Maybe he's weeding in the wrong bed and you missed him behind a tree or something," Janet suggested. "I'll come and help you look."

She stepped through the door and followed Stuart down the path that ran through the centre of the garden. "You go that way and I'll go this way," she suggested, gesturing to the left.

Stuart headed off as Janet suggested, leaving Janet to slowly make her way along the right side of the small grounds. She walked along the side of the house, where low hedges separated their property from the road. Constable Parsons drove past in his police car and gave her a small wave, which she returned cheerily.

She was making her way between the various flower beds,

enjoying their colours and scents, when she heard her name being called.

"Janet? I've found him," Stuart shouted.

Quickly retracing her steps, Janet found the two men standing together near the coach house.

"Is everything okay?" she asked, looking intently at James, whose face was flushed.

"It's fine," James said sharply. "I just took a short walk around the neighbourhood while I was waiting for Stuart, that's all."

Janet shrugged. "If you'd like a cuppa later, ring the bell at the back," she suggested to the men. "Or we could fetch you cold drinks, as it's still rather warm tonight."

"I doubt we'll do much more today," Stuart told her. "We got most of what needed doing sorted out this afternoon."

"Well, the offer is good whenever you're out here," she replied. "I'm sure we aren't paying you enough."

Stuart laughed. "I'm quite happy with our arrangement," he assured her. "And if I don't stop in for tea today, I'm sure I will another time."

"James is welcome as well, if he's still staying with you," Janet said.

"Thanks," James muttered, turning away. He took a couple of steps towards one of the flower beds and then crouched down and began to poke and prod at something that Janet could only assume was weed by the way he was treating it.

"That's meant to be there, mate," Stuart said quietly. "I did these beds yesterday. Let's move over to the other side."

James stood up and followed Stuart across the grass. Stuart waved to Janet as they disappeared from view. She frowned and then turned and headed back to the house. Four strange men in the area, all behaving oddly, she thought to herself. Any one of them could be Peter Smith.

Chapter 9

Janet and Joan settled down in front of the telly. Neither was properly focussed on the American comedy show that was on, however. Janet could tell that her sister was on edge, waiting to see if Michael turned up. She herself was wondering where Edward had rushed off to and when he might be back.

"I'm going to make some popcorn," Janet announced during the advertisements.

"That sounds good," Joan said. "I'll come and help. This is boring, anyway."

Joan switched off the television and the sisters went into the kitchen where Janet pulled a box of microwave popcorn from the cupboard.

"I never thought we'd eat all of that," Joan told her. "It isn't anything we'd normally buy."

Janet laughed. Right after they'd moved in, while Joan had been on her first date with Michael, Janet had made a late-night run to the grocery store for custard cream biscuits. She'd ended up filling a shopping trolley with all sorts of snacks that she and Joan rarely ate. A few bags of popcorn were just about the only things left from the excursion, now.

Janet unwrapped a bag and put it in the microwave. Joan got them each a cold drink while Janet pulled out a large bowl. The loud popping noises that filled the kitchen made conversation impractical. Once Janet had emptied the bag of hot, buttery popcorn into the bowl, the pair sat down at the table.

"You didn't get out separate bowls for each of us," Joan chided, starting to get to her feet.

"Oh, just help yourself," Janet suggested. "It's just us at home. We don't need to be formal."

Janet could see her sister's indecision. While she watched Joan's face, she reached into the bowl and grabbed a handful of popcorn. After a moment, Joan picked up a few kernels herself and ate them carefully.

"So, who do you think is Peter Smith, assuming he's one of the new arrivals to the area?" Janet asked after a sip of soda.

"Leonard," Joan answered firmly.

Janet laughed. "You just don't like him," she said.

"I don't like him, but he could still be Peter Smith," Joan pointed out.

"I think William Chalmers is more likely," Janet told her.

"Let's discuss them one at a time," Joan suggested. "We can start with Leonard Simmons."

"The poor man's only fault is that he's keeping you and Michael apart," Janet said.

"He said he was hiding up here," Joan reminded her. "What is he hiding from exactly?"

"I don't know. But he seems too dull and uninteresting to be a conman. I barely notice him when he's in the room unless he talking loudly about events from forty years ago."

"But that could be an act," Joan said. "He could be just pretending to be boring."

Janet shook her head. "I'm pretty sure he really is boring," she said firmly. "I think he's just an ordinary and dreary man who is currently taking advantage of his friendship with Michael."

"What could he be hiding from, then?" Joan asked.

"His wife? His children? The tax man?"

"It's hard to imagine that he's married," Joan said pensively. "But I suppose he might have been attractive many years ago."

"There's someone out there for everyone," Janet said. "If they want to find someone, that is."

"Yes, well, assuming he's married, why would he need to hide?"

"Maybe he forgot their wedding anniversary or something," Janet said with a shrug. "I don't know enough about marriage to understand its finer points. Maybe he goes away for a week every year, just to give his wife a break from his, um, charming personality."

"Did Michael say what Leonard does for a living?" Joan asked.

Janet frowned thoughtfully. "I don't think so," she said after a moment. "I don't think he said much of anything about the man except that he was an old school friend."

"Interesting," Joan murmured.

"Let's talk about William Chalmers," Janet said. "I don't like him even a little bit and he was very upset that Constable Parsons visited him."

"Yes, but surely the constable would have arrested him if he really were Peter Smith," Joan replied.

"Maybe Robert didn't recognise him, at least not well enough to be certain. I don't think the police can just arrest someone because he might be a conman in disguise."

"He is certainly unpleasant," Joan said. "I wouldn't mind him leaving Doveby Dale, either to go to prison or just to go away."

"I'll second that," Janet said. She looked down at the bowl of popcorn. She and Joan had been munching steadily and it now contained little more than a few unpopped kernels. "And I'll make more popcorn," she added.

While she was making the popcorn, Joan refilled their drinks. "I can't believe we ate the whole bowlful after our big dinner," Joan remarked as they sat back down.

"Me either, but it was delicious," Janet replied, setting the refilled bowl between them. "Now, where were we?"

"We were just trying to get rid of William Chalmers," Joan reminded her.

"Yes, well, if we could find a way to convince Robert Parsons that he's the conman, I'd be happy."

"But I'd still be stuck with Leonard," Joan said sadly.

Janet laughed. "Well, they can't both be Peter Smith," she said.

"Unless they are," Joan said. "Maybe the conman is actually more than one person. That would help explain how he can look so different all the time."

"I suppose anything is possible," Janet said slowly. "But it doesn't seem likely, somehow. I'd like to think the police are smart enough to have figured that out if it were the case."

"I suppose," Joan said with a sigh. "It would be nice to be rid of both of them, though."

"Leonard is leaving soon," Janet told her, patting her hand. "Hang in there."

"What about James Abbott?" Joan asked.

"I don't mind him in the slightest," Janet replied. "He can stay as long as he wants."

Joan smiled. "But could he be the man Robert is looking for?"

Janet shrugged. "I guess so. Stuart said he was an expert gardener, but he didn't seem to know the difference between plants and weeds when I saw him earlier."

"Why couldn't Stuart find him when he first looked?" Joan asked.

"He said he'd gone for a walk," Janet told her.

"I don't know if that's suspicious or not," Joan replied.

"I did see Robert Parsons drive by while I was looking for James," Janet said thoughtfully. "Maybe James was trying to avoid Robert."

"That would certainly be suspicious."

"But it seems just as likely that James was just walking off his dinner," Janet said. "Besides, he's related to Mary in some way. Surely she wouldn't have him in the house if he were a criminal."

"We don't know Mary well enough to answer that," Joan replied.

Janet sighed. "We aren't very good at this detecting thing."

"No, I suppose not," Joan answered. "At least we haven't

managed to get ourselves locked in anywhere this time," she added, staring at Janet.

Janet blushed. "I didn't mean to," she replied weakly. "Besides, you agreed that we wouldn't talk about that ever again."

"And you agreed to stop snooping," Joan retorted.

"We aren't snooping, we're just talking," Janet answered.

"And we still haven't talked about Edward Bennett," Joan pointed out.

Janet felt herself blushing again. "Surely he can't be Peter Smith. He was one of Maggie's boyfriends."

"I'm not sure why that lets him out," Joan replied.

"Stuart and Michael both know him from before anyway. Neither of them seems to think he's anything other than what he claims to be."

"Which is what exactly?" Joan asked. "I've barely spoken to the man. Where is he from? What does he do for a living? Is he married? Does he have children?"

Janet held up a hand to stop the flow of questions. "He works in imports and exports," she told her sister. "Although I'm not sure I know exactly what that means. And he doesn't act as if he's married, but I haven't actually asked him."

"Why on earth not?" Joan demanded.

Janet shrugged. "It simply never came up," she muttered.

"Well, it should have," Joan said stoutly. "You might be dating a married man. That would never do."

"He wouldn't have been dating Maggie if he were married," Janet said as the thought occurred to her.

"He might have been," Joan argued. "We don't know much about Maggie Appleton, but what we do know suggests she led a rather different life to ours."

Janet nodded. It was a good thing Joan hadn't read the letters in the desk yet. Once Joan read them, she'd think Maggie would have been capable of just about anything.

"He did behave oddly tonight," Joan said. "Dashing off like that without any explanation."

"You're right," Janet said miserably. "Maybe it was his wife calling."

Joan shook her head. "I don't think he's married," she told Janet. "But I don't trust him, either. He's hiding something."

"Everyone seems to be hiding something," Janet replied. "Leonard has admitted that he's hiding from someone or something. James did a disappearing act this afternoon and doesn't seem to be who he says he is. William was upset that we told anyone he was here, with an excuse I didn't believe as to why. And now Edward is dashing about Derbyshire with no explanation as to why he had to leave so suddenly."

"So where does that leave us?" Joan asked.

"Nowhere," Janet told her. "We're no closer to figuring out which man is Peter Smith than we were when we started. The only thing we've managed to accomplish is eating two big bowls of popcorn."

Joan looked into the bowl and shook her head. "Where did it all go?" she asked. "I don't feel as if I ate much at all."

"Me either," Janet told her. "But there's nothing left but a few kernels that didn't pop."

"Maybe we should gather all of the suspects together and question them," Janet said after a moment. "That always works in detective stories."

"You know I don't read such things," Joan said. "But I thought the detective got everyone together to dramatically announce who the criminal was. We don't have any idea which man is Peter Smith."

"Who might just as well be hiding in London or Scotland or the Isle of Man," Janet said.

"Indeed, maybe we should alert Bessie," Joan said with a grin.

Janet laughed. "I guess you're right," she admitted.

"I know I'll sleep better at night once Peter Smith is back behind bars," Joan said.

"You mean you'll sleep better once you know he isn't sleeping in our house," Janet told her.

"Well, yes, that's part of it," Joan admitted. "I'm happy we have our very first paying guest, and he's paying handsomely, but if he is a convicted conman, I'd rather not have him in the house."

"And I'd rather not be dating him," Janet added.

"Are you dating him?" Joan asked. "You've been out with him once, but you seem to be trying to avoid him most of the time."

"I don't trust him," Janet told her. "But I wish I could."

Joan nodded. "I think you're better off avoiding him, then," she counselled.

"He's quite interesting, and rather attractive," Janet replied.

The sound of the front door opening made her snap her mouth shut.

"And he's back," Joan hissed. "At least I hope it's him."

The two sisters headed for the sitting room, with Joan in the lead.

"Ah, it is you," she said loudly as she walked into the room.

"It is me," Edward said with a bright smile. "I hope you haven't sat up waiting for me to get home."

"Of course not," Janet said too loudly. "We were just having a snack and chatting. It's only." she trailed off as she glanced at the clock, "…midnight," she added in a surprised tone.

"Where did the evening go?" Joan asked. "I guess Michael never managed to get away."

"Clearly not," Janet said. "Anyway, as it is so very late, I'm off to bed." She headed for the stairs as quickly as she could, not wanting to get caught alone with Edward.

"What would you like for breakfast tomorrow?" Janet heard her sister ask the man. Clearly Joan had realised the reason for Janet's haste and was helping her sister get away. Janet didn't wait to hear Edward's reply.

In her favourite nightgown, with her teeth brushed and her face washed, Janet climbed into bed. She was just finding her place in her book when someone knocked on her door. It had be Joan, she decided. Edward wouldn't visit this late at night. She crossed the room and opened the door a crack, frowning as she realised she was mistaken.

"Janet, we really need to talk," Edward said quietly. "And I'm leaving tomorrow."

"I thought you were staying a few more days," Janet hissed back.

"I thought I was, but my plans have changed again."

"Well, this isn't the time to discuss things," Janet said firmly. "We can talk over breakfast."

Edward frowned. "I don't want to talk in front of your sister," he objected.

Janet shook her head. "Then you'll have to find time for a short conversation after breakfast," she said. "I'm going to bed now."

She shut the door in Edward's face, feeling fed up with the man. Cosy midnight chats were exciting when she was in her twenties, but now she needed her sleep if she were going to be able to function the next day. Tomorrow she was determined to figure out who Peter Smith was, although Edward's recent behaviour seemed to suggest that he might be the man Robert Parsons was looking for.

She climbed back into bed and burrowed under the covers. Half an hour later she threw back the duvet and sat up. I should have just had the stupid conversation, she said to herself. There was no way she was going to be able to sleep without knowing what Edward wanted. She paced around her bedroom, debating what to do. Creeping downstairs for a cup of tea held some appeal, but, having sent Edward away so that she could sleep, she really didn't want to run into him now.

The book on her nightstand didn't appeal in the slightest, but she forced herself to read a chapter from it. When she'd yawned for the tenth time, she slid back down in the bed and shut her eyes tightly. Counting backwards from a thousand, she finally fell into a restless sleep around twenty-seven. Joan was knocking on her door only a short time later.

Chapter 10

"You look terrible," Joan greeted her.

"You don't look so great yourself," Janet retorted. She knew she was a mess, with uncombed hair and tired eyes, but Joan looked as if she hadn't slept either.

"I couldn't sleep," Joan replied. "This Peter Smith thing is starting to bother me."

"I'll just take a quick shower and then I'll be down to help with breakfast," Janet said, yawning. "And while we're cooking, we'll figure everything out."

Joan grinned. "I hope we do," she replied.

Janet shut the door behind her and then raced into the bathroom. After another very quick shower, she got dressed and fixed her hair and makeup. She frowned at her reflection as she added her lipstick.

"You don't need to look your best," she told herself sternly. "The man is leaving."

With that depressing thought echoing through her head, she made her way down to the kitchen. Joan was pottering around, doing nothing much as she waited for Edward to arrive.

"I've put the coffee on," Joan said.

Janet inhaled the heady scent and smiled in spite of her mood. She filled a mug and took a sip, feeling the hot liquid rushing through her system. "I needed that," she told her sister.

"We both did," Joan replied, lifting her own mug to her lips.

Janet heard Edward's footsteps approaching the kitchen, and her heart raced. Before he actually came through the door, the bell on the conservatory door rang.

"I'll go," Janet said, rushing out of the room. She passed Edward on her way and shouted a quick "good morning" at him. He replied in kind, sounding a bit bewildered.

"Stuart, to what do we owe this pleasure?" Janet asked as she opened the glass door.

"I was just hoping that James and I could get a cuppa from you before we get started in the garden," Stuart said. "Mary's had to go out first thing and she's actually taken our kettle with her."

"I'm not sure I want to know why," Janet said with a laugh. "Do come in. Of course you're more than welcome."

"She gone to help her youngest move house," Stuart explained as they walked to the kitchen. "They've the movers in all day and Mary figured the men will need tea at some point, probably after her son's kettle is already packed. She took our kettle, milk, sugar and several packets of biscuits."

"Very sensible," Janet replied. "You do have to keep the moving men happy, don't you?"

In the kitchen, Edward was sitting at the table sipping a hot drink while Joan fixed his breakfast.

"Stuart and James need a drink before they start," Janet told her sister. "I hope you managed to get some breakfast before Mary left," she said to Stuart.

"We didn't, actually," Stuart replied. "I'd love some toast, if it isn't too much bother."

"I can do you both a full English breakfast, if you'd like," Joan said from where she was frying eggs.

"That would be wonderful," Stuart said.

"Yeah, great," James said with a grin as he took a seat at the table.

Janet poured them each a mug of coffee and then tried to figure out how to help Joan without getting in the way. She gave up when she heard the knock on the front door.

"Mr. Chalmers? What brings you here?" she asked, keeping the door mostly shut.

The man gave her a fake smile that made her think of a used-car salesman. "I came to apologise," he said tightly. "I think we got off on the wrong foot and I wanted to make sure that you and your sister didn't have the wrong impression of me."

Janet opened her mouth, ready to tell him exactly what she thought of him, and then snapped it shut. If he really was going to be living in Doveby Dale, she and Joan would have to be able to get along with him. "It's fine, I'm sure," she muttered instead.

"If I could just come in for a minute, I have a few things I'd like to discuss with you."

Janet shook her head. "I'm sorry, but we're in the middle of breakfast," she said. "Maybe Joan and I could stop by your shop one day?"

"Breakfast? I didn't get any breakfast today. I'm staying in that horrid little hotel on the edge of town and they do 'continental breakfast,' which so far has consisted of nothing but day-old bread rolls from some chain supermarket and cold tea. I'll happily pay ten pounds for a hot breakfast and a cup of coffee."

Janet frowned. The last thing she wanted to do was spend more time with the man. But he was offering good money and she would happily sell him her breakfast. She was too tired to be hungry.

"Come on in, then," she said with a sigh.

He followed her eagerly through the sitting room and into the kitchen. Joan was just starting to fill plates.

"Mr. Chalmers is starving," Janet announced. "He's happy to pay for a hot breakfast."

Joan frowned and Janet knew she'd be in trouble later.

"Do sit down," Joan told their new guest. He joined the other three men at the table while Joan cracked more eggs into the frying pan.

"Perhaps we should move into the dining room," Edward suggested. "Otherwise, you ladies have nowhere to sit."

"Oh, stay where you are. We can eat after you've finished," Joan told him.

Janet didn't dare argue with Joan, who was clearly in a bad mood. Hearing someone knock was a relief.

"I'll go," she called out, turning towards the front door.

"Whatever you do, don't invite whoever it is in for breakfast," Joan called after her.

Janet's heart sank when she saw Michael and Leonard on the doorstep. How could she not invite them in?

"I just wanted a quick word with Joan, if that's okay?" Michael said as Janet invited them in.

"She's just making breakfast for, well, everyone," Janet said with a laugh. "Come on in and join the party."

"Oh, I don't want to be in the way," Michael protested.

"If you want to wait in the sitting room for a few minutes, I can send her out," Janet suggested.

Michael and Leonard sat down on the one of the couches and Janet went back to the kitchen.

"Michael is here and he'd like a quick word with you," she told Joan.

"I hope he's had breakfast," Joan murmured as she quickly ducked out of the room. A moment later she was back with Michael and Leonard in tow.

"They haven't eaten," she told Janet, giving her a look that seemed to dare Janet to argue.

"In that case, we'd better move into the dining room," Janet replied.

The six men were quickly resettled. The men who'd already been given plates carried their own breakfast in with them.

"I'll have food out to the rest of you in a just a few minutes," Joan told the others.

Janet was quick to join her in the kitchen.

"Did you set this up?" Joan hissed at her.

"What do you mean?"

"Last night you were saying that you wanted to get all the suspects together and now you have," Joan pointed out. "Did you plan this somehow?"

Janet shook her head. "I'm not that clever," she protested. "And anyway, we're too busy making them all breakfast to ask them any questions."

Joan shook her head. "I still think it's Leonard," she said firmly.

"And I still think it's William Chalmers," Janet replied.

When someone knocked on their door again, the sisters just looked at each other.

"We don't know anyone else," Joan said with a small smile.

"Maybe it's a double-glazing salesman," Janet suggested.

"I bet, whoever it is, he or she is hungry," Joan added wryly.

Janet laughed and headed for the door.

"Constable Parsons? What brings you here?"

"I'm very sorry, but I have reason to believe that Peter Smith is in your house," the man, dressed today in casual trousers and a polo shirt, said. "I'd like to come in and arrest him, if I may."

Janet flushed. "Of course you can," she said, stepping backwards quickly. "But who…."

The man held up a hand. "If you could just show me where everyone is?"

Janet nodded and then led him through the kitchen to the dining room. As the pair entered the room, the six men stopped talking and looked up.

The policeman cleared his throat just before the chaos began.

William Chalmers jumped to his feet. "You called the police on me again?" he shouted.

"He's the cop?" James yelled, jumping up.

"Ethel sent you, didn't she?" Leonard asked in a resigned tone.

Robert cleared his throat again, but James pushed past him and ran.

"Stop him," Robert shouted, chasing after the man.

"Stop him?" Joan echoed from the kitchen, looking confused as the men ran past. "How on earth am I meant to do that?"

Edward now followed James and Robert through the kitchen

towards the front of the house. It took James a moment to get the door open, but then he was down the steps, running full speed towards the road.

Robert wasn't far behind him and Edward had nearly caught up as well. Janet found herself being joined by her sister and the others on the porch where they all stood silently, watching the scene.

A car turned onto the street and nearly hit James. The driver slammed on the brakes, and then James ran around and tried to open the passenger door. When that failed, he spun away from the car, but by that time both Robert and Edward had caught up to him. Robert took his arm and with Edward's help escorted him to his waiting car. Once the man was locked in the back, Robert and Edward had a short conversation, and then Robert waved to everyone on the porch and got into his car.

Edward walked back towards Doveby House slowly while the woman who'd been driving the car that had almost hit James climbed out.

"What's going on?" she demanded angrily of no one.

Janet recognised Mary Long and called down to her. "Mary, come on in and have some breakfast," she suggested.

Mary pulled her car into Doveby House's car park and then joined Janet on the porch. She was short and slender and she looked as if she was in a bad mood.

Everyone else had gone back inside as soon as the police car had driven away. Now Edward joined Janet and Mary on the porch. He gave Janet's hand a quick squeeze before the trio turned and went into the house.

In the dining room, Joan was distributing more plates, each one laden down with delicious breakfast foods.

"I hope someone can tell me what just happened to my brother-in-law," Mary said angrily.

"I thought you were helping Philip all day," Stuart said.

"Yes, well, let's just say Jennifer had other ideas," Mary said sourly.

"Who's Jennifer?" Edward asked.

"Philip's wife," Stuart replied.

"Ah," Edward hid a grin as he sat back down at the table.

"What happened to James?" Mary demanded as she sat down in the single empty seat at the table.

"His real name isn't James Abbott," Edward told her. "And he's a notorious conman."

"Yeah, I know that," Mary replied. "He just got out of prison and came to stay with us while he figures out what he wants to do next. So what?"

"Did he happen to mention how he got out of prison?" Edward asked.

Mary shook her head and sighed. "He escaped again, didn't he?" She shook her head. "That man will never learn."

"How are you related exactly?" Edward asked.

Mary laughed. "I have no idea," she admitted. "We first met about twenty years ago at a family party. He claimed to have been briefly married to my stepsister who had emigrated to New Zealand a few years earlier. He was funny and charming and it didn't really seem to matter."

"And you've kept in touch ever since?" Edward asked.

"Not really," Mary shrugged. "He just seems to pop up in my life every so often. I knew he'd been to prison a bunch of times, but he never stole anything from me and he's wonderful company, really."

Stuart coughed loudly and everyone turned to look at him. "Sorry," he said. "I just didn't find him 'wonderful' in the slightest."

Everyone got on with eating their breakfast while Joan and Janet kept coffee cups filled.

"Who's Ethel?" Joan asked Leonard suddenly.

Leonard frowned and looked down at his plate. "My wife," he said, finally. "I figured she'd sent the police to round me up and send me home."

"You're hiding from your wife?" Joan asked.

"Yeah, well, not really hiding, just having a break, like," Leonard replied. "She's well, she's rather demanding sometimes."

Joan and Janet exchanged looks and Janet bit her tongue. She couldn't imagine what being married to Leonard would be like, so she thought it best not to comment. Instead, she turned to William Chalmers.

"I do wish you'd stop throwing accusations around," she said sharply. "Joan and I most certainly did not call the police on you."

The man flushed. "Sorry," he said. "I think I should be going."

Janet didn't argue, she simply walked the man to the door. He handed her a ten-pound note and then left without saying another word.

"I still don't like him, even if he isn't Peter Smith," Janet said when she rejoined the others.

Edward nodded. "I think Robert Parsons will be taking a very close look at that man," he said. "Anyone who's that bothered about the police is suspect."

It was quiet for a few minutes as breakfast plates were cleared. Janet had a million questions for Edward, but she didn't want to quiz him in front of everyone. Finally Stuart and Mary headed for home with Stuart promising to come back in the afternoon to work on the garden.

"James wasn't any help anyway," he muttered. "He knew nothing about gardening."

Leonard and Michael weren't far behind. "I wanted to tell you that Leonard is heading home tomorrow," Michael told Joan in the kitchen. Janet was loading the dishwasher, pretending not to listen. "I was hoping we could have dinner together after he's gone?"

"I might be able to manage that," Joan said after a moment.

Michael smiled brightly, and then he collected Leonard from the dining room and they left.

"Well, I guess that's that," Janet said as she pushed the dishwasher shut. "It was a rather exciting morning."

"We were both wrong about Peter Smith," Joan pointed out.

"We were close," Janet said with a shrug. "And Leonard is leaving tomorrow anyway."

"That is good news," Joan admitted.

"And I'm leaving today," Edward said from the doorway. "But I'd still like a few minutes of your time if you can spare it," he said to Janet.

Janet felt less reluctant to talk to him now that she knew he wasn't an escaped conman.

"Let's talk in the library," Edward suggested.

She opened her mouth to argue, but changed her mind. It was as good a place as any, she supposed.

She unlocked the library door and then went inside, switching on the nearest light. Sinking into a comfortable chair, she looked expectantly at Edward.

He smiled and sat down across from her, taking her hand in his. "I don't want to leave today," he told her. "But I don't have a choice. You intrigue me and I'd really rather stay and get to know you better."

Janet felt her face turning red. "I've enjoyed getting to know you, too," she muttered, looking down at the floor.

"There are a few things I need to tell you," Edward continued. "For a start, Maggie and I were just friends, although I can't possibly prove that. She wasn't really my type."

"Why not?" Janet couldn't help but ask.

Edward shrugged. "She was loud and flamboyant, all flash and no substance." He shook his head. "We worked well together, but I never wanted a personal relationship with her."

"You worked together?" Janet asked.

Edward nodded. "I'm not really supposed to tell you this, but I think you have a right to know," he said after a moment. "I am supposed to be retired, but I guess I really still work for Her Majesty's government in the security services."

"You're a spy?" Janet tried not to let him see how surprised she was, but she was certain she failed.

Edward chuckled. "I guess you could say that, but that isn't how I would have put it."

Janet pulled her hand away and sat back in her chair, her mind racing. "Why did you come here?" she asked after a moment.

"Maggie very occasionally helped us out by letting people we sent stay here," he explained. "When she died so suddenly, there were some concerns that she might have left information about that lying around."

"So you wanted to go through her papers," Janet said.

"I did, until I found what I wanted elsewhere."

"In the safe?" Janet asked.

Edward nodded and then handed Janet a card that he pulled from his pocket. "Here's the combination," he told her. "I've taken out everything that I needed to remove. You and your sister can go through the rest."

"What's in there?" Janet asked.

"Wait and see," Edward told her with a wink.

"But Maggie died months ago," Janet suddenly recalled. "Why did it take you so long to visit?"

"Her connection to my office was a closely held secret," he replied. "A bit too closely as it happens. I was busy in America and no one thought to notify me about her death until quite recently. I came up as soon as I could, once I heard the news."

"And now you're leaving," Janet said. She was annoyed when she heard the sadness in her voice.

"I am," Edward agreed. "But I can come back and visit again, if you'd like."

Janet shrugged. "I'm not sure," she said truthfully.

Edward nodded. "I know. The nature of my job doesn't lend itself to relationships," he said. "But I am meant to be retired. I'm hoping I'll be rushing around the world a good deal less in the future."

"Well, if you find yourself with some free time, it would be nice to see you again," Janet said after a moment.

Edward smiled. "I'll write," he suggested. "And I'll call when I can. I'm off to Madrid, though, so calling might be difficult."

"Did you often write to Maggie?" Janet had to ask.

"Maggie? I never wrote to Maggie, why?"

Janet struggled to find an answer, but before she spoke, Edward began to laugh.

"I didn't write the letters in the desk," he said eventually. "That was a different Edward altogether."

"You read them?"

"I was looking for my paperwork," he said. "I just skimmed through every sheet of paper I found."

"You could have asked us to let you search the library," Janet said. "You didn't have to break in in the middle of the night."

"I wasn't supposed to tell you who I really am," he reminded her. "I'm only doing it now because, well, because I want you to understand."

"I'll tell Joan," Janet warned him.

"I figured as much," Edward said.

"Sorry to interrupt," Joan said in the doorway, "but there's a man at the door asking for you," she told Edward.

He frowned and got to his feet. "That's probably my ride," he said with a sigh. He offered a hand to Janet. "Walk me out?"

Janet took his hand and they walked to the door together. The man in the doorway looked as broad as he was tall, and Janet had no doubt every inch of it was muscle rather than fat. He had short black hair and he was wearing a black suit and very dark sunglasses.

"Sir, I'm here to take you back to London," the man said. "Danny is coming for your car later today."

"I'll leave the keys with you, if I may?" Edward asked Janet. "When Danny arrives, you can give them to him."

"How will I know it's Danny?" Janet asked as she pocketed the keys.

"He looks just like me," the man in the doorway told her.

Edward grinned and then leaned over and gave Janet a quick kiss. "I'll be back," he whispered in her ear.

So you see, Bessie, we had a rush of gentlemen in the neighbourhood, and only one of them was a wanted criminal. I've taken to the calling the entire episode "The Bennett Case" in honour of our first paying guest. Joan thinks I should call it "The Abbott Case" or "The Smith Case," but I ignore her.

Joan is in much better spirits since Leonard left. I can only sympathise with poor Ethel who has to live with him.

We haven't seen William Chalmers since he had breakfast with us, but I hear he's been busy making enemies of just about everyone he encounters in Doveby Dale. If he ever does get his business up and running, I can't imagine anyone will want to shop there.

As for Edward, I've had one quick note from him. His handwriting is nothing like the handwriting on Maggie's letters from the other Edward. He's hoping to come and visit again soon, but "things keep cropping up," apparently.

I wasn't sure about telling you about his job, but he agreed that I could tell Joan, and I decided telling you was much the same thing. As you are far away on the Isle of Man, you're unlikely to ever meet the man, so I can't imagine it will hurt anything.

Meanwhile, it seems having our first guest has inspired my sister. She is now insisting that we get the business up and running before the end of this month. I hope you can come and stay soon. We'd love to see you!

With all good wishes,

Janet Markham

P.S. The combination that Edward gave me doesn't open the safe after all. Hopefully he will be back soon to give us the correct combination.

Glossary of Terms

- **biscuits** — cookies
- **booking** — reservation
- **boot** — trunk (of a car)
- **car park** — parking lot
- **cuppa** — cup of tea (informal)
- **estate car** — station wagon
- **fortnight** — two weeks
- **high street** — the main shopping street in a town or village
- **holiday** — vacation
- **jumper**— sweater
- **lie in** — sleep late
- **midday** — noon
- **pavement** — sidewalk
- **pudding** — dessert
- **queue** — line
- **saloon car** — sedan
- **shopping trolley** — shopping cart
- **starters** — appetizers

- **ta** — thank you (informal)
- **telly** — television
- **till** — check-out (in a grocery store, for example)

Other Notes

In the UK dates are written day, month, year rather than month, day, year as in the US. (May 5, 2015 would be written 5 May 2015 for example.)

In the UK when describing property with more than one level, the lowest level (assuming there is no basement; very few UK houses have basements) is the "ground floor," and the next floor up is the "first floor" and so on. In the US, the lowest floor is usually the "first floor" and up from there.

When Janet says she might be "brewing something," she means she thinks she might be coming down with a cold or flu.

When telling time, half six is the English equivalent of six thirty.

A double-glazing salesman would be going door-to-door trying to get people to purchase new windows for their homes.

A "full English breakfast" generally consists of bacon, sausage, eggs, grilled or fried tomatoes, fried potatoes, fried mushrooms and baked beans served with toast.

The Chalmers Case

A MARKHAM SISTERS COZY MYSTERY NOVELLA

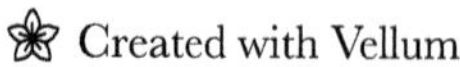
Created with Vellum

For David and Catherine,
because everything I do is for them, really.

Acknowledgments

Thank you to the many people who work with me on my stories.

Denise, my editor, who has better things to do than edit my books, but does it anyway.

Charlene and Janice, my beta readers, who manage to find time to fit in extra reading when I send them yet another manuscript.

My readers, who make what I do so worth it. Please get in touch. I'd love to hear from you. (Contact details are in the back of the book.)

Author's Note

I wasn't planning to write a third story in this series until some time in 2016, but ideas just kept nagging at me until I did it anyway! As always, I suggest you read the stories in order (they run alphabetically), but you don't have to; each story can be read on its own.

If you haven't read the others, you should know that the Markham sisters first appeared in *Aunt Bessie Decides,* book four in my Isle of Man Cozy Mysteries series. Janet has stayed in touch with Bessie, and I use parts of her letters to Bessie to open and close each novella. The letters have nothing to do with the Bessie series, and you don't have to read that series to enjoy this one.

I have used English spellings and terms and provided a glossary and some notes in the back of the book to help readers outside the UK with anything that might be unfamiliar. The longer I remain in the US, the greater the likelihood of Americanisms sneaking into the text, although I do try to eliminate them.

This is a work of fiction and all of the characters are fictional creations. Any resemblance that they may share with any real person, living or dead, is entirely coincidental. The sisters live in a fictional village in Derbyshire. Although some shops or business may bear some resemblance to real-life businesses, that is also coincidental.

Please feel free to get in touch with any comments, questions, or concerns. I have a monthly newsletter that provides updates on new releases. All of the information about subscribing or getting in touch is available on the About the Author page at the back of the book.

15 October 1998

Dearest Bessie,

What an exciting, albeit stressful, life you lead. I can't imagine what it must be like to find a dead body. I know that I invite you to visit in every letter, but it really does seem as if you could use a holiday.

We've finally started taking in a few paying guests, after having our first so unexpectedly last month. I do think Joan is in her element cooking for other people, but I do find it odd having strangers in the house. I'm not sure Joan is as eager to have guests as she once was, though.

You see, having guests led to our own little bit of excitement earlier this month. No one got murdered, but the police were involved anyway. It all started when Joan and I decided to do some shopping that we'd been putting off.

Chapter 1

"How are you getting on?"

Janet dropped the book she was holding and spun around. "I didn't hear you coming," she exclaimed.

"Clearly not, or you would have put the book down and at least pretended to be working," Joan retorted.

Janet flushed. She hated to admit it, even to herself, but her older sister was right. If she'd heard Joan coming towards the small library in the back of their house, she would have stopped reading and returned to work. As it was, Joan had caught her doing what she loved best, rather than doing what she was meant to be doing.

"I'm getting there," she said defensively. "It's a huge job, cleaning and reorganising our library."

"And it will take much longer if you stop to read every book," Joan pointed out.

"I'm not trying to read them all," Janet said. "That one just caught my eye, that's all."

Joan picked up the book from the floor. "*The Missing Picture*," she read off the garish cover. "Not a very interesting title."

Janet shook her head. "It is rather dull, especially compared to the cover," she replied. "I've only read the first chapter, but it's all about art forgery and theft. I'm not sure what the knife dripping with blood on the cover has to do with the story, at least not yet."

"Is he a popular author?" Joan asked.

"I don't think so," Janet replied with a shrug. "From what I can tell, the book was printed by a local printer here in Doveby Dale back in the fifties. I doubt they printed many copies."

"Is it any good?"

"It is, actually, in spite of the boring title and the rather horrible cover. I was quite absorbed in it when you came in."

"Yes, I noticed," Joan said dryly.

Janet flushed again. "Sorry," she said sheepishly. "I'll put it to one side and read later, after I've done some more cleaning. Feel free to help," she added as she took the book from her sister and set it on the desk.

"I'm trying to get lunch ready," Joan replied. "I just came down to ask you if you would prefer to have sandwiches for lunch and shepherd's pie for dinner or have them the other way around."

Janet thought for a minute. "I suppose sandwiches for lunch," she said eventually. "That won't take very long, so I can get even more work done in here before dinner."

"Actually, I thought we might go out after lunch," Joan told her. "I'd like to do some shopping."

Janet frowned. What was her sister planning now? "I didn't know we needed anything," she said, avoiding questioning her sister outright.

"It's high time we found some artwork for the guest rooms. WTC Antiques and Collectibles is having their grand opening today. I heard an advert on the radio while I was tidying the kitchen."

"I don't know that I want to shop there," Janet said thoughtfully. "I really don't like William Chalmers. I'm not sure I want to help support his new business. I think I'd rather he moved away."

The sisters had met William Chalmers, the owner of the new village antique shop, some weeks earlier when he'd come to ask them to sell him some books for his store. He'd been rude and obnoxious each time they'd seen him since and had developed a reputation in the village for being demanding and difficult.

"I don't like the man, either, but Doveby Dale is a small village, and I think that as owners of the only bed and breakfast here, we have to support our fellow business owners, even if they are disagreeable."

"I suppose you're right." Janet sighed.

"Apparently the entire store is on sale because of the grand opening," Joan added. "We could use a bargain."

Janet nodded. The pair had used a small inheritance and the proceeds from the sale of their previous home to purchase Doveby House several months earlier. Although they'd both always been frugal, they'd spent a great deal of their savings on painting and redecorating the seventeenth-century manor house. While they both agreed that a few pictures would enhance the décor in the guest rooms, neither sister wanted to spend much money on acquiring them.

"Okay, I'll work really hard all morning and then, after lunch, we can go and see what Mr. Chalmers has on offer," Janet said.

"Excellent," Joan replied. "Maybe I'll be able to see some progress by the time I come back to tell you when lunch is ready."

Janet waited until her sister was out of sight before she stuck out her tongue. She sighed. Joan was eager to get the library finished. It was the last thing standing in the way of their opening for business. Janet was less enthusiastic about welcoming strangers into their home.

Buying a bed and breakfast had been Joan's idea. The sisters had both retired as schoolteachers from the same primary school in the past year. They'd lived together their entire lives, both enjoying working with children, but neither interested in starting a family of her own. Usually it was Janet who suggested their doing out of the ordinary things, and she had been dumbfounded when Joan suddenly began talking about buying Doveby House and starting their own business.

Now, a few months into owning the house, Janet was running out of excuses to keep Joan from taking in guests. The last bit of the house that needed finishing was the library, and Janet had insisted that she be allowed to do all of the work herself. Joan had agreed, but now she was pushing Janet to get the job done.

Janet was starting by removing the books shelf by shelf and then cleaning each shelf. Then she was dusting all of the books before returning them to their original position. After working intermittently for the past fortnight, she had two walls of shelves finished and two to go. It was tiring work and she was starting to think that maybe she ought to just dust the books in situ and worry about deeper cleaning another time. After the cleaning was done, she'd start sorting the books into categories and seeing exactly what they had. Janet was looking forward to that part.

Resisting the temptation to sigh again, she carefully slid several books off the next shelf. It took a while to remove them all and she had to fight hard against the urge to at least glance at the titles as she stacked them on the desk. Joan was right; if she stopped to read every single book, she'd never get the library done.

"And then we wouldn't have to have guests," she muttered to herself.

The previous month, the sisters had found themselves with an unexpected first guest. He'd paid very well for just a few nights and Janet had found herself being romanced by the handsome visitor who may or may not have been some sort of spy. It had been a strange first experience with a paying guest and Janet wasn't encouraged to try the whole thing again.

She sprayed polish on the now cleared shelf and carefully wiped away the years of accumulated dust and grime. It seemed likely that no one had ever taken down the books from the shelves for cleaning purposes and Janet frowned as she cleared away a dried up spider corpse. The poor thing must have been living behind the books for many years and simply died of old age.

The walls were completely covered in bookshelves, but the shelves were in sections of six feet each, rather than running continuously along the entire wall. Now, as Janet started to dust each book and return it to its place, she noticed that there was something odd about the shelf itself. She was working her way down along the shelving unit along the wall. The top three shelves had been exactly like all of the others, but this one was different.

Where the side of the shelf met the wall, instead of solid wood, there was a small panel of a different sort of wood. Janet ran her fingers along it. She could feel a small gap all the way around the panel. When she tapped on it, she could hear what she fancied was a hollow sound. She rapped on the wood around the panel and was instantly pleased to find that it sounded different. Pulling a few books off the next shelf down, Janet was disappointed that there was only the ordinary shelf behind them. She knocked on it as well, hearing the same sort of sound she'd heard from the wood around the panel.

"What on earth is all that banging?" Joan asked from the doorway.

"I seem to have found some sort of sliding panel or something," Janet said excitedly. "Come and see."

Joan took a couple of steps towards her sister and glanced at the wall. "It's probably a removable section to access a plug socket behind it or something," she said dismissively.

Janet frowned. Her sister was probably right. They'd already found a wall safe, hidden behind a small picture that neither of them had even noticed initially among the sea of books. It was highly unlikely that this was another hiding place. She tapped on it again and then tried to slide it sideways. When it didn't move in either direction, she tried going up and down with it, but that wasn't any more successful.

"It won't move," she told her sister.

"As we don't need to plug anything in, I can't see what difference it makes," Joan said with a shrug. "Lunch will be ready in about an hour. Maybe you can finish that set of shelves before midday?"

Janet nodded, but she was only half listening. She really wanted to get the small panel open. "Maybe there's a button somewhere that makes it slide," she muttered to herself.

"Maybe, if we've just fallen into a James Bond film," Joan said tartly.

"There must be a way to get it open," Janet said.

"Perhaps we should just hire someone to come in and sort out the library," Joan said in a thoughtful tone. "Although I'm not sure we can afford to do that as we are rather broke."

"We aren't broke," Janet said firmly. "We both have our pensions and they are more than adequate to cover our expenses, as long as we're careful."

"But if we had paying guests, we wouldn't have to be as careful," Joan pointed out.

"As if you're suddenly going to start being extravagant," Janet said with a laugh. "You just want to have lots of people tell you what a wonderful cook you are, that's all."

Now it was Joan's cheeks that reddened. "Is that what you think this is all about?" she demanded.

"I don't know what this is all about," Janet replied. "One day we were enjoying our retirement and talking about travelling more and the next day we bought a bed and breakfast. You never did offer me any explanation."

"Do you remember the year we stayed in that little bed and breakfast in Wales?" Joan asked her. "It was a tiny little house almost right on the beach, with only one guest room that we had to share with Mum and Dad."

"With mum and dad?" Janet asked. "How old were you?"

"Oh, maybe eight or nine," Joan replied.

"So I was six or seven," Janet said. "I'm sorry, but I really don't remember. That was over fifty years ago. Why?"

"It was the best holiday I've ever had," Joan told her. "The woman who ran the place was an excellent cook, and as it rained pretty much the entire fortnight we were there, we spent a lot of time in the house. She let me help out in the kitchen and taught me just about everything I know about baking."

"I didn't know that. I mean, I know mum wasn't much for baking, but I didn't realise you learned to bake from a Welsh woman who ran a bed and breakfast."

"She was very kind, and I told mum and dad that when I grew up I wanted to have a bed and breakfast just like hers," Joan said.

"And mum and dad said it was a bad idea and that you should be a teacher," Janet added.

Joan smiled sadly. "Exactly, but how did you know that?"

"Because that's what they told me every time I went to them with yet another idea of what I wanted to be when I grew up."

"I remember you wanted to be a pilot during the war," Joan reminded her. "I think mum and dad were right to discourage you from that."

"That was one of my wilder ambitions," Janet said, smiling at the memory. "I also wanted to disguise myself as a boy and join the army when I was nine or ten, just as the war was coming to an end. Not all of my ideas were foolish, though, but whatever I said, mum and dad always insisted that teaching was best."

"And they were right," Joan said firmly.

"Probably," Janet said after a moment. "But I still wish I'd felt as if I had more choices."

"Women didn't in those days," Joan reminded her. "And mum and dad were doing what they thought was best, anyway. They wanted to be certain that we'd be able to find good jobs, and be able to look after ourselves until we found husbands."

"And we're still working on that one," Janet said with a laugh.

"I'm not," Joan said tartly.

"And yet you're the only one of us who is dating right now," Janet pointed out.

"Michael is just a friend," Joan replied, her eyes not meeting Janet's.

"And he's lovely and smart and there's no reason why you shouldn't be having fun with him," Janet told her.

Michael Donaldson was their neighbour. He lived in one of the pair of semi-detached houses across the road from them. A widower who had once had his own chemist shop, he was retired now. He and Joan had been going out together for several weeks. Joan had never dated before and the pair was taking their relationship very slowly.

"Anyway, ever since that holiday, I've always dreamt of opening my own bed and breakfast, but I never talked about it because it seemed like an impossible idea," Joan said. "And now, after all these years, my dream might just come true. If you ever finish tidying the library, that is."

With that, Joan turned and headed back towards the kitchen. "Lunch is at midday," she reminded her sister from the doorway.

"I'll be there," Janet assured her. After Joan left, she glanced around the room and sighed deeply. Now that she knew what was motiving her sister, Janet felt as if she needed to hurry. She was standing in the way of her sister accomplishing a dream that was more than fifty years in the making. With one last push in every direction, Janet gave up on the mysterious panel and began to quickly dust books and return them to their shelf. By the time the clock in the sitting room began its twelve chimes, she'd finished the shelves by the door and started on the next set.

"I'll do more after our shopping trip," she muttered to herself as she shut the library door and headed towards the kitchen.

Joan was just putting out lunch, and Janet quickly washed her hands before she sat down at the small table that took up one corner of the spacious kitchen.

"If I can get the cleaning done by Thursday afternoon, I can start figuring out a plan for organising the shelves on Friday. Once I've worked out how I want to arrange things, it won't take more than a week to get it done. I suppose you can start booking guests for a fortnight's time," she told Joan while they ate.

"I shall have to go back through the recent requests and see what people wanted," Joan said. "I've been saving them, hoping we might be ready soon. Of course, I've already told them we weren't open, so they all may have made other arrangements already."

"But we get rung up nearly every day with people who want rooms," Janet pointed out. "I'm sure you won't have any trouble finding people who want to come."

"I hope not," Joan said excitedly.

The sisters had been surprised by the amount of interest that was being shown in their little guesthouse. Margaret Appleton, the previous owner, had clearly been very successful and it seemed as if a great many of her former guests were eager to visit again.

Janet forced herself to smile at her sister in spite of her reservations. In a way, she was disappointed in herself. She was always the sister who was looking for new adventures, and now when confronted with one, she was dragging her feet. For Joan's sake, if nothing else, Janet knew she needed to embrace their new lifestyle. They were about to open a bed and breakfast, whether Janet was ready or not.

Chapter 2

After lunch, Janet took care of the washing up while Joan took some measurements in the guest rooms.

"We really do need good names for the rooms," she reminded Janet when she rejoined her in the kitchen.

"I know. Maybe the paintings we find will provide some inspiration," Janet suggested.

"Let's hope so," Joan replied.

Joan was happy to drive the short distance into the quiet centre of Doveby Dale. There was a small car park for the city centre shops, and Janet smiled when she saw how many spaces were available.

"It doesn't look as if the grand opening is drawing much of a crowd," she commented as Joan pulled into a spot.

"Maybe some people walked in from nearby," Joan suggested.

There were a handful houses on the streets around the centre, so it was possible that some people might have walked over to see what WTC Antiques was offering.

The sisters walked slowly along the strip of shops, looking in windows as they went. The first shop was a newsagent and Janet couldn't stop herself from checking the headlines on a few of her favourite celebrity magazines. She didn't buy them often, as Joan didn't really approve. Once in a while, though, when Joan was out with Michael, Janet would buy a few and read them in front of the telly with ice cream and popcorn, two other things that Joan didn't approve of, at least not on a regular basis.

Next door to that was the small chemist shop that used to belong to their neighbour, Michael. He had been bought out by a large chain, and the small shop had been refitted so that it looked nearly identical, on a smaller scale, to just about every other store in their chain.

The next shop was empty, with a large sign in the window giving the details for anyone interested in letting the space. The final shop in the row was the new antique shop. There was a small sign in the window that said "Grand Opening" in an elaborate script that was nearly impossible to read. Janet and Joan stopped outside the door and looked in the window.

There were several large groupings of furniture arranged as if they were in their own small rooms. While many of the pieces were undoubtedly old, Janet didn't see anything that she thought looked like a valuable antique. From where they were standing, there didn't appear to be anyone in the shop.

"Do you think they're open?" Joan asked.

"They must be," Janet said with more confidence than she felt. She stepped forward and pulled on the door handle. The door stuck a bit, but finally pulled open. As it did so, a loud bell sounded somewhere in the building. As Joan and Janet stepped inside, William Chalmers himself came rushing out from a back room towards them.

"Ah, the lovely Markham sisters," he said smarmily. "I'm so delighted you managed to stop by, and when it's lovely and quiet as well. I was just thinking about ringing you, actually."

Janet glanced at Joan before she responded. "It is very quiet, isn't it? I do hope you were busier earlier."

The man flushed under her steady gaze. He was somewhere in his sixties, with grey hair and eyes. His suit was a darker grey. Janet knew very little about men's clothing, but to her the suit looked as if it must have been expensive and tailor-made for the man.

"We had a small crowd when I first opened the door this morning, but it has been quieter since then. I suspect it might pick up again later this afternoon," he told them.

"I do hope so," Janet replied.

"Yes, well, thank you," the man said. "But what brings you in this afternoon? Were you looking for anything in particular or just having a look around?"

"We need some artwork," Joan said.

"Excellent. I have a small gallery in the back room." He beamed at them. "Just follow me."

Clearly the man was trying to show off the various furniture pieces as if they were being used in someone's home, but having so many room-type groupings all around the place made walking through the space incredibly difficult. Janet found herself winding her way through a small sitting room arrangement, dodging a huge dining table with ten chairs and then stumbling over an enormous wooden filing cabinet that was nearly touching the large desk next to it.

The back wall of the room was arranged like a library, and Janet wondered where the man had acquired the huge collection of books that lined the long wooden shelves. She found she was unable to stop herself from taking a closer look. As she approached the shelves, William spoke.

"Oh, I'm sure you aren't interested in any bookshelves," he said loudly. "You have plenty of your own, I'm told."

"Not shelves, but I'm always interested in books," Janet replied. She took another step forward and then frowned. There was something not quite right about the collection of books on display. She reached out to touch the binding of the first book on the shelf. With a frown, she pulled the book from the shelf, finding that the entire shelf full of titles came out together.

"It's just a big empty cardboard box," she exclaimed as she turned the long and narrow box over in her hands.

William quickly crossed to her and took the box from her hands.

"It's a wonderful way to display bookshelves without having to worry about moving a lot of books if someone wants to buy the shelves," he said, sounding defensive.

Janet smiled as she looked again at the shelf. "Prime and Prejudice, Erma, King Lore, Romeo and Julia, Jane Err, Grand Expectations, Middleapril, Lady Chattery's Lover, A Clockwork Apple, The Picture of David Grey." She shook her head and then chuckled. "It's quite funny really. I wish I had time to read them all."

"Yes, well, as I said, it's the perfect way to display shelves. Now if you'd like to follow me?"

Still chuckling to herself over the almost classic titles, Janet followed William and her sister into the back room. As William had told them, it was set up like a small art gallery, and Janet was surprised at the number and quality of the paintings as she glanced quickly around.

"Obviously we'd prefer to use art by local artists," Joan said. "We were wondering if any of them might like to display their work in our guest rooms where we might offer it for sale, actually."

William frowned. "I don't actually have anything by local artists at the moment," he said. "I simply haven't been here long enough to make the necessary local contacts. I've always lived and worked in London, and I feel fortunate to have been able to persuade some of my favourite London artists to let me have some of their work to sell here."

"Perhaps we need to find some local artists ourselves, then," Joan said.

"At least take a moment to have a look around," William suggested, sounding just a little bit desperate. "I have some wonderful pieces that I'm sure would perfectly finish your guest rooms."

Joan looked as if she wanted to argue, but Janet didn't give her the chance. "I really like this one," she told William as she walked towards a large canvas. It was completely abstract, just a swirl of colours making indistinct shapes, and nothing like anything Janet had ever considered purchasing in the past, but there was something about it that appealed to her.

"It's too big for the guest rooms," Joan said dismissively.

"It would fit in my bedroom," Janet suggested.

She looked at the discreetly placed price tag and grimaced. It was several thousand pounds, which was considerably more than she would even think about paying for such a thing.

"I can probably work with you a little on the price," William told her eagerly. "It is my grand opening, after all." He suggested a price that was considerably lower, but still well outside Janet's budget.

"I'm sorry, but I think for today we need to focus on the paintings for the guest rooms," Janet said. She moved past the man and worked her way around the room, firmly blocking the painting she'd liked from her mind.

"I haven't seen anything that's just right," Joan said after several minutes. "And I still really want to find things by local artists, anyway."

"I'm sure I can find something appropriate," William said hastily. "I have so many contacts in the art world. I'm sure I'll be able to find some local artists who'll be interested in showing you their work. Give me a couple of days."

"Why don't we come back one day next week?" Janet suggested. "I'm sure you're busy with the opening and everything, so that gives you some time to see what you can find."

"Excellent," the man said, smiling brightly at them both. "I won't let you down. Now, did you need anything else today?"

"I'd love a look around the rest of the store," Janet said. Really, she was just being nosy, and she also wanted another look at the fake book titles. For some reason she'd found them very amusing.

"We haven't long," Joan said in a no-nonsense voice. "There's so much to do back at the house."

Janet ignored her and strode back into the front room. William and Joan followed.

"I was going to ring you later, you know," William was saying. "I have some friends coming to visit later this week and I was hoping you might be able to accommodate them."

Janet looked over at her sister, but Joan didn't even glance in her direction.

"I assume you'll vouch for these friends of yours," Joan said to William.

"Of course, of course," he said heartily. "Harold is actually a distant cousin and he and Mildred are as much family as friends. They'll be the perfect guests for you."

Janet covered her snort of disbelief with a fake cough as she crossed the room towards a collection of conservatory furniture. There was a small table there that had caught her eye.

"How long would they want to stay? Joan asked.

"Only for a few nights," William replied. "They're planning on arriving on Wednesday and staying until the weekend."

"I suppose we could manage," Joan said, her tone doubtful. "The library isn't finished, though. I hope they won't mind not having access to it, but it's a work in progress, as it were."

"I'm sure they won't mind in the slightest," William assured her. "They're coming to spend time with me and help with the shop for a few days. They won't have time to read."

Janet frowned at the thought of people not making time to read, but she kept her mouth shut. The bed and breakfast was Joan's baby and she wasn't going to interfere in it unless she absolutely had to.

Joan and William crossed the room to the small desk at the back that appeared to be William's office. He and Joan took seats on opposite sides of the desk, presumably making the arrangements for his friends.

"I'm going to take another look at that painting," Janet called to them as she headed towards the back room.

She stood in front of it for a long moment, studying it. If she could work out why she liked it so much, maybe she could persuade herself that she wasn't all that fond of it, she told herself. After a while, she gave up. There was just something about it, the colours, the shapes, the textures, something that she really liked.

Glancing back into the main room, she saw that William and Joan were still talking. With a sigh, she turned and did another circuit of the gallery space, studying each painting in turn, but finding nothing else she especially liked. After a few minutes, she noticed that there was a door along one wall. Undoubtedly it led to storage space or an employee loo.

Firmly telling herself that it was none of her business anyway, she turned and walked briskly away from temptation. A moment later, she was back in front of the door, her hand itching to try the knob. It wasn't that she was nosy, she reminded herself, just incredibly curious. She looked back towards the main room and saw nothing. Already chiding herself for her "curiosity," she tried the knob.

The door opened easily and Janet was quick to find the light switch right inside the door. The room in front of her was small, but still larger than she'd been expecting it to be. There were perhaps half a dozen easels scattered around the space, a partially finished canvas on every one of them. A small table in the centre of the room was covered in painting supplies. Janet was struggling to resist the urge to walk into the room when she heard a sound behind her. Switching off the light, she quickly pulled the door shut again before she turned around.

"That's just storage space," William told her as he strode into the room.

"I was just looking for a loo," Janet said, hoping William didn't realise that she had actually already opened the door.

The man frowned. "I'm afraid we don't have customer, er, facilities," he said.

"Never mind, we aren't far from home," Janet said. She walked quickly past him, back into the main room where Joan was standing near the door.

"There you are," Joan said. "I was starting to think you'd gone out a back way."

"Just admiring that painting one more time," she told her sister. "There's just something about it I like."

"But not the price tag," Joan replied.

"No, I don't like the price tag at all," Janet agreed with a laugh.

"I might be able to let it go for, let's say, half the price on the tag," William interjected.

Janet shook her head. "That's still far more than I can afford to spend on something for just me. If it were for a guest room or one of the public spaces in the house, I might think about it. But if I were to buy it, I'd want it in my room for sure. Thank you for the generous discount, though. I wish I could use it."

"Think about it," William told her. "The offer is good for the rest of this week, at least. If you find you can't live without the picture, stop back."

Janet nodded and then smiled at Joan. "We should get going," she suggested.

"As we have guests arriving on Wednesday, we definitely should," Joan agreed.

The pair made their way out of the shop and back down the pavement in front of the small row of stores. Janet forced herself to keep her mouth shut as they walked, even though she felt as if she might burst.

Chapter 3

"Well, that was interesting," Joan said as she pulled the car out of its parking space. "William seemed like he was trying quite hard to be nice."

"He did, didn't he?" Janet replied.

"I suppose, now that he's having to deal with customers, he's found he must be nicer."

"But didn't William say that he didn't know any local artists?" Janet asked.

"He did, but he said he'd try to find some for us," Joan told her. "Weren't you paying attention?"

"I thought I was, but after I saw what he's keeping in his back room, I wasn't sure I understood."

"Don't tell me you were snooping!" Joan exclaimed.

"I was looking for a loo," Janet said defensively.

"Really?" Joan asked.

Janet sighed. She tried hard not to lie to her sister. "No, not really. I was just curious what was behind the door."

"You're lucky he didn't catch you being nosy," Joan told her. "He would have been furious."

Janet thought back to how disagreeable William had been the

first time they'd met him. She shuddered as she realised how close she came to really angering him. "I just took a quick peek," she told Joan. "And he'd have only been angry if he's hiding something."

"And is he hiding something?"

"I don't know," Janet said with a shrug. "It sort of seems like it, though."

"And you're waiting for me to ask, aren't you?" Joan demanded. "Okay, what did you find behind the door?" she asked in a tight voice.

"It looked like an art studio," Janet replied. "There were a bunch of half-finished pictures on easels, and paints and supplies all around the place."

"Why would William want an art studio in the back of his store?" Joan asked.

"Maybe he has a team of artists making forgeries in there," Janet suggested.

"Maybe you've been reading too many books about such things," Joan retorted. "It seems more likely one of his artist friends is using the space to make pictures for the store. I didn't pay any attention to the names of the artists on the pictures that were for sale, did you?"

"No," Janet admitted. "But why would he have so many unfinished works? Surely artists do one painting at a time."

"As I'm not an artist and can't draw a straight line even with a straight edge, I'm not the one to ask about that," Joan said. "Anyway, it isn't any of our business what he's doing back there."

Janet sat back in her seat and frowned. There was something suspicious going on in that store. If Joan wanted to ignore it, she could, but Janet was determined to find out more about what was happening in WTC Antiques, with or without Joan's help.

Back at Doveby House, over a cup of tea, Joan quickly made a list of what needed to be done before they welcomed their guests on Wednesday. As she filled first one and then a second sheet of paper with chores, Janet remembered why she wasn't eager to start running the bed and breakfast.

"I'll just go and do some more work in the library," she told Joan, getting up from the kitchen table.

"You go and do that," Joan said, clearly distracted by her list making. "But once I've finished the list, you'll have to stop and help with that instead. We can just lock up the library while the guests are here, so it won't matter if you leave a mess in there. The rest of the property has to be spotless, though."

Janet shut the library door and quickly began to pile books against it. With the contents of two shelves stacked behind it, Joan would struggle to get the library door open when she came to get her younger sister. Janet knew she was being childish, but Joan's list had been nothing but tidy this and clean that, which was never Janet's idea of fun.

Joan had never embraced Janet's habit of adding small incentives to her to-do lists. There was nothing Janet liked better than crossing off a chore and finding "have a scoop of ice cream" as the next item on the list, but Joan didn't see it that way.

Now Janet grabbed the furniture polish and went to work on the two shelves she'd just cleared. There didn't seem to be any additional hidden panels. Janet had just returned the last of the books to the second shelf when Joan pushed the door open.

"Ah, it looks like you're in the perfect place to take a break," Joan said brightly, as she watched Janet slide the last book into place.

"If you mean take a few minutes to sit down with my feet up and read a book, I am," Janet replied. "If you mean stop cleaning in here and come and clean somewhere else, well, that's a lot less appealing."

Joan actually smiled before she spoke. "I'm sorry, my dear," she said. "I know this whole bed and breakfast thing was my idea and I know you don't share my enthusiasm for it, but I'd really like to give it a good try. If you really hate it after we've had a few guests, we can talk about selling Doveby House and doing something else with our lives."

Janet thought for a minute before she replied. "It's a little late now for me to start voicing objections," she said finally. "And I'm sorry I haven't been more supportive of your plans. I just hate cleaning and tidying, and it seems like we have an awful lot of that to get done."

"I know you hate cleaning," Joan said. "I thought you might like to go and do the grocery shopping instead, while I start tackling the cleaning?"

"Oh, yes, please," Janet said eagerly. She didn't exactly like grocery shopping, but if Joan wasn't with her, she could at least add a few treats to the trolley as she went. Joan gave Janet a detailed list of everything she wanted from the shops and Janet headed out with the promise of apple crumble for pudding after dinner if she managed to find everything on the list.

Janet drove rather slowly to the large supermarket that was some distance away. She wasn't exactly eager to get the shopping done and get home and it was a lovely day for a drive. Groceries were less expensive at the larger shop than at the smaller store in Doveby Dale, but sometimes the bigger store was unpleasantly busy. Today it wasn't too bad, and Janet found herself in a fairly good mood as she pushed her trolley up and down the aisles.

"We need a cat," she said aloud as she unexpectedly found herself in the pet food aisle after making a wrong turn. She'd always wanted a pet of some kind, but when she and Joan had both been working full-time it seemed unfair to adopt an animal and then spend very little time with it. When they'd retired, they'd discussed the idea briefly, but as they planned to travel, again the thought was dismissed. Now, however, they were clearly staying in one place for a while and the large manor house seemed the perfect place for a cat. Determined to discuss the idea with Joan, Janet carried on with the shopping.

She did very well sticking to her sister's list until the very end. From what Joan had requested, it seemed as if her older sister was anticipating that their guests would be eating their evening meals at Doveby House in addition to breakfast. Perhaps that was part of the arrangement that Joan had made with William Chalmers.

Janet was nearly finished when she reached the ice cream. Joan had requested vanilla, presumably to offer with apple crumble and other puddings. Janet added it to her cart and then found her favourite ice cream in the freezer. Joan wouldn't mind if she brought home a container of that as well, she decided impulsively.

Back at Doveby House, it took Janet three trips to get everything from the car into the house. Janet could hear Joan working hard on the first floor, presumably cleaning the guest rooms. No doubt Joan would put the couple in the east room, as it was somewhat larger than the west room. It was just a shame that they hadn't found any art for the walls yet. Janet was still hoping to come up with better names for the rooms eventually.

Once she'd put the shopping away, Janet climbed the stairs and found her sister in the east room.

"I'm back and the shopping is all away," she told Joan once Joan had switched off the vacuum.

"Excellent," Joan said happily. "I've just been around with a duster and now the vacuum. Tomorrow I'll give the en-suite a quick clean and then give the west room the same treatment. I'm assuming the Stones will want to stay in here, as it's the larger room, but I want to give them a choice."

"Is that their name?" Janet asked. "Stone?"

"Yes, Harold and Mildred Stone," Joan replied. "Apparently Harold is a cousin to William as well as a friend and business associate."

"Lovely," Janet muttered.

The rest of Monday and pretty much all of Tuesday passed in something of a blur for Janet. She helped her sister clean and air the guest rooms, dusted and vacuumed all of the public spaces, and whenever she had a spare minute, worked hard on the library. While these guests might not be interested in reading, she was sure they would eventually welcome a guest who would be interested in their collection of books.

Wednesday morning, Joan was driving herself and Janet crazy with last-minute preparations.

"Are you sure one vase of flowers is enough for the guest rooms?" she asked Janet for the tenth time.

"I'm absolutely certain," she told her sister. "The rooms aren't that large. If we put more vases in them, the guests wouldn't have anywhere to put their things."

Joan nodded and paced back and forth across the kitchen while Janet sipped a cup of tea. "Maybe I should have baked more biscuits," Joan said after a moment.

Janet looked at her for a moment and then shook her head. "We have two dozen different varieties of biscuit. I'm sure they'll manage," she said eventually.

"I feel quite sick to my stomach," Joan confided in her sister. "I can't tell you how badly I want this to go well."

"I know," Janet said. She got up, crossed to Joan and gave her a hug. "It will all be fine, you know," she said soothingly.

William had told them to expect their guests some time after ten, so when midday arrived with no sign of them, Joan rang him at his store.

"It's Joan Markham. I was just ringing to double-check that your friends are arriving today?"

"Oh, they'll be here," William answered. Janet was surprised that she could hear the man from across the room. He must have been shouting into the phone.

The look on Joan's face confirmed that he was speaking very loudly. "I did wonder if you had an idea when they might arrive," Joan said. She held the phone out from her ear and both sisters were able to clearly hear the reply.

"Any time between now and midnight, I suppose," William said. "I'm sorry, but I really must go. Customers, you understand."

He disconnected before Joan replied, leaving her shaking her head.

"I'll bet he doesn't have any customers," Janet said as Joan hung up the phone.

"I'm starting to wonder if he actually has any friends coming to visit," Joan muttered.

Janet insisted that the pair eat lunch at their normal time. "If Mr. and Mrs. Stone arrive in the middle of the meal, they can join us," she told her sister. "I'm not waiting to eat until they get here, especially not until midnight."

Around three o'clock, just when Joan was muttering darkly about ringing William again, this time to give him a piece of her mind, the doorbell rang.

"Oh, dear," Joan said. She headed for the front door, with Janet following behind her. Janet could hear her sister taking slow deep breaths to calm her nerves. As the doorbell rang again, Janet found herself following her sister's lead. Deep breaths weren't much help as the doorbell buzzed for a third time just as Joan reached the door.

"I was starting to think we had the wrong place," the man at the door said as soon as Joan opened the door.

"I'm sorry. I was in the kitchen and it took me a minute to get to the door," Joan apologised. "You must be Harold Stone."

"Yes, that's right," the man said. "And this is Mildred." He nodded towards the woman next to him on the small front porch.

By now, Janet had reached the doorway and she found herself studying their guests.

William had said they were both in their sixties and Harold certainly looked it. His hair was grey and sparse and his skin was weathered and wrinkled. Janet wasn't sure where they'd driven from, but his trousers and shirt were incredibly creased, as if he'd been driving in them for days. He was a few inches short of six feet tall and looked reasonably fit.

Mildred had platinum blonde hair that was caught up in some sort of puff on the top of her head. Guessing her age was more difficult, as her face had a strange stretched and surprised look to it that Janet associated with plastic surgery. Her generous curves were spilling out of a top and trousers that were several sizes smaller than they should have been. Janet blinked and then looked away quickly when she realised she was staring at the woman's heavily made-up face.

"I do hope our room is ready," Mildred said now. "I'm quite anxious to freshen up."

"Of course, if you'll just follow me," Joan replied.

Janet stepped backwards and watched as the man picked up their single suitcase and followed Joan towards the stairs. Mildred trailed along behind them, following a strangely meandering route in her incredibly high heels. As she shut the front door, Janet was torn between following the group upstairs to watch with morbid fascination what might happen next and wanting to be as far away from the new arrivals as she could be.

Before she'd decided what she wanted to do, Joan was coming back down the stairs.

"That was quick," Janet said.

"Mildred wanted to freshen up, so I left them alone," Joan told her.

The sisters exchanged looks that spoke volumes, but didn't speak aloud, uncertain as to how voices might carry in the house. Only a few moments later, before the sisters had left the sitting room, they heard Harold on the stairs.

"Right, well, Mildred will be down in a minute. We're heading off into town to see exactly what William's getting himself up to now," he told the sisters. "We have a key for the front door, don't we? I'm not sure when we'll be back."

"William said you'd want to take your evening meals here," Joan told him.

"Oh, well, maybe another time," he replied with a wave of his hand. "I reckon tonight we should make William buy us dinner in town."

Mildred came down the stairs now. She had exchanged her wrinkled shirt and trousers for a very tight and very short black dress. She tottered over to her husband on yet another pair of skyscraper heels and took his arm.

"Off to see William, then?" she asked.

"Yes, let's go," Harold replied.

"Have a lovely evening," Janet said as the pair headed for the door.

"What time would you like breakfast?" Joan asked.

"Oh, we aren't much for getting up early," Harold replied. "You needn't worry about breakfast for us. We'll probably roll out of bed at midday anyway."

Harold pulled open the door and he and Mildred disappeared through it, leaving Joan and Janet staring after them.

Chapter 4

"I think we bought too much food," Joan said faintly, after a moment.

Janet crossed to the door and checked that it was shut properly. She locked the door and then turned back to face Joan. "They seem nice," she said, a touch desperately.

Joan stared at her for a moment and then began to laugh. "They seem terrible," she corrected Janet after a while. "I should never have said yes to William Chalmers. I don't like him and I can't imagine why I thought I'd like his friends."

"Well, we're stuck with them for now," Janet replied. "We'll just have to make the best of it."

Joan sighed. "Thank you for being nice about this," she told her sister. "I suppose it's my own fault for being so eager to get the place open."

Janet opened her mouth to reply, but a knock on the door interrupted. She turned back around and pulled the door open.

"Constable Parsons, how nice of you to visit," she said brightly to the young man on the porch. "I do hope you haven't come to warn us against anyone this time."

The man shook his head, returning Janet's smile. "Not at all," he assured her. "I was just driving by and I realised I hadn't spoken to you two in a while. I wanted to see how you were doing, that's all."

"Do come in and have a cuppa," Janet suggested. "Joan baked loads yesterday and our guests don't seem interested, so you may as well have some biscuits, too."

Janet stepped backwards and let the man into the house.

"Good afternoon, Constable Parsons," Joan said.

"You both really must call me Robert," the man told them. "No need to be formal with me."

"Why don't you come into the kitchen for that cuppa," Joan said, finding herself unable to add his Christian name to the end of the offer. Although the man was only in his twenties, and looked younger, the sisters had been raised to believe that authority figures commanded respect and that included using their formal titles.

Janet followed the others into the kitchen. Joan quickly put the kettle on while Janet began to pile several different sorts of biscuits onto a large plate. While Joan fixed the tea, Janet set out small plates for each of them and then put the large plate in the centre of the kitchen table. Only a few minutes later they were all settled in with tea and biscuits.

"So, when do you think you'll be open for business?" the man asked after a moment.

"We actually have guests now," Joan replied.

"Do you? I didn't realise."

"They're friends of Mr. Chalmers's," Janet told him. "He asked us if they could stay here for a few days while they're visiting with him."

"Friends of Mr. Chalmers's, did you say? What was the name?"

"Harold and Mildred Stone," Joan answered. "But you don't think there's anything wrong, do you?"

The man took a sip of tea before he spoke. "I'm sure they're lovely people," he said eventually. "I just like to keep track of everyone in my little village, that's all."

"I do hope you won't be expecting us to ring you every time we're going to have guests," Joan said.

"Not at all," Robert replied quickly. "But I've had a few, um, interesting conversations with Mr. Chalmers. I'm more interested in his friends than in most people."

"Have you been to his shop?" Janet asked.

"I have, several times," was the reply.

Janet opened her mouth to ask another question, but Joan silenced her with a look. Janet could tell that her sister thought she was being nosy. I probably shouldn't mention the back room, Janet thought as she nibbled her biscuit. That would definitely make me look nosy.

"They've just arrived today," Joan told the policeman. "In fact, they arrived not long before you did. They did little more than drop off their bags before they headed down to the antique store."

"Perhaps I should pay Mr. Chalmers a visit," Robert said thoughtfully. "Just check in on him and see how business is going."

"It wasn't going at all when we were there Monday," Janet said. "We were there for over half an hour and no one else came in at all."

"I suppose, with the prices on most of the things he's selling, he doesn't need many customers," Joan said. "Just one or two wealthy ones."

"I'm not sure he'll find many of them around here," Robert said. "Doveby Dale isn't that sort of village."

"I wonder why he chose to have a shop here," Janet said.

Robert shrugged. "I was told he was tired of the hustle and bustle of London and wanted a change. You can't get much quieter than Doveby Dale."

"Which is lovely, but not necessarily good for a small business," Janet replied.

"But that's really none of our concern," Joan said firmly. "I'm sure Mr. Chalmers has his reasons for being here. There's little point in our speculating on them, though."

Janet thought about objecting, but she bit her tongue. It wouldn't do to make the young policeman think she was sticking her nose in, after all.

"Did the Stones happen to say where they were from?" Robert asked after he'd finished his third biscuit.

"They weren't here long enough to say much of anything," Janet said.

"I don't remember William Chalmers mentioning it," Joan added. "I got the impression that they were coming up from London, but I don't really know why, now that I think about it."

"It doesn't matter," Robert assured them. "I'll ask them when I meet them in the antique store."

He turned down Joan's offer of more tea and biscuits. "I really must get going. I'm in Little Burton for the rest of this week. Do ring the station if anything out of the ordinary happens, though. Susan will be there to take a message during our regular hours."

"She seemed very nice when we met her," Janet said. "We really must stop and see her, actually. We'd like to put some of her knitted items around the place like Margaret Appleton did. Hopefully, we can help her sell them."

"Oh, please do," Robert said. "Maggie Appleton used to sell quite a few of her blankets and things, and now that Susan isn't making things for selling, she keeps making things for me. I have more jumpers, blankets, and wooly hats than I'll ever be able to use. Susan just knits all the time when it's quiet at the station, which is most of the time."

"She does beautiful work," Joan said. "We'd be delighted to be able to help her find loving homes for her things."

Robert frowned. "I really do appreciate everything she's given me," he told the sisters. "Please don't think I don't. It's just too much, really. I only have one head and she's made me at least a dozen hats."

Janet laughed. "I'll try to stop by to see her this week," she told the man. "Joan will be busy with our guests, but I should have a few minutes."

"Do let her know if anything else comes up," Robert reminded her. "I worry about you two here on your own."

"Michael is just across the road," Joan said. "And so are Stuart and Mary. We aren't exactly on our own."

"Is Stuart still doing all of your gardening for you?" Robert asked as he rose to his feet.

"He is," Joan answered. "And he's doing a wonderful job."

The sisters walked their guest to the front door. "I'll stop back to visit early next week," Robert said in the doorway. "I hope everything goes well with your guests until then."

"They're meant to be gone by that time," Joan told him. "William said they wouldn't be staying through the entire weekend, whatever that means."

"Well, good luck," Robert said. He crossed the porch and headed down the stairs with Janet and Joan watching. Janet continued to watch as he climbed into his car and drove away.

"What did he want?" she asked Joan as the car disappeared around the corner.

"He was just checking in on us," Joan said as she plumped the pillow on the nearest chair.

"Why?" Janet demanded.

"Because that's all part of his job?" Joan suggested. "He's responsible for Doveby Dale and likes to know what's happening all around the place."

"He seemed very interesting in William Chalmers's friends," Janet said thoughtfully.

"They were the only interesting thing we had to tell him," Joan pointed out.

Janet had to laugh. "I suppose you're right," she said.

The sisters spent the rest of the day feeling as if they were just waiting for their guests to return. Janet did some more work in the library, but she wasn't really in the mood. After clearing and cleaning a few shelves, she gave up for the day. After making certain that the mysterious panel was completely covered up, she locked up the library and curled up with her book instead. She was just pages away from discovering who was behind the art forgeries when Joan called to her from the kitchen.

"Janet? We may as well have dinner. We don't know when the Stones will be back."

Janet glanced at the clock and was surprised to find that it was half six. She hadn't realised it was that late. Her tummy rumbled, letting her know that it had noticed the passage of time, even if her brain hadn't.

In the kitchen, Joan was standing in the middle of the room, frowning. "I had meals planned for four people while the Stones were going to be here," she told Janet. "I'm going to have to freeze a great deal."

Before Janet could reply, the sisters heard the front door opening. Janet hurried to the sitting room, reminding herself along the way that the Stones had a key and it was highly unlikely to be anyone else.

"Ah, we're back," Harold Stone said brightly when he spotted Janet.

"I see that," Janet replied.

Mildred looked over at her and gave her a crooked grin. "You said something about food earlier," she said. "I'm starving."

Janet felt herself pressing her lips together firmly. Although she was no expert, it seemed to her that Harold and Mildred were both rather drunk.

"We have shepherd's pie with veggies," Joan announced, having joined Janet. "With Victoria sponge for pudding."

"Oh, I never eat pudding," Mildred said, slurring her words slightly. "Too fattening."

"You know I love you anyway," Harold said loudly. "Have some cake. I want some cake."

"Dinner's just about ready if you want to freshen up, then," Joan announced.

"I'll just do that," Mildred replied. She headed towards the stairs, but it seemed as if she couldn't manage to walk in a straight line. Instead, she stumbled sideways to the left, nearly bumping into Janet, then abruptly back to the right, lurching past the stairs and nearly falling over.

"Oh, never mind," she said brightly. "I'll freshen up later."

"If you'd like to take seats in the dining room, I'll bring the food through to you," Joan said stiffly. She turned and walked back into the kitchen, leaving Janet to show their guests through to the dining room.

"Please sit anywhere," Janet said as she escorted the pair into the room. Harold fell heavily into the first chair he came to at the large rectangular table. Mildred giggled as she brushed past him and sank down in a seat next to him.

"I need a glass of wine," she said loudly.

"I'm sorry, we don't serve alcohol," Janet told her, not feeling the least bit sorry.

Mildred frowned and looked at her husband. "Why are we eating here?" she demanded.

"William said it's included in our room rate," Harold replied, clearly trying to whisper, but failing miserably. He held his hand over his mouth and leaned in closer to Mildred. "The other sister is supposed to be a good cook," he shouted at her.

"Do we get to order now?" Mildred asked Janet.

"Tonight Joan has done shepherd's pie with roasted vegetables," Janet replied.

Mildred made a face. "But why can't I pick what I want?" she demanded petulantly.

"Because this isn't a restaurant," Joan told her as she swung into the room carrying steaming plates. "William asked if I could do evening meals for you as part of your room package and I told him that I could as long as you ate whatever I was already preparing. We aren't meant to do evening meals at all. This is a bed and breakfast."

"I'm sure it's going to be won, er, wonner, er, great," Harold slurred. "Don't mind Mildred; she's just all out of sorts because William wouldn't take us out for a fancy meal."

"Well, we came all this way to see him. I thought it was the least he could do," Mildred said grumpily.

"Where have you come from?" Janet asked casually as the couple began to eat.

"Oh, down London way," Harold replied lightly.

"Coffee or tea?" Joan asked.

"Oh, I want wine," Mildred replied. "Coffee or tea would just make me sober and no fun at all."

"I'm sorry, we haven't any wine," Joan told her. "We do have water or soft drinks."

"Just a glass of water, then," Mildred said with a sigh. "We'll go down to the pub after dinner, I suppose."

"Something fizzy for me, whatever," Harold said.

"So you're William's cousin?" Janet asked as Joan left the room to get the drinks.

"Yeah, somewhere along the way," Harold said with a shrug. "Our family isn't close, like, but we knew each other as boys and then worked together later."

"Worked together doing what?" Janet knew she was being nosy, but she was hoping the pair was too drunk to notice.

"Oh, this and that," Harold said.

Joan returned with the drinks and some fresh bread rolls.

"Oh, those look tasty," Mildred said. She took a roll and spread a thick layer of butter inside it.

Joan watched the pair for a moment and then smiled grimly at Janet. "Do let me know if anyone needs anything," she said tightly before returning to the kitchen.

I'd like some food, Janet thought to herself. Clearly Joan was planning for them to eat after the guests had finished. Janet glanced at the pair and decided that it shouldn't be long. They were clearing their plates at an impressive rate.

A few minutes later Mildred sat back from the table and sighed. "That wasn't half bad," she said with a sniff. She grabbed another roll from the basket and buttered it generously.

"Yeah," Harold muttered as he shoveled his last bites into his mouth.

Janet forced herself to smile at them both. "I'll just get these plates out of the way," she said. "And see about the Victoria sponge."

"Oh, just a very small slice for me, please," Mildred said. "I must be careful."

"Huh," Harold grunted "Maybe if you put on a few pounds you wouldn't flirt with William so much, hey?"

Mildred flushed. "I wasn't flirting," she said with a giggle. "Only maybe just a tiny bit."

Janet was torn between staying to hear more and wanting to get far away from the disagreeable couple. Deciding that duty called, she headed into the kitchen to see about the cake.

"Here," Joan said, handing Janet a tray with two large slices of cake on it.

"Mildred only wanted a small slice," Janet said.

"No, Mildred said she only wanted a small slice. I bet if you take her a small slice she'll complain. She can always leave most of that if it's too much."

Janet shrugged. "I suppose that makes sense."

"Of course it does," Joan told her. "Now hurry them along and then we can have our meal."

Janet smiled at her. "That sounds good."

Back in the dining room, Harold and Mildred were arguing.

"…always flirt, and you always have." Harold said.

"I don't flirt," Mildred said loudly. "I'm just friendly."

"There's a difference between friendly and acting like you'd like to get naked with..."

"Okay, then, cake," Janet interrupted the conversation. "Here we go."

She put the slices of cake in front of each of them and then gave them the biggest smile she could summon up. "Did you want coffee or tea with your cake?"

"We're fine," Mildred told her.

Janet waited a moment and then returned to the kitchen. Joan was busy filling two plates with shepherd's pie and vegetables.

"Did they want anything else to drink?" Joan asked.

"They didn't, but I want a glass of wine," Janet answered.

"I'm not certain we should be drinking with guests in the house," Joan replied with a frown.

Janet thought about arguing, but Joan was right. At least with these particular guests in the house, she thought to herself. With a deep sigh, she turned and walked back into the dining room, bracing herself for the unpleasant conversation she was sure she was going to interrupt.

Instead, she found Harold sitting with his head on the table, fast asleep. He was snoring quietly while Mildred was just spooning up the last of his slice of cake. Her own plate was already scraped clean.

"Oh, dear, I do hope he's okay," Janet exclaimed.

"Oh, he's fine. Just had a few too many, like. He'll sleep it off by morning."

"Not at our dining room table," Janet said firmly.

"Oh, I suppose not," Mildred shrugged. "Help me get him upstairs, will you?"

"Help you? I'm not certain..." She trailed off, feeling totally out of her element.

"Harold, wake up," Mildred said loudly. She gave him a push and he nearly toppled off his chair.

"What? Huh?"

"Come on up to bed," Mildred told him.

"Oh, yeah, hey, did you eat my cake?"

"You ate it before you fell asleep," Mildred told him as she stood up. "Now come on."

She grabbed his arm and the pair stumbled their way out of the room, with Janet following behind. It seemed to take them ages to get up the stairs and Janet wondered at one point if she ought to try giving Mildred a push, but eventually they struggled their way to the first floor.

Mildred managed to spill the entire contents of her handbag all over the landing while looking for the key to their door. Janet swallowed a sigh as she helped the woman collect her things and then opened their door for them. Giving Mildred the keys back, she practically shoved the pair into their guest room and shut the door behind them. Leaning against it, she took several deep breaths before rejoining her sister in the kitchen.

Chapter 5

"Don't say it," Joan greeted her sister as Janet walked in and sat down at the small kitchen table. "I'm so sorry about all of this, I can't even tell you."

Janet looked at her sister and then began to laugh. "I must say, teaching was far easier than running a bed and breakfast," she told her sister.

"It isn't the least bit funny," Joan snapped.

"No, but we might as well laugh," Janet replied. "It's better than crying."

For a moment Joan looked as if she might argue, but then she smiled and then chuckled softly. "I suppose you're right," she said. "We need to be far more particular about our guests."

"I don't know," Janet said. "A little bit of variety is always interesting. They're only here for a few days. I'm sure we'll survive their stay and laugh about it in years to come."

"You're being very understanding about all of this," Joan said. "I don't know that I deserve it."

"Nothing disastrous has happened," Janet pointed out. "Having a couple of unpleasant guests goes with the job. Anyway, it's entertaining in a train wreck kind of way."

Joan shook her head. "I'm not entertained," she said. "I'm starving."

"Me, too," Janet said with alacrity.

The pair quickly ate their meal and very generous helpings of Victoria sponge with vanilla ice cream, a special treat.

"I don't suppose either of them said anything about breakfast," Joan said as she and Janet loaded up the dishwasher.

"No, but I don't think they'll be up very early."

"Harold said when they arrived that they'd probably lie in and that I shouldn't worry about breakfast," Joan said worriedly. "But I don't want them complaining about it if they change their minds."

"Like they did with dinner," Janet finished the thought.

"Exactly," Joan replied.

"I think we'll have to get up and have things ready early, just in case," Janet said with a sigh.

"I think you're right," Joan said sadly.

"Before we go to bed, we need to hide all of the alcohol in the house," Janet told her sister. "I wouldn't be surprised if one or the other of them came down looking for a drink later."

"I'm ahead of you on that one," Joan said with grim satisfaction. "While you were helping them up the stairs, I moved all of our wine into my bedroom. If you need it when I'm not here, it's in the very back of my wardrobe inside the hat box."

Janet shook her head. "If I need it and you're not here, I'd better not drink it."

"You're probably right about that," Joan agreed.

In her room, Janet made certain that she locked her door before she got ready for bed. She slept more soundly than she expected, until stomping footsteps outside her door at midnight woke her. She listened as someone stumbled down the stairs, wondering if she needed to get up and deal with whoever it was. After a few minutes, she heard someone coming back up the steps.

She heard the west room door open and then: "No booze anywhere," Harold said in a disgusted voice.

"We could go to the pub," Mildred replied.

"Too tired," Harold said. "We'll stock up tomorrow for the rest of our stay."

Their bedroom door slammed and Janet slid down under her duvet, hoping the pair might decide to cut their holiday short.

Janet and Joan were up and ready to fix breakfast before eight the next morning. Janet went back to work on the library while Joan fussed in the kitchen, wondering exactly what she ought to do. It was nearly midday before they heard movement from the first floor.

Janet could hear the shower turning on and then off as she dusted shelves and books. About half an hour later, she heard footsteps on the stairs. Locking up the library, she headed towards the kitchen to help Joan.

Harold and Mildred were standing in the kitchen doorway. They both looked as if they felt miserable.

"Good morning," Janet said brightly. "How are you this morning?"

"Oooh, could you keep your voice down?" Mildred asked, wincing. "I took tablets, but they haven't started working yet."

"Oh, dear, I hope you're okay," Janet said, maybe just a tiny bit more loudly than she normally would.

"I'm fine," the woman said through gritted teeth.

"So what about breakfast?" Harold growled. "I just want lots of black coffee and maybe some toast. What about you?" he asked his wife.

"Coffee, that's all," she muttered.

"I'll set a pot brewing," Joan told them. "You can take seats in the dining room and I'll bring you some toast and jam while you're waiting."

"We don't need to sit down," Mildred told her. "Just pour some coffee in a couple of take-away containers and we'll be on our way."

"I don't have take-away containers," Joan told her. "This isn't a take-away."

Mildred opened her mouth to argue, but Harold interrupted before she managed to speak.

"Let's just get something on our way to the shop," he said. "I don't want to wait for the pot to brew anyway."

"But breakfast is included," Mildred argued.

"I don't care," he snapped at her. "I need coffee now."

He stormed out of the room with Mildred following somewhat more slowly. Janet walked behind the pair, happily pushing the door shut behind them and locking it tightly. She leaned against it for a moment, savouring the feeling of having the house to themselves again, if only for a short while.

Deciding that it must be time for some lunch, she turned and headed towards the kitchen. She hadn't gone more than a few steps when someone knocked on the door.

I wonder what they forgot, she thought to herself as she turned back, expecting to find the Stones on the porch. Instead, when she pulled the door open, she found a pair of strangers smiling brightly at her.

"Good afternoon," the man said, giving Janet a slight bow.

"Hello," the woman with him said.

"Um, good afternoon," Janet replied, studying the pair.

They were neatly dressed in clothes that looked well made but weren't new. The man appeared a little bit older than the woman, maybe in his late sixties to her early sixties. They both had grey hair and glasses and looked thoroughly respectable.

"We're awfully sorry to just turn up on your doorstep like this," the man said. "But we used to stay here once in a while when Margaret Appleton owned the house, and, well, we have such pleasant memories of our stays. We were driving through the area, planning to stay in Little Burton, and we thought we might just stop and try our luck with you."

"Oh, I, well, that is," Janet took a deep breath and started again. "We aren't really taking guests yet," she told the couple. "My sister and I just bought the house a few months ago and we're still getting settled in."

"I quite understand," the woman said in a kindly tone. "I mean, taking over a bed and breakfast must be a huge undertaking. Perhaps you'd be so good as to take our details and then, when you are ready for guests, you can let us know? We'd love a chance to stay in Doveby House again. As George says, it has very fond memories for us both."

"Of course," Janet said, feeling flustered. She wasn't sure if she should turn them away or not. "Do come in," she offered. "Let me get my sister."

"Oh, you've done such lovely things in here," the woman said, turning slowly to study the whole room. "I love the colour on the walls."

"Thank you," Janet replied. "We had the entire house painted."

"Except the large bedroom on the first floor, I hope," the man said. "Margaret always told us that it was haunted and that she had to leave the walls purple or the ghost carried on dreadfully."

Janet smiled. "I've heard the same thing," she told them. "Luckily for us, that's my room now and I love the soft lilac shade."

"Janet?" Joan was standing in the doorway, looking confused.

"Oh, Joan, there you are," Janet said. "This is, well, um, I'm sorry, I didn't get your names."

The woman laughed lightly. "We're George and Nancy Harrison," she said. "We were just telling your sister how much we love what you've done with the house."

"You've stayed here before?" Joan asked.

"Oh, yes, many times," George answered. "Mrs. Appleton, well, Maggie, ran an excellent establishment, even if she was a bit, um, well, different," he concluded with a shrug.

"Different?" Janet had to ask.

Nancy laughed. "Did you know her?" she asked the sisters.

"No, not at all. We bought the house from her estate," Janet replied.

"Well, I think what George is trying to say is that Maggie was much more adventurous than we are. She nearly always had a different man living with her, for example. We didn't really approve, but we'd fallen in love with the house, you see, and Maggie was certainly fun to be around. I think we'll enjoy staying here even more with you two here, though."

"Are they staying?" Joan asked Janet in a surprised voice.

"I was just going to get their contact details so that we could let them know when we're open for business," Janet replied. "Unless you had another idea?"

Joan looked at the pair for a moment and then took a deep breath. "The east bedroom is available, if you'd be interested," she said. "Unfortunately it's the smaller of the guest rooms, but the other room is occupied. How long were you thinking of staying?"

"Oh, maybe three nights?" George said, looking at his wife for confirmation.

"Yes, I think that would be about right," she agreed. "And we really don't care which room we're in. We've stayed in them all in the past and they're all lovely."

"Our other guests are having their evening meal here," Joan told them. She quoted them rates for their room, including dinner or with just breakfast. The couple exchanged a look.

"I think we'd rather visit some of the local restaurants for our evening meals," George said after a moment. "If that's okay with you."

"It's fine," Joan said with relief in her voice.

"Let me show you to your room, then," Janet offered.

Joan quickly found the keys to the east room and the pair followed Janet up the stairs.

"You've done a lot of work in here as well," Nancy said happily.

"We have," Janet agreed. "The only thing we haven't done is put up any pictures, but we're working on that."

"Maggie had a sort of still life on that wall," George told her. "It wasn't very attractive, but I suppose it looked better than the blank wall does."

"We'll have something in place by the next time you visit," Janet told them.

"I'll just go and get our bags," George said. "And thank you so very much for letting us stay after all."

"You can thank Joan for that," Janet replied. "Do let either of us know if you need anything."

"I can't imagine that we will," Nancy said happily. "We'll just unpack and then do some sightseeing. We won't be out late. What time is breakfast?"

"Whenever you like," Janet replied. "Joan and I are early risers."

They both laughed. "Maggie Appleton wasn't," George explained. "Breakfast was usually ready some time around ten, if she bothered to make it at all."

"Oh, goodness, I can't imagine," Janet exclaimed. "Joan and I will be up and ready to serve any time after eight, and we can have breakfast ready earlier if you let us know in advance."

"As we're on holiday, I don't think we'll be looking for breakfast any time before nine," Nancy replied. "What time do the other guests get their breakfast? Maybe we can all eat together and save you some effort."

"Today they came down at half eleven," Janet told her. "And all they wanted was coffee."

"Or maybe not," Nancy laughed.

Janet found herself smiling happily as she headed down the stairs. The Harrisons were exactly the sort of guests she'd been expecting them to host when they'd talked about buying a bed and breakfast.

Joan had lunch ready when she got back downstairs. They ate quickly, while talking quietly about nothing much.

"We're just off to do some sightseeing," Nancy said, sticking her head into the kitchen as the sisters were finishing their meal. "We shouldn't be out too late."

"Have fun," Janet called.

The sisters had the house to themselves for the rest of the afternoon. Janet spent a few minutes cleaning the library and then gave in to temptation and read her book instead. Joan fixed a roast chicken with all the trimmings for dinner, and the sisters ended up eating it on their own as their guests didn't return.

After dinner they settled in front of the television. Janet found she wasn't paying attention to the show, as she was too busy listening for their guests. After an hour, she gave up.

"I'm going up to bed," she told Joan. "I'll read up there for a while."

"I don't know what to do," Joan replied. "It wouldn't surprise me if Harold and Mildred turned up and demanded food."

"You can't sit up all night," Janet pointed out.

"No, but I think I'll give them another hour or so," Joan replied.

"If you need me, please shout," Janet told her. "I'll come down and help without any complaints, I promise."

Joan laughed. "I'll hold you to that," she said.

Janet got ready for bed and then curled up with her book. An interesting and unexpected plot twist kept her reading for longer than she'd intended. She couldn't hear the front door from her room, but she heard the voices and footsteps as their guests headed up to their rooms.

George and Nancy were back around nine o'clock, and Janet could tell that they were nearly tiptoeing as they made their way past her door. She heard a whispered exchange, but couldn't make out exactly what was being said. After a moment, their room door opened and then closed again quietly.

A few hours later, just as Janet finished the book, she heard Harold and Mildred noisily climbing the stairs. When they reached the top, they began to shout at one another.

"You have the key," Mildred told Harold.

"No, you took it after I opened the front door," Harold replied.

"I didn't. You put it in your pocket," Mildred snapped back. "And stop shouting or you'll wake everyone up."

"I don't have the key," Harold hissed loudly. "You put it in your bag."

Janet sighed deeply. At least they didn't sound drunk, just angry and loud. She headed towards the door, but stopped when she heard her sister's voice.

"I believe you're looking for these?" Joan's tone was icy.

"Where did you find them?" Mildred asked.

"You left them in the front door," Joan answered. "I'd appreciate it if you were more careful with them in the future."

There was a short pause and then Mildred began to giggle. "We're in trouble," she told Harold.

"Good night," Joan said sharply.

Janet listened to her sister's footsteps going down the stairs as their guests made their way to their bedroom door. It seemed to take them several tries to get the key in the lock and Janet changed her mind about their sobriety. Eventually, she heard the door open and then, a moment later, slam shut.

Janet switched off her light and fell into a restless sleep. A buzzing noise next to her head woke her suddenly. She lay in the dark room feeling completely disoriented.

Chapter 6

Janet sat up slowly, her brain struggling to process the sound. She glanced at the clock and frowned. Two o'clock in the morning. For the past several months, whenever the moon was full, she'd been woken up by the screaming of one of the house's resident ghosts, but the moon wasn't full tonight. Switching on her bedside lamp, she looked around the room and then shook her head. On the bedside table, her mobile phone was buzzing insistently.

"You really should recognise your own ringtone," she said loudly, hoping to wake up her vocal cords before she answered. She'd recognised the number immediately and she knew she was being silly with not wanting the caller to know she'd been asleep, but she was often silly when it came to dealing with Edward Bennett.

"Hello?"

"I'm sorry to disturb you so late," Edward said in a soft voice. "But I just now found five spare minutes and I couldn't think of anyone I'd rather spend them with."

"It's two in the morning," Janet pointed out.

"I know, and I am sorry," Edward said, sounding not sorry at all. "But how are you?"

"I'm fine," Janet replied automatically. "How are you?"

Edward chuckled. "You mustn't just reply without thinking," he told her. "I genuinely want to know how you are."

Janet thought for a moment. "I'm rather tired," she said.

"Oh, dear, and now I've woken you. I'll let you go, shall I?"

"No," Janet replied. "It's nice to hear your voice."

Edward had been their first paying guest, and Janet had been rather overwhelmed by his sophisticated charm. He'd only stayed a few days, telling her when he departed that he worked for the government in some secret capacity.

He'd told her he had been sent to Doveby House to find some paperwork relating to his ties to Maggie Appleton, who'd let him use the bed and breakfast as a safe house on occasion. Janet wasn't entirely sure what to believe about the man, but she found herself attracted to him and she was enjoying their long-distance flirtation.

"Ah, thank you, my dear," he said now. "But I'd rather hear yours. Tell me what's going on in your world."

"William Chalmers has opened his antique shop," Janet began. She told him about the shop and the painting she quite liked. "It's out of my budget, but it's lovely," she concluded. "But I have much more interesting news than that. We have guests. In fact, we're full up with guests."

"Do tell," Edward encouraged her.

Janet spent several minutes telling Edward all about the disagreeable Harold and Mildred and the rather more charming George and Nancy. He asked several questions about both couples that left Janet curious.

"Did you know about our guests before you rang?" she demanded.

"Why would I?"

"I don't know. You just seem very curious about them, that's all."

"I worry about you and Joan," he explained. "This is all new to you and I worry that you'll end up with the wrong sort of guests. There are a lot of unscrupulous people in the world and I don't want any of them to take advantage of you and your sister. When do they all leave?"

"Soon, I think," Janet replied. "Joan handled the bookings, so she knows better than I do. I think the Harrisons said they would be leaving on Sunday morning, and I'm sure William Chalmers said the Stones were only going to be here for a few days. It might feel as if they've been here forever, but I know they'll be gone soon."

"I'd love to say I'm coming to visit, but I'm rather tied up in Greece at the moment," Edward told her. "But I'll ring again soon, if I may."

"Of course," Janet agreed quickly. "Any time."

After she disconnected, Janet lay back in bed and thought about what she'd said. Any time before midnight might have been a better response, she thought now. She switched off the light and eventually fell back to sleep.

The next morning was much like the previous one had been, with the two sisters ready to prepare breakfast well before it was needed. The Harrisons finally came down around ten, full of apologies.

"We meant to be down for breakfast by nine," Nancy said. "But we both overslept. That never happens."

"Would you like breakfast now, then?" Joan asked.

"Only if it isn't too much bother," George replied. "It's close enough to lunchtime that we can wait if we must."

"It's no bother at all," Joan told him.

She got busy in the kitchen while Janet headed out to the garden to cut some fresh flowers for the dining room table. She smiled at Stuart Long, their neighbour who looked after the gardens for them, when she bumped into him in one of the flowerbeds.

"Good morning, Janet. How are you?" he asked.

"I'm very well, thanks. How are you?" Janet replied.

"Oh, can't complain," he told her. "Or rather, I could, but it wouldn't do any good."

"And how is your lovely wife?"

"Mary's good. She's off visiting with her oldest son, Paul, and his wife for a fortnight."

"So Mary's children aren't yours?" Janet asked, flushing when she realised that the question was somewhat rude.

Stuart just laughed. "No, this is a second marriage for both Mary and me. She has three sons and she loves spending time with them and all of the grandchildren. Their wives don't necessarily appreciate it as much as Mary does, but they put up with her once in a while."

Janet grinned. "I can't imagine having a mother-in-law. It must be strange."

"Mary's mother passed away a long time ago. I never met her, but my first mother-in-law was wonderful. She's gone now, too, but we stayed close even after her daughter, my wife, died suddenly. My mother-in-law was a big help with my little girl. I don't know what I would have done without her, really."

"You have a daughter?"

"I do. Marie visits once in a while, when Mary's out of town, like."

Janet opened her mouth and then shut it quickly before another rude question could pop out. Stuart smiled at her.

"Anyway, with Mary gone, I've been spending extra time on your garden. I dug out that bed at the back that was always struggling and planted some new things that I hope will cope better with the amount of shade that bed gets."

Janet nodded. She loved their beautiful garden, but she wasn't especially interested in the details. "Joan is just making breakfast for some of our guests. If you haven't eaten, I'm sure Joan could make something for you, too."

"I made myself a huge breakfast," the man confessed. "But I'll stop by for tea and biscuits later, if I may."

"You know you're always welcome," Janet assured him. While they paid him a nominal amount for taking care of the gardens, he mostly did it because he loved the work. The sisters always made sure to keep him supplied with biscuits and tea so that he knew how much his efforts were appreciated.

With her arms full of flowers, Janet returned to the house. George and Nancy were just tucking into their breakfast. She was surprised to hear footsteps on the stairs as she arranged the flowers.

"Good morning," Harold said as he and his wife wandered into the dining room.

"Good morning," Janet replied. "Are you ready for some breakfast?"

"We told your sister what we wanted," Mildred told her. "She said we should come in and meet your other guests."

Janet quickly introduced the two couples and then headed into the kitchen to help Joan. When she brought Mildred and Harold their plates, the foursome were chatting away like old friends.

"Janet, have you been to this antique store that Harold was just telling us about?" Nancy asked. "Because he makes it sound like a wonderful little find."

"It's a nice little shop," Janet replied. "Mr. Chalmers has some lovely pieces and some interesting artwork as well."

"Then that will be our first stop today, then," George said.

"Excellent," Mildred said. "William will be so pleased."

Janet cleared away dishes and refilled coffee cups while the guests talked about this and that. Once everyone had eaten, the two couples headed out together, apparently on their way to WTC Antiques. Janet carried the last of dirty plates and cups into the kitchen.

"They seem to be getting on incredibly well," she told her sister.

"Who?"

"The Harrisons and the Stones," Janet replied. "Harold and Mildred talked the Harrisons into paying William a visit at his 'charming little antique shop' right after breakfast."

"They're very different sorts of people," Joan said thoughtfully. "Anyway, I'm sure William will appreciate the customers."

"I just hope they don't feel as if they have to buy something just to be polite," Janet said.

"I'm sure they'll be fine," Joan told her. "Anyway, there were lots of little bits and pieces that weren't terribly dear. I'm sure they'll be able to find something affordable if they do feel that way."

"We didn't buy anything," Janet said suddenly. "I suppose we really ought to have."

"You were too taken with that painting to look at anything else," Joan reminded her.

"I was rather," Janet admitted.

"I must say, now that you mention it, I feel quite guilty for not at least buying a useless, dust collecting something or other to help poor William with his business," Joan said.

"But we don't like William," Janet retorted.

"No, but he sent business our way, even if the Stones aren't our favourite guests. I should have thought to purchase something from the man."

"The guests are all out. We could run down now and buy something if it will make you feel better," Janet suggested.

Joan thought for a moment and then nodded. "I really do think we should," she said.

Janet wasn't sure she agreed, but she didn't argue. "Give me five minutes to change into something appropriate for going out," she told her sister.

In her room, she quickly changed and then picked up her handbag. Dropping her phone into it, she remembered the middle of the night conversation with Edward. Why had he rung? What did he really want? She couldn't help but think that he'd rung to find out about their guests. The idea made her feel very uncomfortable.

She locked her bedroom door and then checked both guest rooms. They were both locked.

"Are we supposed to make up the guest's rooms for them every day?" she asked her sister when she got back downstairs.

"No. I told them both that we'd do as much or as little as they'd like, and both couples opted to have us stay out of their rooms until they've gone."

"Is that normal?" Janet asked.

Joan looked at her for a moment and then laughed. "I've no idea," she replied. "They're our first guests."

Janet sighed. "This bed and breakfast thing is turning out to be harder than I expected."

"It's harder than I expected, too," Joan admitted in a quiet voice. "There are so many things to think about."

"Still, it is a good deal more interesting than teaching primary school, isn't it?" Janet asked.

"I'm not sure interesting is the right word," Joan muttered. "I certainly got more sleep when we were teaching."

"They'll all be gone in a few days and then it will be just us again," Janet said. "Unless you've taken more bookings that I don't know about?"

"No. I think after these guests leave we need a bit of a break. We should probably work our way into this gradually, just an odd guest once in a while until we get used to the whole thing."

Janet laughed. "Now you're sounding more like yourself," she told her sister. "And I'm all ready to suggest that we should push onwards and start taking bookings on a regular basis. The only way we'll work out if we like it or if we can actually make a good go of it is if we jump in with both feet."

Joan didn't say anything for a minute and then she sighed. "Let's go and do some antique shopping," she said. "I'm too tired to think about our future anyway. I'm really hoping all of our guests have an early night tonight."

"Perhaps when we have guests, we should take it in turns to stay up with them," Janet suggested. "You stayed up last night, so tonight will be my turn."

"That's very kind of you," Joan said, her tone suspicious. "What's going on?"

"Nothing," Janet replied. "But it is our bed and breakfast, regardless of whose idea it was to buy it. I should do my fair share."

"We can talk about it later," Joan told her.

The pair headed out to the car. Janet sat in the passenger seat lost in thought. She hadn't mentioned her late night phone call, telling herself that she didn't want to worry her sister. Edward had wanted to know about their guests. That suggested that one of the couples had something to hide, something that a man who was quite probably some sort of spy was interested in.

Chapter 7

Joan had no difficulty in finding a parking space in Doveby Dale.

"Is it ever busy?" Janet asked as they climbed out of the car.

"Maybe during the holiday season," Joan suggested. "Although the shops that are here don't really have that much to offer holiday shoppers, do they?"

"Maybe lots of people will want to buy William's antiques for their family and friends this Christmas," Janet said.

"Maybe," Joan replied in a doubtful tone.

The pair made their way down the pavement towards the antique shop.

"Do you know what sort of car Harold and Mildred have?" Joan asked suddenly.

"I really didn't notice," Janet admitted. "I don't know what George and Nancy have, either."

Joan nodded. "I suppose that's something else we're meant to be paying attention to," she sighed.

Janet pulled open the door at WTC Antiques and the sisters walked in. The buzzer sounded, but no one rushed to greet them. The shop looked empty, but after a moment Janet realised that she could hear voices from the back room.

"Everyone must be admiring my painting," she said.

"I'm not sure we can afford both of them, my dear," George was saying to his wife as the sisters walked into the back.

The couple was standing in front of a medium-sized canvas with a few random squiggles on it. Next to it was a second painting done in the same colours, but instead of squiggles there were a handful of very straight lines. Janet shook her head. She hated them both and couldn't imagine why anyone would want them.

"They belong together," Nancy said firmly. "We can't take just one. It would look all out of place without its other half."

"I'm sure we can arrange some sort of price that works for you," William said ingratiatingly. "But first you should look around and see if there's anything else you like. The more you buy, the bigger the discount I can give you, you see."

Nancy glanced at her husband and then smiled. "I don't think George is going to be very happy if I keep looking," she said. "But that won't stop me."

"I rather love this one," Mildred called from across the room. "You should take a look."

Nancy walked across the room towards where Mildred and Harold were standing. Janet cleared her throat, causing everyone to look over at her and Joan.

"Oh, I didn't hear the buzzer," William said, looking flustered. "But it's nice of you to visit again. Did you want to talk about that painting?" he asked Janet.

Janet walked over and looked at the painting again. If anything, she liked it even better now, but she knew she couldn't afford it.

"I'll just keep visiting it here until you sell it," she told the man as he joined her. "Maybe I'll inherit a fortune between now and then and I'll be able to buy it myself."

"We can but hope," William said. Janet guessed that he was trying to sound light-hearted, but the words came out harshly. "If you didn't come for the painting, why are you here?" he added.

"I didn't get a chance to look around the entire showroom the last time we visited," Joan told him. "I'm sure you must have something that would look perfect in one of our rooms."

William glanced over at Nancy who was still talking quietly with Mildred. "If you need anything, come and get me," he called to the women.

"We're fine," Nancy assured him. "I'll just make a list of all the things I want and then you and George can argue about it."

William chuckled weakly and then turned back to Joan and Janet. "Come and have a good look around the other room, then," he said. "I can't wait to see what you think of it all."

Janet followed her sister and William back into the main showroom and then trailed along behind them as Joan looked around. She tried to pretend to be interested in the various items Joan inspected, but she really wanted to go and listen in on the conversation in the back.

The two couples that were their guests seemed like very unlikely friends, and Janet was really curious what they were talking about. As William's friends, she supposed Mildred and Harold were doing their best to sell the others as much as possible. After what felt like hours, Joan finally selected a pair of lamps.

"What do you think?" she asked Janet.

"They aren't bad," Janet replied honestly. They were one of the few things in the place that she didn't hate, at least.

"I thought they'd go nicely on the bedside tables in my bedroom," Joan told her.

Janet nodded. The lamps were very much her sister's style, which made them not really something Janet would care to own.

"While you pay for those, I'll just go visit my painting again," Janet told her sister.

Joan laughed. "I think I may have to buy you that painting for Christmas," she said.

"I wouldn't say no," Janet told her, even though she knew she really would if Joan actually made such an offer. Both sisters were quite frugal and that extended to buying one another gifts. Neither would ever dream of spending that much money on themselves or each other.

Janet walked into the back room and looked around. Harold was standing in one corner, talking on his mobile phone. Otherwise the room was empty. Janet turned slowly, looking for an exit, but it seemed as if the only way in or out of the room was the way she'd just come. Where had the others gone?

Harold looked up from his phone and muttered something under his breath. "Oh, I didn't think you'd be back," he said.

"Where did everyone go?" Janet blurted out.

"They're just in the loo," the man replied hastily. He gestured towards the door in the back wall that Janet had opened on her last visit.

"Oh, is there a loo? I could do with one," she said. She crossed towards the door, but before she got there it swung open. Mildred emerged with George and Nancy on her heels.

"Ah, still shopping?" Mildred asked Janet in a bright voice.

"I was just looking for the loo," Janet told her. "Harold said it's through there?"

"Oh, no, Harold is confused," Mildred said with a laugh. She took Janet's arm and began to steer her out of the room. "That's just a storage space. I saw a little chest of drawers in the very back that I thought Nancy might like, and I just had to show them. Unfortunately, she didn't care for it, but I had to try."

While she'd been speaking, she nearly dragged Janet back into the main room. Joan was just picking up the large box that William had packed her lamps into.

"Ready to go?" Joan asked her sister.

"Yes," Janet replied, knowing that Mildred wasn't going to let her do anything but leave at this point.

"Excellent, perhaps you can open doors for me," Joan suggested.

Janet smiled at Mildred and William in turn. "Thank you," she said. "I'll be back to look at my painting again soon."

"I'll look forward to it," William told her unenthusiastically.

Janet grinned and then rushed forward to open the door for Joan. The box wasn't large and Joan insisted it wasn't heavy, but it was unwieldy. Janet walked in front of her sister as they made their way back to the car.

"I do feel a bit selfish," Joan said once they were on their way back to Doveby House. "Perhaps I should have purchased something for the house instead of for myself."

"Don't be silly," Janet told her. "We've spent a fortune on the house and anyway, you need lamps in your bedroom. Mine came with such nice ones and I've felt just the tiniest bit guilty about that ever since we moved in."

Joan laughed. "I don't believe you've given it a single thought, but I appreciate your telling me that to make me feel better."

Janet grinned. Her sister knew her too well. She'd never thought about the bedside lamps that were already in her almost perfect bedroom when they bought the fully furnished house, but if she had thought about them, she would have felt bad that Joan didn't have a similar set.

"I hope you aren't too sad about that painting," Joan said. "Maybe, if we can keep the guest rooms filled for a few months, you can buy it in the new year."

"Maybe," Janet said with a shrug. "I'm not going to lose sleep over it. There's just something about it that I like, that's all."

"I know. You visited it twice in ten minutes," Joan teased.

"I went back the second time to see what our guests were up to back there," Janet countered. "And they weren't even there."

"What do you mean? Where else could they have gone?"

"Harold was there, on his phone, but the other three weren't in the back. Harold tried to make excuses, but after a moment they came out of the storage room. You know, the one where I saw all those half-finished canvases."

"So maybe they were looking at something back there," Joan said.

"Or maybe they're all part of the art forgery scheme," Janet said excitedly.

"You must stop reading crime fiction," Joan tutted.

"Edward rang last night," Janet said as casually as she could. "He was quite interested in hearing all about our guests."

"Which suggests that he's quite interested in what's happening in your life," Joan said. "I hope you aren't suggesting that he suspects them of something criminal?"

Janet flushed and looked out the car window. "I don't know," she said after a moment. "You have to admit you can see Harold and Mildred being mixed up in something unpleasant."

"Just because I don't like them doesn't mean I think they're criminals," Joan said firmly. "I don't like William Chalmers, either."

"And I'm just as suspicious of him," Janet exclaimed. "Remember how upset he was when he thought we'd sent the police to talk to him?"

Joan nodded. "I do, but that doesn't prove anything. Robert Parsons will have investigated him thoroughly, I'm sure, after that. You just have an overactive imagination."

Janet laughed. "I've been accused of worse," she told her sister.

After a moment, Joan laughed as well. "Anyway, whatever you think of our guests, you must treat them nicely," she said.

"I will," Janet promised.

"And no snooping," Joan added.

As they were just pulling into the parking area in front of Doveby House, Janet was saved from replying, which was fortunate, as she had every intention of snooping if she got the opportunity.

Joan opened the boot of the car and was pulling the box out of it while Janet headed toward their door.

"Let me help," a voice shouted from across the road.

Janet smiled as Michael Donaldson, their other across the street neighbour, rushed across to help Joan. He had been rather busy filling in as a chemist in a shop in Derby for the last week, and Janet knew her sister had missed the man.

Joan had never dated when she was younger, while Janet had dated a great deal, but had never become very serious about any one man. Now Janet was enjoying watching her sister taking baby steps into her first relationship. Michael seemed like a genuinely nice man and Janet couldn't have been any happier for Joan. Now she opened the door for him as he carried Joan's box into the house.

"Where would you like it?" he asked Joan.

"Oh, just put it in my sitting room," Joan replied. "I'll come and unlock the door."

"You've taken to locking your room?" Michael asked.

"We have guests," Joan told him.

"I've missed rather a lot, then, haven't I?"

"You have," Joan agreed. "Are you done working all those long hours now?" she asked.

"I am," he said happily. "The regular chemist is back from his surgery and he's doing very well. I don't know that I'll take anything that demanding again. I'm meant to be retired and I really don't miss working. But that's enough about me. What's going on over here?"

Janet wandered into the kitchen and put the kettle on. She could hear her sister and Michael chatting together as she dug out biscuits and put them on a plate.

"Come and see what you think," Joan called after a few minutes.

Janet walked into Joan's small sitting room. Joan was in her bedroom, looking happily at her new lamps.

"They're perfect," Janet exclaimed.

"They really are," Joan said.

"I put the kettle on," Janet told the others. "Let's have tea and biscuits."

"Just a few biscuits," Joan cautioned. "It's nearly time to start dinner."

"I thought maybe I could take you out," Michael said to Joan. "To make up for being away so much lately."

"We're doing evening meals for some of our guests," Joan explained. "I can't leave Janet with that much work."

Michael looked so disappointed that Janet almost found herself offering to deal with Harold and Mildred herself.

"Why don't you join us for dinner here?" Joan suggested, saving Janet from making an offer she was certain to regret later.

"I don't want to make even more work for you," Michael protested.

"It won't be," Joan assured him. "I'm making spaghetti Bolognese. It isn't any trouble to throw in a bit more pasta and a few extra tomatoes and herbs."

"If you're sure, I'd love to stay," Michael said happily.

"I'm quite sure," Joan said firmly.

"I'll leave you two to get on with the cooking, then," Janet said. "I'll take my tea and biscuits to the library."

She didn't really feel like cleaning, but she wanted to give her sister and Michael some privacy. After drinking her tea she cleared another shelf and gave it a half-hearted wipe while nibbling on a biscuit. While she was dusting each book to return it to the shelf, she stumbled across a book she'd never read by an author she knew she liked. Knowing her sister was busy with Michael, she sat down and began to read. Before she knew it, Joan was calling her for dinner.

"No sign of the guests, yet?" Janet asked as she joined her sister and Michael in the kitchen.

"No, but everything is ready, so I thought we might as well eat. If they turn up while we're eating, we can take turns serving them," Joan replied.

The food was excellent and Janet was delighted when they finished without interruption.

"I know you offered to stay up tonight," Joan said when Janet had finished loading the dishwasher. "But Michael and I want to watch a bit of telly and catch up. You can head up to bed if you like."

Janet thought about arguing, but there was no point in both of them sitting up until the guests arrived home. She headed to bed, curling up with her book until she could barely keep her eyes open. The guests still weren't back when she finally switched off her light and snuggled under the duvet.

Chapter 8

On Saturday, when Janet woke up to her alarm, her first thought was that their guests must have stayed out all night. She showered and dressed quickly and then headed down to the kitchen, where Joan was already fixing breakfast for herself and Janet.

"Did the guests come in last night?" Janet asked, feeling confused.

"They did," Joan confirmed. "And Michael escorted them to their rooms. I believe they were all a good deal more quiet last night than they had been the previous evening."

"They were indeed," Janet said. "I never woke up."

"That's good," Joan said. "They were both back fairly early as well, so I got a good night's sleep. I'm feeling much better today."

Janet wondered how much of Joan's good mood was due to the hours she'd spent the night before with Michael, but she chose not to tease her sister. She was so happy for Joan that it seemed cruel to joke about it.

The sisters chatted about the weather as they ate their breakfast. They were just finishing when they heard someone coming down the stairs. A minute later, all four of their guests crowded their way into the kitchen.

"Good morning, all," Janet said cheerfully. "I hope everyone slept well?"

"Yes, fine, thanks," Mildred replied. "But now I'm starving. Can we have the full English breakfast this morning?"

"Of course," Joan replied. "Why don't you all go and sit in the dining room. Janet can bring in coffee, tea, and juice for you."

"Full English for everyone?" Janet checked as she poured coffee for everyone.

A chorus of "yes, please" sent her back into the kitchen. Joan was hard at work. Janet started making toast and filling toast racks.

"Thank goodness we already ate," Janet commented. "Although everything smells so good, I feel as if I could eat it all again."

Janet carried very full plates of food in to their guests and then refilled coffee cups. Back in the kitchen, she helped Joan with the washing up. When she went back into the dining room, the guests were all getting to their feet and collecting their things.

"We're all off to see the sights," Nancy told Janet. "We're going to show Mildred and Harold a few of our favourite places, as they've never been to the area before."

"That's very kind of you," Janet replied. "You seem to have good weather for it, anyway."

"Yes, it's meant to be sunny all day," Nancy said happily.

Janet walked the foursome to the front door and made sure the door was locked behind them. She jumped when she turned back around and found her sister standing right behind her.

"I didn't hear you there," Janet exclaimed.

"Sorry, I didn't mean to startle you."

"I was just wondering if the police station is open today. We still haven't gone to talk to Susan about her knitting."

"I'd forgotten all about that," Joan said, shaking her head. "We really ought to do that today if we can. I need to go grocery shopping as well. I thought Mildred and Harold were leaving today, but they asked if they could stay one more night, which means one more round of dinner and breakfast for them."

"Let's go now and get the errands run," Janet suggested. "I'd rather be home when the guests get back."

"Yes, I agree," Joan replied.

The local police station was housed in a tiny cottage and going inside always made Janet feel slightly claustrophobic. She didn't know how Susan could work inside the tiny building.

"Ah, the Markham sisters," Susan, a curvy forty-something blonde, said brightly when Janet and Joan walked into the tiny reception area. "Robert said you might be stopping one day this week."

Susan put down the project she was knitting and stood up. "I've been sitting still too long," she confided as she stretched.

"We wanted to talk to you about selling some of your knitted items at Doveby House," Joan said.

"Oh, I wish you would," Susan replied. "I loved the extra bit of income and I have to find some way to get rid of my things. Poor Robert has had all of the hats, jumpers and blankets he'll ever need and far more than he actually wants."

Janet laughed. "I'm sure he appreciates your hard work."

"It's just that I have so much quiet time while I'm here," she explained. "There has to be someone in the office for a certain number of hours each week, but there isn't enough work to keep me busy during those hours. I used to read, but knitting is far more productive. Besides," she added with a sheepish grin, "I used to hate getting interrupted when I was reading. The knitting is much easier to put down."

"I know what you mean," Janet told her. "Everyone always seems to interrupt at the very best part in the book."

"I have a couple of boxes of things here for you to look at," Susan said eagerly. She pulled out and opened several boxes, lifting out blankets, scarves, hats and sweaters and piling them onto the small table against the wall.

"These are all lovely," Joan said.

Janet inspected one of the blankets. At one time she'd done quite a bit of knitting herself, so she knew exactly what she was looking for. The quality of Susan's work was excellent.

"You do wonderful work," she told the woman. "I might have to buy one or two things for myself."

"I'll give you a discount," Susan offered. "Or maybe you could just choose your favourite and you could have it as long as you tell all of your guests how much you love it."

The sisters laughed. "Oh, I'm happy to pay you for a blanket," Janet told her. "And I promise to tell everyone who stays with us about it as well."

"I understand you have a couple staying with you at the moment," Susan said as she began returning items to their boxes.

"Two, actually," Joan corrected her.

"Really? I must tell Robert," Susan said. "Tell me about your new arrivals, then."

Joan told the woman about the Harrisons. "They seem very nice indeed," she concluded. "Even if they've developed a strange relationship with the Stones."

"What's strange about it?" Susan asked.

"That they're friendly with each other at all, really," Janet said. "They don't seem as if they'd have very much in common."

"Perhaps both couples are just feeling out of place in unfamiliar surroundings," Susan suggested.

"The Stones are meant to be visiting with William Chalmers," Janet replied. "I wonder how he feels about them going off to see the sights with total strangers and leaving him to run his shop on his own."

"I don't think he needs all that much help," Susan told her. "It doesn't seem to me that he's all that busy."

As the row of shops that included the antique shop wasn't far from the police station, Susan would have easily been able to keep track of the customers who were coming and going.

"I hope business improves," Joan said.

"I just hope Mr. Chalmers can keep himself out of trouble," Susan replied.

"What do you mean?" Janet asked quickly.

Susan flushed. "I shouldn't be talking about that," she said, shaking her head.

"Should we be worried about Mr. Chalmers?" Joan demanded.

"If he's doing something criminal, I think we ought to know about it."

"He got himself into some trouble in London," Susan said, clearly reluctant to discuss the issue. "All of this is public record, if you know where to look. Apparently some of his antiques weren't exactly as described. He claimed it was all a big misunderstanding, and anyway, he paid his fines and did a short stint in prison. He came up here to start over."

"And we should do whatever we can to support him," Joan added.

"Yes, indeed," Susan replied faintly. "I really shouldn't have said anything. Please don't repeat what I've told you. As I said, it's all public record, but it isn't exactly common knowledge."

"We won't say anything," the sisters said in almost perfect unison.

Joan and Susan talked their way through pricing the knitted items and agreed that the sisters would get ten per cent of the sale prices.

"I hope we'll be back soon to get more from you," Joan said as Susan helped them load several boxes of her work into their car.

"I hope so, too," Susan said. "Although Robert will just be glad that those are out of the office. I've many more boxes full of finished items at home, anyway. Let me know if you need more."

"We'll let you know *when* we need more," Joan corrected her.

Susan smiled at the words and then went back into the police station while the sisters climbed into their car.

"We should have told her about the paintings in the back of the antique shop," Janet said.

"Why?"

"Because then Robert could investigate."

"The man sells artwork," Joan said. "It doesn't seem strange to me that he has a few unfinished paintings in his back room."

"But someone was working in there," Janet said. "Even though he told us he doesn't sell work by local artists."

"Just because someone was working in his back room, doesn't

mean they are a local artist," Joan pointed out. "I think you're just looking for a bit of excitement like in all the books you read."

"Bessie seems to get caught up in murder investigations all the time. I don't see why you don't think William might be doing something criminal. I haven't accused him of murder or anything like that. Just a little bit of art forgery."

Joan shook her head. "Bessie is a dear woman who has had a terrible run of bad fortune lately. I can't imagine how terrible it must be to keep finding dead bodies and discovering people you know are murderers. But sometimes I think you're just looking for something out of the ordinary so you can tell Bessie that our lives are just as exciting as hers."

Janet opened her mouth to reply and then shut it again while she thought about what Joan had said. She didn't envy Bessie Cubbon, the friend they'd made on a recent trip to the Isle of Man. There was such a thing as too much excitement, and it seemed as if Bessie was having rather more than was good for one person at the moment. But Janet didn't think she was being unreasonable in suspecting William Chalmers of doing something illegal in his new shop.

"I still don't like the man," she said loudly.

"I don't like him either, but that doesn't mean he's a criminal."

"Susan told us he's a criminal," Janet reminded her sister.

Joan shook her head. She'd driven them back to Doveby House and now she parked the car.

"There was no point in going grocery shopping with the car stuffed full of Susan's things," she told Janet. "Let's unload them and then one of us can go back out."

Janet pulled the first box from where it was tucked in the backseat. Joan was doing the same on the other side of the car.

"Here, let me help," Janet heard Michael calling from behind her.

"I'll lend a hand as well," Stuart added as he appeared from the garden. "I was just looking for an excuse to take a break from trimming hedges, anyway."

The women were happy to let the men carry the boxes into the house for them. It took them several trips, and Joan had the kettle on before they'd finished.

"Come and have a cuppa, then," she told them after they'd brought in the last box.

"Just a quick one," Stuart said.

"I was just heading out to do some grocery shopping," Michael told Joan. "So I'll want to make it quick as well."

"Why don't you go with Michael and do the shopping and I'll start figuring out where we want to display Susan's items," Janet suggested after they'd all enjoyed tea and biscuits.

"I thought we could use the long table against the wall in the sitting room," Joan told her. "It's not being used for anything else."

"I was thinking the same thing," Janet replied. "I'll just pull out a few examples of each item and try my hand at making a proper display. I'm sure you'll change everything once you get back, though."

Joan laughed. "Let's see how you do," she said.

Janet noticed that she didn't rule out changing everything, which didn't surprise her. Joan would have her own ideas about how things should be displayed and it was unlikely they matched Janet's.

Regardless, Janet enjoyed the next hour. She carefully selected what she considered the very nicest examples of each of the different items that Susan had provided. After pulling out the blanket that she wanted for herself, Janet carefully arranged the display, folding and refolding things until she was satisfied with the results.

There was an old typewriter in the corner of Joan's small sitting room. Now Janet put some paper in it and carefully typed up a list of prices for the items on display. She knew she'd seen some old picture frames in the carriage house, so she headed out there to find one that could hold her neatly typed list.

Stuart was still working in a corner near the building.

"I'm sure I saw some pictures frames in a box in the carriage house," she told him as she walked past.

"There's at least one of just about everything in a box in there,"

Stuart told her cheerfully. "The door's unlocked because I've been going in and out all day."

Janet pushed the door open and switched on the overhead light. It took a moment to come on and did little to help dispel the gloom in the large and windowless space. There were boxes piled up all around the room and Janet sighed as she glanced around. Once she finished with the library, the carriage house was her next priority. There could be treasure in some of the boxes, she reminded herself. She wasn't fooled by the thought. What the boxes were most likely to contain was many, many years worth of accumulated junk.

On previous visits, she and Joan had peeked inside a few boxes and had found nothing even remotely interesting. Of course, now that she wanted one, the old picture frames had suddenly acquired a much higher status in her mind. Shaking her head at her thoughts, she headed into the corner where she thought the frames had been. She was just leaning over what she hoped was the right box when the light went out. A moment later the door blew shut and Janet found herself alone in the dark.

Chapter 9

"Hello? Stuart? Can you hear me?" she called, not daring to move in the cluttered room.

Her words seemed to echo around the space. She heard a noise from behind her and looked around, but couldn't see anything. Her eyes were struggling to adjust to the darkness when the door suddenly swung open.

"Janet? Are you okay?" Stuart called from the doorway. He reached out and switched the light back on.

"I'm fine," Janet told him. "But I don't know what happened."

"I told you before, there's a ghost in the carriage house," Stuart replied. "He or she is harmless enough, but I can't tell you how many times the ghost has turned off the lights and shut me in here."

"I'm just glad you were around to rescue me," Janet said. She quickly bent down and grabbed the first frame she touched. "I'm sure this will do," she said without even looking at it. She nearly ran out the door and back into the autumn sunshine, with Stuart trailing behind her.

"Are you sure you're okay?" he asked, his face full of concern.

"I'm fine," she said, taking a deep breath. "Just a little spooked, that's all."

Stuart laughed. "I've learned to always take a torch in the carriage house with me," he told her. "Then if the lights go out, I can still find the door."

"That's good advice," Janet said. "I'll try to remember it."

Back in the house, she spent a few minutes taking apart and cleaning the dusty picture frame. It seemed as if it had never been used. The photo behind the glass was merely a display photo. Janet slipped her price list into the frame and then put it all back together.

"That looks lovely, though I say it myself," she said as she stood the photo frame in the centre of her display. "And you shouldn't be so frightened by a gust of wind that you're talking to yourself," she added. She wasn't entirely sure how the wind had managed to switch off the light before it pushed the door shut, but that was the only logical explanation.

"Of course you still can't explain the shouting in your bedroom every full moon," she reminded herself.

"Janet? To whom are you speaking?"

Janet flushed as she spun around. Joan and Michael were standing in the sitting room, their arms full of shopping bags.

"I've just finished," she said quickly. "I hope you like the display."

Joan gave her a funny look, but then walked further into the room to take a look. "Actually, it looks very nice," she said after a moment.

"I'm just going to take these bags through to the kitchen," Michael said.

"Oh, of course," Joan said. She followed Michael into the corridor, leaving Janet to fuss over the table for a while longer. Finally deciding that it was as good as it was going to get, she followed her sister into the kitchen.

Michael was sitting at the table with a cup of tea while Joan unpacked the shopping. Janet was very tempted to fix her own tea and join Michael, but she knew Joan wouldn't approve. Instead, she opened the nearest bag and began unpacking it.

"I hope I got enough of everything," Joan said fretfully.

"I'm sure there's plenty," Janet said soothingly. "What are we having for dinner tonight?"

"I thought I'd made a beef stew," Joan told her. "I'll make enough for us, and for the Stones and the Harrisons as well. We can freeze whatever isn't eaten tonight and have it next week when the house is ours again."

"That sounds good," Janet said. "I'll just go out and cut some flowers for the table. I probably should refresh the flowers in both guest rooms as well, don't you think?"

Joan looked at her for a moment and then frowned. "I don't know," she said after a moment. "It seems like we ought to, but both sets of guests said they didn't need their rooms making up while they were here. Maybe we should give them their privacy."

"Surely just changing out their flowers isn't invading their privacy," Janet said. She was excited at the thought of having a peek in each of the rooms now and she was determined to convince Joan to let her do so.

"I suppose not," Joan said, clearly uncertain. "You should make up the vases down here and then just take them up and switch them for the ones that are already in place. That way you only have to spend a minute or two in each room."

"I'll do that," Janet replied. "But first I need to cut some flowers."

She headed out into the garden with a spring in her step. Changing out the flowers wasn't snooping, she told herself. And if she happened to look around a tiny little bit while she was in the rooms, well, that was only to be expected, surely. She shook her head at her own sorry attempts to justify her own nosiness, but now that she'd had the idea, she wasn't going to change her mind.

It only took a few minutes to cut a sufficient number of flowers for the three vases she wanted to fill. Even though it was autumn, their gardens were still full of beautiful flowering plants and Janet was grateful again for Stuart and all of his hard work. Eventually the flowers would fade and she'd have to start buying flowers for the house, but for now she was happy to enjoy their own bounty.

Back in the kitchen, Janet filled a vase and put it in the centre of the dining room table. Then she filled two smaller vases and carried them carefully upstairs.

"Remember, just change out the vases and leave," Joan called after her as she headed for the stairs. "We don't want to anger our guests."

"I know," Janet shouted back, already wondering what she might find in each room.

When she got upstairs, she stood for a moment wondering what to do. She had a vase in each hand and no way to pull out her keys to open the door.

"Well, you didn't think this through, did you?" she asked herself. Shaking her head at herself, she put the vases down on the floor and dug out her keys. She decided to start with the west room, being more curious about the Stones than the Harrisons.

Putting the key in the lock, she turned it slowly and quietly and then laughed out loud at herself. "No one is home," she reminded herself, laughing again when she realised she was whispering.

The smell of alcohol hit her nose as the door swung open. She frowned and switched on the light. The room was far tidier than she'd expected it to be. A quick glance revealed that the smell was coming from an empty wine bottle in the small bin in the corner of the room. While there were a few things scattered around the room, it appeared to be fairly well organised clutter. She peeked into the bathroom and found that it too was being neatly kept.

Janet picked up the vase of half-dead flowers from the side table and replaced it with the fresh ones. Clearly no one had thought to add water to the original vase and the flowers had suffered for it. With the vase in hand, she walked quickly around the room, hoping to spot something interesting, but having no real idea of what she was looking for.

In any event, she was disappointed to find nothing more than the sort of things she ought to have expected. There were a few tissues in one corner, a half-empty wine glass on the bedside table and a scribbled note on the desk with the phone number for WTC Antiques on it.

Feeling disappointed, she walked out and locked the door

behind herself. The east room was almost more disappointing. Aside from two suitcases which were closed up tightly and sitting in the corner of the room, the east room might have been unoccupied. There wasn't a single thing out of place. The bin was empty and there weren't even any toiletries perched on the bathroom sink. Janet swapped the existing vase for the new one, noting that the flowers looked healthy and that someone had obviously been keeping the water topped up.

With nothing to see, she returned to the hallway and locked the room. Carrying the two vases, she made her way back down to the kitchen to empty them.

"Well, what did you find out?" Joan demanded as Janet walked into the kitchen.

"I just changed out the vases. I didn't snoop," Janet said indignantly.

"Of course you did," Joan replied. "But really, what did you find out?"

"Nothing," Janet said with a sigh. "The Stones are much tidier than I expected and the Harrisons have left their room looking almost unoccupied."

Michael chuckled from his seat at the table. "You sound so disappointed," he explained when Janet looked at him. "I would have thought you'd be pleased to have guests who are tidy."

"I suppose I am," Janet said. "I just can't help but feel like the Stones and William Chalmers are up to something they shouldn't be, that's all."

Michael frowned. "I don't much like the man," he told her. "But what do you think he might be doing?"

"William has some sort of art studio in the back room of his shop," Janet explained. "I think they might be making art forgeries."

Michael raised an eyebrow. "Art forgeries? Well, I suppose anything is possible."

Before Janet could reply they all heard the approaching footsteps.

"I know we said we'd eat elsewhere," Nancy said as she appeared in the kitchen doorway. "But we've come back with

Mildred and Harold and we'd love to have dinner here if we may. Whatever you're making smells wonderful."

Joan smiled. "It's beef stew," she told the woman. "And there's plenty for everyone. It should be ready in about half an hour."

"Good, I'll tell the others," she said. She turned and walked away.

"I suppose I should get out of your way, then," Michael said, clearly reluctantly.

"Oh, do stay for dinner," Joan suggested. "We'll feed the guests first, if that's okay, and then we can have dinner ourselves."

"Don't mind if I do," Michael said happily.

Janet made a salad and mixed up dressing while Michael tried to help with everything and mostly got in the way. When the guests came down, Janet took care of getting them drinks while Michael started serving the food.

The guests all seemed quite subdued, and once everyone had been served, Janet couldn't help but comment on it.

"I do hope everyone is okay," she said casually. "You all seem a bit down this evening."

"I'm just so sad that we're leaving in the morning," Nancy said. "We've had such a lovely time and made such wonderful new friends."

"But we'll keep in touch," Mildred said firmly. "And maybe the Markhams will be able to accommodate us again one day soon."

"Oh, I'd love that," Nancy cooed.

"There they go, spending money again," George grumbled good-naturedly to Harold.

"Hm, I wasn't listening," Harold said. "Don't tell me Mildred is going on about that holiday in Paris again."

"I wasn't," Mildred said. "But now that you mention it, we really should all go on holiday to Paris. It's lovely this time of year."

Harold rolled his eyes. "Is it time for the sweets yet?" he asked Janet, passing her his empty plate.

"I'll just go and see if Joan has it on plates yet," she said.

In the kitchen, Joan did indeed have the jam roly poly ready to go. Janet took the tray with the four plates and Michael followed with both cream and custard to give the guests their choice.

"We'll be leaving quite early in the morning," Nancy told Janet as Janet poured tea and coffee. "If you don't mind, we'd love breakfast at seven, but if it's too much bother, just leave it. We can stop somewhere on our way home."

"It's no bother," Janet lied with a smile. "What about you two?" she asked Mildred. "Do you want breakfast at seven as well?"

"Yeah, I suppose that'll work," Harold grunted.

"Now we're off to the pub," George said. "Apparently there's one quite nearby."

Janet carried all of the plates into the kitchen, where Joan was spooning up generous servings of stew for themselves and Michael.

"They all want breakfast at seven," Janet said, watching the happy look on her sister's face fade.

"Seven?" Joan echoed.

"That's what they said," Janet told her. "But they'll probably be late."

Joan made a face. "They'd better not be," she muttered under the breath.

"We'll have an early night," Michael said. "There's nothing on telly anyway."

Joan smiled faintly. "This was all my idea." Janet heard her say to herself as she went back to serving up their dinner. Janet couldn't help but smile at the thought that she'd been thinking herself.

Dinner was delicious, and Janet was surprised that the guests were back from the pub before they'd finished off the last of the jam roly poly.

"We only had just one drink," Mildred said as Janet walked into the sitting room when she heard their voices. "We all have a lot to do tomorrow, you see."

The four guests made their way upstairs, leaving Janet and Joan to finish tidying the kitchen and then have an early night themselves. Janet headed upstairs as soon as she'd helped Joan with the few breakfast preparations they could do the night before, leaving her sister with Michael.

In her room, Janet read for a short while and then switched off the light. She fell into a dreamless sleep, waking at six and wondering for a moment why she'd set such an early alarm. After a quick shower, she dressed and headed down to the kitchen to help Joan.

Joan had all of the preparations done and was just waiting for the guests to arrive to actually start cooking. The sisters sipped coffee while they waited. At quarter past seven, Janet began to feel cross.

"They said seven," she told Joan. "And actually, I haven't even heard their showers running yet."

"Maybe we just can't hear them in here," Joan said. "Or maybe they aren't bothering with showers as they're travelling today. Or maybe they've changed their mind and they're all lying in."

Before Janet could reply, they heard the front door bell.

"Did you invite Michael for breakfast?" Janet asked as she got to her feet.

"No, and he's said many times that he isn't an early riser," Joan replied. She stood up as well and the sisters walked quickly to the front door.

"If it's a potential guest, tell them no," Joan hissed to Janet as she reached the door.

Janet swallowed a smile at the words and then pulled the door open.

"Constable Parsons? What brings you here?"

Chapter 10

The young man smiled. "Mr. Chalmers has some concerns about some of your guests," he told Janet, gesturing towards the man who was standing behind him looking miserable.

"But they're his cousins," Janet replied.

"Not the Stones," William growled. "The Harrisons."

"They haven't come down for breakfast yet," Joan told their visitors.

Janet took a step backwards. "Please come in," she invited them. "They asked us to have breakfast ready for seven, but they haven't actually come down yet."

"They're long gone," William told her. "And you'll be lucky if they didn't take a few of your more portable valuables with them."

Janet and Joan both gasped.

"Now, now, let's not start throwing unsubstantiated accusations around," the young policeman said sternly. "Could one of you check to see if your guests are still here, please?" he asked the sisters.

"I'll go," Janet volunteered quickly. She dashed out of the room before Joan could argue. With her keys in hand, she approached the door to the east room. She knocked quietly, fully expecting the Harrisons to answer the door. When they didn't, she knocked again, more loudly. After a third attempt, she tried the knob. The door opened under her hand.

She pushed it open and stuck her head inside the room. It appeared to be empty.

"Please don't touch anything," Robert said from behind her.

Janet jumped. She'd been so focussed on what she was doing that she hadn't heard him coming up the stairs.

"They seem to have gone," she said.

The only thing out of place in the room was a small pink envelope that was sitting on the table by the door. Someone had written "Joan and Janet" in neat handwriting on it. Without thinking, Janet reached for it.

"Ah, I'd rather you didn't touch that," Robert said. "Or anything else in here. We may well have to have the whole room dusted for fingerprints."

"But what happened?" Janet asked.

"We can talk downstairs," the man told her.

As they exited the room, Janet gestured towards the west room. "We should probably see what's keeping them," she said. "They were meant to be at breakfast at seven as well."

"I suspect they've also gone," Robert replied. "And we'll be wanting to dust that for prints as well."

Janet just stared at him for a moment and then shook her head. "I knew there was something funny going on," she exclaimed.

Back in the sitting room, Joan was fussing over William Chalmers.

"I'm sure Robert will sort everything out," she was saying. "You should have a cup of tea and try to calm down."

"I've worked so hard," he replied. "Everything was going so well. First Harold showed up and tried to ruin everything and then, when I thought that problem was all sorted out, the bloo, er, blasted Harrisons come in and ruin my life."

"Exactly what happened?" Janet asked, looking from William to Robert and back again.

William buried his head in his hands. "I can't talk," he moaned from behind them.

"And I can't tell you much," Robert said. "We're still investigating exactly what happened, but I'll tell you the basics, at least, in exchange for your cooperation with our investigation."

The sisters nodded. Janet reckoned they had little choice but to cooperate, and she was dying to hear the story.

"Firstly, Mr. and Mrs. Stone were former business associates of Mr. Chalmers," Robert explained.

"They were the ones behind the mislabeled things at my last store," William said. "I didn't realise what they were up to until it was too late, or I would have stopped them. We all ended up spending time in prison, even though none of it was my fault."

"Anyway, we were concerned about their visiting with Mr. Chalmers, and it seems our concern was warranted," Robert continued.

"I told you, they were blackmailing me. I've worked hard to achieve a certain social standing here in Doveby Dale and if the good people of the village discovered that I have a criminal record, that would ruin everything. Harold and Mildred threatened to tell everyone about my past if I didn't help them out."

"Help them out how?" Janet asked, ignoring the "keep quiet" look from her sister.

"They still had some questionable merchandise from our London operation," William explained. "They wanted me to sell it in my shop here. I didn't feel as if I had any choice but to agree."

Janet pressed her lips together before she said something she shouldn't.

"There are always choices," Joan said firmly, putting Janet's thoughts into words.

"Yes, I suppose," William agreed with a sigh. "But then Mildred had this great idea. She'd met the Harrisons here and decided that they were the perfect customers for our slightly less than perfect antiques."

"Fakes," Joan said.

"Not exactly fakes," William protested. "Just not exactly as rare and valuable they appeared."

"So they befriended the Harrisons and then tried to get them to buy the worthless stuff?" Janet asked.

"Yes," William said quietly. "I didn't have anything to do with it."

"Except that they conducted their business in your premises," Robert pointed out.

"Yes, well, just that," William muttered.

"So what happened next?" Janet demanded.

"Harold told them that he had a few little pieces he wanted to get rid of and that he could sell them cheap if they were never formally part of the stock in my store. He brought them all to the shop yesterday and showed them to the Harrisons, who agreed to buy the lot. Apparently the Harrisons had a small van and they were all going to meet at eight this morning at my shop to load it up."

"And then?" Joan asked eagerly. Janet smiled to herself. She wasn't the only Markham sister who was just a little bit nosy.

"Mildred rang me at just before six," William said sadly. "She and Harold had just woken up and they were sure they'd been drugged. She told me to check the shop. When I got there, several of my most valuable pieces were missing."

"What makes you think the Harrisons took them?" Janet asked.

"Mildred said she and Harold stopped in the Harrisons' room for a drink last night before bed. That's the last thing she remembers before around half five this morning. Harold's keys were missing. Unfortunately, I'd given Harold a key to the shop so that he could get in this morning. I didn't want to be there for the sale."

"So where is everyone now?" Janet asked.

"Mildred and Harold took off," William said. "They packed their things and snuck away from Doveby Dale before they rang me."

"We're hoping to catch up with them," Robert added. "We have quite a few questions for them."

"But they didn't actually do anything wrong in the end," William pointed out. "The Harrisons didn't buy anything from them."

"We'd still like to speak to them," Robert said sternly.

"And the Harrisons?" Janet asked.

"We're trying to work out what time they left and what direction they were headed," Robert told her. "We're pretty sure they were gone from here before midnight, so they have a good head start. We're pretty certain we know who they really are, but their fingerprints will tell us for sure."

"They seemed like such a nice couple," Janet mused.

William laughed bitterly.

"But what were you doing with all those painting things in your back room?" Janet asked. As soon as the words were out of her mouth, she regretted asking. Joan frowned at her.

William looked at the ground and then up at her. "I was trying out a bit of painting," he told her. "It's something I've always wanted to do, but never tried. I thought maybe I could try putting a few of my paintings in my shop, if they were good enough." He sighed deeply. "Now I just have to hope my insurance will cover the losses from what the Harrisons stole, or I'll be out of business after less than a week."

So our first set of guests weren't exactly what we were expecting, Bessie. I suppose you mustn't judge a book by its cover.

The police found the Stones fairly easily but couldn't charge them with anything. William got rid of all of the questionable antiques and I think Joan and I (and you) are the only ones who heard the whole story.

Most of Doveby Dale is quite sympathetic towards poor William after the robbery, and his shop has been noticeably busier lately. It seems as if everyone is willing to look past his difficult personality in an effort to support him after his misfortune. I will say that he appears to be working hard at being nicer as well.

As far as the police can determine, the Harrisons have vanished completely. The note they left in their room was simply a card apologising for not saying goodbye properly and thanking us for a lovely stay. We aren't sure now if they really did used to stay at Doveby House in the past or not. It is difficult to know what to believe, though they seemed like lovely people.

I've taken to calling the whole sorry affair "The Chalmers Case." Joan prefers to not talk about it at all. We've agreed to take a short break from having guests, just until early next month. I think Joan is starting to reconsider this whole bed and breakfast thing. I haven't told her, but I quite enjoyed the chaos!

Do come and visit, won't you? We'd love to see you again.

With all good wishes,

Janet Markham

P.S. Just yesterday a very large parcel was delivered. It was the painting I'd fallen in love with from William's shop. The card attached said "Just a little something to keep me in your thoughts, Edward." Of course Joan said I mustn't keep such an expensive present from a man I barely know, but the only phone number I have for him has suddenly been disconnected, so I can't tell him that. For now I've hung it in my bedroom and it looks even better than I imagined it would.

Glossary of Terms

- **bin** — trash can
- **biscuits** — cookies
- **booking** — reservation
- **boot** — trunk (of a car)
- **car park** — parking lot
- **chemist** — pharmacist
- **cuppa** — cup of tea (informal)
- **dear** — costly or expensive
- **fizzy drink** — carbonated beverage (pop or soda)
- **fortnight** — two weeks
- **high street** — the main shopping street in a town or village
- **holiday** — vacation
- **jumper** — sweater
- **letting** — renting
- **lie in** — sleep late
- **midday** — noon
- **pavement** — sidewalk
- **plug socket** — electrical outlet
- **pudding** — dessert

- **queue** — line
- **saloon car** — sedan
- **shopping trolley** — shopping cart
- **telly** — television
- **till** — check-out (in a grocery store, for example)
- **torch** — flashlight

Other Notes

In the UK dates are written day, month, year rather than month, day, year as in the US. (May 5, 2015 would be written 5 May 2015, for example.)

When describing property with more than one level, the lowest level (assuming there is no basement; very few UK houses have basements) is the "ground floor," and the next floor up is the "first floor" and so on. In the US, the lowest floor is usually the "first floor" and up from there.

When telling time, half six is the English equivalent of six thirty.

Pensioners are people who are old enough to be collecting a retirement pension. (In the US they are generally referred to as "senior citizens."

A "full English breakfast" generally consists of bacon, sausage, eggs, grilled or fried tomatoes, fried potatoes, fried mushrooms and baked beans served with toast.

A semi-detached house is one that is joined to another house by a common center wall. In the US they are generally called duplexes. In the UK the two properties would be sold individually as totally separate entities.

The Donaldson Case

A MARKHAM SISTERS COZY MYSTERY NOVELLA

Created with Vellum

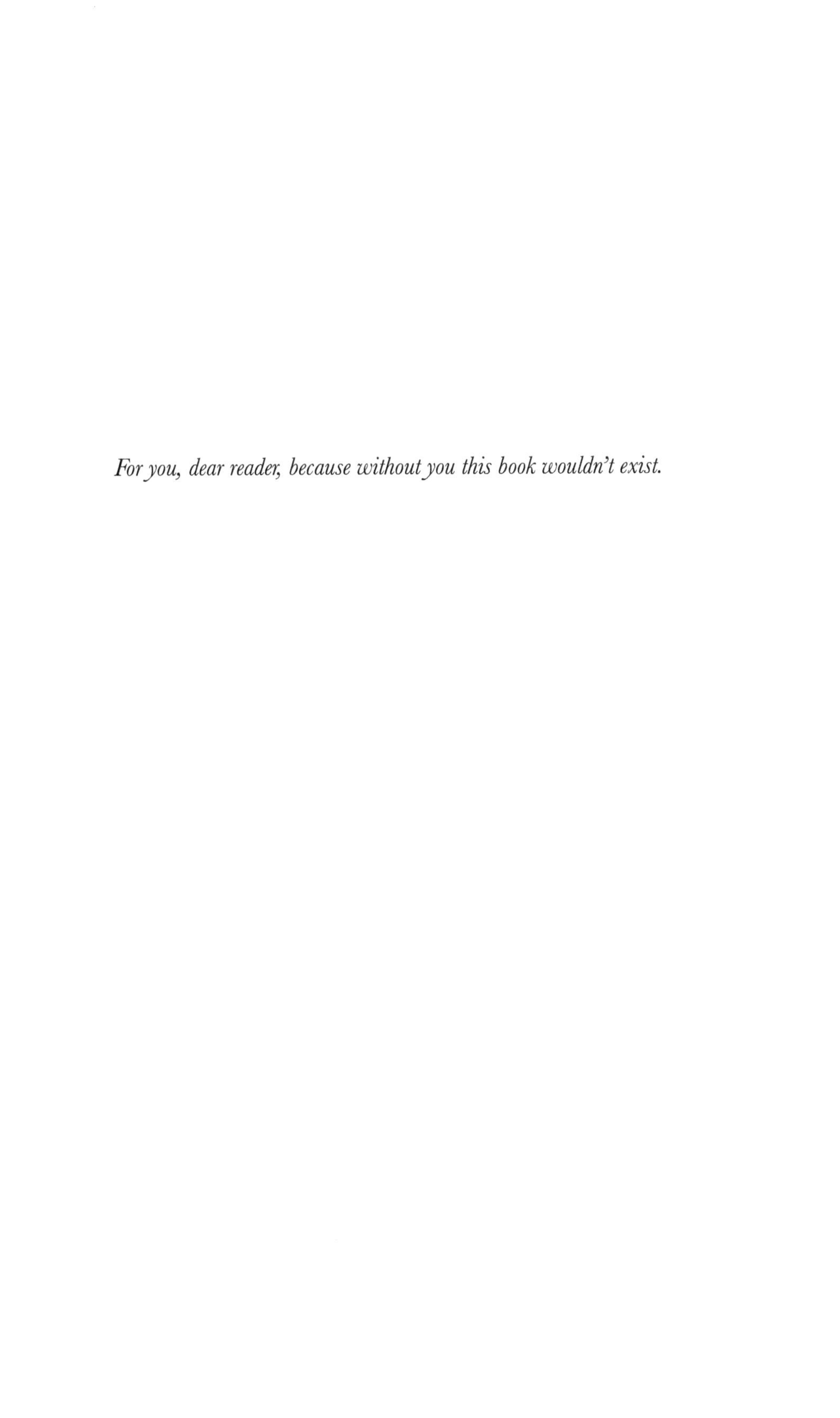

For you, dear reader, because without you this book wouldn't exist.

Acknowledgments

There are so many people who deserve thanks for their efforts.

Firstly, I want to thank my readers. You are the reason I keep doing this, even when I'd rather be eating chocolate in front of the television. (Which is what hubby thinks I do all day, anyway.)

I need to (always) thank my editor, Denise, who puts up with all my grammar foibles and still keeps editing!

My beta readers for this series, Charlene and Janice, are a huge help in so many ways. I always get great feedback from them both and truly enjoy the fact that we've become friends over the course of many books.

I'd love to hear from you. My contact details are in the back of the book. Thank you for your continued support.

Author's Note

I love to write (that may be obvious), and I love every book, story and novella I've ever written, even the really terrible stuff I wrote years ago and have buried in the bottom of my closet! There is something special about this series, though. I'm really enjoying spending time with the Markham sisters.

Maybe it's because I have a sister who is very close in age to myself, so I'm having fun with the relationship between Joan and Janet. It might be the idea that they're doing something totally different with their lives in their "retirement" years. Or maybe it's just because I have so many ideas for them going forward and I can't wait to get them written.

Whatever, welcome to the fourth novella in the series. I suggest you read them in (alphabetical) order, but you don't have to; each novella should stand on its own. The Markham sisters first made their appearance in *Aunt Bessie Decides*, the fourth book in my Isle of Man Cozy Mysteries series.

Since then, Janet (the younger sister) has stayed in touch with Bessie, and each novella opens and closes with parts of Janet's letters to her new friend on the Isle of Man. I use the excerpts from the letters as a way to start and finish each story; you absolutely do not have to read the Bessie books to enjoy this series.

Because of the setting of the story, I have used English spellings and terms. In the back of the book is a glossary and some notes designed to help readers outside the UK with terms that might be unfamiliar. The longer I live in the US, the greater the likelihood of Americanisms sneaking into the text, although I do try to eliminate them.

This is a work of fiction and all of the characters are fictional creations. Any resemblance that they may share with any real person, living or dead, is entirely coincidental. The sisters live in a fictional village in Derbyshire. Although some shops or business may bear some resemblance to real-life businesses, that is also coincidental.

Please feel free to get in touch with any comments, questions, or concerns. I have a monthly newsletter that provides updates on new releases. All of the information about subscribing or getting in touch is available on the About the Author page at the back of the book.

12 November 1998

Dearest Bessie,

Your recent holiday sounds like it was more stressful than your everyday life. I'm glad you finally managed to get away for a few days, although I can't imagine it was very restful, what with the murder and all.

You know that you are always welcome here, if you feel the need for a break. While all manner of strange things seem to go on around here, we've yet to find any dead bodies.

Speaking of strange things, we recently found another hidden panel, which led to an interesting discovery. Joan had her own little excitement early in the month as well, as Michael was very nearly arrested! Suddenly my sister was the one who wanted to play detective, which was quite unusual.

Chapter 1

"I suppose so," Janet said reluctantly, sliding a bite of her apple crumble around on the plate. Her favourite pudding didn't taste quite as nice now that it was obvious that her sister was using it as a bribe.

"We said we'd leave it a fortnight after our last guests left to talk about welcoming more guests," Joan reminded her sister. "That was three weeks ago."

Janet sighed. She knew Joan was right. They'd bought the bed and breakfast with the idea of actually trying to run the business, even if the idea had been almost all Joan's. Thus far, however, the guests they'd welcomed hadn't exactly been ideal, and Janet wasn't sure she wanted to see who else fate might send them.

"I've had a lovely letter of enquiry from a married couple that sound ideal," Joan told her. "They're both artists and they're looking for a quiet getaway so they can spend some time on their art."

Janet narrowed her eyes. "You're hoping they'll do a couple of paintings of the local area for our guest rooms, aren't you?" she asked.

Joan flushed. "We don't really want to spend the money right now," she defended herself. "And those guest rooms really need some artwork. It did cross my mind that the Nicholsons might use their time here to create exactly what we're looking for to put in those rooms, but that isn't the only reason I think we should accommodate them."

"So what else are you thinking?" Janet demanded.

"Just that we should be booking guests on a regular basis. Word seems to be getting out that we aren't taking guests and requests have almost stopped. If we're going to run this place properly, we need people staying regularly."

Janet thought carefully about her answer. She'd been perfectly content, after she and Joan had retired from teaching the previous year, to rest, relax, and travel. It was Joan who'd suggested that they spend a small inheritance and the proceeds from the sale of their previous home on Doveby House, a beautiful seventeenth-century manor house in the small village of Doveby Dale. Janet hadn't known then that her sister had been harbouring a secret desire to own her own bed and breakfast for her entire life. Now that Janet did know that, she felt as if she couldn't stand in the way of her sister's dream, even if the dream was not one that she shared with Joan.

"I suppose the Nicholsons can't be any worse than our previous guests," Janet muttered. "Go ahead and tell them they can come."

"Thank you," Joan said. "I expect they'll be here on Monday. Maybe you can get the library finished by then?"

Janet finished her last bite of apple crumble, swallowing a sigh with it. "I'll get back to work now," she told her sister as she got up from the table. "Unless you need my help with the washing up?"

"No, you go and get to work. I'll just load up the dishwasher with everything."

Janet nodded resignedly. The library was her favourite room in the house and she loved spending time in it. What she didn't love was cleaning it, and that was what needed doing. She'd been slowly working her way around the room, taking row after row of books from the shelves and cleaning each shelf. While she was looking forward to classifying and organising the books themselves, she wasn't allowing herself to start that project until the basic cleaning was done.

Inside the small room, she shut the door behind her and faced the far wall. She'd completed two walls previously and was nearly finished with the third. For a while she'd made good progress, but once their latest set of guests had left, she'd spent more time reading and relaxing than cleaning and tidying. Now she headed for the last tall section on the wall and began to remove the books from the top shelf. Humming softly to herself, she worked as rapidly as she could, doing a quick but mostly thorough job.

About halfway down the wall, when she cleared yet another shelf, she felt a rush of excitement. This section of shelves against the wall had a small inset panel that looked identical to the one she'd found at the opposite end of that wall. She felt her way around the panel, but couldn't find a way to open it. When she knocked on it, she could hear what she was certain was a hollow sound. After trying to slide the panel every which way and failing, she sat down at the desk and stared at the wall.

There has to be a way to open that panel, she told herself.

Joan had suggested, when Janet had found the previous one, that the panels were simply access points for power cables that needed to reach plug sockets behind the shelves. While it was a logical explanation, Janet wasn't fond of it at all. In her mind, the panels must have been put in place to hide something valuable.

"Why do I hear knocking?" Joan asked as she pushed the door open.

Janet jumped to her feet. "I found another of those panels at this end," she told her sister.

"So?"

"So, I still think they must be hiding something."

Joan and Janet both looked at the small picture in the middle of one of the shelves full of books. It was barely noticeable with all of the books around it, but behind it was a small wall safe. Unfortunately, the sisters didn't have the combination to the safe.

Their first paying guest, Edward Bennett, had known all about the safe. When he was getting ready to leave, he'd told Janet that he was some sort of government agent who had occasionally sent people to Doveby House as a safe house. He'd given Janet a combination, but when she tried it, it didn't open the safe. Janet still talked to Edward once in a while, when he rang her, but she'd not yet managed to get the proper combination from him.

"We've no reason to think Mrs. Appleton was hiding anything," Joan said. The sisters had purchased Doveby House from Margaret Appleton's estate after she disinherited her son and left everything to a local charity. The sisters had already discovered that "Maggie" was a colourful character and Janet believed that she had been capable of just about anything.

"We've every reason to think she was hiding things," Janet replied. "She had a hidden safe, after all, and she worked for Edward in some capacity."

"You only have Edward's word for that," Joan pointed out.

Janet sighed. Joan was right. She'd believed everything the man had told her when he was leaving, but now, as time went on, she found herself doubting him more and more.

"I wish I could work out how to open the panel," Janet said, changing the subject.

"It can't be difficult," Joan said. "It probably just slides up or down or something."

"I tried sliding it," Janet told her. "And pushing it and pulling it and just about every other thing."

Joan shrugged and crossed the room. "You never got the other one open, did you?"

"No. But I haven't given up hope on that one, either."

Joan tapped lightly on the small panel and then on the wood around it. "It does sound different," she admitted. "Almost as if it's hollow behind the panel. But that makes sense if it's removable for access."

"I'll let you invite a hundred guests if you can get the stupid thing open," Janet said.

Joan grinned. "There's an interesting challenge." She pushed on the panel and then tried sliding it in every direction. "It seems to move slightly, but not enough," she told Janet after a moment.

"I think there was more movement in the one on the other end," Janet said.

"While we have a minute, let me have a look at that one," Joan suggested.

Janet quickly removed all the books from the middle shelf at the other end of the wall. The panel was still there and when Janet pushed on it, it still didn't open.

Joan walked over and took a good look. "It does move more than the one on the other end," she agreed with Janet after a moment. "It really feels as if it should slide up or down."

"I know. I spent ages trying to get it to do just that when I found it. But then we had guests arriving and I had to work on the cleaning, so I left it."

The sound of their phone ringing interrupted the conversation. Joan went out to answer it while Janet went back to trying to work out how to remove the hidden panels.

"After our chat over lunch, I rang the Nicholsons," Joan told Janet when she walked back into the library a few minutes later. "I left a message on their answer phone. That was them ringing back."

"Have they decided to try the Lake District instead?" Janet asked hopefully.

Joan smiled. "No, they'll be here on Monday for a week-long stay. They'll be having breakfast with us every morning, but prefer to get their evening meals out."

"Well, I suppose that's something," Janet said, trying to keep her tone light.

"I didn't enjoy having guests for dinner," Joan told her. "I won't be suggesting it to guests in the future. It was only because our last guests requested it specially that I agreed."

"So what do you know about our new guests?" Janet asked.

"I think I told you just about everything already. They're a married couple called Fred and Molly Nicholson, and apparently they are both artists. The letter they sent requesting a room said that they were hoping for something of a spiritual retreat."

"Did they say what sort of art they do? I mean, I know you're hoping that they will paint something amazing for our guest rooms, but maybe they do pottery or sculpture or something."

"They didn't say," Joan replied. "And I didn't really think about it."

Janet grinned to herself. Her sister had been so focussed on the idea of getting artwork for the guest rooms that she didn't think the whole thing through. The next week promised to be quite interesting, even if it might not be enjoyable.

"Now let's sort out these panels so you can get back to work on the cleaning," Joan said. She crossed to the panel that Janet had found first and pushed on it firmly.

"There's more movement in the top left corner than anywhere else," she told Janet.

Janet watched eagerly as Joan pushed on the corner and then tried to slide the panel. After a moment, the panel slowly began to slide sideways.

"You've done it," Janet gasped.

"That means we can have a hundred guests," Joan reminded her.

"That was for the other panel," Janet said quickly.

Joan laughed and then crossed to the other panel. Using the same technique, she pushed and slid and wiggled the panel. Nothing seemed to work.

"This one is stuck," she announced after a moment. "But I'm sure it doesn't matter in the slightest. They're bound to be nothing but plug socket access points."

Janet walked over to the now opened panel and glanced inside. "It's dark back there," she told Joan.

"Where's the nearest torch?" Joan asked.

Janet dug one out of the desk drawer and aimed the light into the space. "It's not an access panel," she told her sister excitedly. "It's a small storage space."

"Is there anything in it?"

"Just this," Janet said, reaching into the space. She pulled out the oddly-shaped object and then turned and showed it to her sister.

"It's a piggy bank," Joan said.

"It's a very unusual piggy bank," Janet replied. The small, white ceramic bank appeared to have been hand painted. There were brightly coloured blue flowers on each side of it, and the pig had enormous blue eyes.

"It has ridiculous eyelashes," Joan said.

Janet looked it over and then laughed. "It's rather, um, eccentric, but I think I love it."

"I'm glad you do. I think I hate it."

"Piggy can live in my room," Janet replied.

"You're welcome to her, but maybe not what's inside," Joan said.

Janet laughed. "I was so excited to find her, I didn't even think about what might be inside." She gave the pig a gentle shake and was rewarded by a jingling sound.

"Sounds like there is definitely something in there."

"I just hope we don't have to break Piggy to get it out," Janet said worriedly. She turned the pig around in her hands and was relieved to find a small black rubber stopper in the bottom of the figure.

"You can break it as far as I'm concerned," Joan said dryly.

Janet ignored her as she wiggled the stopper to try to get it out. After a minute, she gave up. "We need something to pry this open with," she said. "Something that won't break Piggy."

The pair went into the kitchen. Janet put the bank on the counter and the sisters dug around in drawers, looking for something that might work to remove the stopper. Janet tried sliding a knife around the edges of the stopper, but it did nothing but move it around.

"Maybe some sort of screwdriver or something?" Janet suggested.

"I think all the tools are in the carriage house," Joan told her.

Janet grabbed Piggy and the sisters quickly headed out to the carriage house, both equally eager to open the piggy bank and see what they'd found.

Chapter 2

The door to the carriage house was open when the sisters reached it.

"Hello?" Janet called as she squinted into the dimly lit building.

"Hello," a voice called back.

Janet smiled as she recognised the voice of their neighbour from the semi-detached house across the street. Stuart Long looked after the grounds of Doveby House for the sisters. He was a retired gardener who loved working with plants and flowers. The sisters paid him a nominal sum for a huge amount of work and supplemented the payments with as much tea as the man could drink.

Stuart used the carriage house for storing the many garden implements that he seemed to need. He kept his things in a very tidy pile by the door. The rest of the carriage house was still the same mess that the previous owner had left. Janet planned to tackle it once she'd finished with the library, but now, as she looked at the piles of haphazardly stacked boxes, she didn't feel in any rush to get started on the job.

"Ah, Stuart, how are you doing?" Joan asked.

"I'm fine, thanks, how are you?"

"We're well," Joan told him. "But we found this piggy bank and we're anxious to get it open."

"That's easy enough," Stuart said. "He looks as if he'll smash without any difficulty."

Janet shook her head. "I don't want to smash her," she said. "There's a rubber stopper in the bottom of her. We need to find a way to remove it."

She handed the bank to Stuart, who turned it over in his hands. "I see," he said after a moment. "Let me see what I have here that might pry that out."

Janet watched anxiously as he tried a couple of different things, but nothing seemed to shift the stubborn stopper.

"Are you sure you don't want to just break it open?" he asked, giving the pig a shake. "There's definitely something in there."

"I really don't want to break her," Janet said. "I quite like her."

Stuart's look suggested that he didn't agree with Janet's opinion of the pig, but he turned it over again and went back to work on the stopper.

"Ah, there you go you little bug…, um, ahem, that is, I think I've got it," he said a short time later. He held up the troublesome rubber piece and then handed the pig back to Janet.

"One of you should turn it over and shake the contents out," he said, sounding as eager as the sisters to see what was inside.

Janet moved a few boxes into a new pile to make a reasonably flat surface to work on. She shook Piggy gently and grinned.

"Coins," she said as the first few items tumbled out of the bank. "What else would you find in a piggy bank?"

A further shake answered her question for her. "A key," she said excitedly. "I wonder what it's for?"

Stuart looked the small pile of coins and the key and then shrugged. "Nothing too exciting in that lot," he said. "I suppose one or two of the coins could be valuable, but if they were you'd expect them to be kept properly, not in a piggy bank."

"Maybe Maggie Appleton didn't know they were valuable," Janet suggested.

Stuart laughed. "You wouldn't say that if you had known

Maggie. She knew exactly what every single thing she owned was worth to the penny. We used to have long conversations about house prices and she tracked every sale in the village so she had a good idea what Doveby House was worth at all times. If those coins were very valuable, she'd have put them in her safe."

"She had a safe?" Janet asked, pretending she didn't know about the wall safe in the office. She was intrigued to find that Stuart knew about it and she couldn't help by try to find out how he'd come to learn of it.

"She had a big old safe that sat on the floor in the storage closet in the sitting room," Stuart replied. "The charity that inherited the house from her probably took it if it isn't there now."

"It most certainly isn't there now," Janet said, trying to hide her disappointment. "I wonder if this key is for that safe?"

"The safe had a combination lock," Stuart told her. "Maggie let me store a few things in that space once, that's why I know," he explained quickly, answering the question Janet had been about to ask.

"I don't suppose you knew the combination?" Janet asked, wondering if Maggie would have used the same combination for both of her safes.

"No, I certainly didn't," Stuart replied. "But if the safe isn't there anymore, why do you want to know?"

Janet shrugged. "Just curious, I suppose," she said. "Sometimes people use combinations that are made up of numbers from their birthdays and the like, and I just wondered if Maggie Appleton did that, that's all."

"She might have," Stuart replied. "But I never knew the combination, or when her birthday was, either."

"Never mind," Joan interrupted. "Thank you for getting the bank open for us. We'll have to have the coins checked out, but I expect they won't be worth any more than their face value, if they're even worth that."

"They're all foreign," Janet said. She was looking through the small pile. "I'm not even sure what country or countries they're from."

"Maggie loved to travel," Stuart told them. "She probably just threw random leftover coins in the pig when she got back from her travels."

"Probably," Joan agreed.

"And you don't know what the key might be for?" Janet asked, holding it up.

"It's just a key, isn't it? I imagine I could be for just about anything," Stuart replied with a shrug.

Janet took the rubber stopper from Stuart and gently wiggled it back into place in the bottom of the bank. "There, good as new," she said happily. "I think I'll put all my change in her every night. It shouldn't take long for me to fill her up."

"She's going in your room," Joan reminded her as they walked back towards the house.

"Oh, yes," Janet agreed. "I wouldn't dare leave her in the public areas. She might get broken."

"That would be a shame."

Janet could hear the sarcasm in her sister's voice, but she didn't care. There was something sweet and loveable about the odd little piggy, and she was going to give her a good home no matter what Joan thought.

"What about the key?" Janet asked once they were back in their sitting room.

"What about it?" Joan replied. She'd put the handful of coins and the key into her pocket for the walk back to the house; now she pulled them all out and put them on a small side table.

"We should work out what it's for," Janet said. "There are some numbers and letters stamped on it, but they're really hard to read. Maybe it opens another wall safe, one we haven't found yet. Or a safety deposit box at a bank. Or a trapdoor hidden in the floor somewhere."

"Or the back door to the house," Joan added. "Or even the front door. Maybe you should start there before you go on another of your flights of fancy."

"It doesn't look like the front door key," Janet argued as she picked up the key.

"It could be a key to one of the guest rooms, perhaps," Joan suggested.

Janet opened the front door and tried to slip the key into the lock. "It doesn't even come close to fitting," she told her sister happily.

"There are lots more doors you can try," Joan reminded her. "Meanwhile, I'd better get some dinner started. At least we have leftover apple crumble for pudding; I don't have to worry about making that as well."

Janet grinned. "Apple crumble for lunch and dinner? It must be my lucky day."

"I think I'll just do spaghetti Bolognese for tonight, if that's okay?" Joan asked. "It's quick and easy."

"That's fine," Janet agreed. "In the meantime, I'm going to try this key in every door in the house."

"And then you can get back to cleaning the library," Joan suggested.

"Yeah, sure," Janet muttered as she headed towards the stairs. Cleaning the library was much less interesting than investigating the mysterious key. On her way out of the sitting room, she'd grabbed her new piggy bank.

In her room, she took a minute to rearrange the top of her dresser to make room for the new addition. She dug around in her handbag and found a handful of coins, which she dropped inside the bank. "Can't have you getting hungry," she told the little pig. After patting the pig's head gently, she turned to her door.

When the key didn't fit into the keyhole, she felt a rush of relief. It would have been a shame to find that the key Maggie Appleton had gone to all the trouble to hide inside the pig, inside a hidden wall compartment, was simply a spare to one of the bedrooms in the house.

Feeling as if the key was the wrong shape for the internal doors at Doveby House, Janet nevertheless tried it in the locks on the two guest bedrooms. Back downstairs, she tried it in the door to the library itself, as well as in the house's back door and even the French doors that opened off the sunroom. It didn't fit into any of them.

"Did you try the carriage house?" Joan asked when Janet joined her in the kitchen.

"Not yet. I thought I'd try that after dinner. And I'll try it in the small lock on the gate that opens into the back lane, as well."

There was a low fence that ran around the large garden that surrounded Doveby House, with a small gate at the back. While there was a lock on the gate, the sisters didn't have a key for it and neither did Stuart Long.

"It would be good if it opened the gate," Joan said. "I've never wanted to go out that way, but it would be nice to have the option."

Janet grinned. There was something weirdly frustrating about having a gate but being unable to use it, even though, like Joan, she'd never yet actually wanted to get through it.

"I can't help but feel that it's the key to something more important than that gate, though," Janet said.

"That's because you have an overactive imagination," Joan replied. "I'd much rather have a key to the gate than a mystery key taking up space in a drawer."

Janet sighed. Joan was always so boringly practical. Neither sister had ever married and they'd always lived together. Just sometimes Janet wondered what her life might have been like if she'd separated herself from her sister when they'd been younger. Joan was two years older and she'd always seemed to feel responsible for her younger sister, which had allowed Janet to enjoy being less responsible and more whimsical. Perhaps both sisters could have benefitted if they'd lived apart rather than together.

"Anyway, dinner is ready," Joan interrupted her sister's thoughts. "You sit down and I'll serve."

Janet smiled to herself as she sat down at the small kitchen table. As a steaming plate full of spaghetti was put in front of her, she remembered why she'd lived with Joan for all these years. Joan was an excellent cook.

"There's garlic bread," Joan told her, opening the oven.

The smell of melted butter and garlic made Janet's mouth water. The bread was Joan's own homemade loaf, split lengthwise and covered in a very generous layer of butter mixed with garlic and herbs. Joan sliced it into several pieces and Janet grabbed a slice the moment Joan set it on the table.

"This is wonderful," Janet said after her first bite of the crunchy and buttery bread.

"Make sure you leave room for the apple crumble," Joan reminded her.

"I always have room for apple crumble," Janet said with a laugh.

After dinner and crumble, Janet helped her sister load their plates into the dishwasher before heading out into the garden with her key. Although Joan insisted she didn't really care what the key was for, she did follow Janet out into the garden.

"It's a lovely night," Joan said.

"It is," Janet agreed. "It feels far too warm to be early November. Are you going to sit in the garden for a while?"

"I thought I might," Joan replied. "Michael said he might stop over, and I thought I might just wait for him outside. We won't have many more warm nights."

Michael Donaldson lived in the other half of the semi-detached property across the street from Doveby House. He was widower in his sixties, and both sisters had been surprised when he'd begun courting Joan. While Janet had dated extensively in her youth, Joan had been content to focus on her career as a primary schoolteacher, so this was her first experience with dating.

Janet was enjoying watching the relationship between her sister and their handsome neighbour develop slowly. Michael was a retired chemist, and just lately he'd been filling in at the local chemist's shop for a sick colleague. Janet knew that Joan had missed the man when he'd been too busy to stop by and visit.

"He's done working in Doveby Dale, then?" Janet asked.

"He worked until midday today and then a proper substitute arrived to cover until Owen is back on his feet."

Janet nodded. She'd only met Owen Carter a few times when she'd called into the small local chemists for plasters or headache tablets, but he seemed like a nice man. She'd been shocked to hear that he'd needed a rather serious operation at the young age of forty-seven.

"You enjoy the weather, then," Janet said. "I'll just check the carriage house and the back gate."

Joan settled on a bench while Janet made her way towards the carriage house. It really was an unseasonably warm night and Janet decided that she'd join her sister on the bench once she'd tried the key. They'd be stuck indoors soon enough when the winter weather arrived.

The carriage house was locked up tightly. Janet had already compared the key she'd found in Piggy with the actual carriage house key and she knew they were nothing alike, but she tried the mystery key in the lock anyway, mostly to satisfy Joan. It didn't fit.

It wasn't far from there to the back gate, but Janet took her time, enjoying wandering through their gardens. Stuart did an excellent job maintaining the many flowerbeds and grassy areas and keeping the paths neat and tidy. Janet didn't like to think what they'd have to pay someone else if he ever decided he didn't want to help them anymore.

The lock on the gate was rusty and Janet wondered if she'd manage to get the key to fit, even if it was the right key. When she tried the key in the lock, though, it was quickly apparent that the key was much too small for the lock on the gate, rusty or otherwise. She sighed and then turned and headed back towards the house.

As she walked, she saw something over the low fence that had her quickening her pace. When she reached Joan she took a deep breath before she spoke.

"I'm not sure what's going on," she told her sister. "But there are two police cars at Michael's door."

Chapter 3

"I didn't know we had two police cars in Doveby Dale," Joan said after a moment.

"No, I didn't either," Janet agreed. "But what could they want with Michael?"

"Are you sure they're at Michael's? Maybe they are visiting Stuart and Mary," Joan suggested.

"I suppose they could be," Janet admitted. "Although the cars are parked at Michael's end of the street. I couldn't see anyone in either house, though."

"I'd much rather think they're talking to Stuart and Mary than Michael."

"Yes, me, too. And if someone is in trouble, I do hope it's Mary and not Stuart."

Joan nodded. The sisters didn't dislike Stuart's wife, Mary, but they didn't exactly like her either. This was a second marriage for both Stuart and Mary, and Mary seemed to spend a great deal of her time visiting one or another of her three children from her first marriage who were scattered around England. From what they could gather from Stuart, her children appreciated the frequent visits, but their various spouses were less enthusiastic.

Joan and Janet often felt like they'd done little more than say the odd "hello" to the woman. Her regular absences allowed Stuart more time to work in the Doveby House gardens, for which the sisters were grateful, but they also meant that the sisters ended up giving Stuart breakfast, tea breaks and sometimes even evening meals while she was away.

"Perhaps we should take a short stroll around the neighbourhood," Joan suggested now. She stood up from the bench and stretched. "We really haven't been taking nearly enough exercise, have we?"

Janet hid a grin. Joan was trying not to appear nosy, but Janet knew her sister was burning up with curiosity. As that exactly mirrored Janet's own feelings, she didn't argue.

"I was just thinking we should be doing more walking around our lovely neighbourhood," she replied. "Especially on these last few nice nights of autumn."

The sisters linked arms and walked slowly around Doveby House. Although it was highly unlikely that anyone was paying any attention to them, they deliberately strolled the long way around, as if they weren't the least bit interested in what was happening across the road. They walked slowly down the path at the front of their property, trying hard to not to stare at the two police cars that were still in place.

"Where to now?" Janet whispered as they reached the corner where their short cul-de-sac met a slightly busier road.

"I suppose we could walk up towards the main road," Joan suggested. "There's a pavement."

And that path would take them behind the semi-detached properties, perhaps affording them a look in their back windows.

They'd only just crossed the road when they heard a door opening. Janet gasped as she realised it was Michael's front door that they'd heard. She and Joan stood still and watched as their local neighbourhood constable, Robert Parsons, walked out of Michael's house. There were two other men with him, one in a police uniform and the other in normal clothes, like Robert. The trio stopped next to the two cars and chatted for a moment before the two strangers got into one car and drove slowly away.

Robert climbed into his own car and followed them slowly back towards the main road. At the corner, he stopped suddenly and put down his window.

"Good evening, ladies," he called. "Out enjoying the last of the warm weather?"

"We were," Janet agreed. "I do hope everything is okay," she added, earning a stern look from her sister.

"Everything is fine," Robert told her. "I'll stop by to see you both tomorrow. I haven't done that for a while."

"I'll bake something special," Joan told him.

"I'll stop by around two," the policeman replied before putting up his window and driving away.

"He thinks we were being nosy," Joan said in a cross voice.

"We were, rather," Janet replied.

"It's worrying when there are police cars in our neighbourhood," Joan said. "Of course we wanted to know what was going on."

"Maybe we should just ask Michael," Janet suggested.

"Oh, no, we can't do that," Joan said, clearly shocked by the suggestion.

"Why on earth not?" Janet demanded.

"It would be, well, nosy," Joan told her. "If he wants us to know what's going on, he'll come and talk to us about it."

"I was thinking I might stop over and ask him if he recognises our mystery key," Janet said. "Stuart didn't, but maybe we should ask Mary as well."

"Is Mary here?" Joan asked.

"There's only one way to find out," Janet said in a determined voice. Before Joan could stop her, Janet turned and made her way to Stuart and Mary's door. She knocked loudly, ignoring the disapproval that was radiating off of her sister when Joan joined her on the doorstep.

"Good evening, ladies. This is a pleasant surprise," Stuart said when he opened the door. "What can I do for you?"

"We're still trying to work out what the key we found in the piggy bank might open," Janet told him. "I know you took a look and didn't have any ideas, but I wondered if Mary might recognise it."

"She's visiting her youngest this week," Stuart told her. "His wife is away for work, so it seemed like the best time for Mary to visit."

"Oh, well, we can ask her when she gets back," Janet said, eager to have a chance to talk to Michael. "Thanks anyway."

"Did you want to come in for a cuppa?" Stuart asked.

Janet exchanged glances with Joan. It was clear from Stuart's voice that he was hoping they'd agree. The man must have been lonely with his wife away. The ringing of a telephone saved Janet from answering.

"Oh, that'll be Mary," Stuart said brightly. "I'd better go and answer it. See you soon."

He very nearly shut the door on Janet's nose in his haste. She stepped back quickly and then shook her head. "It's just as well we didn't want to have that cuppa," she muttered as she turned away from the door.

"We shouldn't bother Michael," Joan said now.

"Nonsense," Janet replied. "We'll just ask about the key. It won't take more than a minute or two." She could tell her sister was going to protest more, so Janet hurried across the small space between the two front doors and knocked on Michael's door.

A moment later the door slowly swung open and Janet gasped. "Michael, what's wrong?" she asked, staring at the man, all thoughts of the odd key gone as she took in his appearance.

Michael blinked back at her and then shook his head. "You should come in," he said, stepping backwards to let the sisters into the house. They followed him down the short corridor into the kitchen, where Michael fell heavily into a chair.

"Please, sit," he said, waving a hand.

Janet sat down across from him while Joan took a seat next to him. As she shifted in her chair, Janet took a good look at the man. She'd always considered him rather handsome, but tonight he was pale and looked several years older than normal. He looked like a man who had just been given some shocking and bad news. Janet began to feel guilty about their suddenly dropping in. Sometimes being nosy wasn't a good thing, she thought.

Michael sighed deeply and then took Joan's hand in his. "I'm glad you stopped by," he said.

"I could make some tea," Janet suggested.

"That would be perfect," he replied.

No one spoke while Janet filled the kettle and switched it on. Michael answered her queries with monosyllables as she searched the cupboards for cups and teabags. Eventually, Janet managed to assemble everything and serve the tea.

"Have extra milk and sugar," Joan told the man. "You seem to have had a shock."

"I have, rather," Michael agreed, spooning sugar into his cup with grim determination. Joan finally took the spoon away from him after he'd added a seventh spoonful.

"Did you come over because you saw the police were here?" he asked after a few sips of tea.

"Not at all," Janet replied with forced cheer. "We found this key, hidden in a piggy bank, and we were hoping you might know what it's for." She held up the key.

Michael barely glanced at it. "I've no idea," he said.

"What's going on?" Joan asked in a quiet voice.

Michael sighed. "I assume you saw the police cars," he said.

"We did," Joan confirmed.

"They wanted to ask me a few questions," Michael said. "Questions about, well, my work."

"Has something happened at the shop?" Joan asked.

"When the man from the head office arrived, the first thing he did was an inventory. Apparently there is a somewhat large discrepancy between his inventory and what the shop's records show should be there."

"And he contacted the police about it?" Janet thought that seemed like an overreaction to what might be a simple accounting error.

"When it comes to controlled substances, it's wise to involve the police at the earliest possible moment," Michael told her.

"Even if someone just hasn't been keeping very good records?" Janet asked.

"It's more than just bad record keeping," Michael told her. "As chemists, we're trained to keep very detailed records, anyway. Bad record keeping is almost as much of a crime as stealing drugs."

"Really?" Joan asked.

Michael shrugged and shook his head. "No, not really, but it is very serious. The items we dispense are carefully controlled for a reason, or rather many reasons. It's vital that we always know exactly what we have and what we're giving to our customers."

"I assume something is missing, rather than there being too much of something," Janet said, earning a "hush" look from her sister.

"Actually, it's a bit of both," Michael said with a frown.

"That suggests it really is bad record keeping," Janet said, ignoring yet another look from her sister. "Like maybe someone isn't tracking the incomings or the outgoings properly."

"Yes, that's what worries me," Michael said with a sigh.

"I thought Owen always seemed incredibly professional," Janet said. "I can't imagine he'd make mistakes."

"Everyone makes mistakes now and again," Michael replied. "And Owen hasn't been feeling quite right in the last few months. It's easier to make mistakes when you aren't one hundred per cent."

"So the police think Owen is behind the problem?" Joan asked.

"The police are investigating," Michael replied. "Which means they are looking at Owen, but they are also talking to everyone who has worked in that shop in the last couple of months."

"Which includes you," Janet said.

"Indeed, I've covered for Owen several times due to his poor health," Michael agreed.

"But you aren't the only one," Janet said. "There was some strange little bald man in there one day when I was there."

Michael chuckled. "George Hawkins, though he won't thank you for describing him that way."

"He was rather, um, different," Joan said. "He kept humming and talking to himself the whole time we were there."

"George is a lovely man, but he's quite eccentric. He had his own little shop on the outskirts of Derby and his regular customers loved him. Unfortunately, his wife became quite ill and he ended up selling the shop and looking after her full-time until she passed away. Now he fills in at various shops around the area when people are ill or on holiday, although there are a few shops that won't have him back because of his, well, oddness."

"That's a shame," Janet said. "I didn't mind him being a bit peculiar. He gave me excellent advice about a cream for my dry skin."

"He's very good at his job," Michael said. "But these days that isn't enough for the big chain stores. They want you to interact with your customers, and persuade them to buy lots of extra things they don't need. It's a very different job to what I did when I had my little shop."

"Is there anyone else who's been filling in besides you and George?" Joan asked.

"Ethan Bailey did a week or two last month," Michael replied. "I don't know if you were in the shop while he was there or not. If you were, you might not have noticed him."

"But surely he was the only one in there," Janet said. The tiny local shop didn't get enough business to have a shop assistant in addition to the chemist. The chemist was expected to handle all transactions, from filling prescriptions to ringing up nappies and baby food.

"Well, yes, but I've always thought of Ethan as an almost invisible person," Michael said. "He's just the sort of man who blends into the background wherever he is. I've never heard him raise his voice or seen him get flustered or upset about anything. Every time I see him I spend several minutes thinking he looks familiar before I finally work out who he is, and that includes days where I know we're going to be working together. He just has the most unmemorable face and personality of anyone I've ever met."

Janet laughed. "Now I hope I get to meet him at some point.

You must let me know the next time he's going to be working locally."

"I don't know that anyone will be working there for a while," Michael said gloomily. "The police have shut the whole place while they do a more thorough inventory."

"That sounds a lot more serious than I was thinking this was," Joan said thoughtfully.

"It could be very serious," Michael replied.

"So could George or Ethan have been the making all of the mistakes?" Janet asked.

"The mistakes don't look genuine to me," Michael told her. "That's why I'm so upset."

"What do you mean?" Janet demanded.

"From what the police told me, it seems like the mistakes aren't really mistakes," Michael explained. "It looks more like someone has worked very deliberately to make it appear like random mistakes have been made.

Chapter 4

"Who would do that? And why?" Janet asked.

"For the moment, the police have to question everyone who might have done it," Michael told her. "That means I'm as much of a suspect as Ethan, Owen and George. As for why, there is a huge market on the street for controlled substances."

"Someone in Doveby Dale has been stealing drugs from the local shop and selling them on the street?" Janet took a deep breath when she realised she was almost shouting. Joan glared at her.

"Of course, whatever is going on is nothing to do with you," Joan said to Michael in a soothing voice.

"Unfortunately, that isn't true," Michael said sadly. "I've worked in that shop quite regularly lately. It was my shop, after all, before I sold it to the big chain. Luckily, when I sold it they did a very thorough inventory and everything came back exactly right."

"Of course it did," Joan said stoutly.

"The police can't seriously suspect you," Janet said.

"They have to suspect everyone. That's their job," Michael replied. "Oh, young Robert Parsons has been very nice about the whole thing, but really, he has to do his job."

"Robert is very nice and he seems very good at what he does," Janet said.

"From what I've seen, I'd agree," Michael replied. "He's just awfully young, that's all."

Joan nodded. "What about the other people who were with Robert?" she asked. "Who were they?"

"Investigators from Derby," Michael said. "They've been sent over to help Robert with the case, as it's rather serious. They were the ones who searched the house."

"They searched your house?" Joan asked in a shocked voice.

"With my permission, yes," he replied. "I have nothing to hide, after all."

"It still feels, well, rather invasive," Joan said. "But at least they didn't find anything. That should let you out, shouldn't it?"

"I wish it was that easy. If I really was supplying controlled substances to people without prescriptions, I suppose I wouldn't keep any of the evidence at my own home, would I?"

"I certainly wouldn't," Janet said.

"It seems likely that all of the sales were simply handled through the shop," Michael said. "That's how I would do it, if I decided to turn criminal."

"So how can they investigate? Fingerprints on the bottles of missing tablets?" Janet asked.

"Since all of us who work there have probably, at some point, handled just about all of the bottles in the entire shop, there's no way to check such things. We're talking about large dispensing bottles, after all, and fairly common medications. I'm sure I've filled prescriptions for most of them most of the days I've worked down there."

"What makes you think it's deliberate, exactly?" Janet asked.

"Robert probably wasn't supposed to show me the lists, but he let me have a quick look at the inventory that Matthew Rogers took and the report from the main office of what the shop was meant to have in stock."

"And Matthew Rogers is who exactly?" Janet interrupted.

"Sorry, he's the young man from head office who is here to cover for Owen for the next six weeks. The corporate bosses decided that was preferable to having various different people filling in for him on a day-to-day basis."

"I suppose that makes sense," Janet replied.

"It's somewhat unusual, though. When I first heard that they were sending someone, I thought they were sending him to take a good look at the shop and maybe think about closing it. It can't be making them much money. Now I'm wondering if they had some reason to be suspicious and sent Matthew to investigate."

"Would someone coming in for a short time like that usually start work with an inventory?" Janet asked.

"It isn't unusual, and again, if they were thinking of closing the shop, it would be something they'd want done."

"What did you learn from the two different lists, then?" Joan asked.

"I didn't get to study them at length," Michael told them with a frown, "but from what I could see, there were discrepancies all over the place. For a few items we had more stock than we should have, but not by much. More often, we were short, in some cases by a considerable amount."

"So if someone was making mistakes, they were making a lot of them," Janet mused.

"And most of the missing drugs were ones with street value," Michael added. "All drugs have street value, I suppose, but some are more in demand than others. Nearly all of the missing drugs were what I would consider highly in demand."

"And there's no way to tell from the store's records when the drugs went missing?" Joan asked.

"That's what the investigator from Derby is going to be doing next," Michael replied. "He's going to go through the store sales reports and prescription records with a fine-tooth comb to see if he can spot anything."

"So we have to hope that the person who made the pretend mistakes also made some real mistakes?" Janet asked.

Michael gave her a wry grin. "Something like that," he agreed. "The more I think about it, the more worried I get, though. In a small store with only one chemist working at any given time, it wouldn't be all that hard to steal a few drugs now and again. If Owen hadn't fallen ill, it might have been some time before anyone did a thorough inventory. Someone could have made themselves a tidy fortune."

"So the police will be looking at everyone's bank balance?" Janet asked.

"The last place I'd put any illegally acquired funds is in my bank account, but I suppose the police will look at that anyway."

"And find out if you've suddenly started having exotic holidays or you recently bought a luxury home in the Canary Islands, or maybe a fancy sports car," Janet said.

"I think that's quite enough," Joan said sharply. "Michael hasn't done any of those things."

"I did go on a long weekend to Edinburgh in May," Michael replied. "I don't think that's especially exotic, though."

"Scotland is such a beautiful place, the police can't be suspicious of anyone going there," Janet said.

"Why Edinburgh?" Joan asked.

Michael flushed. "My wife and I honeymooned there, many years ago. I try to go back once in a while to, well, reminisce."

Joan looked down at the table. Michael squeezed her hand, but didn't seem to know what to say. Janet jumped in before the silence could be more awkward.

"So, who do you suspect?" she demanded.

Michael shook his head, looking at her in surprise. "That's just it, I don't suspect anyone. There are only four people who could have done it, Ethan, Owen, George, and myself, and until about an hour ago I would have sworn none of us would ever do such a thing."

"What about this Matthew Rogers?" Joan asked.

"Robert said he told them that one of the reasons he was sent was because of the large number of issues the store has been having lately. He came to investigate."

"What sort of issues?" Janet asked.

"Bottles of tablets being reported as damaged and unusable,

issues with the till being opened repeatedly but no sales being registered, missing items being reported from our shipments, unusually high levels of returns on merchandise, all sorts of things, really. No one thing that caused any alarm, but all together it seems to suggest that there is something out of the ordinary going on at the shop."

"Have you noticed anything unusual when you've been in the store?" Janet knew she was being pushy, asking all these questions, but as long as Michael was willing to answer, she wasn't going to stop.

"Not really," Michael said. "The last time I was there when a shipment came in from head office, I remember there were a few items missing that the invoice claimed has been sent. It happens from time to time and the driver just noted it on the paperwork before I signed for the delivery. Other than that, it's all been business as usual, as far as I know."

"So what do you think is going on?" Joan asked quietly.

"I wish I knew," Michael said with a sigh. "For now we'll just have to wait and see what the police can find out, I suppose. Robert wasn't sure when the shop will be allowed to reopen. I gather Matthew is arguing that he should be able to offer at least a limited service immediately, even if they want to shut up the pharmacy itself."

"The good people of Doveby Dale will be up in arms if they can't get their headache tablets and baby food," Janet remarked. Those were the two items that someone always seemed to be buying whenever she was in the store, anyway.

Michael chuckled. "You're right about that. We're convenient for the locals who don't want to drive all the way out to the grocery store, even though it's only a few minutes further away. We get a lot of mums who need nappies or baby food and a great many folks who run out of headache tablets and can't bear the thought of driving anywhere until they've taken some."

"What can we do to help?" Joan asked.

"Nothing," Michael said, shaking his head. "For the moment, there's nothing anyone can do. We just have to wait and see what the police find out. Whether the shop is open or not isn't my concern. Matthew will be dealing with that. I just have to get on with my life."

"With a dark cloud hanging over you," Janet said.

"Janet, I hardly think that's appropriate," Joan scolded.

"Janet is right, though," Michael said. "I do feel as if there's a cloud hanging over me. Let's hope Robert and his associates are good and quick."

"I'm sure Robert will do his best," Janet said. "That is, I'm sure he'll get it all worked out quickly," she added, feeling as if the first statement wasn't encouraging enough.

"Let me see that key, then," Michael said. "I didn't take a proper look earlier."

Janet dug the key out of her pocket and handed it to the man. He turned it over in his hands and then shrugged. "There's a number on it," he pointed out. "1226; I would think it must be for a safe deposit box or a locker somewhere or something."

Janet nodded. She'd noticed the number herself, but that didn't seem to get her any closer to solving the mystery. "Thanks for looking, anyway," she said as she took the key back.

"If I think of anything, I'll let you know," Michael said.

"I don't suppose you know where Maggie Appleton did her banking?" Janet asked.

"She had an account at the bank next to the grocery store," Michael said, referring to the local branch of a national chain. "I used to run into her there once in a while when I was doing my own banking."

"Do they have deposit boxes?"

"They do. I even have one," Michael replied. "But the keys don't look exactly like that."

He dug around in his pocket and pulled out a ring of keys. He flipped through them and then stopped and held up a key. "See? They're a little bit smaller and the numbers are done differently."

Janet took the key and studied it for a moment. Michael was right. The key was just different enough from hers that it seemed unlikely they were keys for the same bank deposit boxes.

"There are lots of other banks around, though," Michael said as he returned his keys to his pocket. "Just because she had an account at one bank doesn't mean she didn't have other accounts elsewhere."

Janet nodded. "Maybe I'll have time to try a few banks over the next few days," she said thoughtfully. "We don't have guests until next week."

"You're having more guests?" Michael asked, giving Joan a surprised look.

"We have a nice young married couple arriving on Monday," Joan told him. "I'm sure they won't be any trouble at all."

Michael and Janet exchanged doubtful looks, but neither voiced their thoughts.

"If you want a hand with breakfast or anything, let me know," Michael said. "Now that I'm not covering at the shop, I have lots of free time."

"I'm not sure we have money in the budget for staff just yet," Joan told him. "But we'll keep it in mind."

Michael laughed "I wasn't necessarily looking to get paid," he told her. "I'd be happy enough just getting fed some breakfast of my own after the guests were taken care of. I was really just trying to find a way to spend a bit of time with you because you always get so busy when you have guests."

Joan flushed. "We'll see," she said evasively.

Michael nodded. "I suppose you might not want to spend time with me while I'm being investigated by the police," he said sadly. "I understand."

"Don't be ridiculous," Joan snapped. "I know you've not done anything wrong. I just, well, that is, I mean, we don't have guests until Monday. Maybe we could have dinner tomorrow or something?"

Michael smiled and Janet felt relieved to see him looking better than he had since they'd arrived. "I'd really like that," he said eagerly. " Do you want to go somewhere fancy?"

"Oh, good heavens, no," Joan replied. "I'll cook and we can just relax. With all the cleaning and everything that needs doing before

Monday, I won't have time to get all dressed up for something fancy."

"A quiet night in sounds wonderful," Michael replied.

"And my women's group has a meeting tomorrow night, so you can have the house to yourselves as well," Janet said. She'd recently joined the Doveby Dale Ladies' Club, a small group of retired women who got together once a month to discuss everything that was wrong with the world. Sometimes Janet found the other women a bit annoying, but she did enjoy having an evening out without her sister.

"Oh, I'd quite forgotten about that," Joan said. When she looked away from Janet as she spoke, Janet knew she was lying. Clearly her elder sister had deliberately planned the evening, wanting to be alone with Michael. Janet smiled to herself as she stood up to go. She liked Michael and thought he and Joan were well-suited.

"Let us know if you hear anything more about the, well, unpleasantness at the shop," Joan said at the door as Michael showed them out.

"I will," he promised. "And I'll see you around seven tomorrow."

"Perfect," Joan replied.

The sisters walked back across the road to their door, both lost in their own thoughts.

"It's getting late," Janet remarked when she saw the sitting room clock.

"It is, and we have a busy day tomorrow," Joan replied.

"Let me guess," Janet said without enthusiasm. "We have to start cleaning for our guests."

"Oh, maybe," Joan said airily. "But more importantly, we have to start investigating the goings-on at the chemist shop."

Chapter 5

"We what?" Janet asked, staring at her sister.

"I'm sure Robert is going to do his best," Joan said, flushing. "But I did think that maybe we could, I don't know, ask a few questions here and there. Just to see if we can find out anything useful."

"You never want to stick your nose in," Janet reminded her.

"I've never had a good reason to stick my nose in," Joan retorted.

"But now you want to help clear Michael's name," Janet suggested.

Joan flushed again. "It just seems a shame that the police are considering him a suspect. He's such a wonderful man. I just want to help get everything cleared up as soon as possible."

"So where do we start?" Janet asked.

Joan shook her head. "You're the one who reads all those stories about murder and mayhem. You tell me."

"I think the first thing we need to do is get a good night's sleep," Janet said after a moment.

Joan looked disappointed. "I'm not sure I'll sleep very well," she muttered as Janet headed towards the stairs.

"The shop is shut now anyway," Janet pointed out. "We can't

very well go knocking on people's doors at this hour of the night with nosy questions. We'll have to work out how to approach the suspects and work from there."

"I just hope we can help Michael," Joan said anxiously.

Janet was on the bottom step, but now she crossed over to her sister and gave her a hug. "I'm sure it will all be okay," she murmured. "Robert's very good at his job, and with us poking around as well, I'm sure the culprit will be behind bars in no time."

"At least one of us is optimistic," Joan said, stepping back from Janet. "Go and get some sleep. I'll have breakfast ready at eight."

Janet nodded and then climbed the stairs. Her mind was racing as she tried to work out how she could help her sister in her quest to aid Michael. She was sure she'd have a good idea if she slept on it, or at least that's what she told herself as she climbed into bed. When her alarm rang the next morning, she was disappointed to find that no wonderful idea had come to her in the night.

After a quick shower, Janet got dressed and combed her hair. Neither sister generally bothered with makeup. Now Janet stared at herself in the mirror. It seemed as if everyone they met thought the sisters looked a lot alike, but Janet couldn't really see it. While Joan was slender and always looked slightly disapproving, Janet was curvy and smiled almost constantly. Today the smile looked a bit forced as she thought about Michael's problem.

"I think the first thing we should do is head into town and see what's going on at the shop," Joan announced after she'd set the breakfast plates on the table.

Janet sat down and picked up a fork. She frowned down at her plate. Joan was an excellent cook, but today's breakfast was not up to her usual standards.

"Sorry about breakfast," Joan added. "I can't seem to concentrate on cooking."

Janet ate without complaining, but where before she had been interested in getting involved in Michael's case because of her inherent nosiness, now she was determined to get the matter resolved for far more selfish reasons. While she didn't mind cooking for herself once in a while, there was no way Janet wanted to take on cooking for the bed and breakfast when they had guests on the way. If Joan was too upset to cook properly for their guests, Janet wasn't sure what they'd do.

Janet washed burnt toast down with bitter coffee, trying to pretend that she hadn't really noticed anything unusual. "What do you think we can accomplish by stopping at the shop?" she asked as she loaded the breakfast plates into the dishwasher.

"I want a word with this Matthew Rogers. He's the one who's stirring up all the trouble, after all."

Janet nodded. As she hadn't come up with a better idea, she couldn't argue. "Maybe, while we're there, we should stick our heads in at the bank and see if the key we found is for one of their boxes," she suggested.

"I suppose," Joan shrugged.

Janet could tell that Joan didn't want to spend any time on anything other than helping Michael, but the key intrigued Janet. She really wanted to find out what it opened.

A few minutes later the pair were heading into Doveby Dale with Joan at the wheel.

"Of course Owen is laid up in hospital," Joan said, swerving back into the correct lane when she noticed the approaching car.

"Why don't you let me drive?" Janet suggested.

"I'm fine," Joan snapped. "Just a bit distracted."

The loud honking of a car horn told both sisters that Joan had just missed a stop sign. Joan sighed. "Okay, maybe I'm too distracted to drive."

Luckily it was only a short distance into the small city centre of Doveby Dale. Janet sighed with relief when Joan slid the car into a parking space.

"I'll drive home," Janet said firmly as they exited the car.

"Yes, I think you should," Joan agreed.

Joan had parked across two spaces, but as the car park was nearly empty, Janet didn't think it mattered overly much. The pair walked quickly towards the short row of shops. It seemed very quiet as they strolled past the newsagent. The chemist shop had a sign in the window.

Closed due to unforeseen circumstances. We will reopen on Monday at nine.

"Well, that's that, then," Janet said.

"I wonder if William knows anything?" Joan replied, walking past the chemist and down to the end of the strip.

WTC Antiques was owned by William Chalmers, a somewhat disagreeable man with a shady past. Strangely, it seemed as if the sisters were becoming something like friends with the man. Now Joan pushed open the door to his shop.

Janet winced at the loud buzzing noise that filled the room as they walked into the shop. A moment later William appeared in the doorway to the back room.

"Ah, Janet and Joan Markham, what a pleasant surprise," he said in an artificially bright tone. "To what do I owe this pleasure?"

"We were just in the neighbourhood," Janet said, wrinkling her nose as she realised her own tone was just as false sounding as his had been.

"I do hope you are enjoying your painting," he replied, smirking at her.

Janet flushed. She'd fallen in love with a painting in the store when it had first opened, but it was far too expensive for her. Edward Bennett had purchased the painting and had it sent to Janet as a gift. As Janet didn't really know what to think of Edward, she wasn't sure how she felt about the expensive gift. She'd not had a chance to speak to Edward since the painting had been delivered, and the subject was somewhat uncomfortable for Janet.

"It's a lovely picture," Joan said now, clearly trying to help her sister during the awkward pause.

"It is, yes," William agreed. "But I have a few paintings coming in soon by local artists, if you're still interested."

"Oh, yes," Joan said. "Do let us know when you have something."

William nodded and then looked expectantly at them both.

"We were hoping to get a few things from the chemist," Janet said. "That's why we came into town."

"Oh, I did see that it was shut. I wonder why," William said.

"I can't imagine," Janet lied, feeling relieved that William obviously hadn't heard anything about the missing drugs yet.

"I know Owen had some surgery or something, didn't he?" William asked. "But I thought your neighbour was covering for him."

"We'll have to ask Michael what's going on," Janet said with a shrug. "Anyway, we won't bother you any further today. Do ring us when you've something for us to see."

She turned and pulled Joan out of the store. On the pavement, Joan shook her head.

"How do you do that?" she demanded.

"Do what?"

"Lie, that's what," Joan replied. "You pretended that you didn't know anything about why the shop was shut. I was afraid if I opened my mouth I would say something I shouldn't."

"It's probably best if only one of us is a good liar," Janet muttered. "Anyway, he didn't seem to know anything. That's the good news."

"I was hoping he might say that he'd seen someone stealing drugs from the store," Joan replied. "That would have been better news."

The pair were walking slowly away from the short row of shops, down the pavement towards the small local bank. "Still determined to find out about that key?" Joan asked as they reached the entrance.

"I am," Janet replied. "You can wait here if you want."

Joan sat down on a small bench just outside the door, while Janet made her way inside. A moment later she was back, a frown on her face.

"No luck?" Joan asked.

"Honestly, when did they start hiring twelve-year-olds to work behind bank counters?" Janet demanded. "She glanced at the key and said 'nope, not ours,' and then went back to gossiping with the girl at the next window. I'm awfully glad we don't bank there."

"So where to now?" Joan asked her.

Janet sighed. They'd made their way to the car and she simply couldn't think what they could do next to help Michael.

"Derby's a long drive, if we want to visit Owen in hospital," Joan said, thoughtfully.

"We should talk to Michael before we drive all that way. The poor man might not even be allowed visitors," Janet pointed out. "And we don't know where to find the other two men at all."

"Michael might be able to help us out there as well," Joan said. "Maybe we should head back to Doveby House and see if he's home."

"Maybe, since you're having dinner with him, we should do some work around the house before he comes over," Janet suggested. "Robert is meant to be stopping by and we have guests arriving on Monday, after all."

Joan flushed. "Of course you're right," she said. "But lunch with Michael would be better than dinner. I'd really like to get his troubles sorted out before the guests arrive, if we can."

Janet drove the pair back to Doveby House. As soon as they were in the front door, Joan rang Michael. She hung up with a frown.

"No answer," she said.

"And you didn't leave a message."

"I didn't know what to say," Joan replied. "Anyway, let's do a bit of cleaning and then I'll try again."

Janet started on the public spaces, dusting and vacuuming her way from room to room. She hadn't finished the deep cleaning in the library yet, but she ran a duster over the shelves that she'd yet to tackle and then vacuumed the space. If their guests had any interest in seeing the library, it was at least presentable. When she finished, Janet shut and locked the library door, hoping that their guests wouldn't even notice the small room.

"Tomorrow I'll finish cleaning the upstairs," Joan said over a lunch that wasn't much better than breakfast had been. "Then Saturday we can go and do the shopping for the beginning of the week. I don't want to buy too much until we find out what our guests are going to want for breakfast each day."

"That sounds good," Janet replied. "Maybe Sunday we can head into Derby and visit poor Owen in hospital, then."

"We'll have to work out a good reason for doing so," Joan mused. "It isn't like we actually know the man, after all."

"Maybe Michael will have some ideas," Janet suggested.

"I don't really want, that is, I'm not sure," Joan took a deep breath and then shook her head. "I'm not sure I want Michael to know that we're doing a bit of, well, snooping," she said eventually.

"But we need him to tell us where to find all of the suspects," Janet pointed out.

"Maybe we can find a way to get the information from him without him suspecting what we're up to," Joan said.

Janet couldn't imagine how they'd manage that, but she didn't voice her doubts to her sister. Joan was obviously finding the whole thing very stressful. The scorched soup at lunch proved that. Janet didn't want to do anything to add to her sister's upset.

Joan tried Michael's number a dozen more times during the afternoon, but with no luck.

"You don't suppose he's been arrested?" she demanded eventually.

"We'll have to ask Robert that when he's here," Janet replied.

Only a few minutes later, Robert rang them. "I'm awfully sorry, but I'm not going to be able to come and see you this afternoon," he told Janet. "I'm just too busy. I'll stop and see you soon, though."

"What's he so busy doing?" Joan asked when Janet repeated the conversation.

"Let's go and visit the police station and see if we can find out," Janet suggested.

Joan turned pale for a moment and then smiled. "We can visit with Susan and pay her for the blankets that you and I bought."

The sisters had agreed to try to sell some of the woman's knitted creations at Doveby House, but aside from buying a blanket each for themselves, they hadn't sold anything yet.

"Exactly," Janet replied. "And see if she knows anything."

Janet drove again, parking right outside the tiny police station.

She took a deep breath of crisp autumn air before walking into the former cottage that made her feel quite claustrophobic.

"Good afternoon, ladies," Susan said from her usual post behind the small reception desk. She was, as ever, knitting something.

"Good afternoon," Janet replied.

"We've brought you payments for the blankets that Janet and I bought," Joan told her.

"I was hoping you'd sold out by now," Susan said with a laugh.

"We haven't really had very many guests," Joan replied in an apologetic tone. "We're still quite new to the whole bed and breakfast thing. If you'd rather have your things back, we'll return them. I don't know how much we'll sell, especially as we're only taking a booking here and there."

"Oh, goodness, no," Susan said. "You keep what you have. I've been working up a storm since then and I'll soon have as much again. There was a sale on knitting wool, you see, so I stocked up."

Janet laughed. "We have guests arriving on Monday," she told the woman. "We'll do our best to get them to buy something."

"Thank you for this," Susan said, taking the money from Joan. "I suppose I should put it away for a rainy day, but I suspect I'll soon be back at the shop buying up more wool."

"We tried to stop at the chemist earlier," Janet said, trying to sound casual. "I don't suppose you know why it's shut?"

Susan smiled. "Owen, that's the chemist, had some surgery a while back. I gather they're having trouble finding someone to fill in on a regular basis, so the head office just decided to shut for a few days until they can sort it out."

"Really?" Janet asked, surprised by the story she knew wasn't totally true.

"Well, that's what I was told," Susan replied.

"We should ask Michael," Janet said, keeping her tone thoughtful. She watched the other woman's face, wondering if the man's name would spark a reaction.

Susan shrugged. "I know he fills in sometimes. It was such a nice little shop when he had it, you know. It just isn't the same now it's part of that chain."

The sisters both nodded.

"Well, thank you for your time," Janet said, feeling discouraged.

"Stop by any time," Susan replied with a laugh. "I'm always here, and always knitting."

The sisters were silent on their way back to Doveby House. Janet was trying to come up with a plan, and she knew her sister was fretting.

Chapter 6

Back at home, Janet was delighted to see Michael's car parked in front of his house.

"Michael's back," she said happily.

"I'll just ring him and see if he wants to come over early," Joan replied.

Janet went into the kitchen to put the kettle on while Joan was on the phone. A moment later her sister joined her.

"He'll be here at six," she told Janet. "Although he took a lot of persuading. He's very upset about this whole thing."

"I don't blame him," Janet replied. "You'll have to try to cheer him up over dinner."

"I wish you weren't going out tonight," Joan said.

Janet went into the sitting room and played through the messages on their answering machine and then laughed. "Your wish just came true," she told Joan when she rejoined her in the kitchen. "My meeting has been cancelled. Nancy has the flu."

Joan smiled slightly. "I'm sorry for you, but pleased for me," she said quietly.

Considering her sister's current mood, Janet decided it was the perfect night for her to help out with dinner. They kept it simple and

Janet watched carefully and kept pots turned up or down as needed, so that by the time Michael arrived the food was ready and nothing was spoiled.

"I'm not really in the mood for company tonight," Michael said as a greeting. "I'm sorry."

"Don't be sorry," Janet said. "You're worried about the mess at the shop. That's totally understandable."

"I'm trying to put it out of my mind," Michael said sadly. "But I'm failing miserably."

"So let's talk about it over dinner and see if we can't work anything out," Janet said.

Joan gave her an angry look, but Janet ignored it. She knew Joan didn't want Michael to know they were investigating, but they couldn't do much of anything without some help from the man.

"I'd rather talk about just about anything but the shop," Michael said.

"I think everything is ready," Joan interrupted. "Let's eat."

"You two sit down and I'll serve," Janet said firmly. Joan looked as if she might argue, but after a moment she sank down onto one of the chairs at the small kitchen table. Michael sat down next to her and sighed.

"Let me open a bottle of wine," Janet suggested.

While none of the three drank often, wine sounded like exactly what they needed tonight. Janet dug a bottle of red out of the small cupboard in the corner and opened it quickly. She poured and served the wine before passing around a large bowl of salad.

The conversation felt stilted at first, but gradually everyone began to relax. Janet mentioned a television programme she'd seen a few nights earlier and the trio settled into a chat about the quality, or lack thereof, of television these days. Janet served generous portions while the conversation ebbed and flowed and the wine disappeared.

"I didn't make a pudding," Joan said as Janet cleared the dinner plates.

"We can have ice cream," Janet suggested. "There are a few different types in the freezer."

"Ice cream sounds good," Michael agreed easily. "Do you have chocolate?"

"Chocolate or chocolate with chocolate chips," Janet answered. "I love ice cream," she added as he considered the choices. "There's mint chip as well, and vanilla."

"Just plain chocolate is fine with me," he said with a smile. "And not too much, as I ate an awful lot of dinner."

Janet spooned several scoops of ice cream into a bowl for him, fixing herself a bowl of mint chip and then putting a single scoop of vanilla into another bowl for her sister.

"Thanks," Joan mumbled as she took the bowl and the spoon Janet offered.

"Shall I open another bottle of wine?" Janet asked as she topped up Michael's glass with the last of the first bottle.

"I don't think so," Joan said. "I think we've had enough."

"Joan's right," Michael said with a grin. "This ice cream will finish me off nicely and then I'll be ready for bed."

"We were thinking of making a trip into Derby on Sunday," Janet said, trying to sound offhand. "Is Owen still in hospital there?"

"He is," Michael confirmed. "Why?"

"I thought we might stop by and see how he's doing," Janet said with a shrug. "He always seemed like such a nice man and I thought you said once that he hasn't any family here."

"He doesn't," Michael agreed. "He married quite young, but his wife died only a few years later. They never had children and he never remarried. I don't suppose he's had any visitors, aside from the police, of course."

Joan flinched when Michael said the word 'police,' but Janet ignored it. "So he might be quite happy to see us," she said. "It seems like something we should do for our local business colleague."

"I suppose so," Michael said, but he looked doubtful.

"In the meantime," Janet pressed on, "I'm out of a few things and the local shop is shut. Where is the next closest chemist shop?"

"There's a lovely little shop in Little Burton," Michael told her. "Ethan Bailey is actually working there at the moment, covering for their regular man who's taken an extended holiday."

"We'll have to try to get there tomorrow," Janet said, almost to herself. "I'm nearly out of headache tablets."

"If you can wait, George Hawkins is covering at a shop in Derby. You could get your tablets when you go to visit Owen," Michael said.

"I'll just write down the details for both shops and we'll see how we get on," Janet said. Michael gave her the names and addresses for the two shops and Janet wrote them down.

"I suppose I should get home," Michael said after he'd eaten the last of his ice cream.

"Why don't you two watch a bit of telly together," Janet suggested. "I'm going to have an early night."

She headed up the stairs before either her sister or Michael could object. From the way the conversation had gone, Janet felt sure that Michael knew exactly what she and Joan were up to, and she didn't trust herself to keep quiet about their intentions if she spent any more time with the man. In her room, she curled up with a book and read until she was tired enough to sleep.

The sisters spent most of Friday cleaning and tidying Doveby House for their guests. Janet didn't ask Joan what she and Michael had discussed the previous night. She assumed that Joan would share what she felt she should. By the time they sat down to their evening meal, the house was just about ready.

"I think we've earned a day off tomorrow," Joan said as they put their dinner dishes into the dishwasher.

"Let's drive up to Little Burton and see what Ethan Bailey has to say for himself," Janet said.

"That's exactly what I was thinking," Joan agreed.

The weather was cool but dry as the sisters left Doveby House the next morning. Little Burton was only a short drive away, but they'd decided to make a day of it and explore not only the chemist shop, but also the other shops the small village offered.

Janet drove, easily finding a parking space in the small village centre car park when they arrived.

"I wonder if they have any shops that might have artwork by

local artists," Joan said as they walked along the short shopping street.

"This looks like the best bet for that," Janet remarked. She was looking into the window of a small antique and collectables shop.

Janet reached to open the door, but it was locked. "They aren't open," she said in surprise.

"On a Saturday?" Joan said. "Are we too early?"

Janet read the sign on the door. "Apparently they are only open regularly in the summer months. If we want to shop, we'll have to book an appointment."

Joan shook her head. "That seems a strange way to do business," she said. "But what do I know?"

There were only a few other shops to explore and the sisters soon felt as if they'd exhausted pretty much everything that Little Burton had to offer, aside from the shop they'd come to visit.

"I suppose we should visit the chemist shop, then," Joan said as they stood at the far end of the street, opposite the shop in question.

"There's a bank," Janet said, pointing down a side street. "Let's try that first."

The girl behind the desk at the bank was very kind, but she was certain that the key they'd found wasn't from one of their boxes. "Ours are only three digit numbers, as well, even if the key did look like one of ours, which it doesn't," she said.

With nothing else left to do, the sisters headed in to see Ethan.

"Ah, good morning," the man behind the counter told them.

Janet looked at him for a long minute. She could instantly see what Michael had meant. The man had no distinguishing characteristics. He had brown hair and brown eyes and he looked like just about every middle-aged man she'd ever met.

"I've run out of headache tablets," she said now.

Ethan walked her over to the display and talked her through the various choices. When Janet finally settled on her usual brand, he led her back to the counter.

"We usually shop in Doveby Dale," Janet said as he pushed buttons on his till. "But that shop is shut at the moment."

"I'd heard that," he muttered. "Some problem with staffing, I think."

"That's a shame," Janet said, digging around in her purse for exact change. "The chemist there always seems so nice. I do hope he's okay."

"Oh, I'm sure Owen, er, Mr. Carter, will be just fine. He's had a few health problems, that's all. He'll soon be back, I reckon," he replied.

Janet took her bag and smiled brightly. She couldn't think of anything else to ask, so she turned and walked out of the shop with Joan following.

"We didn't learn anything," she complained to Joan when they reached the car. "I'm terrible at this. I couldn't work out what to ask."

"You did better than I did," Joan told her. "I didn't say a word the whole time."

"We'll have to work out what we want to ask George and Owen before we see them," Janet said as they began their drive home.

"I thought we were going to have lunch in Little Burton," Joan said a moment later.

Janet laughed. "I forgot," she exclaimed. "But I'm sure there will be a pub or something between here and home."

Joan muttered something under her breath, but Janet ignored it. She knew her sister didn't really like eating in pubs, but Janet preferred them to the little tea rooms that Joan favoured. She'd genuinely forgotten about their plans to have lunch in Little Burton, but she wasn't sorry if it meant a nice pub lunch rather than sandwiches at a tea shop in Little Burton.

Even with their pub lunch, they were back at Doveby House before they'd expected to be. "I suppose we should finish getting the house ready if we're going into Derby tomorrow," Joan said as Janet parked the car.

"I suppose," Janet said without enthusiasm.

"What shall we do for lunch tomorrow?" Joan asked. "I'm not sure I want to eat in another pub."

"Maybe we could try that American chain that just opened a

branch in Derby," Janet suggested. "I understand the restaurant is quite near the hospital."

Joan looked as if she might object, but then she smiled "If that's what sounds good to you, then I suggest we go there," she said. "It's the least I can do for you since you're snooping on Michael's behalf."

Janet grinned. She wasn't going to argue with Joan, not when Joan was going out of her way to be agreeable.

The pair worked their way through the house, tidying and cleaning the entire thing. It was time for their evening meal when they'd finished.

"After that big lunch, I'm not very hungry," Joan said as she and Janet stood in the middle of their kitchen.

"Me, either," Janet agreed. "But we should have a little something. Do we have to go grocery shopping tonight?"

Joan frowned. "I forgot about the shopping," she said. "I suppose we should, though I hate going out this late."

Janet laughed. "Let's have something light and then I'll go into town and get the shopping. You can relax. You've had a long day."

"If you do the shopping, I'll finish in the guest rooms," Joan countered. "They could both do with a little bit more polishing."

"They're perfect," Janet disagreed. "You'll wear yourself out trying to make them any better. Just relax."

"I can't relax," Joan told her. "I'm too worried about Michael. It's better I keep busy."

Janet thought about arguing, but her sister's frown kept her from speaking. Joan obviously had deeper feelings for their troubled neighbour than Janet had realised. Janet could only hope that she could do something to help.

After a meal of bread and soup, Janet headed to the nearby grocery store with a short list. After Monday or Tuesday, when they had a better idea of what their guests would prefer, Janet would drive over to the larger and less expensive store on the outskirts of the village. She could stock up then on all of the things they needed.

When she returned to Doveby House with the shopping, Joan was vacuuming the guest rooms for the third time.

"I think that's enough vacuuming," Janet said, taking the machine away from her sister. "It's time for bed."

"I'm not tired," Joan complained.

"Then read a book," Janet suggested. "Grab something at random from the library and read until you fall asleep."

"I only read the classics," Joan argued.

"Maybe it's time to try something new," Janet replied. "I suggest Agatha Christie. She's a classic anyway, in her genre."

"Detective fiction," Joan sniffed. "Not really my cup of tea."

"Stop being such a literary snob," Janet said. "There's nothing wrong with reading just for fun."

Joan looked as if she was going to argue, but Janet spoke again.

"Think how wonderful it would feel to simply lose yourself in a book right now," she said persuasively. "Get lost on the Orient Express. I highly recommend it."

Before Joan could argue further, Janet rushed up to her room and found the book. She handed it to her sister with a smile.

"Really, try it," she said. "If you hate it, you can stop reading after chapter two."

"I'll think about it," Joan said stiffly. She took the book and walked away towards her bedroom.

Janet smiled as she watched her go.

Chapter 7

When Janet's alarm went off the next morning, she climbed out of bed and took a longer than normal shower. They weren't in any great hurry to get to Derby, she told herself. And once the guests arrived, showers would be hurried affairs. Joan had breakfast ready when Janet finally made her way down to the kitchen.

"I was starting to think you'd overslept," Joan said in a mild tone.

Janet could tell that her sister wasn't happy. "I'm sorry. I took a long shower to make up for all the quick ones I'll have to take once the guests arrive."

"I wish I'd thought to do that," Joan muttered as she put plates of food on the kitchen table.

"Maybe you should have a nice long bath tonight," Janet suggested. "You prefer baths, anyway, and we should be back from Derby in plenty of time."

"I might just do that," Joan said. "I just hope, I mean, oh, never mind."

Janet knew exactly what Joan was hoping; that by the evening they'd have Michael's problem all sorted out. Joan wouldn't be able to relax properly until the police had the drug thief in custody.

They ate quickly, with little conversation. Joan had pulled out their maps of the area and had already worked out a route to the hospital in Derby. Now she showed Janet what she'd found.

"This little side street is where the chemist shop is," she said, showing Janet. "We should be able to park at the hospital and walk from there. It isn't far."

Janet nodded. "I think I'll drive," she said softly.

Joan looked as if she might object, but then shook her head. "You probably should," she agreed.

The drive wasn't a bad one and traffic was lighter than Janet had feared. They were in Derby earlier than they expected and quickly found the hospital and its vast and confusing car park.

"Do we know which building Owen is in?" Janet asked as she turned onto the road that went around the hospital complex.

"I didn't realise the hospital was this large," Joan replied. "I have no idea."

They drove slowly around the entire facility, trying to read signs as they went. Eventually Janet shrugged. "I suppose we can walk if we have to," she said.

"Let's try the main building," Joan suggested. "We know he isn't in the maternity hospital or the children's wing, after all."

Janet pulled up to the gates for the car park for the main hospital and took a ticket from the machine. After a moment, the gate lifted and she drove through it. It took the women a few minutes to find an empty space and Janet sighed with relief as she turned the car off.

"I love to drive," she said. "But I hate having to park."

Joan laughed. "I know what you mean," she said sympathetically.

The pair made their way towards the hospital's nearest entrance. Once inside, they followed signs for "information."

"Good morning," Janet said to the elderly woman behind the information desk. "We're here to visit Owen Carter."

The woman shrugged and then slid her finger down the list she had in front of her. "He's on the surgical ward," she said after a moment.

Janet and Joan exchanged glances. "Perhaps you could give us directions?" Joan asked politely.

The woman sighed deeply and then opened a desk drawer. She pulled out a map of the hospital building. "You just have to go down this corridor, take the lift to three, walk down to the end of the hall, turn left, go through the double doors, turn left again and then turn right and then left again."

While she talked, she traced the route on the printed map. As soon as she was finished speaking, she slid the map back into her desk drawer and gave the sisters a huge fake smile. "Okay?" she asked.

"Thank you so much," Janet said gushingly. "You've been ever so helpful. I can't tell you how much we appreciate your kindness."

As the pair walked away, Joan chuckled. "You can't tell her how much, because we didn't appreciate it at all," she whispered.

Janet shook her head. "The sign said she's a volunteer. I'm not sure why she bothers as she so clearly hates the job."

"Maybe she enjoys being difficult," Joan suggested.

"I'm sure she does," Janet agreed. Between them, the sisters were just able to remember the directions they'd been so hastily given.

"She gave us the right directions, anyway," Janet said as they walked into the surgical ward.

"Let's just hope Owen is really here," Joan replied.

The aide at the nurses' station smiled brightly at them. "Oh, Owen doesn't get many visitors," she said. "He'll be thrilled to see you. I'm sure he's in the lounge, watching a bit of telly. He's just about ready to be sent home, you see, so he's able to enjoy himself a bit."

"What are we going to say to him?" Joan hissed as the sisters walked towards the lounge.

"I have no idea," Janet replied, trying to sound unconcerned. With every step, she was frantically trying to think of a good excuse for their unexpected visit.

Owen was alone in the lounge, listlessly flipping through the channels on a small television. Janet knew he was in his late forties.

He had a full head of brown hair, and his eyes, behind thick glasses, were also brown. He stood up and Janet remembered that he was quite tall. She had forgotten how he towered over them when they were in the shop.

"Ah, the Markham sisters," he said as they walked into the room. "Michael told me you might drop by. He's ever so worried about the missing stock from the shop. I think he's concerned that I might be equally bothered."

"And you aren't?" Janet asked.

"Not really," Owen shrugged. "I know I haven't done anything wrong, you see." He smiled at them. "And I know Michael hasn't done anything wrong, either. But it used to be his shop. I think he still feels responsible for it, even though it's nothing to do with him."

"So who do you think has been stealing drugs from the shop?" Janet blurted out.

Joan looked shocked at the blunt question, but Owen just shrugged.

"I've had a lot of time to sit here and think," he replied. "And I don't think I'm any closer to figuring that out. Obviously, it wasn't me. And there's no way you'll ever convince me it was Michael, either. If he wanted to get up to no good, he had plenty of years to do so while he owned the shop."

"So that leaves Ethan Bailey and George Hawkins," Janet said. "Does either of them strike you as likely culprits?"

"I've known both men for many years," Owen told her. "I simply can't see either of them stealing. And it isn't just that. All chemists have a healthy respect for the controlled substances we work with. The idea of one of us selling them on the street is just crazy."

"How are you feeling?" Joan asked after the awkward silence that followed Owen's pronouncement.

"I'm fine," he said with a wave of his hand. "Really, they should have let me go last week, but I've no one to go home to and they don't want me totally on my own for a while. I'm lucky it's pretty quiet in here and they haven't had to ship me off somewhere else."

"I'm glad you're doing so well," Joan replied.

"I'll still be signed off work for another six weeks or so," he told her. "That's why they sent this Matthew Rogers up. He's meant to cover for me."

"Could he be the culprit?" Janet asked.

"I've never met the man, but the bosses at the central headquarters seem to think very highly of him." Owen shrugged. "As I understand it, he was only here for about an hour before he rang the police. Changing all of the records and things would have taken quite a bit of time. I can't see how he'd have managed it."

"Michael said there have been a lot more returns and other little issues lately as well," Janet said, hoping she wasn't being too nosy.

"There have been too many people in and out of there since I've been unwell," Owen told her. "I wanted Michael to cover for me, but head office kept chopping and changing things. Michael did a few days and then they called George and he did a week, but before he was properly settled in they called Ethan for the next week. It's hardly surprising that a few little errors occurred."

Janet nodded. "Have you spoken to the police?" she asked.

Joan shook her head, but Janet ignored her.

"They've been to talk to me a couple of times," Owen replied. "But I haven't had much to tell them."

"We should have brought you a book," Joan exclaimed. "I do hope you have plenty to keep you busy while you're here."

Janet sat back and let her sister chat with the man about the relative merits of crossword puzzles and science fiction novels. She had dozens more questions to ask, but she didn't want to be rude. After twenty minutes, a nurse stuck her head in.

"Sorry to interrupt, but the doctor would like to see Mr. Carter now," she said.

"We should be going anyway," Janet replied, standing up quickly. "It's been lovely to see you, though."

"Likewise," he said. "I do hope you'll stop to visit me at the shop once I'm back to work."

"Of course we will," Janet assured him. They walked with him down the corridor to his room, as it was on their way out.

"Thank you both for stopping by," he said at his door. "It's always nice to have visitors."

"It was nice to see you, too," Janet told him. "We'll see you back in Doveby Dale soon."

"Are we still planning to walk to the shop where George Hawkins is working?" Janet asked as the sisters boarded the lift.

"I suppose so," Joan replied. "It isn't raining and it doesn't look far on the map."

They stopped at the car to check the map again and then set out, happy that they had a better idea of where they were going than they had in the hospital. The walk was longer than they'd expected, however, and Janet was quite pleased to finally see the shop in the distance after several minutes of making their way through the busy city streets.

At the door to the shop, Janet paused. "I don't know what to say here either," she told Joan. "I'm so glad that Michael told Owen we were coming. That broke the ice nicely."

"Maybe he's told George as well," Joan suggested.

"Oh, dear. I was just planning on doing some shopping and then trying to start a conversation. If Michael's told him we're coming, that makes it awkward," Janet said.

Before they could debate further, a young woman interrupted. "If you're not going in, do you think you could move along? I need some nappies."

Janet flushed and then stepped back, holding the door open for the young woman and her large pushchair. The baby inside was adorable, but as Janet smiled at him she got a whiff of something that suggested the mum needed the nappies quite urgently.

The shop was only a little bit larger than the one in Doveby Dale, surprisingly small for a big city store. Janet and Joan wandered around for a few minutes while the woman bought what she needed. Janet found herself watching George as she pretended to browse the shelves.

He was probably somewhere in his sixties. As he walked back and forth through the shop, helping the woman find what she needed, he mumbled constantly to himself, often stopping to rub the top of his head, which was completely lacking in hair. He had a pair of glasses in his hand and he was forever putting them on to study something and then pulling them back off again.

"Now, what can I help you ladies with?" he asked, smiling vaguely in their direction after the woman left.

"We just need some headache tablets," Janet said a bit desperately.

"Headache, headache, headache," the man muttered as he walked around the counter. "This is what we have," he told Janet, gesturing to the appropriate shelf.

"We usually shop in Doveby Dale," Janet said as she looked over the choices. "But the store there is shut for some reason."

"Is it?" George replied. "I suppose there must be a good reason. Derby's a long drive for you, though. Surely you could have found headache tablets somewhere closer."

"We were coming up to visit a sick friend," Janet told him.

"Oh, well, I suppose that makes sense," he said.

Janet selected her usual brand and handed them to the man. "I'll take these," she said.

"Very good," he replied. He rang up her purchase while still talking quietly to himself. "Thank you," he said loudly at the end.

"Thank you," Janet replied. She glanced at Joan, who shrugged, and then they exited the shop.

"Well, that didn't go well," Janet said with a deep sigh as they headed back to their car.

"On the other hand, you won't need to buy any more headache tablets for the next five years," Joan retorted.

Janet chuckled. "I know. It was a dumb choice, but I couldn't think of anything else. I suppose I'm just not cut out to be a detective."

"You did better than I did," Joan admitted. "I didn't do or say anything, after all. And I'm the one who's concerned about Michael."

"Yes, well, I think we did our best. Maybe we'll have to just leave everything up to the police," Janet said.

"I really want to meet Matthew Rogers," Joan said in a thoughtful tone. "Maybe he's the one behind all of this."

"He's only just arrived in the area," Janet pointed out.

"Which makes him the perfect suspect," Joan replied. "We don't know him, so we don't like him and we won't mind if he's arrested."

Janet laughed. "I suppose, when you put it that way, he's the perfect suspect."

"Yes, he is," Joan said.

Janet drove to the restaurant they'd agreed to visit for lunch. The food was excellent and Janet was pleased to see her sister relaxing, at least a little bit. The drive back to Doveby Dale was uneventful.

Chapter 8

"So what do we do now?" Joan asked over their light evening meal.

"I suppose we should be getting ready for our guests," Janet replied.

"But what about Michael?" Joan demanded.

"I don't know," Janet said. "We've talked to all three of the suspects. What did you think of them?"

Joan's reply was interrupted by a knock on the door.

"I'll go," Joan said, jumping up from the table.

"It must be Michael," Janet muttered as she took another bite of her sandwich. Joan didn't rush to the door unless she was expecting him.

A few minutes later Joan was back with Michael in tow. "I really don't want to interrupt your dinner," he was protesting.

"It's just a light meal," Janet told him. "We had a huge lunch in Derby."

"Ah, yes, Owen told me you'd visited when I rang him earlier," Michael replied.

"We had a lovely little visit with him," Joan said.

"And did you stop and see George as well?" Michael asked.

"We did," Joan confirmed.

"So, have you worked out who has been stealing from the shop?" Michael asked eagerly.

Janet looked at Joan and then both sisters shook their heads.

"They both seem like nice men," Janet said. "I find it hard to believe that either of them is capable of such a deplorable thing."

"Yes, I'm finding it hard to believe anything bad about either of them," Michael agreed.

"Has Robert been back to see you?" Janet asked.

"He stopped by with a few more questions earlier today," Michael replied. "Really, we just went back over the same things again." He sighed deeply. "I just feel so helpless. There should be something I can do to help Robert work this out."

"Surely the inspector from Derby is meant to be doing that," Joan said.

"I suppose," Michael said with a shrug. "But they don't seem to be getting very far, at least not yet."

"It's only been a few days," Janet said. "Investigations take a long time."

Joan shook her head. "On what are you basing that assumption?" she demanded.

"In the books I read, investigations take a long time," Janet answered defensively. "The detective always follows a few false leads and suspects the wrong person for a while before he or she works it all out."

"Maybe they do suspect me, then," Michael said. "As I'm the wrong person."

"They always catch the criminal in the end," Janet said reassuringly.

"If only we lived in a fictional world," Joan said dryly.

Janet flushed. "I'm sure there are similarities," she muttered.

The trio chatted about nothing much for several minutes while Janet and Joan finished their meal. Joan fixed tea for everyone and put out biscuits, but it was clear that everyone was distracted. Michael didn't stay long.

"I'm sorry, but I'm not very good company tonight," he told the sisters as they walked him to the door. "Anyway, you'll want an early night with guests coming tomorrow."

"What time are you expecting our guests?" Janet asked her sister before she headed up to bed.

"Sometime after midday and before three," Joan replied. "Mr. Nicholson was a bit vague when I talked to him. I suppose a lot will depend on traffic."

"I think I'll have a very lazy start tomorrow, then," Janet said. "Since we'll have to be up early while the guests are here."

"That's a good idea. Maybe I'll try to lie in as well," Joan replied.

Janet knew that her sister would probably be up at six, just as she nearly always was. Even in childhood Joan had never been very good at having lazy mornings. As she climbed the stairs, Janet was again reminded of how much she loved Doveby House. In their old cottage, with its single bathroom situated between the two small bedrooms, Janet had always been woken when Joan got up for the day. Now, the sisters were on separate floors and each had her own bathroom. Janet could sleep even when her sister couldn't.

It was nearly midday before Janet made it down the stairs the next morning. She felt refreshed after several extra hours of sleep and a long shower. She found her sister in the kitchen.

"You look terrible," she greeted Joan, who didn't look as if she'd slept at all.

"I couldn't sleep," Joan replied, refilling her coffee mug as she spoke.

"Oh, I am sorry," Janet said. She gave her sister a quick hug. "Why don't you go and lie down for an hour or two before the guests arrive?" she suggested. "I'll do some work in the library where I'll hear the door if they arrive early."

Joan shook her head. "I've had too much coffee now," she said with a small laugh. "I'm just hoping the guests have an early night."

"I'll stay up with them," Janet said quickly. "You can have an early night, regardless."

"We'll see," Joan replied.

Joan nearly always insisted on doing most of the work for the bed and breakfast, and Janet knew that was because Joan was the one who'd wanted to buy Doveby House in the first place. For the most part, Janet was happy to let her sister do the lion's share of the cooking, cleaning, and sitting up late with the guests, but now she felt guilty as she looked at her sister's tired face. She didn't argue, but she was determined that Joan was going to have an early night.

"Are you still hoping our guests might do some artwork for us?" Janet asked.

"It would be wonderful," Joan said. "But after our previous experiences with guests, I'm not getting my hopes up."

Janet nodded. It was best not to have any expectations of guests. That way they wouldn't be disappointed.

After an early lunch that was also a late breakfast for Janet, the sisters did a last minute tidy up of the house. Janet vacuumed down the centre of each room while Joan dusted and plumped pillows. They were seated in front of the telly, trying not to watch the clock, when someone knocked.

Joan rushed to the door, while Janet followed at a more leisurely pace.

"Welcome to Doveby House," Joan said.

Janet reached the door and added her own welcome while she took a good look at the new arrivals.

"I'm Fred," the man with long blonde hair and a ring through his nose said. He nodded at the girl next to him. "This is Molly."

Molly's head was shaved and she also had a ring through her nose. "Hey," she said quietly.

Joan stepped back to let the couple in. Fred dragged a large suitcase in behind him. He was very thin, in skin-tight jeans and a T-shirt that had seen better days. Janet wondered if he could actually lift the case that looked very heavy.

Molly was very slender as well and was wearing an almost identical outfit, except her T-shirt had long sleeves. Janet could see various tattoos on Fred's arms and she wondered if Molly also had some. There was no polite way to ask, of course.

"You have your choice of two guest rooms," Joan said. "I would suggest the larger one, but you can choose."

"We'll have to see which one feels right," Molly told her seriously. "We're creative. The energy has to be right."

"Yes, well, if you'd like to follow me, I'll show you the rooms," Joan replied.

Janet followed the trio up the stairs. Fred half-carried and half-dragged the case along as they went, bumping it up the stairs. Joan opened both guest rooms and let the couple inspect them.

"This one," Fred said after several minutes. He pointed to the east room. "It feels better."

"Of course," Joan murmured, handing him the key. She locked up the west room. "We'll just leave you to freshen up," she said. "I'll put the kettle on if you'd like some tea in a short while."

"Great," Molly muttered. "We'll be down."

In the kitchen, Joan looked at Janet and shrugged. "They seem nice, I suppose," she said hesitantly.

"I've never met artists before," Janet whispered. "They're sort of what I expected and sort of not."

"I know what you mean," Joan replied.

It wasn't long before the couple joined them in the kitchen. Joan quickly made the tea and set out a large plate of biscuits.

"So you're both artists," she said once everyone was settled in.

"We are," Fred confirmed.

"We're quite eager to find some paintings of local scenes for the guest rooms," Joan said. "If either of you does anything like that, we'd love to see it."

Molly snickered and shook her head. "That sort of art isn't for us," she told Joan. "We didn't come up here to paint the scenery."

"So why are you here?" Janet asked. As soon as the words were out of her mouth she felt as if it was a rude question, but the couple didn't seem to mind.

"We're looking for inspiration," Fred told her. "A change of scenery always helps inspire our work. A week here should recharge our creative batteries."

"What sort of art do you do?" Janet couldn't help but ask.

"I'm a poet," Molly said proudly.

"Really? I've heard it's frightfully hard to get poetry published," Janet said.

"I don't worry about such things," Molly said airily. "I write for myself, not for others."

Janet bit her tongue before she asked how the woman paid her bills. Even she knew that was a question too far.

"Let me share something with you," Molly said. "A poem that I wrote on our drive here." She shut her eyes and then cleared her throat. "I've called it The Drive;

Long
Tedious
Tiring
Inspiring
Trees
Dogs
Soil
Snails
Biscuits
Darkness."

She sat back and took a sip of tea.

Janet looked at Joan and then smiled brightly. "That was lovely," she said with as much enthusiasm as she could muster. It wasn't much different to her tone when she'd told her class of eight-year-olds how talented they all were when they'd had their first attempt at writing a poem.

"Thank you," Molly said. "But I'm quite exhausted. I think I might just go and lie down for a bit."

"She's always worn out after she has these creative bursts," Fred told them.

"Are you a poet, too?" Janet asked. As soon as the words were out of her mouth, she was sorry she'd asked. What if he wanted to share something with them as well?

"No," he said. "I'm a sculptor. I work with natural materials."

"Like marble?" Janet asked.

Fred laughed. "Like soil and twigs and rocks," he told them.

"How interesting," Janet managed to say. She didn't dare look at her sister. She could only hope that the couple had paid in advance. She couldn't begin to imagine where their income came from.

"So, do you have a telly?" Fred asked as the sisters tidied away the tea things.

"I can show you to the television lounge," Janet offered.

"Great. I'll just hang out there until Molly's feeling better. Then we can head out and explore Doveby Dale. I'm sure it will be inspiring."

With the man happily settled in with the remote in hand, Janet headed back to the kitchen to make sure Joan didn't need any help.

"Well, we could always try putting a copy of one of her poems on the wall, instead of a painting," Janet suggested as Joan started the dishwasher.

"I couldn't even manage to say anything," Joan said with a shudder. "It was just so, well, incomprehensible."

"I'm almost afraid to ask what Fred's sculptures look like," Janet replied.

"Maybe they're both really famous and we just don't realise it," Joan said.

"Maybe," Janet said doubtfully. "At least it will make us feel better to think that," she added.

"They paid cash in advance," Joan told her. "Just in case you were wondering."

"I was, rather," Janet admitted.

It was a couple of hours later when they heard footsteps on the stairs. Molly wandered down to where the sisters were reading in the sitting room.

"Where's Fred?" she asked, sounding disoriented.

"He's watching telly," Janet told her. She showed the woman into the next room, and Molly sank down next to her husband on the long sofa.

"We should go out," Fred said, glancing at Molly. "I'm hungry."

"I'm not," Molly replied with a yawn. "I'd rather just stay here and watch telly."

Janet excused herself and returned to her book. A few minutes later the couple emerged.

"Where can we get a quick meal?" Fred demanded.

Joan gave him directions to the nearest café. As soon as the guests were gone, she started making dinner for herself and Janet. They were still eating when they heard the front door open.

"I'll go, you eat," Janet told Joan.

"We're back," Molly said brightly as Janet walked into the sitting room.

"If you're in for the night, I'll put the chain on the door," Janet said.

"I don't think we're going anywhere else tonight," Fred replied. "We're just going to watch some telly and relax."

Several hours later Janet insisted that Joan head to bed. "I'll wait up in case the guests need anything," she said. Janet was surprised when Joan actually agreed. Clearly her sister was exhausted.

After another hour, Janet decided to check on the Nicholsons. In the lounge, Fred and Molly were both fast asleep. Molly was snoring gently. Janet considered her options and then sighed. She'd have to wake them.

She picked up the remote from the floor. It must have fallen out of Fred's hand. After switching off the telly, she knocked loudly on the door. The guests both sat up quickly.

"Good evening," Janet said. "I wanted to make sure you were both okay and found you asleep. Surely you'll be more comfortable upstairs."

"I wasn't sleeping," Fred said grumpily. "I was watching telly." He glanced at the now black screen and frowned.

"It was a long day," Molly said. "The drive took ages."

"Yes, well, why don't you both head up to bed?" Janet suggested.

"Yes, let's," Molly said. She got to her feet.

"I wanted to watch the rest of the programme," Fred protested as Molly pulled him up.

"It's probably finished," Molly said. "Let's get some sleep."

Janet took a moment to tidy the lounge behind them, hoping

they'd be tucked up in their room before she got upstairs. Their bedroom door was just closing as Janet reached the top step. She let herself into her room with a sigh of relief. Having guests was a strange mix of excitement, tension, stress and chaos. She wasn't sure whether she liked it or not.

Chapter 9

Janet was up, showered, dressed and ready to help her sister make breakfast before eight the next morning.

"They said they'd probably be up around nine," Joan reminded her as Janet paced around the kitchen. "You should have slept later."

"I will tomorrow," Janet said. "Except they'll probably be up early tomorrow."

It was nearly half nine when the couple came down the stairs.

"Full English breakfast?" Joan asked them when they appeared in the kitchen doorway.

"Oh, I just wanted coffee and maybe some toast," Molly replied.

"We're vegetarian," Fred said.

"An omelet?" Joan suggested.

"I know some vegetarians eat eggs, but we don't," Fred told her.

"Beans over toast?" Janet asked.

"Just toast is fine," he replied. "And lots and lots of coffee."

Joan nodded. She'd made coffee earlier; now she poured some into mugs for the guests. Janet got busy at the toaster, filling two toast racks as quickly as she could.

"I have several jams and marmalades. What do you prefer?" Joan asked.

"Nothing for me, thanks," Molly said. She took a bite of her dry toast and washed it down with coffee. "This is good."

"I'm fine as well," Fred said.

Joan set a fresh pot of coffee brewing. After a moment Janet excused herself. There was no point in her watching the couple eat and nothing she could do to help Joan with the coffee. She made her way to the library and pulled the books away from the panel they'd not managed to open. For several minutes she worked on sliding it in every direction, but it simply wouldn't budge. When she heard movement in the sitting room, she put the books back and locked up the library.

"They've gone for the day?" she asked Joan, who was just shutting the front door.

"Yes, off to soak up inspiration from the dales, I gather."

"If all they're going to want is toast and coffee every day, breakfast will be easy," Janet remarked.

"Indeed," Joan said. "Easy and boring."

Janet grinned. "You can make me an omelet every morning, if you get bored."

Joan laughed. "I'm not that bored," she replied.

Back in the kitchen, it only took a moment for them to tidy up.

"Maybe we should get some different types of bread," Janet said thoughtfully. "If that's all they're going to eat."

"That isn't a bad idea," Joan replied.

They headed to the closest grocery store, and Janet selected several different loaves of bread while Joan picked up a few other little things.

"That's quite a collection," Joan said when she rejoined Janet.

"There were so many different choices and they all looked and smelled wonderful," Janet replied. "I got a little carried away."

"Let's just hope Mr. and Mrs. Nicholson like a bit of variety," Joan said.

As they drove slowly through Doveby Dale, Janet suddenly pulled into the car park for the small row of shops.

"Did we need something here?" Joan asked.

"I thought we could see if the chemist is open," Janet replied. "And maybe meet Matthew Rogers."

"I'm glad your brain is working," Joan said. "I've been so preoccupied with worrying about our guests that I forgot all about Michael's little problem."

Janet knew that wasn't strictly true. Even when Joan was fussing over the guests, she had been preoccupied.

They made their way along the pavement and Janet was happy to see that the shop was open when they arrived. A soft buzzer sounded as they made their way through the door. After a moment a man walked out from the back of the store to greet them.

"Good morning, ladies, although it might be afternoon by now. I've rather lost track," he said with a bright smile.

Janet smiled back. The man was younger than she'd expected, probably in his thirties, with blond hair and blue eyes. If she'd been thirty years younger, she might have found him attractive.

"What can I help you with today?" he asked.

Joan looked at Janet and Janet found herself caught in the same lie yet again.

"I just need some headache tablets," she said.

She heard Joan smother a laugh as the young man turned and showed her to the appropriate display. As Janet followed, she glanced around and wondered to herself why she hadn't requested any one of the thousands of other products in the shop. She shook her head at her own stupidity as she walked past facial tissues, cosmetics, shampoo, soap, and the myriad of other things such stores carried. In front of the tablets, she made the same choice she always made.

"We tried to stop in last week, but you were shut," Joan said as the man rang up Janet's tablets.

"We had a small staffing issue," the man replied.

"Oh, really?" Joan remarked. "We were quite used to Mr. Carter. He always took good care of us. I do hope he's okay."

"He needed a bit of surgery, that's all," the man replied. "He should be back in another month or so."

"And will you be here until he returns?" Joan asked.

Janet looked over at her sister, feeling slightly stunned. All this chattiness was very out of character. Joan was focussed in the man behind the counter.

"I should be, yes," the man said. "I'm Matthew Rogers, and I've been sent from the head office to cover for Mr. Carter until he's well enough to return to work."

"There have been ever so many different people in here," Joan said in a confiding tone. "It's quite disconcerting to find a new man here every time we come in."

"Yes, well, that's why I'm here," Matthew said soothingly. "I shall be in place for the foreseeable future."

"I'm quite sure the man who was here last week gave me some rather bad advice," Joan said. "I had a cold, you see, and he suggested some sort of over-the-counter medicine that didn't help in the slightest."

"I am sorry," Matthew said smoothly. "Head office is aware that the coverage in this shop hasn't been the best. Again, that's one of the reasons that I'm here."

Joan nodded. "Well, we'll look forward to seeing you again," she said. "Ready?" she asked Janet.

Janet picked up her bag and nodded. She quietly followed her sister out of the store. When they were back at the car, she finally had to speak.

"What just happened?" she asked Joan.

Joan flushed. "I don't know what got into me," she said, a bit sheepishly. "I just started talking and I couldn't help myself. I think I'm just so eager to help poor Michael that I got carried away."

"Well, you did very well," Janet said. "I don't think we learned anything, but it was interesting watching how the man reacted to the questions."

"He seemed like a very pleasant young man," Joan said.

"He did," Janet agreed. "But that leaves us without any suspects at all."

Joan nodded. "Yes, I realise that," she said, sighing.

"But what's going on now?" Janet asked. They'd been standing next to their car, talking, and Janet could still see the front of the chemist shop. She watched as Matthew walked out of the shop. He looked up and down the street and then went back inside.

"It looks as if he's locking the door," Joan whispered.

"And he's turned off the open sign," Janet said. "Maybe it's time for his lunch break?"

"I think he's up to something," Joan said. "Come on."

Joan walked off quickly, leaving Janet to catch up. "Where are we going?" Janet demanded.

"To see what's happening," Joan told her.

Janet shook her head. Her sister was behaving entirely out of character. Joan slowed her steps as they walked past the shop. The sign on the door now read "closed," with no note of explanation. Joan kept walking, past the shop and then down past William Chalmers's antique store. There was a small, single-lane road after that, which appeared to turn and run behind the row of shops.

"Let's go," Joan whispered, pulling Janet along the road.

Janet was about to object, but stopped herself. There was no way she wanted to start being the sensible sister. That was Joan's job. If Joan wanted to start being more adventurous, Janet was going to simply go along.

The road was more of a narrow lane with small parking spaces for each store. The first door along the back of the building had a small sign that read "WTC Antiques."

"It should be the next door, then," Joan hissed.

They crept forward slowly, with Janet hoping that Joan knew what she was doing. Janet didn't have a clue.

There was a low wall that separated the space between the shops. It was no more than three feet tall and about ten feet long. Now Joan ducked behind it. Janet rolled her eyes and then joined her sister, wincing as she crouched down.

"Now what?" Janet demanded.

"I don't know," Joan whispered. "I just wanted to see what Matthew is doing."

"He's probably sitting in the back room, eating his lunch," Janet said.

Before Joan replied, the door at the back of the chemist shop swung open. Janet gasped, earning a stern look from Joan.

"Of course I still love you," Matthew was saying. As he emerged from the doorway, Janet could see the mobile phone in his hand.

"I'm just stuck up in Doveby Dale, otherwise I'd be there for your birthday. You know that," he said.

Matthew lit a cigarette and inhaled deeply. "We can celebrate in a few weeks," he said. "I'll buy you something really special to make it up to you."

The sisters watched as he finished the call and then punched in another number. "Hey, I got your message. What's wrong?"

A second cigarette was lit from the first as he listened. "Ah, honey, you know me better than that," he said after a while. "I'm stuck in Doveby Dale, working, otherwise I'd be there to go with you to your cousin's wedding. You know I love you."

Janet looked at Joan and they both shook their heads. As Matthew paced back and forth, talking and smoking, Janet felt her leg muscles begin to cramp. After another minute, the smoke that was slowly filling the small lane began to make her nose tickle.

"I need to move," she hissed at Joan.

Joan shook her head.

"I'm going to sneeze," Janet said, struggling to control her nose.

Joan rolled her eyes and then went back to watching Matthew. He hung up from the call and punched in another number.

"Hey, baby," he said in a sexy voice. "I was thinking of you all morning." He turned his back and then walked back into the store. The moment he disappeared, Janet jumped up and began to walk back the way they'd come. Joan followed.

They'd only gone a couple of steps when they heard Matthew's voice again. Janet glanced back. She could just see him standing in the doorway of the shop. Suddenly the distance between them and the end of the row of shops seemed enormous. They were going to get caught. Janet just hoped that Joan had an explanation ready when the man spotted them.

Joan grabbed Janet's arm and then pulled her towards the building. They heard Matthew still talking on his phone as Joan tried the handle on the back door to the antique shop. A moment later the sisters were staring at a very surprised-looking William Chalmers.

"Um, good afternoon?" William Chalmers's words sounded like a question rather than a welcome.

Janet sneezed several times in a row. Joan handed her a tissue when she finished.

"Sorry about this," Janet said to William. "We were trying to find a shortcut back to our car and ended up in the lane behind the shops. Something or someone made a loud noise and startled us both so we just ducked in here."

"It was probably the guy on the end," William said. "He's always throwing things around back there."

Joan was studying a few of the pictures on the easels that were spread around the small storage room.

"These are very good," she said.

Janet looked at the nearest picture, happy that her sister had changed the subject. She was surprised to find that she agreed with Joan. "I know just where this is," she exclaimed. "Joan and I went walking the other day and we were right there."

"I love painting the dales," William said, his face bright red with embarrassment. "I take photos of scenery I like and then paint them back here. I don't try to paint outside."

"You're very talented," Joan told him. "Do you have anything that's finished?"

William shook his head. "I never seem to, that is, well, finishing is the hard part," he told her. "I get them nearly done and then, for some reason, I can't bring myself to do those last few touches. I keep starting new paintings rather than finish the old ones."

"Well, if you finish these two," Joan said, gesturing, "I'll buy them from you, assuming we can agree on a fair price."

William flushed. "Oh, you could have them," he told her. "I don't, that is, I'm not really ready to start charging for my work."

"They're quite good," Janet said. "You said you know a lot of artists. Have you ever shown them anything you've done?"

"That's just it," William told her. "I've never finished anything to show anyone. I think it's my way of avoiding having to find out what others think of my work. I'm generally very confident and self-assured, but when it comes to my art, well, I never think it's good enough."

"Finish these two," Joan said. Janet recognised her elder sister's "stern teacher" voice. "I'll be back at the end of the month to collect them. We can discuss prices then."

William looked as if he wanted to argue, but Joan didn't give him a chance. "I think we probably should be going," she said to Janet.

Janet nodded. "Our guests might be back by now and it's definitely time for some lunch."

"And I want to ring Robert and have a word," Joan said as they walked through the shop to the front door.

Chapter 10

Joan was quiet on the drive back to Doveby House. Janet was curious to know what her sister wanted to talk to the police constable about, but she didn't want to ask. It had been a strange day, with Joan acting all out of character. Janet drove silently, wondering what her sister was thinking.

There was no one at the house when they arrived home. Joan fixed a quick lunch and then rang the police station. Janet could only hear Joan's end of the conversation, which was short.

"Hello, Susan, how are you?" Joan began.

"Yes, well I'd be ever so grateful if you'd ask Robert to ring or stop by Doveby House when he has a minute."

"Yes, thank you."

When she disconnected, she smiled at Janet. "She's going to ask him stop by," she told her. "He's out with the investigator from Derby now."

"He isn't going to bring the investigator here, is he?" Janet demanded.

"She didn't say," Joan said.

Joan seemed unconcerned, but Janet wasn't sure the investigator from Derby would appreciate their interfering in the case.

As it happened, it was only Robert who turned up a short time later.

"Good afternoon," he said. "What can I do for you ladies today?"

Joan insisted on fixing him a cup of tea. She'd piled dozens of biscuits on a plate before he'd arrived and now she urged him to take several. Once he was settled in with his snack, Joan began.

"I want you to make sure you take a very close look at Matthew Rogers," she told the young constable. "I think he's behind whatever's gone wrong at the chemist shop."

Robert nearly choked on his biscuit. "Well, that's very, um, interesting," he said. "I appreciate you taking the time to share your thoughts with me."

Janet didn't think he appreciated it at all, but she didn't say anything.

"I'm quite worried about Michael, you see," Joan went on in a confiding tone. "But I'm certain he hasn't done anything wrong. That Matthew Rogers, though, he isn't an honest person."

"His company thinks very highly of him," Robert told her. "They sent him here because there were issues with the store. I can't quite see how he could be behind the problems as he'd only just arrived when they were discovered."

Joan shrugged. "I'll leave the detective work to you," she said. "I'm just telling you where to look."

Robert swallowed a sip of tea and then nodded. "And do you share your sister's opinion?" he asked Janet.

Janet nodded slowly, trying to think of how to word her reply. "He seems like a very nice man when you meet him," she said after a moment. "But he's not nearly as nice as he appears. I wouldn't be surprised if he was doing something criminal. Besides, the other suspects are all such lovely men."

"They are very nice and I hate having to investigate them," Robert admitted. "But that's my job. I must say, they've all been very cooperative."

"What about Matthew? Has he been cooperative?" Joan demanded.

"Very," Robert replied.

Joan frowned. "Well, I do think if you dig a little bit beneath the surface, you'll find all sorts of nastiness there," she said.

"Thank you for sharing your thoughts," Robert said again. "I'll definitely take a closer look at the man."

Janet showed Robert out while Joan tidied in the kitchen. When she rejoined her sister, Joan was humming quietly.

"You seem to be in a better mood," Janet remarked.

"That's because it won't be long now before the whole unpleasant business is wrapped up and Michael's name is cleared," Joan replied. "In the meantime, we have guests to keep us busy."

The guests didn't keep them all that busy, but Janet did tidy and vacuum their room every day. Joan kept trying to find things they might enjoy for breakfast, but they never ate more than dry toast, no matter what she offered.

The pair usually went out each morning and were back at the house by seven or eight. They'd watch a bit of telly and then head to bed just as Janet and Joan were getting tired. By the time they left, Janet had decided that if all guests were like Fred and Molly, she and Joan should welcome guests more often.

Joan was back to her normal self, cooking and baking nearly perfect meals and treats every day. Michael visited often and seemed to share Joan's conviction that the police would have the matter sorted very soon. Janet found herself eager to investigate further, but with no clear idea of what to do.

A week after their visit with Robert Parsons, the day after their guests had checked out, Janet found him on their doorstep again.

"Come in," she invited the man.

She shouted for Joan, who quickly invited the man to have a cuppa.

"I can't stay long," he told them. "But maybe just a quick one."

Janet fixed a plate of biscuits while Joan arranged the tea things. Within minutes, they were all sitting together at the kitchen table.

"What can we do for you?" Joan asked the young man.

"I just came to tell you that you were right," he told her.

"About Matthew Rogers, you mean?" Joan asked.

"Yes, he's been arrested, and the charges will be significant," Robert replied.

Joan nodded. "I knew he couldn't be trusted."

"But how did he manage it, if he'd only just arrived?" Janet asked.

"Ah, it was all tricked up on the computer," Robert said. "From what we can tell, he had access to the store's computer records and he started making changes in them many months ago, about the same time that Owen told the head office that he was going to need several months of sick leave."

"He really planned ahead, then," Janet remarked.

"He did," Robert agreed. "He changed orders, created phantom returns and did a lot of other things to make it look as if there were problems in the store. Then he persuaded his manager that he should come up here and sort everything out."

"Clever," Joan murmured.

"He was a bit too clever," Robert said. "He made so many changes to the drugs records that even he didn't know what the store had. He was stealing from their inventory before it was shipped and then altering the records so that the store here didn't notice, but as I understand it, he started getting overconfident and ended up making a few mistakes. When he arrived here, the first thing he did was an inventory which showed what a mess he'd made of it."

"But why ring the police?" Janet asked. "Why not just fix the records?"

"I gather his boss ordered him to do the inventory before he did anything else and there were so many mistakes in it that he knew he didn't have time to fix it. I'm not totally clear on how it all works, but he said something about not having access to the company's main computers here, so he couldn't change things on that end. Anyway, apparently he decided to ring the police, thinking that he couldn't be blamed as he wasn't even here when the drugs went missing."

"But you were able to find evidence," Joan said happily.

"Well, no," Robert replied. "After I talked with you, I started watching him more closely." The young man flushed. "The investigator from Derby was convinced that someone else was guilty and he was concentrating on that angle, so I just kept my mouth shut and watched Matthew Rogers. After a few days I started to notice a few things about how he was running the shop. Let's just say it didn't take long for me to catch him doing something illegal. After that, his story began to fall apart."

"Well, that's one mystery solved," Joan said briskly. "Michael will be pleased that he isn't a suspect any more."

"He was never a suspect in my eyes," Robert told her.

"Yes, well, I suppose Owen and George will feel better as well," Joan said.

"And that just leaves us with this mysterious key," Janet said, pulling it out of her pocket. She'd taken to carrying it around with her just in case she happened to find herself at a different bank where she could ask about their deposit boxes. So far, that hadn't happened.

"Mysterious key?" Robert said. "Why is it mysterious?"

Janet handed him the key. "We found it inside a piggy bank in a hidden compartment in the library," she explained. "But we don't know what it's for."

Robert turned the key over his hands. "I haven't seen one of these in a few years," he told the sisters. "See the stamp on this side? It says 'DDBS' in very faint letters."

Janet took the key back and studied it. She thought she'd inspected the key in great detail, but she hadn't been able to make out the very small and lightly etched letters.

"What does it mean?" she asked Robert.

"It's a key for the safe deposit boxes at the Doveby Dale Building Society," he told her.

"But where is that?" Janet asked excitedly.

"They tore it down about five years ago," Robert replied.

Janet sat back in her chair, feeling crushed. "So it's a key for nothing?" she asked.

"The place was old and in bad repair," Robert told her. "By the time they tore it down, everyone was happy to see it go. If Maggie

Appleton had anything stored there, she moved it elsewhere before the demolition."

"At least now we know," Joan said. "Thank you."

Janet muttered something similar, but she wasn't feeling grateful. She'd had such high hopes of finding a great treasure when they discovered what the key was for, and instead it turned out to be worthless.

Joan showed Robert out while Janet tidied up. She popped an extra biscuit into her mouth in an effort to improve her mood. It didn't help much.

So after all that the key was worthless, which still irritates me slightly. Joan is now convinced that she's a very clever detective, but we both knew Matthew Rogers wasn't a very nice man after all those phone calls to different women. Still, she's claiming all of the credit for his arrest. I don't really mind as it means she can't complain when I want to investigate something in the future.

Besides, I've taken to calling the whole episode "The Donaldson Case," which annoys her no end. She keeps saying that, as Michael was totally innocent, his name shouldn't be associated with it. I just ignore her.

I don't think I mentioned the lovely presents our guests left for us. Fred made us a sculpture out of twigs and grass. Unfortunately, when we tried to relocate it to a suitable location, it rather fell apart.

Molly wrote us a poem:

Doveby House
Warm
Inviting
Telly
Bright
Sneezes
Tuesday
Needs a cat.

I don't understand it, but I quite agree with the sentiment. I've just about worked up the nerve to ask Joan about getting one. I'll keep you informed.

With all good wishes,

Janet Markham

Glossary of Terms

- **bin** — trash can
- **biscuits** — cookies
- **booking** — reservation
- **boot** — trunk (of a car)
- **car park** — parking lot
- **chemist** — pharmacist
- **cuppa** — cup of tea (informal)
- **fizzy drink** — carbonated beverage (pop or soda)
- **fortnight** — two weeks
- **high street** — the main shopping street in a town or village
- **holiday** — vacation
- **jumper** — sweater
- **lie in** — sleep late
- **midday** — noon
- **pavement** — sidewalk
- **plasters** — adhesive bandages (Band-Aids)
- **plug socket** — electrical outlet
- **pudding** — dessert
- **push chair** — stroller

- **queue** — line
- **saloon car** — sedan
- **shopping trolley** — shopping cart
- **telly** — television
- **till** — check-out (in a grocery store, for example)
- **torch** — flashlight

Other Notes

In the UK, dates are written day, month, year rather than month, day, year as in the US. (May 5, 2015 would be written 5 May 2015, for example.)

In the UK, when describing property with more than one level, the lowest level (assuming there is no basement; very few UK houses have basements) is the "ground floor," and the next floor up is the "first floor" and so on. In the US, the lowest floor is usually the "first floor" and up from there.

When telling time, half six is the English equivalent of six-thirty.

Pensioners are people who are old enough to be collecting a retirement pension. (In the US they are generally referred to as senior citizens.)

A "full English breakfast" generally consists of bacon, sausage, eggs, grilled or fried tomatoes, fried potatoes, fried mushrooms and baked beans served with toast.

A semi-detached house is one that is joined to another house by a common center wall. In the US they are generally called duplexes. In the UK the two properties would be sold individually as totally separate entities.

The story continues in…
The Ellsworth Case
A Markham Sisters Cozy Mystery Novella

The bed and breakfast is now up and running and Janet and Joan are looking forward to welcoming their last guests before they take a break for Christmas. The news that someone is passing counterfeit currency around Doveby Dale is worrying.

Both couples that arrive at Doveby House seem odd to the sisters and so does William Chalmer's new friend, Karen Holmes. The library keeps turning up surprises, including a beautiful oak tantalus, while the police keep turning up more counterfeit twenty pounds notes.

Is it possible that some of their guests are counterfeiters? Why is Karen Holmes interested in the much older William Chalmers? And what other secrets will the library reveal?

Also by Diana Xarissa

The Isle of Man Cozy Mystery Series

Aunt Bessie Assumes

Aunt Bessie Believes

Aunt Bessie Considers

Aunt Bessie Decides

Aunt Bessie Enjoys

Aunt Bessie Finds

Aunt Bessie Goes

Aunt Bessie's Holiday

Aunt Bessie Invites

Aunt Bessie Joins

Aunt Bessie Knows

Aunt Bessie Likes

Aunt Bessie Meets

Aunt Bessie Needs

The Isle of Man Ghostly Cozy Mysteries

Arrivals and Arrests

Boats and Bad Guys

Cars and Cold Cases

Dogs and Danger

The Markham Sisters Cozy Mystery Novellas

The Appleton Case

The Bennett Case

The Chalmers Case

The Donaldson Case

The Ellsworth Case

The Fenton Case

The Green Case

The Hampton Case

The Irwin Case

The Isle of Man Romance Series

Island Escape

Island Inheritance

Island Heritage

Island Christmas

About the Author

Diana Xarissa lived in Derbyshire, and then on the Isle of Man for more than ten years before returning to the United States with her family. Now living near Buffalo, New York, she enjoys writing about the island and the UK.

Diana also writes mystery/thrillers set in the not-too-distant future under the pen name "Diana X. Dunn" and fantasy/adventure books for middle grade readers under the pen name "D.X. Dunn."

She would be delighted to know what you think of her work and can be contacted through snail mail at:

Diana Xarissa Dunn
PO Box 72
Clarence, NY 14031.

Find Diana at:

www.dianaxarissa.com
diana@dianaxarissa.com

CPSIA information can be obtained
at www.ICGtesting.com
Printed in the USA
LVHW041835081218
599778LV00020B/812/P

9 781530 965694